The truth of this moment weighs upon me.

I am not merely calling my people to embrace a more ambitious criminality. I am sounding the clarion for war.

"In our darkest hour, all of our closest galactic neighbors treated us like vermin. They acted as if our suffering meant less than theirs, for no better reason than we live beneath our own banner. They ignored our wounded and our hungry. Turned their backs on our dead. Left us to dig through our own ashes and watch our skies *burn*.

"They counted on us to die.

"Now it's time for us to show those *fegoru* that we are still predators! That we are not so easy to kill—and that we will not be forgotten. Not by them. Not by their children. Not by the galaxy. We are Nausicaans! And we will take back what is ours!"

My people's cheering hits me like a tidal wave.

I know I have them. Their hearts are on fire. They know what's at stake.

All that we have left in the universe is on the line now. All that we are. All that our people still hold dear. All that we might yet be.

We never saw the Borg coming. Never had a chance to defend our world. Our people.

Today, those of us who remain will stand as one. And we will be counted.

Live or die, win or lose . . . we will make certain that history remembers us.

STAR TREK
THE NEXT GENERATION®

Collateral Damage

David Mack

Based on *Star Trek*®
and
Star Trek: The Next Generation
created by
Gene Roddenberry

GALLERY BOOKS

New York   London   Toronto   Sydney   New Delhi   Nausicaa

G

Gallery Books
An Imprint of Simon & Schuster, Inc.
1230 Avenue of the Americas
New York, NY 10020

First Gallery Books trade paperback edition October 2019

GALLERY BOOKS and colophon are registered trademarks of Simon & Schuster, Inc.

For information about special discounts for bulk purchases, please contact Simon & Schuster Special Sales at 1-866-506-1949 or business@simonandschuster.com.

The Simon & Schuster Speakers Bureau can bring authors to your live event. For more information or to book an event, contact the Simon & Schuster Speakers Bureau at 1-866-248-3049 or visit our website at www.simonspeakers.com.

Manufactured in the United States of America

10 9 8 7 6 5 4 3 2 1

Library of Congress Cataloging-in-Publication Data is available.

ISBN 978-1-9821-1358-2
ISBN 978-1-9821-1359-9 (ebook)

to dreams outgrown but never forgotten

HISTORIAN'S NOTE

This story's prologue takes place in February 2381, a week after the end of the Borg Invasion (*Star Trek Destiny*).

The events of the main portion of this story take place in January 2387, approximately eight weeks after the *Enterprise*'s mission to intercept the Nejamri generation ship (*Star Trek: The Next Generation: Available Light*) and ten weeks after the public exposure of Section 31's crimes (*Section 31: Control*).

Charity begins at home—but if it ends there, what good is it?

PROLOGUE
February 2381

It's been seven days since my world died. Since it was murdered. Cut down like a mad cur, left to burn without a living soul to mourn its dead. Destroyed for no reason.

From the top of Nausicaa's highest mountain I look down upon a charred cinder. A blackened orb, silent and empty. A haze the color of rotting flesh lingers over the plains below. It matches the pallor of our once radiant skies, hidden now by a permanent blanket of brown dust and gray smoke ejected into our atmosphere by the Borg's pitiless barrage.

Where I should see the city of my birth, the land of my fathers, the home of my family . . . all I see is a smoldering crater, its nadir still aglow with the green fires that made it. A smoky wound in the landscape. An empty space, both literally and figuratively.

I want to scream. To howl out my anguish and my fury. But grief steals my voice, chokes me like a tourniquet on my throat. My mandibles quiver. My eyes burn with rageful tears, but I need to stay strong. I am all my people have left. If I am weak, the last of us perish.

I cannot falter. I must not fear. I must find a way forward.

Behind me, others succumb to their grief. The women and the younglings I let weep. The men bellow their voices raw, as if they hope their shouts can pierce our world's deathly shroud. They need this, to know they poured out their *tegoli* to the Four Winds and were not heard.

Our gods will never hear our cries again. They have abandoned us, or they are dead. Either way, they no longer matter. All that I know now to be true is that we are alone.

And that I should have been here.

I should have died beside my mates and our brood. Yawa, can you ever forgive me? Baru? Do you hear the regret in my voice? I wish I hadn't lived to see a day without you both. Without our willful, passionate younglings. Were you grateful I was offworld? Did you hope I would avenge you? Or did you leave this world cursing my name? Calling me a coward?

I swear on your *tegoli* that I am no coward. Had I been here, I would have shown the Borg the very essence of *guramba*. I would have made them pay in blood for this horror.

That's more than what the Federation did—which was *nothing*. Not a single ship came to defend Nausicaa.

For all their big talk, where was the Federation when we needed them? The Borg were *their* enemy. A nightmare they spawned. A catastrophe they unleashed on the galaxy.

Where was the Federation when our world was being laid waste?

Where was the Federation as our monuments were vaporized, as every trace of our history, our culture, our literature, our music, our heritage was disintegrated? They were in retreat, scrambling to protect their precious Earth.

The great and vaunted Starfleet was running scared while the Borg churned my world's oceans into sludge with the burning ashes of six billion Nausicaans.

Now there's nothing left. Not a single survivor on the planet's surface.

The only Nausicaans left in the galaxy were those who were offworld when the Borg arrived. A handful of rogues, scavengers, and independent merchants. The closest thing our people had to a military died with this planet. Along with our fractious government and every last trace of wealth we possessed as a civilization.

We have always been a proud species. Strong. Independent. Fearless.

But now there are so few of us. One bad decision could drive us extinct.

I grew up knowing that Nausicaans never ask for anything. Not for help, or favors, or mercy. What we want, we take. What we have, we keep. That is our way. But how do we take back our own past? Our own identities? Thousands of cycles of history, mythology, music, art, literature, poetry, and faith . . . all dead and gone.

All that we were. Destroyed in a flash of light and heat.

Now the last of us are adrift. Too proud to beg. Too weak to conquer. The Nausicaan people have become debris swept away by time's cruel and endless current.

Killed for no reason. Not because we had something the Borg wanted, or represented something they feared. But because our star system was situated between the Azure Nebula, the Borg's arrival point in the Alpha Quadrant, and their ultimate target, the Sol system.

Earth.

Our world was murdered because it was on the Borg's most direct route to Earth.

My people never challenged the Borg. They never showed any interest in us, or in our technology. They left us in peace, and we did the same. Until they met the Federation. That was when everything changed. Once the Federation and its Starfleet made contact with the Borg, it was only a matter of time before something like this happened.

Always the same story with Starfleet. So superior. So sure of themselves.

And now billions of my people are dead. Exterminated like vermin. And on other worlds, the same sad story, over and over again. Tens of billions burned alive, every last one of them a sacrifice on the blood-soaked altar of the Federation's arrogance.

Some want to blame the Borg for this atrocity. But the Borg are gone. Absorbed into the Caeliar gestalt. Absolved of responsibility, all their sins forgiven.

So be it. I know who's really to blame.

I turn away from the endless fields of destruction and face the few dozen lives that are now my sacred responsibility to defend in a brutal, uncaring universe. "Enough!" My voice is hoarse. I point toward my ship, the *Seovong*, which sits parked on a small alpine plateau nearby, its aft landing ramp open. "We go."

My first officer Kradech sidles over and advises me in a confidential tone. "Kinogar? The women and younglings need more time."

He has always been less hard-hearted than me. I shake my head.

"Weep for an hour, weep for a day. When our tears run dry, our world will still be dead." I tilt my head toward the ship. "Get them on board."

I watch, my expression blank but my heart howling, as Kradech and my other trusted men shepherd the handful of our grieving kin back inside the ship. Some of them clutch tiny mementos of our lives-that-were; one lucky woman has a book written in our native tongue. I spy a youngling who has a woodwind instrument that she might not know how to play but has been told nonetheless to treasure and keep safe.

As far as I know, we are all that remain of the Nausicaan people.

For their sakes, I will make the Federation pay for all that we have lost.

Holding back my burning tears, I board my ship and take to the stars, leaving behind the corpse of my world—and with it, a piece of my *tegol*.

JANUARY 2387

1

———◆———

The collar of Jean-Luc Picard's dress uniform was as snug as a noose against his throat. He slipped his index finger behind it and gave a gentle tug in search of some slack. *I don't recall this being quite so tight.* Out of the corner of his eye he saw that he had drawn the attention of his wife, Doctor Beverly Crusher, who sat beside him in the shuttlecraft *Galileo*. He let go of his collar and turned his gaze forward to see the towers and spires of San Francisco slip past outside.

Crusher also wore her dress uniform. Picard had reminded her that there was no need for her to endure this discomfort, but she had insisted. "We're in this together, Jean-Luc," she had said an hour earlier, while they were dressing in their quarters on the *Enterprise*.

I can only hope that doesn't turn out to be true.

They had not spoken since boarding the *Galileo*. Their flight down from Earth orbit had been brief but fraught with anxiety about what awaited them at its end. This was a journey they had postponed for as long as possible—first with excuses, and then with a mission far beyond the Federation's border. But the time for delays and evasions was past.

I can't run from this any longer. It's time to account for my actions.

Members of the Federation Council had been demanding Picard's presence for several weeks, ever since the public exposure of Section 31—and, with the uncovering of all its crimes, foreign and domestic, the revelation that Picard and several flag officers of Starfleet had played key roles in the coerced removal from office of Federation president Min Zife over seven years earlier. What had shocked Picard as much as anyone had been the news that

Section 31 had taken the additional step of executing Zife as well as his top advisors immediately afterward.

If only I had known . . . That thought led him nowhere. When he revisited those fearful, violent days, and tried to imagine what he might have done differently, he found himself at a loss. The Tezwa crisis had been some of the darkest days of his Starfleet career. Millions of lives lost, a planet and a people left in ruins, all for naught. He had hoped never to think on it again, yet its horrors had chased him everywhere since, as inescapable as his own shadow.

A shift in the shuttlecraft's artificial gravity and a downward pitch of its bow alerted him and Beverly of what was coming a few seconds before their pilot, Lieutenant Allison Scagliotti, said over her shoulder, "Captain, we're on final approach to Starfleet Command."

"Thank you, Lieutenant."

He shifted his hand just far enough to link his fingers with Crusher's.

She reciprocated the gesture, a small but significant show of support.

Over the *Galileo*'s comm, Picard heard the voice of a flight control officer at Starfleet Command give final instructions. Just as Picard had expected, the shuttle had been directed to the landing pad nearest the office of Starfleet's top-ranking officer, Chief Admiral Leonard James Akaar. It made sense, and not just for its convenience; that pad was secured from external observation, and no nongovernmental civilians were permitted there.

In other words, no press.

Galileo touched down with barely a bump. The droning of its impulse engines fell to a soft purr but did not go quiet. It had orders to return to the *Enterprise* as soon as Picard and Crusher were delivered safely to Starfleet Command.

Scagliotti replied to Starfleet Command's flight control officer, "Command, *Galileo* is secure. Passengers going ashore now. Requesting clearance for immediate departure."

"Clearing you a lane. Stand by, Galileo.*"*

Picard and Crusher unfastened their safety harnesses and rose from their seats. Scagliotti opened the shuttlecraft's portside hatch ahead of their approach, and then the young woman swiveled her chair to face them as they disembarked. Tears shimmered in her green eyes as she tucked a lock of red hair behind her ear. With hope and sincerity she said, "Good luck, sir."

What could he say? He didn't want to give her false hopes.

He acknowledged her kind wish with a small nod. "Thank you."

And then he led his wife off the shuttlecraft, into the blinding glare of a crisp, clear winter morning in San Francisco, California.

Side by side they walked across the landing platform to the double doors that led inside Starfleet Command. As soon as they were clear of the platform's red zone, they heard the *Galileo*'s engine drone rise in pitch. Neither Picard nor Crusher looked back, but he saw the ascending shuttlecraft reflected in the mirror-perfect façade of Starfleet Command's windows.

The double doors parted ahead of them as they approached. A tall Starfleet officer stepped out from the other side to greet them—a youthful-looking male Pacifican, with a liquid-respiration mask over his nose and mouth, prominent webbing between the long, slender digits of his hands, and elegant multicolored fins extending from the top and sides of his head. As he neared to conversational range, Picard saw that the man wore a lieutenant commander's rank insignia, and he spoke through a special translator module built into his respirator mask.

"Greetings, Captain Picard." He faced Crusher. "Welcome, Doctor Crusher." He gestured toward the open doors behind him. "I'm Lieutenant Commander Boyelip, senior aide to Chief Admiral Akaar. You're both expected. Follow me, please."

Boyelip turned and led them inside.

Far from a hero's welcome. Not that I had any reason to expect one. Not this time.

In the sterile white corridors, they passed officers of various ranks, species, and genders on their short walk to the office of Star-fleet's ranking admiral. Picard was certain that he felt the weight of everyone's stares as he did his best to avoid acknowledging them. Eschewing eye contact, he'd learned, was the key to dodging unwelcome queries. So he did his best to keep his focus in front of him, on where he was going, what he was doing, whom he was talking to.

But still he felt the stares. The looks of accusation. Everywhere he went. And their weight grew with each passing day. Soon it would be too much to bear. He had to shed this burden.

Boyelip opened the door to Akaar's office, but he remained outside as Picard and Crusher entered, and then he closed the door behind them.

Akaar stood at his floor-to-ceiling window, his broad back to Picard and Crusher. The tall, white-haired Capellan—who was still well muscled, despite being over one hundred twenty years old—gazed out at the beauty of San Francisco Bay. He spoke with the solemnity of a Bajoran *vedek* reading a prayer for the dead. "So it begins." He looked at Picard. "You will never know how dearly I'd hoped this day would never come."

Picard had traveled too far to succumb to maudlin impulses. His only succor now was to be found in the rituals of protocol. He stepped forward and said the words he had rehearsed so many times over the last eight weeks, in preparation for this moment.

"Admiral, per your order and at the request of the Starfleet Judge Advocate General, I present myself as a material witness in the ongoing criminal inquest into the actions of Section Thirty-One during the Tezwa crisis. I am prepared to offer testimony regarding my role in those events, and to take full responsibility for my actions."

Akaar absorbed that news with admirable sangfroid. Then he looked at Crusher. "And to what do I owe the pleasure of *your* company, Doctor?"

"I'm here to do what he won't."

"Which is?"

"Look out for his best interests."

"Then that makes two of us." The admiral gestured at the guest chairs in front of his curved desk. "Please, sit." He settled into his own chair and waited for them to be seated before he continued. "Captain, I appreciate your respect for the formalities. I will see to it that your gestures are properly noted and logged for the JAG's files."

"Thank you, Admiral."

"You're more than welcome. Now, let me tell you why I insisted that you present yourself to me, rather than directly to the JAG. I did my best to keep you and the *Enterprise* out of the inquiry's reach during its early phases. I'd hoped they might find enough to be satisfied without dragging your name through the mud. That hasn't been the case.

"The people of the Federation are understandably spooked by the discovery that they and their ancestors lived for more than two centuries in a surveillance state run by a sociopathic artificial superintelligence. And that, I'm sure, would have been the greatest of their concerns were it not for the exposure of documents alleging that Starfleet led a coup against the president who won the Dominion War, and then turned a blind eye to his murder.

"I did all I could to shield you from the media shitstorm these past few weeks, but my ability to give you cover is at an end."

Picard nodded. "I expected as much, Admiral. And I'm prepared to face the music."

"Hold that thought. Because your predicament is worse than you think." Akaar picked up a padd, called up a file, and passed it across the desk to Picard so that he could peruse its contents. "At oh-nine-hundred this morning, Federation attorney general Phillipa Louvois petitioned the Federation Council and President zh'Tarash to remand all Starfleet personnel involved in the Section Thirty-One inquiry to the civilian justice system, rather than permit Starfleet to conduct its own separate proceedings under courts-martial, as required by the SCMJ."

That news made Picard sit up, alarmed. It stank of a witch hunt. "And?"

"I pushed back. Hard. The legal autonomy of Starfleet is a privilege I am not willing to surrender, and there is no legal precedent for such a shift in authority. The good news is, the Federation Supreme Court rejected Louvois's request. The catch is, this means our official inquiry must be absolutely beyond reproach. Do you understand what I'm saying, Captain?"

"Yes, Admiral."

"Just in case, let me spell it out for you. I summoned you so that I could be the one to tell you that I have referred the investigation of your role in the allegedly coerced removal from office of President Min Zife, and any culpability you might bear in his alleged subsequent murder, to the Starfleet Judge Advocate General's Corps, with my official request that they convene an Article Thirty-Two criminal inquiry under the terms of the SCMJ."

"Understood, Admiral."

Akaar frowned as if he had just swallowed something distasteful. "Be advised that while you are not being charged with any specific offense at this time, as your superior officer, I strongly advise you to retain expert legal counsel as soon as possible, and to treat this inquiry with all of the caution and gravity that you would any criminal proceeding. Understood?"

"Perfectly, sir."

"Then we're done. Thank you for coming in. Dismissed."

Akaar stood, which cued Picard and Crusher to rise from their chairs. The admiral shook Picard's hand and then ushered him toward the door, which opened. From its far side Boyelip beckoned Picard and Crusher to follow him. He escorted them back to the nearby landing platform, where a small shuttlepod stood waiting. As they all paused in the open doorway to the platform, Boyelip asked Picard, "Do you need me to arrange accommodations for you, sir?"

"That won't be necessary." Picard took his wife's arm and walked with her to the shuttlepod. Boyelip watched from the doorway as they boarded. Only when the hatch was sealed did Boyelip head back inside the building.

The shuttlepod pilot, a fresh-faced young Andorian *shen*, asked, "Destination, sir?"

"The Château Picard Winery in La Barre, France," Picard said as he and Crusher took their seats and fastened their safety restraints. "Take me home."

It was home, and it wasn't. The original farmhouse that Picard had remembered from his youth had burned down years earlier, claiming the lives of his older brother, Robert, and Robert's teenaged son René, in whose memory Picard and Crusher had named their own son. Robert's widow, Marie, had survived the fire, and in the years since the tragedy she had rebuilt the house and carried on the running of the winery. The vineyard, thankfully, had remained unchanged.

Picard could not say the same for the house. It had been reconstructed atop the original foundation, but Marie had taken the liberty of revising its floor plan. She had enlarged the kitchen to include a spacious cooking island with a prep sink, and had reconceived the ground level into an open concept that had unobstructed sight lines from the kitchen to most of the rest of the floor. As a result, the rebuilt home felt expansive, and it was filled with natural light.

It was beautiful and functional—but it wasn't the home that Picard remembered.

He couldn't begrudge Marie the right to remake her own home, especially when he considered all that she had lost. It would have been selfish of him, or of anyone, to expect her to rebuild the house exactly as it had been. Which would not have been possible, anyway. No replica would ever have been perfect enough to fool anyone who had lived there. So why try?

It reminded Picard of an old philosophical riddle: If one replaces the parts of a ship one at a time—a plank here, a bolt there, a sail, a rudder, a wheel—and if, at some point, one realizes that not a single piece of the original vessel remains . . . is it the same ship?

Was this the same home? He shook his head.

A question best left to scholars.

One thing was still the same: the tantalizing aroma of a wheel of brie, topped with cranberry relish and wrapped in puff pastry, baking in the oven. Its sweet fragrance filled the house and wafted outside through open windows to the porch, putting a contented smile on Picard's face. A baked brie and a bottle of Cote du Rhône, or perhaps a bottle from the Languedoc . . . those sparked fond memories for him. Of nights at the dinner table with his parents and his brother, of roasted chicken and mashed potatoes, sautéed spinach with garlic, and warm baguette, fresh from the oven . . .

The house's front door opened behind him. For a moment, sounds of mirth escaped from inside—the giggles of Picard's young son, René, playing with his aunt Marie.

Crusher eased the door shut behind her and moved to stand with Picard, looking out at the vineyard. "Your sister-in-law can't stop doting on our son."

"Can you blame her?"

"I guess not." Crusher planted her hands on the railings and looked out into the fading twilight. "I took the liberty of unpacking our bags."

He rested his hand atop hers. "Thank you." He looked back and smiled at the sight of Marie and little René playing with a plush stuffed rabbit. "When is dinner?"

"Promptly at eight, Marie says. She's opening a bottle of Château Picard's best vintage ever, in celebration of your return home."

Picard was surprised that his eyes filled suddenly with tears. Being reminded of how long he had been away brought back memories of his contentious last encounter with Robert, in the wake of Picard's violent psychological and physical domination by the Borg.

"Twenty years," Picard said, his voice catching as sobs built within his chest. "Since Robert knocked some sense back into me. Made me face what the Borg took from me. Helped me remember who I am." He wiped away grateful tears with the back of his hand. "Four years later, he was gone. He and René." A deep breath brought back a semblance of dignity. "Part of me would give anything to have them back. If only they wouldn't have to see me like this."

Crusher laid one arm across Picard's shoulders. "They would still be proud of you, Jean-Luc. Just like I am."

He turned his back on the vineyard and regarded the unfamiliar home that had supplanted the dwelling of his memories. "There were times I thought I'd never see this place again. Even when I thought of retirement, I never considered coming back here. This is Marie's home now. Her legacy more than it was ever mine." Pulled by undertows of memory, he turned once more toward the orderly rows of the vineyard. "My connection to this land, to its history . . . it's all too distant for me to feel any real sense of ownership, for any of it."

Crusher joined him in regarding the vines. "I understand. But I think it's important that our son has a chance to experience this place for himself. To form his own memories. It's a part of his history—and no less important to his identity than our life on the *Enterprise*."

She was right. He looked through a window to watch Marie play with René and was struck by a profound feeling of nostalgia, by memories of his own mother's love—there, in the kitchen that had been, that would never be again, that he would never forget.

"I wish my brother were here. I wish he could have seen me as a father. That our boys could have had a chance to know each other, to form that special bond cousins enjoy." A dark turn forced itself upon Picard. "But not if it meant they'd see me like this. Disgraced. Accused of betraying my president. My government. My people."

Crusher took his arm in a gentle grasp. "Before the news broke, you never told me what really happened on Tezwa, or with Zife. I'm still not sure you have."

"You're safer that way." Assailed by memories of black days and desperate times, of compromises he wished he had never made, Picard looked away into the gathering night. "Bad enough that I might need to face justice. If I were to confide all that I knew of this grim affair, you might face the same legal jeopardy." He put his hand to her cheek in a gesture of tender care. "For the sake of our son, one of us must remain beyond reproach."

"But does it really matter at this point, Jean-Luc? By the time your hearing's over, all of the details are going to be public anyway."

Picard felt his hard frown deepening the lines on his face.

"That's what I'm afraid of, Beverly."

2

—◆—

Wind-blown muck clouds my suit's full-face visor. I wipe it off with my gloved hand, then shake my hand mostly clean. It's hard to see through the night's raging storm of acidic rain and corrosive dust. The gale is strong here at the edge of town thanks to the machine-made crater behind us. The excavators run through the night, filling the ground with tremors and the air with rumbles, as if a storm lurks forever on the horizon, ever threatening but never breaking.

Kamhawy Freehold is large enough to be a city, but it's more like a massive cluster of prefab buildings and jury-rigged power plants, huddled together for protection at the edge of a jungle filled with horrors. The only thing keeping the wilderness at bay? A perimeter force field.

Life is dangerous on Celes II, always has been. A decade ago this world belonged to the Romulans' legions of automated mining machines. Then Shinzon murdered the Romulan praetor, and their Star Empire forgot all about this place. Celes II declared its independence, and a bunch of disaffected wildcatters set up an "independent mining consortium." I'm sure they felt mighty proud of themselves—right up until the day the Borg vaporized this planet's other cities in a matter of minutes. Then the 'catters wasted no time begging the Federation to set up terraforming reactors to fix the atmosphere. From what I've seen, it's a waste of time. This equatorial island is one of the last patches of living biomass on this planet. I say let it die.

Still the Federation clings to this blasted rock. The rest of the world yawns dead around it, but as long as this crater yields duranium ore and raw dilithium, the 'catters and their guests will keep this rusted heap of scrap metal stocked with food, drink, and distractions. Comfort for themselves, death for everyone else. A lesson they learned from the Federation.

Viewed from outside, Kamhawy glitters like a jewel. It looks radiant, powerful, and untouchable behind its invisible force field. But I know better. Like so much that the Federation builds, this shield is weaker than it looks. It's full of flaws. Soft spots.

It's a bubble. Bubbles are easy to pop, if you know where to poke.

I activate my helmet's transceiver. "Kradech, report."

My brother-in-arms answers on our secure channel. *"Kradech here. Go ahead, Kinogar."*

"Are the charges in place?"

"Setting the last pair now." The foul weather and the planet's wild magnetic disturbances make our comms crackle with static. *"Arming detonators in sixty seconds."*

I check the time in my faceplate's holographic display. We're ahead of schedule. "Take your time. Do it right. No second chances."

"Understood." The channel closes with a soft *click*.

A few paces from me, one of my shooters, a quiet thinker named Drogeer, studies his targeting scanner. Even though he's young, I've learned to keep him close and take his advice. He's rare among our kind: a snowblood—*venolar* in the old tongue. No passion in him, no fury—but no shortage of *guramba*. No fear. Just cool blue reason. Ice water in his veins.

I open a private comm channel from my helmet to his. "Drogeer, report."

His voice is monotone, steady. *"Target holding position. Wide range of life signs. Assorted small arms, several active alarm systems. Tracking one new hostile in the strike zone."*

"Any comm chatter from station security?"

"Nothing on their regular channels. Nothing flagged by our comms filter."

"Tell me if any of those change."

"I will." He continues scanning. He never looked up from the device the whole time he was speaking to me. I terminate our private channel and move down the line.

My engineer Majaf busies himself making final adjustments to an array of devices placed near the city's edge, all facing one of the force-field emitters. He has done a fine job this evening. With little help he has installed three subspatial distortion generators and a cluster of demolitions. It all has to work together, some parts of it on a rigidly timed schedule, others only upon demand. If any piece of it fails, none of us will get off this rock alive.

I stand beside him and admire his work. Over a secure channel, I ask, "Ready?"

"Pull the trigger and we'll find out."

I walk away cursing the Four Winds for sending me an engineer who thinks he's funny.

Minutes later I reach the rendezvous point. Kradech and Drogeer are already there, along with half a dozen more of our brothers. I do a head count. Check their names in my visor's display. Then I switch to the tactical overview and confirm that all of our external preparations are placed and armed. It all looks good.

I power up my disruptors, one rifle and one pistol. At the hatch that leads underground into a smuggler's tunnel and then inside the city, I pause to verify one last detail. I switch to my primary secure comm channel: "Kinogar to *Seovong.* Status report."

Haylak, my ship's top pilot, replies, *"Standing by to launch on your command."*

"Remember: Engines off until I say 'go.' If you start early, station security will see."

"Understood. Seovong *out."*

I open the hatch and lead my team down into the tunnel, and then into the peripheral quarters of Kamhawy. We stay for as long as we can in the service tunnels—the access spaces beneath the main thoroughfares, pipe-lined conduits below and between buildings' foundations.

When at last we dare to emerge from hiding, we are in one of the darkest sections of the city, amid the tenements that the filthiest of the station's laborers call home. The streets are lined with distractions for the miserable and overworked: a slew of bars, arcades, and brothels. For those who are even less fortunate than their downtrodden neighbors, there are pawn shops.

But most important of all are the unmarked doors. What lies behind those depends on who you are. For the weak, there is nothing on the other side of these portals but pain and death. But for the strong, the bold, the born predators . . . these doors are gateways to opportunity.

Following the signal on Drogeer's tracker, we arrive at just such a door.

I kick in the door and storm inside, guns blazing.

My men charge in with me, their own weapons shrieking.

No *guramba,* no glory.

"I don't know," Kima said. The Orion woman looked me up and down, and as she crossed her legs I caught the sweet hint of her pheromones swirling around me. "What's the catch, Okona?"

I played it cool. Pretended to be light-headed, just for a second, so she wouldn't suspect that I'd long since been immunized against her species' form of gender-specific mind control. "No catch," I said. "What you see is what you get: a Husnock military Omega-particle cannon." I waved my hand above my wares like an overeager used-hovercraft salesman. "Fresh from a poorly secured Breen weapons depot on Salavat."

Kima circled the crate. We were past the point of trust-but-verify. I had let her tech-nerd minion scan every inch of the OPC to make sure it was genuine and capable of wreaking utter havoc on scales too terrible to imagine. And I'd been completely candid about the precautions I had taken before bringing them to this backwater ball of mud. No one could use the OPC until I removed its biometric restraint—a step that I would take only after my RIO—remote intelligence officer—confirmed that payment in full had been received, as agreed.

All I had to do now was close the deal. And not get shot. Or blown up.

I heard the twitching of anxious fingers against triggers all around me while Kima paced in front of the open crate. "I have to admit, this represents a unique opportunity. On the black market, it could be worth an absolute fortune."

"*Could?* As if there's the slightest doubt? This thing's a latinum mine."

"Anything this valuable comes with risks."

"Such as?"

"Reprisals, for one. How do I know the Breen won't come looking for payback?"

"Who'd pick a fight with someone who holds one of these?"

"You jest, Okona, but—"

"Please, call me Thadiun."

"No." She eyed the merchandise. "As lucrative as this might be, trying to move it would be suicide. The Breen will be looking for it, and so will Starfleet. And the Klingons. And anyone else looking for an edge in the latest interstellar arms race."

I could tell that I was losing her. And after all I had done to bait the hook! I put on my best mask of innocence and pressed one hand to my chest, to signal that I was speaking from my heart. "I hear what you're saying, Kima. The OPC is gonna draw a lot of heat, and you don't think the profit is worth the risk. But what if I cut my price twenty-five percent?"

Her eyes narrowed and her nostrils flared, like an aquatic predator smelling blood in the water. She drifted closer to me, her smile almost wide enough to show her teeth. "What if you cut your price by sixty percent?"

"Be reasonable, Kima. Getting it out of Breen space wasn't easy, or cheap. I can't cut my price any more than thirty percent."

"Fifty-five."

"Thirty-five and I'm losing money on the deal. Final offer." It was a classic case of dueling bluffs. We both had good poker faces. I waited several seconds. She didn't blink, so I closed the lid on the OPC and started securing the locks.

She put her hand over the crate's control panel. "Forty percent."

"What? Am I subsidizing you now? No, thanks." I brushed her hand aside and finished locking the crate. "If you don't mind, I have an appointment with some serious buyers on—"

"Thirty-five, done." Kima turned toward her consigliere, a brawny Zibalian whose face, neck, and arms were completely covered in intricate tattoos. "Kadan, pay the man."

For about three seconds, I felt pretty good about myself.

Then the front door of Kima's hideout exploded inward.

The lights flickered and went dark. An apocalyptic thunderclap shook the building and rained dust from the rafters into my eyes. My sphincter clenched as disruptor blasts screeched by on either side of me, mowing down Kima's men. When the shriek and whine of weapons fire ceased a few seconds later, most of the Orion Syndicate's muscle in the room had been reduced to half-cooked meat on the floor. Only Kima and I were left standing to greet the squad of heavily armed Nausicaans in armored tactical suits who charged inside and spread out around us.

The one in charge pointed his rifle into Kima's face. His voice was filtered through a speaker on the front of his helmet. "Weapon! Where is it?"

"Weapons?" She waved at her men's small arms on the floor. "Take your pick."

The boss Nausicaan pressed his rifle's muzzle to Kima's throat, just above the notch in the center of her clavicle. "Cannon. Give it to me."

She glared at him, her voice and body rock steady. Which I found funny, because I was shaking like a leaf in a storm. Kima looked into the ugly bastard's face. "Do you have any idea who I am? Or who you're stealing from?"

The Nausicaan's fanged mandibles twitched inside his helmet while he waved his rifle around like a madman. "You? Kima. This place? Orion Syndicate." He pulled his trigger and blasted a fist-sized hole through Kima's torso. Her body flew backward and landed in a heap against the back wall. "Me, one in charge."

When he looked at me, I flashed a dumb smile. I don't know why. I couldn't help it. To be honest, it's almost become a reflex at this point. As if smiling like a moron were some kind of universal semaphore for *please don't hurt me.*

He pointed his rifle at my face. "Cannon."

I pointed at the crate. "In there. The code for the lock is nine-six-one-alpha-three."

He kept his weapon aimed at me while one of his men opened the crate. They scanned the OPC and signaled him that they had what they had come for. I did my best to look small and nonthreatening, with my right hand folded over my left wrist in front of me, where he could see. With a tilt of his head, he beckoned the rest of his men toward the crate. "Prep for transport."

"You'll need to move it outside first," I said, drawing a glare from the boss thug. "The Orions scan-shield their compounds. No beaming in or out."

It took a second, but one of his men confirmed my report. The squad of goons started looking for handholds on the outside of the smooth polymer cargo crate.

"Your best bet is to grab it from the bottom," I said. "And remember to keep your backs straight. Lift with your legs. And don't—" I caught a glower from the boss. "Never mind."

As the goon squad hefted the crate toward the open front doorway, I activated the escape protocol that I'd hoped would not be needed that evening. Luckily for me, I've never walked into a room without a plan for how to get out of it.

A tap on my wrist chrono sent out a signal to a series of small explosives—two that I had insinuated into the compound's fire-suppression system and its hydro plumbing, and one on the locked side exit door three running strides from my chosen negotiating position.

A rapid series of flashes and pops, and the room filled with hot vapor and blinding firefighting foam—all as the side door's lock and hinges were blown to bits. I heard the Nausicaans fire their weapons in the choking fog behind me, but I was already moving. My shoulder hit the side door. It broke free of its frame and tumbled into the alley outside, with me on top of it. I caromed off the wall on the other side of the alley and kept running.

By the time I reached the street I was hauling ass and looking for cover—because the disruptor shots slashing through the air above my head made it clear the Nausicaans weren't going to let me get away anywhere near that easily.

I ran until I couldn't breathe and my lunch started climbing back up my throat. Anything that gave me cover, I used: piles of garbage, an abandoned freight pod, a holographic ad display.

The Nausicaans stayed with me. Hectored me with disruptor shots. One singed the hair above my right ear. Another nicked my left heel and left me trailing smoke for half a block.

All I wanted was to put a little more than five seconds between us. Just enough time for me to trigger my emergency transporter recall and not risk getting shot while waiting for the beam to take hold and spirit me away. But the long-legged bastards were fast.

Booking around a corner, I saw a three-way intersection ahead of me. It was time for one of the classic tricks. I pulled a miniature combo charge from my belt and chucked it behind me on the move. It detonated with a blinding white pulse and a bang that shook my guts against my aging bones before it choked the alley with dense gray smoke.

Finally, a few seconds of cover.

I hooked left and ducked down a stairwell to a door below

street level. Triggered the transporter recall and started counting the seconds.

From back the way I'd come, I heard the Nausicaans come to a clumsy halt, all grumbles and battle-rattle as they collided with one another in the tight space. I couldn't make out what they were saying, but I was pretty sure they were arguing.

Then they were in motion. And coming my way.

I drew my Nalori-made blaster and put my back to the wall.

In my head I'd counted five, but I didn't feel the comforting embrace of the transporter's annular confinement beam. Was my count off? Had my signal been delayed? Or were the Nausicaans jamming the city's signal repeaters?

If that recall signal doesn't go through, this is about to get ugly.

Through thinning curtains of smoke I saw the Nausicaans— just shadows at first, then silhouettes. Their edges sharpened with each step they took in my direction.

How had they followed me? Dumb luck? Or were those helmets of theirs better equipped than they looked? I feared I was about to find out—the hard way.

I raised my blaster and got a bead on the point man.

My finger curled around the trigger—

A stifling sensation of pressure, a paralyzing hug. The confinement beam. A few seconds late, but just in time to give away my position. *That's just great.*

I froze. Firing my weapon then would have been suicide—the charged plasma would be trapped inside the confinement beam, where it would ricochet a few thousand times and turn me into a well-done shredded steak. My view of the Nausicaans faded as I was cocooned in shimmering particles, but in my final moment before transport I saw the point man fire at me. His disruptor shot rebounded off the confinement beam and hit the Nausicaan behind him.

Everything went white—and then I was in the transporter nook of my ship, a beat-up-looking Mancharan starhopper named the *Tain Hu.*

The confinement beam released me. Praying there was still time to fix this mess, I holstered my blaster and rushed out of the nook, then forward through the center passage to the cockpit. I arrived just in time to see what looked like a Nausicaan ship making a high-speed run—straight into the city's force field.

Are they nuts? If they hit the shield, they're as good as—

Searing-white flashes lit up numerous points along the edge of Kamhawy Freehold. Secondary explosions followed. The energy shield, normally invisible, flickered golden for a fraction of a second before it stuttered and perished.

I watched the raiders soar away and cursed under my breath. Then I powered up *Tain Hu*'s sensors and got a lock on their vessel long enough to confirm that its crew was composed entirely of Nausicaans—and that they had the Husnock weapon on board.

I leaped into my flight chair and reached forward to power up *Tain Hu*'s engines and run the bastards down. Then a force field blocked the front of my docking bay. It shimmered an ominous crimson, and my vessel quaked, rudely snared by a tractor beam.

An automated message from the city's security office appeared on my status monitor:

Lockdown in progress. No arrivals or departures permitted at this time. All docked vessels may be subject to inspection. Remain where you are until further notice.

I sighed. *Perfect. I am so screwed.*

It was a good bet Kamhawy's signals control office was blocking all the regular subspace frequencies. Luckily for me—or maybe not, considering my predicament—*Tain Hu*'s hidden quantum comm didn't operate on any frequency that the station would be able to block or intercept. I powered up the quantum transceiver and set the channel for my compatriots, who I knew were not going to like what I had to tell them. As usual.

An indicator light flashed green, confirming the channel was open and secure. "Expositor, this is Agonist. Do you copy?"

I'd once asked why we had to use code names on a comm that

was supposed to be impervious to eavesdropping. The answer was exactly what I'd expected: *Always assume someone is listening.* Even when they can't possibly be listening? *Especially then.*

A bright, feminine voice replied over the comm, *"This is Expositor. Go ahead, Agonist."*

"I presume Suzerain is on the line?"

A rich, masculine voice answered, *"Of course I am. What's your status, Agonist?"*

"Operation: Marrakesh has gone sideways."

"What a surprise," Suzerain said. *"Details, please."*

I brushed burnt bits of hair from the side of my head. "The meet was raided by Nausicaan bandits. Well armed, well trained, and they knew what they were looking for."

Expositor groaned. *"Oh, no. Please tell me they didn't take—"*

"The OPC? Afraid so. One of Kima's people must have talked."

"Can you pursue?" Suzerain asked.

"Negative. The Nausicaans shot their way out, made a hell of a mess. I'm stuck in lockdown with the rest of the city for God only knows how long." I checked my sensor logs. "Their last-known bearing was two-five-eight mark twelve. But they could be going just about anywhere, and they didn't leave anybody for me to question, so we're in the dark while they're in the wind." Exhaustion and the inevitable adrenaline crash hit me, and my hands started to shake. It was past time for a stiff drink. "So what now, guys? Any suggestions?"

Suzerain was not happy. *"For the man who just lost a Husnock weapon that can frag a planet? Try seppuku."*

"A job well done! Drink up!" I pour half a bottle of Risan wine down my throat, swallow, and belch loud enough to tremble the bulkheads. Then I laugh while Kradech slaps my back, and I pass the bottle to Majaf. No one cares how rare the wine is. Or that Risa is just as dead as Nausicaa, and that grapes will never grow there again. All we know is that the wine tastes good, and it's rich in ethyl alcohol, which sweetens the taste of victory.

Even our young hotspur Grendig is whooping it up, and that *keebets* got shot by my ricochet. He downs his second can of Tiburonian liquor and shows off his "battle wound" to Kiruna. She's twice the sharpshooter he'll ever be, but she humors him because it's been a long while since either one of them has had a chance to couple. I pity their bunk neighbors tonight.

Drogeer keeps to himself as usual. He sits on the deck with his back to the bulkhead, breathing in narcotic vapors through a liquid-cooled pipe that's all the rage on Ferenginar these days. The misty drug suits our *venolar* brother. It makes him somber. Deepens his calm.

Me? I'll stick to booze.

Kradech comes back from his quarters with a pair of Earth drums he says are called *bongos*. They sound ridiculous to me, but once they blend into the rhythm of all the other improvised percussion instruments my crew has amassed over the years, I don't care. It's all just part of the beat. Part of the song. Everyone chants along at some point—everyone except Drogeer, of course. But I see him bobbing his chin, keeping time. He plays it cool, but I know he feels the tempo in his blood, just like the rest of us. Deep inside, he is still Nausicaan.

Roars of laughter fill the mess hall. I look over. Kradech has the floor, and he's holding court, born showman that he is.

"And then Kinogar kicks in the door," he bellows at the younglings, as if they haven't heard this story twice already tonight, "and he lights! them! up!" He mimes firing a disruptor rifle on autopulse, strafing the cluster of younglings, who shriek with amusement as they topple and collapse in a heap, cheerful in their pantomime of violent death.

I watch them and wonder if someone, somewhere, ever made such sport of the end of Nausicaa. Got such a rave review by mocking the slain. Then I banish my self-pity. Blame the alcohol for making me maudlin. It's a night to party! We are victors, flush with spoils.

Meanwhile, Kradech runs circles around the younglings, his tale not yet done. "And then we chased the *hyoo-mon* through the streets! Through the alleys! Up stairs and down the sewers! And all the way he's whining and crying and acting like a scared little *yefu*! And why?"

The younglings shout as one, "Because he's a HYOO-MON!"

I grab a fresh bottle of wine and open it by smashing off the top of its neck against the jamb of the doorway. Half of it splashes down the front of my shirt and vest as I walk aft, emptying the scarlet booze into my gullet in one long pour. I let my booted feet stomp the deck, my footfalls like thunder, announcing my presence as I move aft and then descend through the ladderway into the cargo hold.

Down in the hold, our chief medic, Doctor Veekhour, and my second officer, Zenber, review the inventory of all we took from the Orions.

I hold my nearly empty bottle over my head. "Counting widgets again? Don't you two know there's a party in the mess?"

Veekhour looks up at me. His mandibles twitch with mild annoyance. "We'll be there soon." He catches a look from Zenber, and then he adds, "Since you're here, come see this."

These two are such sticklers for detail. Careful logs. Precise counts. I make fun of their love of paperwork, but the truth is that without them, we would long ago have starved, wound up adrift without fuel, or worse. I join them next to the cargo pod we took from Kima's hideout. "What is more important than celebrating with the rest of us?"

Zenber hands me a data slate with his updated inventory. "Good haul tonight. Latinum. Weapons. Rare drugs, all in demand on the black market. But this"—he looks down into the open crate—"too hot for us."

"What are you talking about?" I look down. And then I'm confused. I feel the lines in my brow deepen as I scowl at the alien device inside the gray polymer crate. "What is it?"

"Artillery," Zenber says.

"What kind? Not Federation. Or Klingon. Not Romulan. Not Breen."

I see the worried look that passes between Zenber and Veekhour, and then Zenber spills the bad news. "Husnock."

The blood drains from my face as piss fills my bladder. We're sitting on a fortune, but at the same time it's putting a target on our backs. "The fixer said we would score something special. Never said Husnock."

I pace around the crate to the other side, not for any good reason, just to burn off nervous energy. My mind races. This could be the key to our long-delayed revenge. Or a path to dynastic wealth. Maybe both. If it doesn't get us all killed.

Zenber stares at the weapon as if he expects it to speak to him. Then he shakes his head. "This is bad. Remember Slokar and the Patriots of the Wind?"

"Slokar was a fool," I say, my voice dropping to a growl. "Sloppy. No discipline."

Veekhour remains wary. "He has a point, Kinogar. Dangerous people want this. Starfleet, Klingons, Romulans, Breen—not to mention Orion Syndicate, and now the Dashkari Barons. Any one of them would exterminate us for this."

"We can't even sell it," Zenber says. "The moment we admit to having it, we become the most wanted fugitives in the galaxy. Every one of us marked for death."

I wave off their petty fears like I'm swatting at flies. "Enough! No more talk of running scared. If you've lost your *guramba*, get off my ship." I grasp the sides of the crate and consider the deadly bounty that has found its way into my hands. "I agree, Zenber: we cannot sell it. But I also cannot throw it away. We took it by force. That makes it ours. And I intend to use it."

The doctor's eyes widen. "*Use* it?"

"Without hesitation or pity." I reach down and caress the cannon. "Too long have we lived on the fringes, stealing from soft targets, plundering the weak. Now the Four Winds have granted us the strength to take our fight to those who most deserve to feel our wrath. For Nausicaa and all her people, we will make the Federation pay for its arrogance and its indifference. After all these years . . . we will take what we are owed."

3

———•———

There were few assignments in Starfleet as routine as a core-systems patrol, a roughly elliptical journey plotted to take a vessel within medium sensor range of the five populated star systems in closest proximity to the Federation's capital in the Sol system. This was one of the most heavily defended sectors of space in either the Alpha or Beta Quadrants. No surprises here.

That made core-systems patrol the deployment of choice for Starfleet vessels deemed less than fully mission ready, for whatever reason. Got a crew full of midshipmen cadets? Still working out the bugs from a shakedown cruise? Testing a bunch of unreliable new refits? Congratulations—you just earned a turn on the galaxy's dullest milk run.

Commander Worf did his best to push those notions from his head as he reviewed the day's third fuel-consumption report. *The* Enterprise *was made for more than this.*

From any reasonable perspective, there was nothing wrong with the *Enterprise* or its crew, except for the absence of Captain Picard. And in his final conversation with Worf before his departure, Captain Picard had done his best to cast the *Enterprise*'s temporary orders in a positive light. "This is a good sign, Mister Worf," he had said. "If the powers that be really thought my command was over, you'd be putting another pip on your collar right now. As it is, they clearly just want you to keep the ship ready until I return."

"I hope so," Worf had said. And that had been that.

Now the feedback tones and ambient hums of the bridge enfolded Worf, who had in a short time come to appreciate just how perfectly attuned the bridge's center chair was to all that happened around it. Every console alert, every flicker of new activity caught his attention.

Commander Geordi La Forge lingered aft, near the bridge's master systems display, reviewing some sensor logs with Lieutenant Dina Elfiki, the ship's senior science officer. Though La Forge had always preferred to work from main engineering whenever possible—a request that Captain Picard had generally granted, since La Forge had been chief engineer long before taking on the additional role of ship's second officer—for the time being Worf had made it clear that he needed him on the bridge. With Worf serving as the ship's acting commanding officer, La Forge also enjoyed a temporary promotion, to acting first officer. Which meant that, whether he liked it or not, his duty station was here on deck one.

On the main viewscreen, warp-stretched stars flowed toward the *Enterprise* and then vanished out of frame. Routine comms chatter issued from the security console, which was tended by Lieutenant Aneta Šmrhová. Dark-haired, dark-eyed, and darkly serious about her work, she alone of the other officers on the bridge seemed to share Worf's distaste for being tasked with the mundane, regardless of the spin one put upon it.

At the forward stations, senior flight control officer Lieutenant Joanna Faur leaned toward operations officer Glinn Ravel Dygan. In a confidential tone of voice she asked the Cardassian exchange officer, "Did you get a chance to try that holonovel I recommended?"

Dygan gave Faur a sly sidelong look. "The one with branching narrative paths?"

"That's the one."

He grimaced. "I tired of it. Nothing but happy endings."

"Well, what did you expect? It was a romantic comedy."

He shrugged. "Plenty of romances end in murder-suicides. Lovers get separated by wars. Calamities. Accidents of fate."

"Then it wouldn't be a comedy."

"I disagree. I think it's all in how you play it."

Their discussion drew the attention of Lieutenant T'Ryssa Chen, a half-Vulcan, half-human woman who served as the ship's senior first-contact specialist. "She has a point, Dygan. In the Western literature of Earth, there are classical divisions between comedy and drama—or comedy and tragedy, as they used to define them."

Lieutenant Rennan Konya looked up from his tactical console, visibly intrigued. "Can't a story have elements of both?"

"Sure," Chen said, splitting her focus between the Betazoid deputy chief of security and Dygan at ops. "But according to the ancient Greeks, a story's goal was either laughter or tears."

Faur looked back from the conn and shook her head. "I prefer the Elizabethan standard. Tragedies end in death, comedies end with weddings."

Dygan frowned. "That seems needlessly reductive."

Chen reacted with feigned shock to his protest. "This from a man whose culture calls *The Never-Ending Sacrifice* the epitome of literary accomplishment. Nearly two million words of leaden prose about seven generations of a family all serving in drudgery and then dying."

"When any of *your* cultures produces anything even *remotely* so profound in form or subtext as the repetitive epic, I will deign to have this debate with you—but not *until* then."

Out of the corner of his eye, Worf saw La Forge and Elfiki being drawn toward the debate like moths to a rhetorical flame. *Please do not let them get involved.*

"You know," La Forge interjected, "I haven't read a lot of Cardassian literature, but from what I have read, I've noticed a few recurrent themes that might be relevant here. First—"

Worf did his best not to let his hand curl into a fist. *Fek'lhr, kill me now.*

An alert shrilled from Šmrhová's console, and the comms chatter went wild.

"Stations," Worf said, sitting up straighter at the promise of action.

The bridge crew snapped into action, all hints of small talk abandoned.

Šmrhová silenced the clamor from her station. "Captain, we're receiving a mayday. From the Kamhawy mining freehold on Celes II." She activated a small transceiver attached to her ear and listened to the message. "They say they've been attacked by Nausicaan raiders and have sustained serious damage to their municipal shield."

Another alert sounded, this time from Konya's console. He muted it, checked his panel, and then looked up at Worf. "Captain, new orders from Starfleet Command. 'Proceed at best speed to Celes II and investigate the attack on Kamhawy Freehold. Render aid and take other action as deemed prudent or necessary.' Signed by Admiral Kernova, sir."

"Helm, set course for Celes II, warp nine, and engage. Lieutenant Konya, compile a record of recent pirate activity in this sector. Flag any that involves Nausicaans." Worf swiveled his chair just far enough to lay eyes on La Forge. "Number One, find out what vessels are in this and adjoining sectors. We may need help pursuing the attackers."

La Forge gave a quick nod. "I'm on it."

"Lieutenant Šmrhová. Run a battle drill within the hour."

"Aye, sir."

The ship's artificial gravity wavered for a moment as the *Enterprise* accelerated to high-warp speed, turning the streaks of starlight on the viewscreen into a blurred wash of swirling light. Through the *Sovereign*-class vessel's spaceframe and deck plates, Worf felt the vibrations of its warp engines pushing their limits, and around him the low chatter of a bridge crew on a milk run had given way to the tense murmurs of a crew on its way into danger.

Some of the officers would feel put out because their relaxing core-systems cruise had turned into a serious mission, but for Worf, whose Klingon heart bristled at the very notion of leisure, this was exactly what he had been craving: a chance to do something that mattered.

In his book, there was nothing better.

After years of responding to door chimes aboard starships, something about the sound of a simple knock on a wooden doorjamb struck Picard as oddly atavistic.

He set his padd on the table next to the front room's sofa and got up. Attired now in the simple clothes and plain shoes of a rural vintner, Picard walked to the house's front entrance. There the inner door stood open, enabling him to see his visitor through the screened outer door. Like a sailor spying land after months at sea, or a thirsting pilgrim laying eyes upon an oasis after endless days in the desert, Picard smiled at the sight of his old friend William Riker, gray-bearded and dressed in civilian garb. "Will!"

Picard opened the door and stepped out onto the porch. Riker returned his smile. "Jean-Luc. It's been too long." When Picard threw open his arms in welcome, Riker stepped into his embrace. Picard found great comfort in Riker's presence. After all the years they had served together, all that they had endured side by side, Riker had come to feel like a son to Picard. Even after the birth of René, his flesh-and-blood scion, Picard had retained an almost paternal affection for Will Riker. Though he had never explicitly said so aloud, he truly loved him.

"It's good to see you, Will. Or should I say *Admiral*?"

Riker answered with a good-natured shake of his head. "There are no ranks between us."

"Quite right." Picard stepped back. "What brings you here?"

"I heard you'd been called home."

"I stayed away as long as I could."

"And now I'm the one who needs to go. But I didn't want to leave Earth without seeing you." Riker gestured toward the sprawl of vineyards. "Walk with me?"

"Of course."

The two of them descended the porch stairs, crossed the dirt road that separated the house from the vine rows, and continued on, into the rows of naked vines. It was winter, and the vines were resting. Soon spring would return, and the vines would turn green with leaves before bearing new fruit, the first steps toward another vintage of Château Picard wines.

Underfoot the ground was rocky and dry, and each step that Riker and Picard took kicked up short-lived clouds of dust in their wake. Overhead the sky grew dark, shifting from violet to black, as the last rays of day faded beyond the nearby hills.

Once they were a few dozen meters from the house, Picard thought it safe to broach sensitive topics. "Something on your mind, Will?"

"I'd be lying if I said I wasn't worried for you." He squinted toward the horizon. "They grilled me pretty hard a few months ago. Asked me a lot of questions about you. What I knew about what you'd known, that sort of thing."

It troubled Picard to think that any actions of his might have blown back upon Riker. "They didn't try to smear you, did they?"

Riker shook his head. "Not directly. The majority of their questions concerned the end of the Tezwa crisis. And I was a POW for most of that."

A sudden pang of conscience nagged at Picard. "Will, should we be discussing this?"

"It's all right, Jean-Luc. I spoke with my lawyers before I came here. It's perfectly legal for us to meet and talk about what we went through together on Tezwa."

"That's reassuring, I suppose."

Riker let his fingertips brush against the dry, barren vines as they strolled onward. "I have to be honest, Jean-Luc. I'm worried."

"Because?"

"I'd always thought there was something odd about the way Min Zife resigned his presidency, but until the JAG questioned me about it, I'd never really considered the possibility that you had anything to do with it." When he glanced toward Picard, there was fear in his eyes—not for his own fate, but for Picard's. "Then I read Ozla Graniv's exposé in *Seeker.* And her follow-up piece about everything that happened on Tezwa." A sharp intake of breath preceded a long sigh. "Now I don't know what to think."

Picard didn't need him to spell out his concerns. He shared them. "Will, I know what you want to ask me. And I—"

"Jean-Luc, stop." The moment turned awkward, heavy with mistrust and apprehension. "Don't tell me anything I'd have to lie about under oath."

Picard kept his expression neutral in spite of feeling wounded that Riker thought him capable of such perfidy. "I would never put you in that position. Will, I *give you my word*—as your former captain, as your brother-in-arms, as your *friend*—I never for a moment harbored even the slightest suspicion that Min Zife had been murdered. The moment I read that in Graniv's article, I was gutted. I felt *betrayed.* I never wanted that. You must believe me."

Riker stopped walking, and Picard halted beside him. They faced each other. Riker looked into Picard's eyes . . . and then he grasped Picard's shoulders. "I believe you."

It was a small act of affirmation, a personal gesture that would mean nothing in a court of law, but to Picard it meant everything. "Thank you, Will."

"So . . . what happens now?"

"I don't know."

Riker resumed walking, and Picard kept pace at his side. "If my experience with the JAG was any guide," Riker said, "what comes next won't be pleasant. They're looking for a scapegoat, Jean-Luc. They *need* one."

"And you think they mean to sacrifice me upon their altar."

"Maybe. Given your public stature, maybe they think you're the kind of martyr who could wash them clean of this mess." His shoulders slumped as if suddenly burdened with an oppressive weight. "The only thing I can tell you for certain is that you need a real defense lawyer. Not some JAG-assigned defender whose next promotion hinges on letting you get burned at the stake. You need a barracuda, Jean-Luc—professional legal defense counsel, one that knows how to work within the Starfleet judicial system."

"Given that my inquest is set to start at any moment, I really don't have the time to vet defense counsels, Will."

"Then it's a good thing I've already done it for you." He stopped, reached into his coat pocket, and pulled out a small business card of clear polymer with an embedded isolinear chip. "This is a man I trust." He handed the card to Picard. Laser-etched onto its face:

JONATHAN EZOR, ESQ. – CRIMINAL DEFENSE LAWYER

"You need an expert," Riker said. "I've told him to expect your call."

Picard smiled and pocketed the card. "After all this time, you're still watching my back."

"And I always will," Riker said. "Because I know you'll do the same for me."

4

———

I hated running. I wasn't a young man anymore, and I had long since learned the bliss of staying still. But someone always found a reason to make me run—either because they were chasing me, or, in this case, because they were selfish enough to make me chase them.

She had been working a simple grift in the middle of Kamhawy's open-air market. An alien version of a game I'd first learned as three-card monte. Some folks liked to call it "Follow the Queen," but I'd always found that confusing because it was also the name of a seven-card poker variant. All that matters is that she was running a sleight-of-hand card scam on the street, and she'd found a whole bunch of wet-behind-the-ears young punks off some Federation merchant-marine cargo hauler who all thought they'd be the one to beat her. Nearly thirty minutes into the con, none of them had figured out how Pinch was palming the money card. She was a few minutes away from the most lucrative night she'd seen in half a cycle.

Then I came along and ruined it.

I'd tried to lay low, but I don't do inconspicuous. It's a family thing—we Okonas have always had a knack for stealing the spotlight. Still, I'd done my best. And yes, I'd had a job to do, but that didn't mean I had to be a jerk about it. Just my shit luck, between rounds of fleecing the gullible, Pinch spotted me across the way. As soon as she could stuff the latinum strips into her pockets, she was off like a ship jumping to warp.

Then I was running, for the second time in less than a day.

And damn, she was fast. And small. She slipped under and

around things that I had to jump over or bash through, and after the second mound of garbage my shoulder started to ache.

The fact that she ran told me she was the one I needed to find. If she'd been any other run-of-the-mill lowlife on this blister at the ass end of space, she'd have stood her ground, told me off, maybe even tried to shoot me fair and square. Instead she'd taken off at the first sign that someone had put two and two together and found her name in the sum. That spelled *guilty*.

One thing I'd always loved about backwater rocks like Celes II was that you could chase people like this, and no one ever interfered. No good Samaritans here. No one stuck out a foot to trip you. The big idea here was, *Stay out of other people's shit.*

The downside was that when a nice gal like Pinch tried to shoot off chunks of my skull with a disruptor, no one cared about that, either.

Did I mention she was fast? She was half a block ahead of me and opening her lead.

Please don't let me lose her. I'll never hear the end of it.

Fate was about to laugh at me and crap in my hat when a garbage hauler turned the corner in front of Pinch and chugged her way, blocking the whole damned street, as they always do in this shitty 'burg. She was cut off, her lead was wasted, and she knew it.

She turned back and unleashed a wild barrage in my direction. I ducked behind a parked transport that ended up taking most of the punishment. Lying low, I peeked underneath it and saw Pinch's feet as she darted into a narrow passage between a couple of garages. When I stood, I saw that the vehicle I'd used as a shield had been reduced to a smoking total loss. I pitied its owner, who would have to explain all of this—first to the city patrol, and then to some wincing insurance investigator with a mandate to invalidate claims whenever possible.

But most of all, I felt bad for Pinch, because I knew something she didn't.

She had retreated into a dead end. Unless she had a transporter recall beacon—which would be a hell of a trick, since she had no ship that I knew of—she was *stuck*.

That didn't mean she was helpless. Lessons you learn the hard way are the ones that tend to stick; I'd learned at a young age that cornered animals are dangerous. Now I had Pinch's back to a wall. I drew my blaster and moved into the dead-end alley slowly.

Heaps of debris and bagged garbage filled the air with an unholy stink of rotting meat, spoiled dairy products, and the excrement of vermin. Broken machine parts jutted from piles of wet refuse, and the pavement shimmered with oily residues, lit from high above by cold blue floodlights. Steam rose from grated vents, obscuring my view of the end of the alleyway.

"Pinch?" I hoped that calling out her name might calm her a bit. Tell her that I was an acquaintance and not some random assassin. "No need to shoot. I'm not looking for a fight. Don't want to take you in. Just want to talk to you. Ask a few questions on the down low."

A disruptor pulse screeched through the mist and blazed past my head, close enough that I felt its heat on my cheek and smelled the scorched air in its wake.

I froze. "Come on, Pinch. It's me, Okona. Hold your fire."

Her voice trembled. "Okona?"

"Yeah."

"You still owe me twenty strips of latinum, you sonofabitch."

Did I? I honestly couldn't remember. "What if I said I was here to pay up?"

"I'd know you were lying."

"I have it on me, Pinch. And more. Let's put down our weapons and talk."

"You first."

I holstered my pistol. "Done. My gun's back in its leather. Come on out."

I raised my empty hands as Pinch emerged from a cloud of mist with her weapon raised and pointed at my face. It took her a second to see I'd told her the truth.

Grudgingly, she holstered her piece. "What do you want?"

"First, let's settle my debt." With one hand still raised, I made a point of reaching with only my thumb and forefinger under my jacket. Carefully, I pulled out a spindle of latinum strips. I let her watch as I pulled off twenty in a row. I took a few slow steps forward, set the latinum on the ground, and then backed up. I kept both hands raised as she moved forward to collect the money, and then she retreated, never once taking her eyes off of me.

The strips disappeared inside her coat. "All right. Talk."

"Sources tell me you helped a bunch of Nausicaans find one of the smugglers' tunnels."

"Don't believe everything you hear."

"Yeah, I know. But this had the ring of truth. So spill it, Pinch. Who's their leader? What's the name of his ship? And how do I find them?"

The short human woman smirked and gave me a derisive snort. "How stupid do you think I am, 'Kona? Ratting out Nausicaans is a good way to end up dead."

I tossed a fistful of latinum strips to the ground in front of her. "It's also a good way to end up rich. And far away from here."

She squatted and scooped up the bribe.

"The merc you're looking for leads the largest all-Nausicaan gang in the galaxy."

"Where does he hang his hat?"

"How the hell should I know? They've got no home port. They're nomads, always moving. They strike and move on, like killer pilgrims."

That sounded right to me. I'd dealt with Nausicaans more than once since the Borg Invasion back in '81. They were renegades now. Wanderers. Pirates with no home.

But even pirates had to find harbor somewhere.

"Last question, I promise: Where would they have gone from here?"

"Why would they tell me?" A sly smile tugged at the corner of her mouth. "And if they did, why would I be dumb enough to remember?"

She'd said enough. I lobbed another spindle of rolled latinum at her feet.

Her coy smirk widened into a grin. "Wait, I think it's coming back to me . . ."

The side hatch of the runabout *Colorado* slid open, and Lieutenant Aneta Šmrhová stepped out before the gangplank had finished extending in front of the open hatchway. By the time the plank touched the landing platform on the roof of Kamhawy Hall, she was already off it and moving to greet the freehold's chief of patrol, a human in his forties with deep brown skin, a shaved head, and the broadest shoulders she had seen in a long time.

His handshake was firm, his eye contact steady, his voice clear. "Lieutenant Šmrhová? I'm Kenneth Sapp, chief of patrol. Or mayor, depending on the situation."

"Which title do you prefer?"

"I prefer Ken."

"Whatever you like, Ken." Šmrhová gestured with her arm as she introduced the other three members of her *Enterprise* away team, who exited the *Colorado* and gathered behind her. "Allow me to present the rest of my unit. Lieutenant T'Ryssa Chen, sciences. Lieutenant Robert Mars, security. And our pilot, Lieutenant Ally Scagliotti."

"Welcome to Kamhawy, and thanks for getting here so fast."

Šmrhová was eager to get to work and made no effort to hide it. "You said you had a developing situation?"

"Copy that. Someone's been trying to crack the firewall on our flight-ops server all day." Sapp motioned with his head for the away team to follow him inside the station's command center. "C'mon, I'll show you what we've got so far."

Mars and Chen fell into step behind Sapp, who led them inside the municipal control center. Šmrhová waved off Scagliotti. "Stay here. Keep the motor running."

The pilot registered the security chief's mood. "Dust-off or intercept?"

"Either. And get a transporter lock. Just in case."

"You got it, boss." The svelte, red-haired woman turned and ducked back inside the runabout, while Šmrhová followed Mars, Chen, and Sapp inside the control center.

Dreary did not begin to describe the patrol group's headquarters. It was a cathedral devoted to obsolescence. Outdated banks of workstations stood on two circular tiers around a pit designed for the shift's watch officer. Massive two-dimensional holograms were projected in front of a black wall opposite the landing-pad entrance, which was visible through tall floor-to-ceiling windows that were transparent from the inside and mirrored on the outside. Tangled wires drooped like jungle vines from gaps in the ceiling, linking all the systems together.

It's a wonder this place hasn't blown its EPS conduits. Or just burned down.

Sapp led Chen, Mars, and Šmrhová into the command well at the room's center. Despite the antiquated nature of the systems, the readouts were clear, and the amount of useful information available to the watch officer at any given moment was enough to impress Šmrhová.

The patrol chief pointed to one screen. "We've been digging into the sabotage committed yesterday. The explosives that ripped open our dome and helped the Nausicaan bandits escape."

Chen cut in, "Are you sure they were Nausicaans?"

"Check the sensor logs for yourself." Sapp punched in commands on his master console and directed Chen to a screen of data. "No evidence of signal jamming or spoofing. Plus, we had witnesses say Nausicaans were part of a running gun battle last night in Haligon Sector, and we found Nausicaan genetic material at a few different sites related to yesterday's fracas. If this wasn't them, somebody went to a lot of trouble to frame 'em."

A curious expression furrowed Mars's brow. "Were you able to ID the ship?"

"She had a Nausicaan registry, but most pirates do these days. Mostly because there's no Nausicaan government to verify the transponder."

"Not that they were ever much help," Mars grumbled.

"True." Sapp called up new screens of information. "We thought they might have accomplices, so we set a general lockdown the moment they breached our energy shields."

Chen moved to a systems monitor and keyed in new commands. "Ken? When did someone start trying to hack your firewall?"

"About six hours ago. We tried to narrow down the source, but they gave up before we could pinpoint their location."

Šmrhová sidled over to Sapp. "Does your station's secure transmitter still work?"

"I think so. Why?"

"I'd like to have the *Enterprise* analyze your server logs. The hacker might have eluded your security software, but I doubt they can hide from ours."

Sapp rolled his shoulders. "Sure, why not? I've got nothing to hide." He called out to one of his people on the lower tier, "Pérez! Open a channel for the *Enterprise*. Full admin privileges. Put it on socket three, port one-twenty."

"Comin' right up, Chief."

Šmrhová tapped her combadge. "Šmrhová to *Enterprise*. Stand by to patch in to the Kamhawy Freehold mainframe on local socket three, port one-twenty. I need a priority-one analysis of attempts to hack its flight-ops system a few hours ago."

La Forge's voice answered over the comm channel, *"Understood. Patching in to their system now. Stand by for—"* When his transmission cut off midsentence, she wondered if they had lost contact. Then he continued, *"Lieutenant, those attacks on the flight-ops system never stopped. They're still going on. Hang on while we track them back to their source node."*

The look on Sapp's face was a combination of surprise and admiration. Around him, the staff in his command center reacted with everything from embarrassment at being shown up to fierce determination to see this threat to their security and reputation brought to justice.

"Whoever your hackers are, they're good. They've almost cracked the system, and they did it while completely evading detection."

Šmrhová rolled her eyes. "We can pin a medal on them later, sir. Where are they?"

"Malka Sector, docking bay bravo seven."

"Copy that." Šmrhová faced Sapp. "Have a security team meet us there ASAP." Before the man could protest, she drew her phaser and tapped her combadge. "Šmrhová to *Colorado*. Away team site-to-site transport. Malka Sector, docking bay bravo seven. Meet us there."

"On my way," Scagliotti said over the comm, just before the runabout's transporter beam dematerialized Šmrhová, Chen, and Mars—

—and reassembled them inside a dingy, cramped, and poorly lit docking bay. Parked in front of them was a beat-up rattletrap of a ship. Šmrhová's best guess was that thing had to be almost a century old, and she was willing to bet it was held together by crude welds and prayer.

She aimed her phaser at the ship's port side and advanced with her eyes on the flight deck, which was housed in the nose assembly at the end of a neck-shaped length of its fuselage. "You in the ship! Come out, now!"

Behind her, Chen and Mars drew their phasers and spread out to either side, both of them aiming at the strange beat-up ship in front of them.

The canopy of its flight deck was tinted to shield its interior from view, but Šmrhová felt certain there was someone inside. Her suspicion was confirmed by the first purrs of activity from inside the ship's thrusters—its engines were being powered up for lift-off.

"Don't even think about trying to launch!" She fired a warning shot with her phaser—a short blast on a heavy stun setting—into the port-side fuselage behind the canopy. Just enough to shake the ship and leave a minor scorch on the outside of the vessel. She tapped her combadge. "Šmrhová to Kamhawy flight ops. Patch me through to the ship in Malka bravo seven."

"Channel open, Lieutenant. Go ahead."

"Attention, crew of—" She realized she didn't know the ship's name. Looking aft, she saw it stenciled beneath its rear atmospheric stabilizer fins. "Crew of the *Tain Hu.* This is Lieutenant Aneta Šmrhová of the Starfleet vessel *Enterprise.* Stand down. If you attempt to escape or open fire, you will be fired upon."

On the far side of the docking bay, large doors slid open. A team of armed Kamhawy patrol officers charged in with rifles braced and ready for combat. Within seconds they had fanned out and surrounded the battered old Mancharan starhopper.

There continued to be no response from inside the ship.

"Crew of the *Tain Hu,* this is your final warning. Stand down or be destroyed."

Outside the docking bay's threatening red force field, the runabout *Colorado* dropped into view and pivoted to face the ship in the docking bay.

Scagliotti said over the open channel, *"Colorado is in position, shields up and weapons hot. Standing by for your order, Lieutenant."*

"Hold position, *Colorado. Tain Hu,* respond or be fired upon."

The starhopper's engines shut down. Their deep rumbling purr became a fading whine.

An aft hatch on the ship's underside fell open, shrouded in a fog of hydraulic vapors and waste heat from its thermal exchangers. As the ramp touched the deck, a lone man ambled down through the misty veils, his pace languid, his body language fluid and relaxed.

Šmrhová sidestepped right to put herself at the bottom of the ramp to meet him.

The man emerged from the haze. He was tall, thin, handsome

in a boyish way, and clean-shaven. Fair skinned with brown hair showing ample signs of gray, he greeted Šmrhová with a smile of the most perfectly white teeth she had ever seen. "Well, hello. I'm Thadiun."

She grabbed him by his wrist, flipped him onto his back on the deck, and put her knee into his chest. "No. You're under arrest."

If I were being honest, I'd have to admit that she turned me on. Truth is, I'd always been a sucker for strong women. I just love 'em. Probably because my mom was smart and tough. She didn't take any guff, I'll tell you that for nothing. She had principles. A code. That's important. You gotta have a code in life. Something you stand for. Lines you won't cross.

And I got the feeling this dark-haired, brown-eyed beauty from the *Starship Enterprise* was a woman who had a lot of uncrossable lines. From the moment she took me into custody, I knew she was something special. Fast? Like a striking cobra. Strong? Like a *mugato*.

But her interrogation methods could've used some work. She took it so seriously. It was unhealthy. That kind of thing leads to high blood pressure. Insomnia. Irritable bowel syndrome.

All the same, I loved watching her work. Even with my hands magnetically manacled and stuck to a table in the *Enterprise*'s brig.

Spittle flew from her lips as she shouted questions into my face. "Where were you during the Nausicaans' attack on the station?"

"I don't remember."

She started lifting holographic videos from the padd in her hand and flinging them into midair above us, where they played out while she continued. "Security cams saw you in close proximity to the warehouse attacked by the bandits." She conjured up footage of a running battle: the Nausicaans chasing me through one vapor-shrouded alleyway after another. "Is this you?"

"Can't tell. They didn't get my good side."

Lieutenant Šmrhová pounded her fist on the table. "You think this is funny, Okona? I've got the *Enterprise*'s forensic teams going over this footage right now. Not to mention every square centimeter of your ship, and every crime scene down below. We *will* tie you to this. And what do you think happens *then,* smartass?"

"I've always relied upon the kindness of strangers."

"Well, I doubt you'll find any here."

"Then we should go someplace else. I know the most charming little café on Bolarus. They make a *sikenberi* crêpe that will knock your socks off."

"Are you making a pass at me?"

"Depends. Is it working?"

She bolted from her seat, growled like a Vulcan *le-matya,* and stormed out of the interview room. As the door slid closed, I asked, "Was it something I said?"

There was no reply. She was playing hard to get. I respected that.

When the door opened again, I was pleased to see someone I recognized: Geordi La Forge. It had been a long time since he and I had last crossed paths—more than two decades, in fact—but I never forgot a face, even one that used to be hidden behind a visor but now sported a pair of metallic cybernetic eyes. I smiled at the sight of him. "Geordi!"

He frowned back at me. "Okona."

"Why do I get the feeling you're not here to bring me good news?"

"We've got you red-handed trying to hack the systems inside Kamhawy flight ops. So why don't you come clean and tell us what you're doing here?"

"All right, if you insist. I'm here as a talent scout. Looking for backup dancers for an interstellar review of Klingon traditional music for kids called *What's Opera, gagh?*"

"I could put you out an airlock and no one would ever know."

"Not true. *You'd* know. And it would consume your soul."

La Forge sighed in frustration. "Please don't make Worf come in here."

"Is that supposed to be a threat? No offense, Geordi, but in the last few weeks alone I've been shot at by mercs of every stripe and species, bitten by a Gorn, rudely probed by Tholians, drugged by Romulans, and used for a punching bag by a Balduk with a drinking problem. At this point, I seriously doubt there's anything that Starfleet would or could do to me that I'd see as anything worse than a boring day in grade-school detention. So unless Lieutenant Šmrhová wants to get back to planning a night out for two . . . piss off."

My spiel didn't make Geordi mad. He just shook his head at me.

"That's how you want to play it? Fine. Just tell me this: What do you think I'm gonna find when I search your ship?"

I smirked and made an effort not to laugh.

"Assuming you don't set off the booby trap? *Nothing.*"

The crawlspace beneath the *Tain Hu*'s cargo deck was tight enough to make La Forge feel claustrophobic. He had gone through the trapdoor head-first and shimmied on his belly to the only point of direct access to the booby trap. To reach it he had pulled himself under low cross struts and through gaps in walls of ODN cables, all while pushing his tool kit in front of him. *At least I can see in the dark without a palm beacon. One less thing I need to carry.*

Several long, overheated minutes after reaching the device, La Forge severed the last connection in its trigger assembly. He exhaled in relief as the miniaturized explosive's detonators deactivated. The protective sensor-jamming field surrounding him cycled down with a soft, falling hum. He slipped his hand under his chest and tapped his combadge. "La Forge to Elfiki. Do you read me?"

Her comm voice reverberated inside the cramped space. *"Go ahead, Geordi."*

"Bomb deactivated, force field down. Beam me out, please."

"Stand by."

A transporter beam enfolded La Forge in shimmering particles that flared white—

—and when details returned, he was standing in the cargo hold of the *Tain Hu*, along with Elfiki and half a dozen forensic-investigation specialists from the ship's security division. She arched a thin, elegant eyebrow at La Forge's lubricant-stained uniform. "Are you okay?"

"I'm fine." He brushed some gunk off his trousers. "But if it hadn't been for that thing's sensor jammer, I'd have been just as happy to let a 'bot handle that job."

"Harder than you thought?"

He harrumphed. "Hardly." But he was lying. The device had been far more sophisticated than what he'd expected to find. A drifter like Okona? Jury-rigging half his own systems? He should have had some amateurish plasma charge linked to the deuterium tanks. Instead, La Forge had found a trilithium charge with quantum triggers, set to frag the antimatter containment system and rupture the fuel tanks in a picosecond.

One mistake down there and I might've destroyed Kamhawy Freehold.

He was about to tell Elfiki the truth about the bomb, but they were interrupted by Ensign Rockwell Ingersol, an awkward young forensic investigator with an unkempt mustache and a tendency to speak too quickly to senior officers. "So we just finished a full sweep? I'm talking, y'know, bow to stern? And there's, like, nothing here. I mean *nada*. Zilch. Ziparooskie."

La Forge tried to project calm. "Slow down, Roc. You mean there's no contraband?"

"Forget contraband, man. I'm saying there's *nothing* on board. Period. No cargo, legal or otherwise. Every crate in the hold? Empty. Nothin' in the hidey-holes under the deck plates. Not even a tooth under his pillow." Ingersol flinched at the silence with which Elfiki and La Forge met his spiel. "Y'know, because of the tooth fairy? And—"

Elfiki made him talk to her hand. "We got it, Roc."

Hoping to distract the well-meaning motormouth, La Forge

pulled Ingersol aside. "Do me a favor, Roc. Take the rest of the team through the ship again, and scan for signal-latency artifacts. See if this ship has any compartments that are better hidden than the ones under the deck."

"Aye, sir." Like a puppy afflicted with nervous tics but still eager to please, Ingersol hurried back to the rest of the forensic team and relayed La Forge's orders.

As the specialists split up into pairs to search the small merchant ship, La Forge took Elfiki aside and lowered his voice. "No cargo? Does that seem odd to you?"

"A little. But maybe he came in with a load but didn't have an outgoing contract yet."

"I'd be more willing to believe that if we hadn't caught him trying to escape."

Elfiki tilted her head. "Maybe we should have a look at his manifest."

"Couldn't hurt."

They climbed the ladder to the main deck and headed forward to the cockpit, which was barely large enough to accommodate four average-sized humanoids—two up front, at the flight and command consoles, and two behind them to either side—one for sensors and navigation, the other for comms and onboard computer systems.

La Forge sat down in the command chair and tried to access the ship's logs and manifest. "We're still locked out. I was hoping the forensic team would've cracked this by now."

Elfiki planted herself in front of the main computer interface. "Let me see if I can bypass the lockouts with some backdoor commands built into its root kit." Her fingers flew against the interface, entering insanely long strings of esoteric commands—the kind of thing La Forge had seen Data do more than once. Elfiki was nowhere near as fast as Data, of course, but the fact that she could attempt feats such as this was nonetheless impressive to La Forge.

She shook her head, mildly frustrated. "This ship's data banks aren't running on any of the systems I'd expect to see on this kind of hardware. For that matter, nothing on this ship runs on standard-issue tech."

La Forge looked around the cockpit, which seemed as if it were being held together with spit, promises, and bits of wire. "Makes sense. Who knows what Okona had to do to keep this heap of crap flying?"

"That's not what I'm saying." Elfiki tapped the display above her head. "I'm saying all this stuff has been made to look old and lousy. But it's all cutting edge."

"Are you serious?"

"The encryption on the main computer is stronger than anything I've ever seen in civilian hands. And I'll bet you a month's pay that if we pull open the bulkheads, we'll find state-of-the-art tech underneath. This ship is a diamond dressed up like a lump of coal."

"Well, I'll be damned." La Forge turned in a small circle, admiring the shabby disguise of the *Tain Hu,* and marveling at what it might conceal. "Maybe we—"

His combadge chirped once, and then: *"Ingersol to La Forge."*

"Go ahead, Roc."

"Sir? I think we found something, under the pilot's bunk. A secret panel. We're cutting it open now."

"Be careful, Roc. It could be trapped, and we don't know what's in there."

"Hang on, sir. Almost in."

Elfiki and La Forge traded looks that said, *He's going to get us killed.*

Ingersol's voice pitched upward with excitement. *"It's open! Sir, we've got a cache of small arms, compact military ordnance—and what I'm guessing is a small fortune in latinum."*

His report put a smile on Elfiki's face. "Let's hear Mister Okona explain *that.*"

"Good work, Roc."

"Thank you, sir. We're gonna bag-and—"

The lights inside the *Tain Hu* went out, plunging the ship's interior into darkness. In a blink the cockpit's canopy tinted itself black, blocking all light from outside. La Forge froze. "Roc? Are you still there?" No response. La Forge tapped his combadge. It let out the sad, dysfunctional chirrup that meant it was offline. Switching to more old-fashioned methods, La Forge shouted through the cockpit's aft-facing exit, "Roc! Can you hear me?"

Ingersol shouted back, his voice muffled by bulkheads. "I hear you, sir!"

"Report!"

"We're all fine here! What happened to the lights?"

"We were gonna ask you that. Hold your position, until we—" La Forge stopped speaking when a red light activated on the command console. The indicator blinked three times, and then it remained on. Its glow was bright enough that it enabled La Forge to see Elfiki's face in the dark. "Any idea what that might—"

A voice bellowed from the speaker above La Forge's head: *"Worf to La Forge!"*

It took La Forge a moment to realize that all comms were being routed through the *Tain Hu.* "La Forge here."

"Order the forensic team to cease work immediately."

"Okay. Does this have—"

"Return to the Enterprise. *Right. Now."*

Turning down the temperature in the brig to keep prisoners agitated and awake was an old trick and a useful one, as long as it wasn't taken too far. With Okona down to trousers, a light tunic, his socks, and a thin pair of shoes, Šmrhová figured that the current temperature of thirteen degrees Celsius would have him eager to cooperate in no time.

Instead she found him seated at the table in the interview room, his hands clasped behind his head, legs stretched out in front of him, seemingly as cozy and as chipper as could be.

It made her want to slap his smug face.

She sat down across from him and called up a slew of files on her padd. "Do you know what I have here, Okona?"

"The galaxy's angriest diary?"

She let his jibe pass without comment. "I have your whole life in the palm of my hand. Your first brushes with the law. Your last run-in with Starfleet, on the *Enterprise*-D. And decades of suspect behavior after that."

A rakish grin. "Let me guess: you plan to use it for bedtime reading."

"I'm glad *you* think this is funny. Because now that I've got you, I don't plan on letting you slip away on a technicality."

"That's sweet of you, but we've only just met. I think it's a bit early for us to be making any serious commitments."

Her hand curled into a fist all on its own.

She took a deep breath, counted silently to five, and willed her hand to open. "Trouble follows you, Mister Okona. You've been implicated—though never formally charged—in literally *dozens* of unsolved heists, kidnappings, hijackings, and acts of violent sabotage, on more than four dozen worlds both inside and outside the Federation." She turned the padd so he could see its litany of his alleged offenses. "What can you tell me about that?"

A small shrug and a devil-may-care smirk. "As you said . . . I was never charged."

As God is my witness, I am going to kill this man with my bare hands.

"Mister Okona, I want to know what you were doing here at Kamhawy Freehold. Why you were seen fleeing the same Nausicaan bandits who sabotaged the force field. And—"

Okona waved his hand to cut her off. "Enough about me. Let's talk about *you*."

"Let's not."

"Why? Because you were taught at a young age to hide your feelings? Who drilled that into you? Your dad?" He squinted at her. "No—your mom. Your dad skipped on you, right?"

How could he know that?

His gaze was charming, hypnotic. It took effort for Šmrhová to look away and put her focus back on the padd and his dossier. "You were born in the Madena system. And your species appears to be descended from the Argelians—"

"Your mother taught you not to trust other women. And your dad? All you learned from his vanishing act was that you want approval from male authority figures. So much so that you mimic them. Swagger and talk tough like them. You'll do whatever it takes to make sure that when people see you, all they notice is the steely blade—never the silken sheath."

She felt exposed, revealed, vulnerable. It pissed her off.

"Amateur psychobabble? Is that the best you've got?"

"Sorry, sweetheart, but I *am* improvising here. That said, if you're free for dinner—"

Only then did she perceive the utter wrongness of the scene in front of her. "Where are your manacles?" A quick glance revealed them in the corner of the room. "How did you get them off?" She bolted from her seat and backed up to give herself room to move in case he attacked. "Who are you?"

"I'm just a boy . . . sitting in front of a girl . . . asking her to feed him."

Šmrhová was torn between an urge to flee and a desire to attack—but her rational mind, the part that had been trained by Starfleet, told her to stay calm, stand her ground, and figure this out. Okona was still seated. Except for his mouth, he had barely moved since she had come in. His eyebrows had been more animated than his hands. He was the epitome of calm.

She took control of her emotions. Relaxed her shoulders. Returned to the table and sat down across from Okona. "Why did the Nausicaans chase you?"

"Did they? I don't recall that."

Just like that, I'm back to wanting to hit him.

"Tell me about your ship."

"The *Tain Hu*? She's a beauty, ain't she?"

"She's a warp-speed eyesore. But she has more power than any hundred-year-old starhopper I've ever seen. Almost as if someone put an ugly old shell on a much newer ship."

"That would be a clever trick, wouldn't it?" He widened his disarming smile. "You don't date much, do you? That's a shame. I bet you've got—"

"Finish that sentence and you'll be shitting out your teeth for a week."

"No offense, but you really need to work on your small talk."

That's it.

Šmrhová was on her feet and circling the table to slap some sense into Okona—and then the interview room's door slid open. La Forge entered first, carrying a small bundle under his arm. He walked toward Okona.

Worf followed him in and placed himself in front of Šmrhová. "Lieutenant. This interview is terminated. All records of it have been deleted."

La Forge helped Okona to his feet and handed him his personal effects. Okona accepted them with a polite nod and a smile.

Šmrhová's temper started to rise. "Captain? What the hell is going on?"

"Mister Okona is not a suspect, a person of interest, or even a witness. And if anyone asks, he was never here."

As Okona strapped on his belt and sidearm, La Forge faced Šmrhová and explained with a disgruntled frown, "Lieutenant, say hello to Agent Thadiun Okona of Starfleet Intelligence."

5

—◆—

"Agent Okona has been released, as ordered." Because Worf was alone in the captain's ready room, he dared to add, "But I wish to object, for the record."

"Denied." The holoscreen image of Admiral Akaar captured the centenarian's dour scowl with startling clarity, even from across many light-years. *"Because there will be no record of Okona's detention on the* Enterprise, *nor his release from it."*

Worf was no stranger to the demands of operational security, especially as it concerned the safety of undercover intelligence operatives such as Okona. But he hated to see good opportunities wasted. "Admiral, the *Enterprise* was sent to Celes II to capture a gang of Nausicaan pirates. I believe Agent Okona is tracking those same Nausicaans. His information coupled with our resources could—"

"Commander Worf, the Enterprise *was also sent to Celes II to render aid to Kamhawy Freehold. I suggest the* Enterprise *focus on that aspect of the mission, for now."*

The admiral's implication was clear, but Worf was unwilling to accept it. "Letting Agent Okona leave this ship without compelling his cooperation in our investigation would be a mistake."

"No, it's an investment. One of many we've made in Mister Okona since his recruitment nearly two decades ago." Akaar paused. *"I need you to understand this, Commander. Okona is not just any agent. He's valuable to us because he's not a Federation citizen. That gives him a freedom of movement and association even our best NOC agents can't match."*

"It also means he has no diplomatic protection if he gets caught."

"True. Okona is a deniable asset, one that can be lost or captured

in foreign space without incurring a military reprisal against the Federation. But that remains true only so long as Agent Okona can't be linked, even tangentially, to Starfleet or the Federation—for instance, by being seen or suspected of aiding a Starfleet investigation or capture mission."

All of what the admiral had said was true; Worf had heard the same explanation given in defense of many other nonofficial cover, or NOC, agents through the years. But something about this case and Okona in particular continued to rouse Worf's suspicions.

"Deniability alone would not make one man so valuable. What service does Okona provide that warrants this kind of amnesty?"

"Commander Worf, you literally do not possess a high enough security clearance to be granted access to that information." With a heavy sigh the admiral added, *"Release Agent Okona and his ship from your custody in the next ten minutes. That is an order. Akaar out."* The chief admiral terminated the transmission, and his snowy-haired visage was replaced by a white Starfleet emblem on a field of azure.

Worf had never liked dealing with admirals. This encounter had not changed that.

He leaned forward and rested his left hand over his right fist on top of the desk. "Commander La Forge, please report to the ready room."

Within seconds the door to the bridge slid open with a soft hiss. The ambience of computer feedback tones and comms chatter filtered in briefly as La Forge stepped inside and approached Worf at the desk. Once the door closed, La Forge asked, "How'd it go?"

"As expected. Is the tracking device ready?"

"Tucked inside *Tain Hu*'s reserve deuterium tank. It'll activate in thirty minutes."

"Are you sure Okona will not detect it?"

"It's highly unlikely. We're using ultra-low-frequency subspace bursts. Even if his sensors could pick those up, they'd look like routine long-range comms static."

"Good. Tell Okona he is free to go. Then, keep me apprised

of every move he makes. He *will* help us find the Nausicaans—whether Starfleet likes it or not."

I climbed the aft ramp into the *Tain Hu*'s cargo hold and made my way forward to the cockpit. The inside of my ship looked like it had been ransacked by a gang of ill-tempered animals, because it had been. Bulkhead panels had been pulled down, cabinets emptied onto the deck, drawers rooted through and their contents scattered. I hadn't seen the inside of the *Tain Hu* in such disarray since my last wild weekend on Risa—back in the days when Risa still existed.

Mess or no, I was grateful to be leaving Celes II. The local hospitality had left much to be desired, and I'd quickly found the conversation repetitive and dull.

A quick scan of my biometric signatures released the ship's myriad lockouts. I settled into the pilot's chair and fired up the engines. Thrilling vibrations coursed through the deck and spaceframe. *Tain Hu* wanted to get back into open space just as badly as I did.

I flicked open the comms. "*Tain Hu* to Kamhawy flight control. Requesting permission to depart." I knew what they'd want next, so I sent it before they had to ask: my flight plan. Not my real one, of course, but one innocuous enough to free me from their clutches.

A woman's voice answered in clipped tones over the comm: "*Tain Hu, you are clear to launch. The tractor beam has been deactivated, and your docking bay force field is down. After launch, hold to heading three-five-five mark nine until you pass through the municipal shield. From there you will be free and clear to navigate.*"

"Thank you, control. This is *Tain Hu*, lifting off."

I gave the thrusters a nudge, just enough to lift my ship off the deck. Then I guided her forward through the docking bay's entrance. For one brief moment I thought about gunning my impulse drive and hot-rodding out of there, but I must have been feeling my age, because discretion triumphed over ego. I left at one-quarter thrusters, nice and easy, and slipped through a gap in the freehold's shield before settling into my flight path, where I accelerated to half impulse.

After I'd reached orbit, a glance at the sensors confirmed the *Enterprise* wasn't actively scanning me. I took that as a good sign. It helped sometimes, having friends in high places.

"Computer, systems check, level one."

"Running," the computer replied in a pleasant feminine voice. *"All systems nominal."*

"Just what I wanted to hear." I programmed my first warp jump into the helm. After a few seconds the computer confirmed that its calculations for FTL travel were complete. With a tap on the panel I engaged the warp drive, and the *Tain Hu* jumped away from Celes II.

I kept my eyes on the passive sensors for a few minutes. Then I powered up the quantum transceiver and waited for the green light. It snapped on. The channel was open.

"Expositor, this is Agonist. Do you copy?"

"Loud and clear, Agonist. Did you enjoy your time off?"

"You mean my incarceration on the *Enterprise*? It was all that I'd hoped for and less. I trust you've made some headway analyzing the intel I sent before my unplanned detention."

"Not as much as you might hope."

"Give me something. Anything."

"A few leads from COMINT. *Local LEOs report a handful of Nausicaans causing a ruckus on Argelius. Throwing money around, making a general nuisance of themselves."*

"Typical behavior for Nausicaans. What's our interest?"

"One of them was heard boasting about a big score on Celes II."

"Okay, *that* I can work with. Get me last-known locations, ASAP."

"Already uploaded."

"Nice work. Thanks, Expositor."

"Before you go—"

"Don't say it."

"—Suzerain needs to talk to you. Tootles." There was a soft *click* as Expositor relayed the conversation to our ever-dissatisfied superior.

"You really put your foot in it this time, Agonist. Losing the OPC was a disaster all by itself, but then you got nabbed by Starfleet? Do you have any idea how close you came to having your cover totally blown?"

"I have some idea, yes. By the way, how long should I wait before I disable the tracking device La Forge's people hid in my reserve deuterium tank?"

"Why haven't you done it already?"

"Partly because I made the questionable decision to check in with you first, and also because La Forge and his team must feel really clever right now, and I hate to take that away from them."

"I wish you showed the same regard for my *feelings—not to mention my career, and Expositor's. You're one bungle away from getting us all disavowed."*

"I know, and I'm sorry. Really. But I'm gonna fix this, I promise."

"Fine."

"Are we done? If we are, put Expositor back on."

Another barely audible *click* on the quantum channel. *"Expositor here."*

"Just a heads-up, I'll be changing course for Argelius as soon as I remove the *Enterprise*'s tracking device." I glanced at the data screen and saw the constabulary reports from Argelius's main spaceport city. *"Tain Hu* needs a new transponder ID—the Argelians know all of my aliases. And I'll need an inbound flight plan, backdated, along with a new legend."

"All in the next few hours? Geez, anything else?"

"Yes, actually. If it wouldn't be too much trouble, could you have the *Enterprise*'s quartermaster replicate a nice bouquet of flowers and send them to the quarters of security chief Aneta Šmrhová?

And have them add a card: 'Thanks for the lovely time. We must do it again. Love, Thadiun.' Oh, and get a vase, too. Something fancy."

"You've got to be kidding. Tell me you didn't—"

"No, I didn't. That's what makes it funny."

"Or suicidal."

"Just send them, please."

"Fine, but it comes out of your pay. If Suzerain sees that on the budget he'll hit the roof."

"Thanks, Ex."

"You're welcome. Now be careful this time, would you?"

I laughed. "C'mon, you know me—I'm *always* careful."

6

The man outside Picard's door looked exactly as he had expected he would: average height, a physique rounded by middle age, his pate bald on top with a ring of buzz-cut salt-and-pepper over his ears and above his neck. His complexion had the pale cast of a man who had spent much of his life indoors, hidden from natural light. The creases of his suit were perfect, as were the Windsor knot of his silk tie and the mirror-perfect polish of his oxfords. He toted a briefcase.

Picard offered the man his hand. "Commander Jonathan Ezor, I presume?"

"Retired, but yes." He shook Picard's hand. "I have my own practice now."

"So Will said." Picard stepped back and ushered Ezor inside. "Do come in. The dining room's been prepared for us."

Ezor stepped inside. "I hope you didn't go to any trouble."

"Not at all. Just tea."

"Oh. That would be perfect. After you, Captain."

They retired to the house's dining room, where Marie had set out her tea service. A silver pot filled with hot water rested on a matching tray. Two ancient china cups stood ready beside a box with a selection of loose teas, and beside the tray were a bowl of sugar, a saucer with some lemon wedges, and a small milk jug.

One cup was already filled, its tea ball submerged, the brew steeping. "I'd taken the liberty of starting my Earl Grey. Do you have a preference?"

"Yorkshire Gold, if you have it."

"Naturally. Second from the right."

They settled into chairs across one corner of the table. Picard removed the strainer from his cup and added the faintest squeeze of fresh lemon. He sipped quietly while Ezor prepared his own beverage. Judging from the surety of his actions, Picard surmised that Ezor was, like himself, no stranger to the etiquette and mysteries of proper English tea.

Once the lawyer's tea was steeping, Picard decided it was reasonable to proceed to business. "I understand you were a Starfleet JAG officer."

"Yes, for just over twenty years. I resigned in eighty-one, after the—" He caught himself as if he were about to commit a faux pas.

"You can mention the Borg. It's no longer the open wound for me that it once was." He set down his tea. "How do we begin?"

"Have you stood for an Article Thirty-Two hearing before?"

"No, but I have faced summary courts-martial. Both were routine inquiries—the first for the loss of the *Stargazer* under my command in 2355, the second in 2371, following the loss of the *Enterprise*-D."

"Okay, so you're familiar with the rudiments of military court procedure. That's good. An Article Thirty-Two hearing is more of an inquiry—"

"I know what it is," Picard interrupted, and then he felt embarrassed. "My apologies."

"I understand, Captain. This is a stressful time for you."

"That doesn't grant me a license for rude behavior. At any rate, I'm familiar with Article Thirty-Two hearings as the preliminary step to a court-martial."

"Correct. It's analogous to the preliminary hearings used in civilian criminal courts, to determine if sufficient evidence exists to warrant formal charges." Ezor lifted his briefcase into his lap, opened it, and took out a large padd. He set the briefcase back on the floor, and then he showed the padd to Picard. "The JAG Corps appointed an investigating officer to your case roughly two months ago. As you can see, she's been busy."

"Quite."

"As I'm sure you know, the rules of evidence in a military court differ from those that apply in the civilian judicial system. By the same token, different standards apply regarding the admissibility of witness testimony. One protection that still applies, however, is your right against compulsory self-incrimination."

The implications of Ezor's statement troubled Picard. "Shouldn't I be allowed to present my side? Explain my actions?"

"You're certainly *allowed* to do that, but I wouldn't *advise* it. As your legal counsel, my professional advice is that you not take the stand at any time, for any reason."

Picard took a moment to process that. "I see." He reached inside his jacket and withdrew his own padd. After unlocking it with a seven-digit code, he handed it to Ezor. "For your files. My logs, both command and personal, covering the entirety of the *Enterprise*'s mission to Tezwa in late 2379, as well as the period up to and including the resignation of President Min Zife."

Ezor looked at the padd as if it were a freshly excreted mass of feces. "What am I supposed to do with these?"

"I would hope that they might prove exculpatory."

"That's doubtful, Captain. If anything, your statements in these logs, combined with everything that's already been declassified because of the Section Thirty-One exposé, would only serve to tighten the noose around your neck." He nudged the padd back across the table to Picard. "This is of no use to us. And I'd suggest you refrain from rereading any of it."

"But it's evidence."

"Which the investigating officer has already subpoenaed. Trust me, Captain: there's nothing you can enter into evidence at this point that the JAG doesn't already have." Returning to his own padd, Ezor continued, "Walk me through everything that you remember about those events, starting—"

Picard held up a hand. "Wait. Before we submerge into details—" He waited until he had Ezor's full attention. "Don't you want to ask me whether I'm guilty?"

Ezor shook his head. "I never ask. And part of the reason why is that criminal culpability in a matter such as this is far more complicated than you can imagine. To be honest, Captain, it's possible that *you* might not know for certain, one way *or* the other.

"You might think yourself guilty, only to discover exculpatory factors. Or you might think yourself *not* guilty, only to find out that you've committed crimes of which you were unaware. But most important of all: It's irrelevant. Because all that matters when this mess is done is what the state can *prove*—and on what facts we can cast reasonable doubt.

"The rest . . . is just theater."

7

We drift in deep space, running in low-power mode. Cold and dark. Ghosts in a void that even the Four Winds cannot touch. Our voices echo inside the *Seovong*'s cargo bay as we huddle and debate. I let my people speak. All deserve to be heard. This concerns all of us.

The cargo bay reeks of body odor, dirty clothes, and foul breath. The air is hot from all our talking, thick with all the carbon dioxide we've spewed. Our own stink has grown strong enough to bury the bitter stench of burnt wiring, the chemical fumes of spilled lubricants and leaking hydraulic fluids, the lingering reek of our malfunctioning waste-reclamation system.

Zenber stalks back and forth like a caged predator. He slams his gloved fist on top of the crate holding the Husnock cannon. "Weapons like this change *everything*. No target is too hard for us to crack. No enemy too strong to face. This will make us *all* rich!"

Growls and rumblings of approval. His rant strikes a chord with the others. I feel their hunger. Their resentment. They want to make others hurt the way we do. I want that, too—but I also want more reward. Zenber yields the floor to Grendig, who beats his chest like the old heroes we all sang about as younglings. "Think of all the jobs we had to let pass because we didn't have the firepower! All that we could have taken! All we could have been!" He points at the sealed shipping container. "This makes us strong! Makes us a power to be reckoned with!"

More howls of support. A few of the younger guns slap the deck or stomp their feet. The older ones, like me and Doctor Veekhour, and the uniquely cold-blooded Drogeer, listen and consider the matter in silence. Do they really not see what is right in front of them?

It's Kiruna's turn to speak. She works the crowd, prowls its nearest edge, makes eye contact while she makes her argument. "No more hit-and-runs for us! With firepower like this, we can take a whole world hostage! Ransom it back for everything we'd need—and then use the cannon to keep ourselves safe!"

That gets a big roar. Passions are running hot now.

I've heard enough. I stand. Motion for Kiruna to step aside and sit down.

"Too small. All your plans. All your dreams. *Too. Small.*" I stand behind the crate. Rest my hands on top of it, as if it were an Altar of the Winds. "This is a gift. Not just to us. But to all our people. The Four Winds have trusted us with the fate of our kind. No more small targets. No more small jobs. We must dream bigger. Aim higher. Be more daring. Find our *guramba.*"

Majaf the engineer bolts to his feet, his pride wounded. "You say we have no *guramba*? How long have we fought for you? How many have died? How much have we bled?"

His protests ignite a chorus of complaints.

At the first sign of a break in the clamor, the ship's pilot steps out of the crowd to take the floor. "Six years we have clung to life! Hung on by our fingernails! With our fangs! Kinogar talks of dreams. Of plans. The only plan I care about is the one that feeds us all *tonight.*"

I like Haylak, but right now I want to choke him silent. Not because he is wrong, but because I need my people to do something they are in no condition to do: *make sacrifices.*

At the aft end of the bay, leaning against the bulkhead, Drogeer looks up. "Haylak is not wrong. We have a right to survive here and now." Then he nods toward me. "But Kinogar is also right. We have been lucky. Great power has come to us. We could use it just for ourselves. But that would make us no better than the Federation. We could use it to destroy without reason or care, but then we would be the same as the Borg." He steps forward, through the wall of bodies, some standing and some seated, to take the floor. "Or we could stand for all of our kind."

You beautiful, reasonable *venolar*. No one makes an argument like a snowblood.

"This is what I am saying!" I raise my voice to claim the room's attention. "This weapon did not come to us by accident. We captured it because our redemption has come at last. The Four Winds have given us the mission of helping every Nausicaan who still draws breath to reclaim their birthright. To take back their pride! To give them back their *guramba*!"

I lift my voice louder, as if to fill the ship and shake the stars. "The Four Winds have blown away the storm clouds that have haunted us since the death of our world. Now they sing the old songs and call us forth. To remember our *true natures*!"

I lock eyes with each of my people as I circle the room.

"We were not born to be scavengers! Nausicaans are a people of pride. Power. Courage. Now our time of darkness is at an end! We have been called to rise up, to step into the light, to be seen and counted as the new heroes of our people!"

The truth of this moment weighs upon me. I am not merely calling my people to embrace a more ambitious criminality. I am sounding the clarion for war.

"In our darkest hour, all of our closest galactic neighbors treated us like vermin. They acted as if our suffering meant less than theirs, for no better reason than we live beneath our own banner. They ignored our wounded and our hungry. Turned their backs on our dead. Left us to dig through our own ashes and watch our skies *burn*.

"They counted on us to die.

"Now it's time for us to show those *fegoru* that we are still predators! That we are not so easy to kill—and that we will not be forgotten. Not by them. Not by their children. Not by the galaxy. We are Nausicaans! And we will take back what is ours!"

My people's cheering hits me like a tidal wave.

I know I have them. Their hearts are on fire. They know what's at stake.

All that we have left in the universe is on the line now. All that we are. All that our people still hold dear. All that we might yet be.

We never saw the Borg coming. Never had a chance to defend our world. Our people.

Today, those of us who remain will stand as one. And we will be counted.

Live or die, win or lose . . . we will make certain that history remembers us.

There were many aspects of his service with Starfleet Intelligence that Commander Sam Lavelle found rewarding and productive, but attending the daily intelligence services briefing at the Palais de la Concorde was not one of them.

No one had to explain to him why the daily gathering was necessary. Coordination of activity between the Federation's various internal and external intelligence agencies was vital to maintaining their respective and collective effectiveness, and to safeguarding the security of the United Federation of Planets, its extraterritorial possessions, and its allies.

But the bureaucratic red tape that arose from that coordination nearly drove him to apoplexy on a daily basis. The sheer volume of paperwork was maddening. And it was daunting to know that every operational decision he made—some of them in the heat of life-or-death action—would be second-guessed in committee every day for the rest of his career. His only solace was that on most days he did not have to be there to endure it in person.

Today was not one of those days.

Lavelle breezed through security on his way into the building. He had become a well-known presence in the Palais since his promotion to operations management inside of Starfleet Intelligence, which served as the Federation's primary agency for gathering foreign intelligence. As he entered the third-floor conference room that had been designated for the daily reports from the Federation's intelligence community (whose members often referred to themselves collectively as simply "the Community," complete with capital *C*), he recognized several of his peers from the UFP's civilian intelligence and counterintelligence agencies.

Settling in across the table from him was Patton Gibson, a spymaster with the Federation Security Agency, which held jurisdiction over internal counterintelligence operations. Whereas Gibson was squat, pudgy, pasty, and bald, Lavelle was tall, trim, tanned, and blessed with a full head of hair that had only recently become salted with gray at his temples and above his ears.

A few seats to Lavelle's left, but on the same side of the long table, was J. Chapman Shull, a fortyish woman with hair the color of cold steel and a fierce will to match. A proud daughter of the American South, she had worked her way up through the ranks of the obscure but vital Federation Reconnaissance Office. Though it employed no operatives in the field as SI did abroad and the FSA sometimes did domestically, the FRO was responsible for monitoring nearly every observable segment of the galaxy—and beyond. Its technology and the specialists who maintained it were the ever-watchful eyes and ears of the United Federation of Planets.

Lavelle took his seat and called up Okona's latest report, which included an after-action summary by Lieutenant Naomi Wildman—a.k.a. Expositor, Okona's tactical support, analysis, and remote intelligence officer—on his padd.

No sooner had Lavelle gotten comfortable when he was compelled to stand by the arrival of Bera chim Gleer, the security advisor to President Kellessar zh'Tarash. The burly male Tellarite had earned a reputation for being cantankerous during his decades representing Tellar in the Federation Council, and he had made no secret of his political opposition to former president Nanietta Bacco. Though he had been publicly critical of President zh'Tarash in the weeks that had followed her election and inauguration, that had not stopped the Andorian *zhen* from appointing Gleer to this vital cabinet post, nor had it dissuaded Gleer from accepting the job. In spite of their obvious ideological differences, Gleer had become one of zh'Tarash's most trusted advisors—a partnership that had paid dividends in the form of improved political relations between their respective worlds, which previously had spent centuries as bitter rivals.

Gleer took his place at the head of the table. "All right, sit down." Everyone took to their chairs. Gleer's persona was gruff, but also efficient.

Lavelle leaned back, hoping to hide himself behind his peers and postpone his turn in the spotlight. *Please don't let him start with me. Please don't let him start with—*

"Commander Lavelle," Gleer said, his voice booming. "Explain to me how one of your assets lost possession of a Husnock Omega-particle cannon."

Dammit.

Lavelle sat forward and cleared his throat. "NOC agent Agonist was using a Husnock OPC—which had been replicated by the Breen from original schematics they stole last year—as bait to expose and neutralize an Orion Syndicate black market cell operating on Celes II. In addition, Agonist's orders were to track the Husnock weapon after it left the Orions' hands, in order to expose and neutralize potential non-state terrorist groups suspected of operating within the Beta Quadrant."

Even from a distance of several meters, Lavelle felt Gleer's scathing stare, as if it gave off a stinging heat that prickled his skin. The Tellarite harrumphed. "If you had already planned to track the weapon, how did your asset manage to lose it?"

"The transaction with the Orions was interrupted by a band of heavily armed Nausicaans. They killed the Orion cell members—including Agonist's inside man, who was going to plant a tracker on the crate after it had been scanned—before a tracking device could be insinuated."

"Where is the OPC now, Commander?"

"We're still working on that, sir."

Gleer's lean face scrunched into a portrait of pure anger. "In other words, you don't know. A catastrophically powerful weapon is loose inside local space, in the hands of non-state actors with unclear motives, because you and your team bungled a cakewalk op. Tell me, Commander: How am I to explain this to the president without telling her that you and your team have completely humped the *targ*?"

All eyes were on Lavelle, and he felt his face redden with shame. "I think that might be a bit unfair, sir. I mean, if we were to rate this on a scale, with a perfect op at one end, and a total *targ*-hump at the other, I think we'd—"

"Save it. This is one gigantic bowl of *plurk* you've brought us, so you're the one who has to eat it. Because I damned well won't be. Just answer me this: What is your team doing *right now* to recover that weapon?"

"Our analyst, Lieutenant Wildman, is coordinating with Agonist to track all activity by Nausicaan pirates and agitators within forty light-years of Celes II, and we're monitoring all subspace frequencies for any chatter that might suggest the Nausicaans are either trying to sell the weapon, or use it as a recruitment tool."

"Good. But this asset of yours—Agonist? Tell me that's not who I think it is."

"I'm afraid it is, sir. But I assure you, he's the perfect agent for the job."

"Is your man following protocols, at least?"

"Absolutely, sir."

"And he made sure the Nausicaans didn't acquire an operational device?"

"That's my understanding," Lavelle lied, knowing the truth would get him demoted.

Gleer looked at least slightly mollified. "Is your agent's cover intact?"

"Yessir. I made it very clear to Agonist that his discretion is absolutely vital. At my request, he is doing everything he can to maintain a low profile."

The Balduk's fist hit my jaw hard enough to rattle my teeth, split my lip, and fill my mouth with blood. The blow sent me sprawling into a table. It splintered beneath me. I crashed to the floor in a mess of broken wood, shattered glass, and spilled drinks. Bruised and sluggish, I tried to push myself up from the floor. That's when the Chalnoth's steel-tipped boot slammed into my ribs, cracking bones and forcing the air out of my chest.

I was starting to think these guys didn't like me.

I rolled with the kick and counted myself lucky that the folks ducking out of the bar were nimble enough to hop over me as I tumbled underfoot like an abused slab of meat.

Every part of me hurt as I got up. My left eye was swollen shut. My torso was a map of deep, dull aches punctuated with the sharp jabs of fractures threatening to break through the skin. A grinding sensation in my right hip told me that it was out of its socket again. And my hands felt like they weighed a hundred kilos each— no matter how hard I tried to raise them to protect my head, I couldn't make my arms obey my commands.

The Balduk, the Chalnoth, and their Antican cohort had done a great job of softening me up. So good a job, in fact, that even though their species looked nothing alike—the Balduk were lupine brutes whose long faces looked like they wore their skulls on the outside; the Chalnoth resembled bipedal lions with great manes and tusks that protruded from their mouths; and the Anticans had a canine quality to their appearance, but would never deserve the praise of being "good dogs"—I was so far past double vision that I could no longer tell them apart.

Which meant it was time for their cowardly Nausicaan ring-leader to come and take his free shots at my undefended chin.

I waited for him to get close. He didn't let me down. The big bastard put both pairs of his fangs right into my face and gave me a heavy dose of his rotted-fish breath. "Skinny *hyoo-mon*! Start fight you can't finish. Not smart."

"Forgive me, but you're wrong." I shrugged and smiled. "I'm not human."

It was just the goading the Nausicaan needed. He grabbed the front of my shirt with one beefy mitt and pulled the other back, winding up to land the mother of all punches.

Then I struck.

I ducked and twisted, seized his wrist, and freed myself from his grip. Bent his thumb backward just far enough to force him to his knees.

His buddies charged in to attack. With one hand I kept the pressure on the Nausicaan's finger. With the other I drew my blaster and stunned the goons in three snap-shots. They collapsed on the deck with minor scorches on their outer garments but stunned well enough that I knew they wouldn't be getting up any time soon.

Then the Nausicaan slipped free and sprang at me, reaching for my throat.

My free hand deflected his, and I stepped backward to foul his balance. He stumbled forward and began to fall. I kicked my knee into the bottom of his jaw and savored the crunch of breaking teeth. For good measure I . . .

I wondered whether anyone would believe that story. It was so much more satisfying than what *really* happened after I got my big whiff of ugly fish-mouth.

He buried his fist in my gut and I folded over like a cooked prawn.

I staggered and fell forward. Slumped against the Nausicaan. Tried to hang on to him, but he backpedaled and let me face-plant into the bar's piss-sprayed floor.

His three friends chortled and whooped with laughter at my expense.

Then came the click-and-whine of an energy weapon being charged at the bar. With my one good eye, I watched the quartet that had been kicking my ass moments earlier freeze. They turned to face the bartender. The Argelian lass was tall but thin as a rail. She held a Tellarite-made charged-plasma scattergun pointed at the Nausicaan's head. "Get outta my place."

The Nausicaan grinned. It wasn't a friendly gesture among his species. Baring teeth and fangs was how Nausicaans challenged people to fight.

I winced as the bartender fired and cooked half of the Nausicaan's right leg in one shot. He roared, his minions shrieked in fear, and the scattergun's blast echoed inside the bar's confines. Smoke softened the room's edges as the air thickened with the stench of charred meat.

The bartender recharged her scattergun. "Out. *Now.*"

One fried limb was all the persuasion the Nausicaan and his friends needed. Wary of the scattergun, they back-stepped toward the bar's main entrance. The Antican was the first one out, followed by the Balduk and the Chalnoth. The Nausicaan paused just long enough to deliver a final taunting grin before he, too, retreated from the bar.

Several seconds after their departure, the bartender shut off the scattergun. She set it back into its hiding place behind the bar top, and then she poured a pair of shots of Andorian gin.

"Get off the floor," she said, as if I weren't then more bruise than man. "I have to mop."

I groaned and struggled not to shed tears as I pulled myself up onto a bar stool. As I sat at the bar and sipped my gin, the bartender eyed me with suspicion. "Guess what?"

"I dread to ask."

"Last man standing gets the bill."

I nodded, too weary to argue. "Sounds fair." I reached inside my coat. Pulled out a credit chip loaded with Federation virtual currency. Slapped it on the bar. "This should cover it."

"Drinks *and* damages, tough guy."

"That's fine."

I could tell she still didn't really believe me. Part of her wanted to, but she couldn't even start to hide her distrust. Nonetheless, she took the chip, and as she walked away she grumbled, "This better not be a scam."

"It's good, you have my word."

She said nothing. Chip in hand she repaired to the bar's back office, to see just how much value she could extract from the thing.

I waited until she was gone from sight before I pulled from my pants pocket the comms device that I had stolen from the Nausicaan. It had been one of the easiest lifts I'd done in years. It had helped that I'd been able to distract him by collapsing on him like a half-conscious wino. Curious, I switched on the device to see what kind of lock I needed to beat. It loaded the main interface without delay, and I laughed.

Typical careless Nausicaan. Doesn't secure his tech.

I hid the comm inside my coat and called it a good night's work.

8

If you want to be left alone, go where no one else wants to go. That's what her father had always said. At first glance it had struck her as glib, like the kind of prattle that passed for wisdom between drunkards or fools. But the longer that Juneau Wright had lived with those words, the more she had come to embrace them as her mantra. There was a truth in them. After all, hermits remained isolated by choosing to dwell in places bleak and hard to reach.

So she had chosen to do the same, just with more company.

Raising the capital had not been easy on a Starfleet warrant officer's salary. After three decades of frugal living and a string of savvy investments, she had come up with only a fraction of the funds she'd needed to effect this escape from civilization. It all would have been so much easier to do had she been willing to seek an underwriting grant from the Federation. But that would have defeated the point. The whole idea of this project was to live without allegiance, to be an island with its own flag and no political obligations. To be independent. To be free.

The answer had been to find several thousand like-minded beings who were willing to pool their resources to turn Wright's dream into a reality: Stonekettle Station, a commune of scientists, scholars, philosophical theorists, and countless others from all manner of professions, all united in their desire to live as citizens of the galaxy.

Twenty years later, Stonekettle Station had not only come into being, it had become renowned as a bastion of free thought, technological innovation, and sensible self-governance, and it had grown to the size of a small city. In spite of its reputation, however, few people ever chose to visit. The reason why was no secret.

Wright had constructed her new community on Skarda, one of the harshest, least hospitable worlds she had been able to find in the Beta Quadrant—a choice that had made the planet almost affordable, at least as planets went. It was an airless, geologically inactive rockball orbiting a red giant star. Its rotation was slow enough that a single day, or "sol," on Skarda was roughly equal to six days on her native world of Earth. A core of superdense elements had given the planet more mass than its size would have suggested, but its gravity was still only sixty-nine percent of Earth standard. Inside the station, artificial gravity generators made up the difference and provided more natural-feeling environments for its humanoid residents.

A massive dome of transparent aluminum sheltered Stonekettle Station from the majority of hazards the universe at large tended to throw their way. By night it fended off the cold of space— temperatures routinely dipped as low as negative one hundred seventy-nine degrees on the dark side of Skarda—and it protected them from a variety of cosmic rays, magnetic storms, and impacts by objects up to half a meter in diameter. Larger threats were dealt with by a variety of methods, including nadion-pulse cannons, quantum torpedoes, and ultra-tech drone interceptor ships, remotely controlled from Stonekettle Station, that could either alter the courses of incoming asteroids or obliterate them outright.

By day, however, the dome alone was not enough.

Because of Skarda's proximity to its star, portions of its surface would melt within two hours after sunrise. Within four hours, the temperature on the sunlit surface exceeded eleven hundred degrees Celsius, and a few remote sensors had registered temperatures close to thirteen hundred degrees at midday. As strong as transparent aluminum was, temperatures that intense would turn it into a scorching puddle of liquid metal.

For that reason, the scientists of Stonekettle Station had from the start shielded the dome's exterior with a sophisticated mesh of high-energy force fields. That had soon yielded its own challenge, however. An enormous amount of energy was required to fend off the deadly heat of Skarda's red-giant star, more than the city's main generators could provide without leaving the rest of the facility in the dark. To address that deficiency, Wright and her engineers had invented a miniaturized and extremely powerful portable matter-antimatter reactor, or PMAR. Now in its fifth and final year of testing, it was proving to be a major leap forward in municipal power generation, one that promised to grant Stonekettle Station financial security for generations to come once it was licensed out to cities and starbases across the galaxy.

Beneath the great dome, the station-turned-city was subdivided by sixteen colossal bulkheads of transparent aluminum. These had been installed as a precaution against the risk of a dome breach, so that in an emergency, endangered areas could be evacuated and sealed off to protect the rest of the station. It was a system that Wright prayed never had to be used. Even though the internal bulkheads were reinforced by the same force-field mesh as the main dome, she didn't want to imagine the fiery hell that Skarda's star would bring down upon her people if anything ever happened to that dome.

Except on the days when she prayed for it to implode and put her out of her misery.

Wright had only one regret about spearheading the creation of Stonekettle Station, and that was the fact that she spent more time administrating it—or, as she liked to say, "putting out fires"—than she did working on her own research projects. A never-ending stream of tedium flowed across her desk and threatened to drown her in boredom. If it weren't for the oddballs with which she'd surrounded herself in Ops, she might have resigned in disgust years earlier.

Her deputy administrator, Keer glasch Pov, was a perpetual pessimist and master of gallows humor. At over a century, he was also the oldest Tellarite she had ever known.

Wright slapped the back of Pov's chair, which was mounted on a swing arm attached to a gimbal, a setup that enabled him to move between several workstations without getting up. "Hey, Keer. How many disasters today?"

"Should I count the ones that rolled over from yesterday?"

"Forget I asked."

"Already have."

The next station Wright passed on the way from the turbolift to her office was the master systems console. It was tended by an engineering liaison, which was a polite way of saying "person who is a functional incompetent with tools and code alike." The current first-shift exile from her chief engineer's domain deep in the bowels of the central core was Kootis Denn, a young Arkenite. A slender headset encircled his prodigious, three-lobed bald noggin; it was called an *anlac'ven,* he'd told Wright, and he needed it to help his inner ear compensate for the lack of wave motion when he was working in terrestrial environments.

If only there were a headset that could teach him how to use a dyno-spanner.

"Everything still working, Kootis?"

He answered without looking up from the day's offworld news. "Yup. Until it isn't."

"Filling me with confidence, kid, as always."

The last duty post between Wright and her office was comms, the nerve center of the whole level—which, inexplicably, was occupied by Yoon-ta, a nervous but well-meaning Thallonian woman with burgundy-red skin and flowing, bone-white hair.

"Yoon! Whadda ya hear?"

"Um, nothing. I mean, plenty, sure, but nothing strange. All good, ma'am." She winced, remembering too late that Wright hated being called *ma'am.* "I mean—all good, boss."

"All right. I'll be in my office if anyone—"

An alert signal beeped on Yoon-ta's console. She swiveled toward it, slapped the console to mute the noise, and then she poked at the panel's interface until she had news worth sharing. She looked up at Wright. "Boss, we're getting a distress signal."

"From . . . ?"

Yoon-ta coaxed the info from her system. "A small cargo ship. The *Jameela*. A *Beaumont*-class frigate, Denevan registry."

"In other words, impossible to verify."

Though she knew it was uncharitable of her, Wright had learned in recent years to be suspicious of any vessel that used a registry from a world that had been wiped out by the Borg. Many such vessels were run by legitimate merchants who simply had been lax in finding new ports of registry for their ships. But just as many, if not more, were being used by pirates to maintain their anonymity and get within striking distance of targets—and such attacks had been on the rise in this sector. If ever a situation called for caution, Wright figured, this was it.

Pov shouted from his command post, "Is it a general hail, or one sent to us?"

Yoon-ta covered the tiny transceiver in her ear while she listened to the SOS again. "It's directed at us. They're asking for permission to land."

"That can't be right," Denn deadpanned. "No one ever comes here."

Something about this bugged Wright, but she couldn't say what it was. "Permission denied. We'll send out a repair team on a shuttle."

The Ops team waited while Yoon-ta relayed Wright's answer to the ship in trouble. Then the young woman looked back at Wright. "They say they don't have time to wait, and can't make these repairs in space. They say their life-support system is failing, and their environmental suits are depleted. If they don't land in the next ten minutes, they're all going to suffocate."

Wright shot a look at Pov. "Check it out."

"Scanning." Within seconds, the gruff old Tellarite harrumphed. "Checks out. Their exchanger's shot, and CO_2 levels inside the ship are borderline toxic."

Everyone was looking at Wright, waiting for her to say something. She checked the station's clock. It was the thirtieth hour of darkness, just six hours shy of the literal middle of the night on Skarda. There would be no safer time for them to open a small portal in the dome. That should have allayed her concerns, but instead it made them worse.

Perhaps sensing her equivocation, Pov added, "Boss? Interstellar law requires us to render aid to ships in distress. We might not fly a flag, but we still need to respect that."

He was right. She knew it—and very likely, so did whoever was on that ship.

"Yoon, tell the *Jameela* to power down. We'll bring it in with a tractor beam." A smooth pivot toward system ops. "Kootis, extra power to the force field. I don't want to lose any air when we open the dome, and I want to keep that ship contained until it lands." She issued her next orders on the move, heading back toward her deputy. "Put the *Jameela* into docking bay forty-seven. Send a team of engineers and at least ten armed security officers to meet it. And lock down the main corridor outside the bay."

Pov raised one bushy white eyebrow, and his porcine nostrils flared. "Overkill?"

"Let's call it *an abundance of caution.*"

So trusting. So foolish. Cry for help and the gullible fools open their doors. As we descend through the station's briefly opened dome, I point at Drogeer. He dispatches a small cloud of tiny drones loaded with explosives from the *Seovong*'s torpedo tubes. The devices are too small to register on most sensors, and when they operate in passive mode, most defensive systems mistake them for small bits of harmless debris.

The dome closes above us. Our ship continues its smooth glide into a docking bay, cradled in a tractor beam. I swat Majaf's shoulder. "Make sure to knock out their tractor beams before we take off."

He raises a padd and taps it with his index finger. *"System hack loaded and ready."*

It's all about being prepared. Kradech steps forward to stand at my left, his rifle in hand. A platoon of battle-hardened Nausicaans lines up behind us in the ship's cargo hold. High-pitched whines overlap in the crowded space—the sound of disruptors' pre-fire chambers being primed for combat. It is especially shrill today, because our weapons are set to kill. We will need to blast through some heavy barricades to reach the station's PMAR core facility. Those who get in our way are about to be reunited with their ancestors.

I feel the tremors in the deck beneath my boots as the ship touches down. We have every reason to expect the bay outside the ship is pressurized with breathable air, but I'm taking no chances. We all wear pressurized suits with visors enhanced by tactical holographic overlays. In a blink I see where all of my people are, assess the field of battle, and react accordingly.

"Grendig, take Squad One left. Zenber, take Squad Two right. Squad Three, with me. We'll halt on the ramp and cover the bay's main entrance. Kradech, Squad Four is the rear guard. Don't advance until my team clears the ramp. Everyone clear?"

Nods of assent from my squad leaders.

"No prisoners. Keep moving until we reach the PMAR. Then we split up: Squads One and Two recover the PMAR. Squads Three and Four disable the station's comms and tractor beams. Rendezvous here. Anyone not back by the time we load the PMAR gets left behind."

Pilot Haylak's voice cuts into our helmet comms: *"Bay pressurized. Opening aft hatch."*

"Find cover, then fire and advance." In front of us, the ramp starts to lower. "May the Four Winds blow at your backs."

The ramp touches down. My men charge. Fan out across the docking bay. I lead my team down onto the ramp. We crouch until we're all on one knee, rifles braced against our shoulders.

On the far side of the docking bay the doors open with a sharp hiss. I let the station personnel rush in. By the time they see the trap, it's too late.

I fire the first shot. Blast a hole through a Trill toting a phaser rifle.

Then all of my men fire, unleashing an angry red barrage. Smoldering bodies litter the deck. A few of the station's people get shots off, take down a couple of my soldiers. But the fight in the docking bay is over in a matter of seconds. After the last echoes of weapons fire fade away, the grating bleat of station alarms assails us from unseen speakers overhead.

I lead my squad off the ramp and across the bay, toward the entrance to the station's core structure. "This way. Demolition techs, to the front. Get us through the barricades, and then into the main turbolift shaft. From there we'll use antigravs to make our descent to reactor control."

Majaf rounds up the explosives experts and joins them on the sprint to the force-field–reinforced blast doors that have sealed the main corridor outside the bay. There was no sound of them being deployed while we were in the bay. They must have been in place before we landed. This station's commander is every bit as shrewd and paranoid as I've been warned.

Good. That will make my victory all the more satisfying.

My engineers work quickly. They slap shaped demolition charges all over the blast door that blocks our way to the nearest turbolift hatch. Majaf shouts, *"Fire in the hole!"* When I see him running for cover, I know to follow him, and so do the rest of my people.

We crouch and cover our heads.

Even through closed eyes, the moment of detonation feels like staring into a sunrise while being pummeled with thunder. The shock wave hits us like a great charging animal, bowls us over, sends us all rolling. When we come to a stop and look around, we are swamped in smoke. Hunks of white-hot metal debris—the remains of the blast door—litter the deck.

I spring to my feet. "Move!" My men get up, and we run.

The enemy will respond. They have the advantage of numbers. We need to be faster.

By the time I reach the doors to the turbolift, Drogeer and Grendig are prying them open. The two halves of the portal separate with a hydraulic gasp and a shriek of metal grinding against metal. My men force the halves of the door back into the bulkhead. On the other side yawn black chasms both above and below. Only after I engage the night-vision function of my suit's visor am I able to see the architecture of several parallel shafts in the great open space beyond.

Kiruna asks me, *"How far to reactor control?"*

I note the symbol denoting this deck's location. It takes me a second to translate the Federation-standard characters in my head, and then do the math. "Twenty-three levels down."

The fog around us shifts, disturbed by a new surge of fresh air. Someone has opened the next blast door. I raise my weapon. "Incoming!" I point in the direction from which the new air comes, and my people lay down suppressing fire.

Orange phaser beams slice through the vapors and cut black scars along the walls and ceiling. The station's security people are fast and well armed. I can only hope I haven't underestimated them.

"Squad Two, move up! Squad Four, cover the rear! Don't let them split us up or cut us off! Squad Three, into the shaft!"

I step in first, surrender to free fall for a few seconds, until I feel my stomach lurch into my throat. Then I switch on my suit's antigrav circuit to slow my fall. By the time we reach reactor control at the bottom, we land like feathers on a hot summer day.

I don't have to look up to know my people are with me.

They are my blood. My bone. My brothers and sisters.

Where I go, I know they will follow.

We are the wind.

"Where the hell are they?" Wright stood behind her deputy and tried to make sense of the alerts and tactical reports that flooded his screens. "Why don't we have eyes in the docking bay?"

Pov gave himself a push and swung his chair over to the security monitors. "Their ship is jamming us. Started just after they touched down." He swatted a console that was showing him nothing but garbled machine language. "Now it's hashing internal comms."

"Damage report," Denn shouted. "Main-shaft turbolifts are off-line."

Yoon-ta reacted as if that were good news. "Sounds like they're stuck."

"Don't count on it," Wright said, moving to review the updates on Denn's screens. "If they knocked out the lifts, they must be using the shafts to reach their target." She leaned closer to the Arkenite engineer. "Kootis, monitor all damage-control circuits. Tell me where the intruders breach, and maybe we can figure out where they're going."

He looked confused. "Without sensors, how do we know they're even *in* the shaft?"

"Because that's the route I'd use if I wanted to make a fast attack without fighting my way through thirty levels of enemy personnel." Frustrated by the lack of new intel on the master systems display, Wright hurried to the communications station. "Yoon-ta, fire up the emergency hard line to the security office. I need to talk to Chief Gilmour, on the double."

"I'll try, but we're getting tons of static, even on the hard lines."

"Just do it, and patch it through to Keer's station." Wright returned to her deputy's side, still no wiser and far more aggravated. "What are they here for?"

"Hard to say." Pov called up a station directory. "Nausicaan bandits usually go for soft targets. Exposed equipment. Fuel or water. Food shipments. The really gutsy ones have taken down a few latinum transports. But these guys must be some combination of highly motivated, tragically stupid, or clinically insane, because no matter why they came here, there's no way they're getting out alive. The dome's already closed and the energy shield is up."

Denn interjected, "New damage report! Turbolift doors breached on level seventy-five."

Wright's stomach twisted with horrified realization of what was happening. "They're going after the PMAR. Kootis, prime the backup generators! Keer, push the PMAR into overdrive, make it too hot for them to grab. And Yoon-ta, get Gilmour on the horn! We need everybody who can hold a weapon in reactor control! *Right. Now.*"

I breach the door to reactor control and fire a quick burst of disruptor pulses as I enter. Most of my shots hit consoles, filling the air with smoke and sparks, but one rips through a skinny Caitian woman's left elbow and leaves the lower half of her arm dangling. She yowls, adding to the chaos. By the time the two armed guards posted to the reactor room know what's going on, my men are inside the confined space and have them covered.

"Take their weapons," I tell Drogeer and Grendig. Then I point at Majaf. "Get the PMAR ready to move." I turn toward Kiruna. "Distractions. Now."

My people move fast and speak little. Nolok and his brother Lokun disarm the station's reactor security guards—and then stun them for good measure. Last thing we need now are fools trying to be heroes.

An angry growl draws my attention. Majaf grabs two of the station's engineers—a pair of Bynars—by the fronts of their jumpsuits and lifts the tiny bipeds off the floor so he can look them in the eye while he threatens them. *"Shut down the PMAR and release it from the chassis!"*

"Not that easy," says the first Bynar.

The second adds, "Multistep process."

Majaf shakes the Bynars. *"Lies! Made to be portable! Fast shutdown and removal."*

"Quick installation—"

"—difficult removal."

I wrap my hand around the throat of the second Bynar and glare at the first. "Want to feel this one die? No? Shut down and remove PMAR in the next two minutes."

I tighten my grip for emphasis.

"Need my partner—" The Bynar is terrified and struggling to adapt to not having his thought finished by his linked partner. "—to perform procedure."

I let go of Bynar Two, who lands in a crumple on the deck. "Work."

Confident that Majaf has the Bynars under control, I move to stand behind Kiruna, who has taken over reactor control's master systems board. "Report."

"Closing emergency bulkheads on all engineering levels." She punches in more commands. *"Launching all emergency escape pods into the red giant."* She plugs a trio of isolinear chips into slots on the board, and then she keys in more functions. *"Closing and locking all docking bay emergency doors except ours."* With a flourish, she enters her final sequence. *"Triggering overloads in the command systems. That will slow them down, make it harder for them to fix my sabotage."*

I slap her back. "Good job."

At the center of the cramped space, the Bynars and their engineering team race to turn off the portable matter-antimatter reactor. Grendig returns with one of the station's junior people, whom he has forced to retrieve the PMAR's traveling case.

A few paces away, Zenber is anxious. He checks the chrono. Then he checks it again. The sound of plasma torches cutting through emergency bulkheads on the next level above ours resounds through the station's skeleton.

I beckon Kiruna and Grendig. They jog up to me, eager to serve. "Go to the top level of this section. Set proximity bombs for anybody who forces in from above."

The duo take off running. Fearless. No questions. True Nausicaans.

That will buy us a few more minutes. More than enough time to remove the PMAR.

Zenber sidles over to me. *"When are you going to tell us the exit strategy?"*

I take a breath and savor the moment. "When it's time to go."

"They did what?" Wright prayed she had heard her deputy wrong.

"Fired all the escape pods into the sun," Pov said. "And locked down all the docking bays except their own before frying the command network with a major overload."

"That does it. Close the outer door on the bandits' docking bay manually, on the double."

Pov nodded. "On it."

On the inside, Wright boiled with rage, but she had to keep a professional face, no matter what. Being in command meant being in control—not just of one's people and one's assignment, but also of oneself. That didn't mean taking abuse lying down.

"Clear all sections adjacent to that ship, then have security get in there and hit it with everything we've got. Mess up the bay all you want, but I want that ship in pieces."

"Order relayed," Pov said. Then he added under his breath, "Fingers crossed."

Vexed by the paucity of information she was getting about the attack, Wright moved to the master systems console and crowded in next to Denn. "Where are they now?"

"Still in reactor control, I think."

"You think? You mean you don't know?"

The Arkenite flapped his arms at his screens. "Can *you* make sense of this? Because I certainly can't. Power surges, sensor grids offline, comms are fouled . . ."

Yoon-ta interrupted, "Engineering reports they're closing the docking bay blast door now, but it's going to take about thirty sec—"

An ominous roar thundered through the station, rattling the core down to its frame. The sudden tremor sent Wright and her crew stumbling into consoles and walls. Flashes overhead—overloaded EPS conduits blew out ceiling panels and dislodged bundles of cable, which tumbled into the operations center amid great firefalls of sparks and white-hot plasma.

Wright was done pretending to be calm. "What the hell was that?"

Pov struggled to make his array of consoles yield anything but static and nonsense. "I'll tell you as soon as I know."

Smoke filled the operations center as hot plasma melted through the deck plates. Wright sprang to the closest emergency locker and pulled it open. She pulled out a full-face mask with a small portable air tank, and a handheld fire suppressor. Walking back to the smoldering points that were spewing the most toxic fumes, she set the suppressor for "plasma fire" and sprayed the trouble spots with a pressurized stream of fire-choking chemicals.

In less than half a minute the fires were out, but the cloud of vapors choking Ops had become thick enough to reduce the team to silhouettes even at short distance. Wright pulled off her face mask, and the stench of scorched wiring and overheated metal filled her nose. "Any word yet what hit us?"

Denn was the first to speak. "The bandits' ship shot its way out."

"Where is it now?"

This time Pov had the report: "Navigating beneath the dome. Way too close to the habitats for my comfort."

"Well, we can't just shoot it down. Any chance the tractor beams are back online?"

"Sorry, still borked. But maybe we can trap them in a shield pocket if—" A rapid series of high-pitched beeps shrilled from Pov's console. "We've got a sighting of the bandits! They're still in reactor control." He looked almost excited by the news. "There's no way out of there. It's scan-shielded. We've got them pinned down."

Wright felt the coming disaster in her bones, but prayed she was wrong. "Tell Gilmour to get down there and negotiate. Maybe if we ask for their demands, we can stall them until—"

Darkness fell, and the feedback tones of the computers went silent. For several seconds the only points of light were sparks tumbling from ragged gaps in the overhead. Then dim red and orange emergency lights powered by local batteries snapped on, bathing the operations center in a ruddy glow. The consoles remained offline, and Wright became suddenly aware of the absence of a white noise she had long taken for granted: the hum of the ventilation system.

"Yoon-ta, find a personal comm. See if you can raise anybody in reactor control."

"Yes, ma'am—I mean, boss."

Damn, this went pear-shaped fast.

Outside one of the operations center's broad transparent aluminum windows, which looked out and down upon the sprawl of buildings that constituted Stonekettle Station, the bandits' ship sped upward, as if on a collision course with the great dome.

"What the hell are they—?"

A searing flash forced Wright to shut her eyes and turn away.

Then a blast wave rocked the core like a high-magnitude earthquake. There was no riding it out, no grabbing something heavy. Wright and her crew and everything around them tumbled madly for several seconds, like dice shaken inside a cup.

When the light and thunder faded, Wright forced her bruised and aching body off the deck and turned to look out the window—to see her worst nightmare come true.

Something had disintegrated a jagged swath of the dome. Enormous slabs of bent transparent aluminum rained onto the structures far below. Wright's stomach turned at the sight of it. Thousands of tons of debris plunged from a dizzying height. There was no telling the number of buildings that would be destroyed, or how many people hurt or killed.

Even from inside Ops, Wright heard the wails of sirens—
station alarms warning of falling atmospheric pressure, the cries
of emergency-response vehicles, and the steady trumpeting bleats
that signaled the dome's interior partitions were being sealed to
isolate the exposed sections. Far below, flashing lights pierced the
veils of smoke and dust that rose from the devastation.

Though she couldn't see them through the haze, Wright knew
that thousands of people must have been scrambling to evacuate
the compromised sectors of Stonekettle Station.

When she looked up, she saw a prismatic pulse of light—the
bandits' ship jumping to warp and abandoning her critically damaged station to its fate.

Around her, the Ops crew looked dazed. She needed them
working, and quickly.

"Yoon, are we clear of the bandits' jamming?"

It took the young Thallonian woman a moment to collect herself. "Hard to say without the main subspace transmitter, but I
think so."

"All right. Kootis, get a line to engineering. I want *everybody*
working to repair the subspace transmitter. Let Yoon-ta know the
second it's back online. We need to send an SOS."

Confusion creased the engineering liaison officer's brow. "What
about the dome?"

"The dome's fragged. If we don't get help before the sun comes
up in twenty-nine hours . . . everyone in this station's gonna die."

9

The normal low buzz of activity that filled the bridge of the *Enterprise* had gone quiet as soon as the ship assumed orbit above Skarda and the fractured dome of Stonekettle Station. Worf and the ship's other senior officers had listened with rapt attention as Juneau Wright described the brazen attack on her facility—and the impending disaster it now faced as a consequence.

"That was roughly six hours ago." Wright's face filled the forward viewscreen. *"We now have just under twenty-four hours until sunrise hits us. If we can't restore the energy shield by then, the heat from the red giant will vaporize the station and everyone in it."* She massaged her forehead and brushed aside a sweat-soaked lock of her steel-gray hair. *"Please tell me there's something the* Enterprise *can do to help us."*

Worf leaned forward in the command chair, his demeanor pensive. "Can you evacuate?"

"Not really. We've got more than sixty thousand people down here, most of them permanent residents without personal transportation. All of the ships that were able to bug out did, each of them packed to the bulkheads, but that only moved about six hundred people." She raised one eyebrow to telegraph her doubt of her own next question. *"I don't suppose you've got room for a spare sixty thousand people?"*

"We do not." The situation looked grimmer with each passing moment. Worf looked toward La Forge. "Are there any ships nearby that can aid the evacuation?"

La Forge keyed information into his command console, and then he frowned. "The nearest ships with the necessary extra life-support are over seventy-two hours away."

The dismay on Wright's face mirrored Worf's mounting frustration. "If we cannot get the people out, we need to protect them in place. Lieutenant Šmrhová, can we use the *Enterprise*'s shields to cover the damage in the station's dome?"

The security chief shook her head. "No, sir. The breach is too large."

"That wouldn't be enough, anyway," Wright cut in. *"The heat from the star will melt the dome without our energy shield to back it up. And if you can't shield the breach, there's no way you can shield the whole dome."*

Worf sighed. "What will it take to restore the energy shield?"

"We'll need to replace our PMAR core."

With a knowing grimace, La Forge said, "Let me guess: You don't have a spare."

"It's a complex piece of engineering." Wright looked and sounded a bit embarrassed as she continued. *"My chief engineer has been pushing us for years to build a backup, but we're always stretching our budget as it is. Living on borrowed time and shrinking credit. I had to make a command decision, and keeping the rest of the station running had to come first."*

Nodding, La Forge said, "We have a few dozen portable fusion generators on board. Could those help?"

Wright shook her head. *"Sorry. You could have five times as many and it wouldn't be enough to raise even part of the shield."*

Worf stood. "Then we must either recover your PMAR, or build a new one."

His declaration left Wright slack-jawed. *"Build a new one? You can't be serious. It's a miniaturized matter-antimatter reactor. It took the best engineers and physicists in local space years to make it work, and* months *to build the last one from the ground up."*

"That might be true. But your team did not have the resources of the *Enterprise*. Do you still have the schematics for the device?"

"We might be able to dig them up. But if you're suggesting we share them—"

Her reluctance irked Šmrhová. "Do you want our help or not?"

"I won't let our most valuable patent fall into the wrong hands."

The station leader's stubbornness was about to rile Worf's temper, but then La Forge stepped toward the viewscreen. "Does your PMAR contain anything that can't be replicated?"

"Only about forty specialized components and ten unique compounds. Why?"

Her news deflated La Forge's trademark optimism. "So much for the easy way."

From the aft section of the bridge, Elfiki spoke up. "Sirs? Maybe we're looking at this the wrong way. We might not have to replace the PMAR if we can replace the power it provided."

"That's a good point," La Forge said. "Commander Wright, can your team send us some ballpark figures for how much power it takes to run your energy shield?"

"Sure. Hang on." To someone off-screen she said, *"Keer, send the shield's power-usage specs to the* Enterprise." Then, to La Forge, *"Should come through in a moment."*

La Forge faced Šmrhová. "Relay that data directly to Elfiki's console."

Once more looking hopeful, La Forge hurried aft. Worf followed him. They flanked Elfiki at the aft sciences console and waited while she analyzed the new data. She highlighted a few columns of information, singled out other sums, and nodded. "It'll be tight, but we might be able to jury-rig a solution that'll keep one section of their shield up."

That sounded less than ideal to Worf. "One? How large a section?"

Elfiki pointed out details as she continued. "One-sixteenth of the shield on the dome, and two of the internal bulkheads beneath it." A humble shrug. "Best we can do in the time we have before sunrise." To La Forge she added, "We'll need to pull the warp cores from two of our runabouts, yank the override safeties, and rewire the station's reactor core to accept them."

"In less than twenty-four hours? That's cutting it pretty close, Dina. And how are they supposed to cram sixty thousand people into a sliver of the station made to hold four?"

Elfiki lifted her hands in a gesture of surrender. "I solved the problem in front of me."

Worf clapped a hand onto Elfiki's shoulder. "Well done." He turned back toward the main viewscreen, and La Forge followed him as they moved in front of the command chair. "Commander Wright. With your permission, I would like to send Commander La Forge and an engineering team. We have a plan to restore part of your energy shield."

"We'll take all the help we can get, Captain."

"I also plan to find the bandits who stole your reactor core—and bring it back." He swiveled his chair toward La Forge. "Number One, assemble an away team, and proceed to the station on the runabouts *Irrawaddy* and *Colorado*. Take whatever you require."

"Aye, Captain." La Forge moved toward the aft turbolift. "Elfiki, you're with me."

Elfiki handed off her station to Lieutenant Corinne Clipet and followed La Forge into the turbolift. As they made their exit, Worf settled back into the command chair.

"Good luck, Director Wright."

"Thank you, Captain. Stonekettle Station out."

She ended the transmission, and the screen reverted to a view of the night side of Skarda—and the one feeble gleam of life clinging naked to its surface.

Worf shot a glance toward the security console. "Lieutenant Šmrhová. You are now the acting XO. Please take over that station."

"Aye, sir." She handed off the security console to Rennan Konya and moved to the standing console on Worf's right. "Sir, if we recover the stolen core but fail to bring it back here before sunrise, that might present a new problem."

"How so?"

"Assuming La Forge and Elfiki can patch a runabout's warp core into the station's energy shield—if it's raised when we get back, we won't be able to land a ship or beam through it. Which means whatever they rig up has to hold for sixty hours, until sunset. But if it doesn't—"

"Assume that it will," Worf said, seeing no value in pessimism. He stood and headed for the ready room. "We break orbit as soon as the runabouts are away. And the moment we do, I want to hear your plan for hunting down the Nausicaans who did this."

Stepping out of the runabout *Colorado* into a docking bay near the top of the station's core, La Forge shivered at the bitter chill in the air and marveled at the sight of his breath condensing into vapor. Looking back at the other engineers and specialists debarking from the runabout, he saw them clench in reaction to the cold—gritting their teeth and pulling their arms to their sides. Reflexively, La Forge did the same, hugging his satchel of tools a bit closer to his flank.

A hatch opened on the far side of the bay. The station's director strode in, followed by one of the tallest Andorians La Forge had ever seen. Wright wore a heavy jacket and gloves, but the Andorian seemed comfortable in his loose shirt with the sleeves rolled up past his elbows, showing off his sky-blue skin and reminding La Forge that the Andorians hailed from a frigid homeworld. The lanky Andorian *thaan* carried a padd in his left hand.

La Forge waited for Elfiki to exit the runabout and join him before he walked over to meet Wright and her associate. He extended his hand in greeting. "Commander Geordi La Forge, chief engineer and acting XO, *Enterprise*." A half nod toward Elfiki. "This is our senior science officer, Lieutenant Dina Elfiki."

"A pleasure." Wright shook La Forge's hand and then Elfiki's before introducing her colleague. "This is Doctor Peshalan th'Fehlan, our director of engineering."

"Thank you both for coming," th'Fehlan said with a polite smile and a small twitch of his antennae. He handed his padd to La Forge. "As per your request, this is a complete inventory of all parts, equipment, tools, and raw materials available here on the station. I regret that we can't run the replicators while the station is on emergency battery power."

"We understand, believe me." La Forge paged through the inventory lists, his eyes scanning for critical items in each category. "This looks good."

Wright looked past La Forge and Elfiki to watch nearly two dozen *Enterprise* engineers begin dismantling the runabouts. "What are your people doing?"

Elfiki shot a wary look at La Forge. "Gotta tell 'em sometime."

That quip stoked Wright's suspicions. "Tell us what?"

La Forge reached into his satchel, pulled out his padd, and handed it to Wright. "We plan to restore one segment of your shield by powering it with the warp cores from our runabouts."

Th'Fehlan's antennae wobbled. "One segment? You mean just one of the sixteen?"

"Correct," Elfiki said. "That plus the core is all we can manage."

La Forge continued, "For this to work, we need to move everybody into one sector of the station, under the strongest surviving section of the dome."

Wright looked doubtful. "That's gonna be pretty tight quarters."

"Which is why we need your people to prioritize saving lives and information, but let physical possessions go. We're gonna need every square centimeter we can get, and fast."

That directive made th'Fehlan wince. "Commander, this station is packed with unique prototype inventions. Do you really expect our people to sacrifice years or even decades of research and effort on just your say-so?"

"Only if they want to live."

Wright put herself between La Forge and th'Fehlan. "That's why we'll move all the databanks into the safe sector, Pesh. Our people can rebuild, but not if they're dead."

The Andorian hung his head in surrender, then he nodded. "Fine."

Once more Wright looked at the runabouts, whose engine cores were half-exposed. "You guys must be sure this'll work."

Elfiki shrugged. "Pretty sure. It works in theory, at least."

Alarm widened the Andorian's pale eyes. "In *theory*?" He shot his own worried look at the runabouts. "What if your theory's wrong? You'll get cooked to death with the rest of us."

The science officer played it cool. "That's okay. I don't have any big plans."

Wright looked stunned. "Commander, is she serious?"

"In her way. But truth? This is no joke. If this doesn't work, we have no exit strategy. So you should know: My team and I are in this all the way. If you go down, we go down with you."

That seemed to reassure Wright. "Nothing like having skin in the game. So where do you want to start working this miracle of yours? Ops or engineering?"

"Engineering," La Forge said. "We need to see how the PMAR was hooked up, and then we'll design and fabricate an adapter that'll let us connect our warp cores in its place."

Wright and th'Fehlan nodded in agreement, and then the engineer gestured toward the hatchway behind him. "Follow me. I'll take you down to reactor control."

Elfiki fell in beside La Forge, and then she motioned for him to fall back a stride so she could whisper something to him. "I lied about not having any plans. Please don't get us killed."

He shot her an accusatory look. "*Me?* This was *your* plan."

She sighed, shook her head, and quickened her pace. "I *knew* you'd bring that up."

10

Heavy rain scoured the windows of the courtroom. Instead of golden sunlight and blue skies to greet the proceedings, the chamber's high vantage of San Francisco's metropolitan sprawl was obscured by low-lying black clouds and dense curtains of mist.

Lightning and thunder had shaken Picard's transport pod on its approach to Starfleet Headquarters. He had weathered too many brushes with death to be alarmed by something as mundane as a thunderstorm, but he had held Crusher's hand for comfort all the same, and he'd been thankful that she had felt no need to remark upon it after they'd landed.

Ezor awaited them inside the courtroom. He stood at the table reserved for the defense, setting out his padd and some printed notes. Spare padds had been set out in front of the second and third chairs. The second chair was occupied by Lieutenant Galen Tam, a youthful Bajoran woman assigned to Picard's defense by the Starfleet JAG; the third chair was for Picard.

At the prosecution's table sat a fortyish Efrosian man with a golden mane and a matching long mustache and chin tuft. He wore a white Starfleet dress uniform bearing a commander's rank insignia. He had but a single padd in front of him, and no associates.

Crusher sidestepped to a seat in the front row of the lower gallery, directly behind the defense's table. Ezor turned and opened the gate in the banister that separated the active area of the courtroom from the spectators' benches. "Good morning, Captain. Please, have a seat."

"Thank you." Picard shuffled behind the chairs, paused to shake Galen's hand, and then settled into his chair. As he'd expected, the room had no jury box, just a dais with a table from which an admiral would preside. At either end of the dais, behind the table, stood two flags: to Picard's left, the blue and white stars-and-laurels flag of the United Federation of Planets, and on the right, the banner of Starfleet.

A commotion behind him turned his head. The doors of the courtroom were opened wide, and members of the public and media hurried in to find seats. A similar clamor occurred above him, in the upper gallery. In less than half a minute all available seats were taken, and the doors were closed once more. The courtroom was packed with stares of morbid curiosity.

Crusher leaned forward and confided to Picard, "Nothing like being popular."

"Or infamous."

A door to the left of the dais slid open, and the hearing officer entered. As expected, she was a Starfleet admiral with whom Picard had no prior associations, either personal or professional. She paused a moment beside the dais to confer with her aide.

Ezor leaned over to speak confidentially to Picard. "Remember what we talked about. Be aware of your own reactions. Maintain a calm presence. Be attentive without—"

Excited murmurs filled the galleries as the rear door of the courtroom opened once more. Picard—along with everyone else—looked back to see who had just arrived.

And all of his hard-won composure turned to nauseated dread.

Phillipa Louvois, the Attorney General of the United Federation of Planets, the same woman who had prosecuted him at his court-martial after the loss of the *Stargazer* and who had nearly cost Data his freedom as a sentient being, strode up the center aisle, her visage stern. She pushed past the gate and took her place—in the first chair of the prosecution's table.

Picard's pulse thumped in his ears, and sweat beaded on his brow. He did his best to keep his voice to a whisper, but his urgency made it almost impossible. "Jonathan! What's going on?"

The defense lawyer looked as shocked as Picard felt. "We're about to find out."

The admiral ascended the dais. Another Starfleet officer stepped forward and announced, "All rise!" Everyone in the courtroom stood. "These proceedings are now in session." As soon as the admiral took her seat, the officer before the dais declared, "Be seated." As the participants and spectators settled, the bailiff withdrew to a post in the corner of the room.

Picard watched the admiral, a middle-aged humanoid—he knew better than to presume she was human, despite her appearance—thrice ring the small brass bell on her table.

"This proceeding will come to order. This preliminary hearing is convened by Admiral Leonard James Akaar, Chief Admiral, Starfleet, by the appointing order dated January sixteen, 2387. My name is Admiral Marin Liu. I am certified in accordance with Article Twenty-Seven B and sworn in accordance with Article Forty-Two A of the Starfleet Code of Military Justice. I have been detailed as preliminary hearing officer under Article Thirty-Two B of the Starfleet Code of Military Justice, to inquire into the matters set forth on the charge sheet dated January ninth, 2387, in the case of Captain Jean-Luc Picard, the accused. Copies of the charge sheet and appointing order have been furnished to me and all counsel, and will be inserted into the record as PHO Exhibits One and Two, respectively.

"Present at this hearing are myself, Admiral Marin Liu, the detailed preliminary hearing officer; the accused, Captain Jean-Luc Picard; defense counsels, Mister Jonathan Ezor and Lieutenant Galen Tam, Starfleet JAG; and as counsel for the government, Commander Uli Tymel, Starfleet JAG, and Ms. Phillipa Louvois, Federation Department of Justice."

Liu looked at Picard. "Are you Captain Jean-Luc Picard, the accused in this case?"

Picard replied. "Yes, Admiral."

"Thank you." Liu continued, "Lead counsels, at this time please state your legal qualifications, status as to oath, the authority by whom you were appointed and/or detailed, and any disqualifying capacity in which you may have acted." She nodded at Louvois.

"I am Phillipa Louvois, the Attorney General of the United Federation of Planets. I am certified in accordance with Article Twenty-Seven B and sworn in accordance with Article Forty-Two A of the Starfleet Code of Military Justice. I've been detailed to this preliminary hearing by direct order of the Federation Council, and with the consent of Starfleet Command, the convening authority. I have not acted in any disqualifying manner."

"I'm Jonathan Ezor, civilian counsel for the defense. I'm certified in accordance with Article Twenty-Seven B and sworn in accordance with Article Forty-Two A of the Starfleet Code of Military Justice. I've been detailed to this preliminary hearing at the request of the accused, and with the consent of Starfleet Command, the convening authority. I have not acted in any disqualifying manner."

"Mister Ezor, I see we have your contact information on file. Would you please tell the court where you are presently licensed to practice law?"

"Admiral, I'm a member in good standing of the Earth, Vulcan, and Rigel bars."

"Mister Ezor, do you affirm that you will faithfully perform all the duties of defense counsel in this case now in preliminary hearing?"

"Yes, Admiral."

"Very good. It appears that defense and government counsels have the requisite qualifications to proceed. Is the accused or counsel for either side aware of any grounds that might disqualify *me* from conducting this preliminary hearing, or does either side desire to question me, or raise any challenge now?"

Louvois shook her head. "No, Admiral."

Ezor followed suit: "No, Admiral."

"Mister Ezor, are there grounds to assert that the accused was not mentally responsible for his actions at the time of the offenses charged, or that the accused is not mentally competent to participate in the defense of his case in this preliminary hearing today?"

Ezor replied, "No, Admiral."

"Captain Picard, Attorney General Louvois has been appointed as counsel for the government at this preliminary hearing. She is not acting as counsel for the preliminary hearing officer. She is here solely to represent the government. She will not advise me as to my determination of probable cause, or what disposition I will recommend in this case, as those decisions rest with me alone. After completing this preliminary hearing, I shall make determinations and recommendations I deem appropriate for matters disclosed at this proceeding. Do you understand?"

Picard nodded. "Yes, Admiral."

"Are there any questions by any party concerning my function or the function of government counsel?"

A quick chorus of "No, Admiral" moved things along.

"Captain Picard, you've chosen to retain civilian counsel at your own expense, and to retain the advice of military counsel in second chair. Do you have any questions about your rights to counsel, or their respective functions in this proceeding?"

"No, Admiral."

"Very well, then. Let's proceed. Captain Picard, do you have a copy of the charge sheet in front of you?"

"Yes, Admiral."

"Captain Picard, please follow along on your copy of the charge sheet as I inform you of the general nature of the charges that I will be reviewing at this preliminary hearing. You are alleged to have committed the following violations of the Starfleet Code of Military Justice:

"Specification One of Charge One alleges that Captain Picard was an accessory to the murder of President Min Zife, Starfleet commander-in-chief and elected head of state of the United Federation of Planets, in violation of Article One-Eighteen of the SCMJ.

"Specification One of Charge Two alleges that Captain Picard knowingly engaged in a conspiracy with other Starfleet officers to murder President Min Zife, in violation of Article Eighty-One of the SCMJ.

"Specification One of Charge Three alleges that Captain Picard knowingly abetted acts of espionage carried out by an entity known as Section Thirty-One, in violation of Article One-Zero-Six A of the SCMJ.

"Specification One of Charge Four alleges that Captain Picard knowingly suborned and abetted sedition against the United Federation of Planets, by attempting to coerce the unlawful removal of sitting President Min Zife, in violation of Article Ninety-Four of the SCMJ.

"The name of the accuser is Admiral Leonard James Akaar, as sworn to before Admiral Marta Batanides. A copy of the charge sheet will be appended to the record as PHO Exhibit Three. Does either counsel desire that I read each charge and specification in full, or desire further review of the charge sheet before we continue?"

Louvois and then Ezor both replied, "No, Admiral."

"Captain Picard, under Article Thirty-Two of the Starfleet Code of Military Justice, you have the right to remain silent and to refuse to make a statement regarding any offense of which you are accused or suspected and that is being investigated. The fact that you may choose to exercise this right cannot be used against you in any way, and I may not consider your silence as evidence. Do you understand your right to remain silent?"

"Yes, Admiral."

"Captain Picard, I am going to explain to you the purpose of this preliminary hearing and the rights which you have in this forum. If you do not understand what I am telling you, let me know and I will explain it again until you and I are both satisfied that you understand.

"The purpose of this preliminary hearing is to review the charges against you, to determine if there is probable cause to believe the charged offenses were committed and whether *you* committed the offenses; to determine if there is court-martial jurisdiction over the offenses and over you; to consider the form of the charges; and to recommend to Admiral Akaar what action should be taken regarding the charges.

"I have been appointed to conduct a formal preliminary hearing under Article Thirty-Two of the Starfleet Code of Military Justice. I know nothing at all about your case except for the information contained in the charge sheet and in the order that appointed me to investigate these charges. I have also met with your counsel and with government counsel to discuss some of the legal issues that might arise during this preliminary hearing, to identify the witnesses who are expected to testify, and to mark the exhibits which may be offered.

"I have formed no opinion as to probable cause, jurisdiction, or what I will recommend. I will make a recommendation to Admiral Akaar solely on the basis of the evidence that I receive during this preliminary hearing. You will have an opportunity to review the report in which I will submit my recommendations, and you will have an opportunity to object to it, as well.

"This preliminary hearing is *not* a trial, and I am not a judge. I am not here to determine your innocence or guilt. It is my duty to impartially weigh the evidence to determine probable cause, jurisdiction, and the form of the charges, and to formulate a recommendation. I will consider all matters within the scope of the hearing that tend to exonerate you, and all matters that tend to implicate you, in violations of the SCMJ. I might recommend that the charges against you be referred for trial at a general court-martial, special court-martial, or summary court-martial. I also might recommend that the charges, or some of them, be dismissed or disposed of at a forum other than trial by court-martial.

"Admiral Akaar is not bound by my recommendation. For example, if I recommend that a charge against you should be dismissed, he might still decide to send that charge to a court-martial. Because my recommendations are only advisory in nature and are not binding on the convening authority, he will make the final decision on the disposition of the charges in this case.

"Do you understand the purpose of this preliminary hearing?"

"Yes, Admiral."

"Captain Picard, I advised you earlier that you have the right to remain silent, and that you do not have to make any statement regarding the offenses of which you are accused and that any statement you do make may be used as evidence against you in a trial by court-martial.

"You also have the right to testify under oath, or to make an unsworn statement. If you testify under oath you may be cross-examined by the government counsel and questioned by me. If you decide to make an *unsworn* statement, you may *not* be cross-examined by government counsel *or* questioned by me. You may make an unsworn statement orally or in writing, personally or through your counsel; you may make a statement with respect to some charges or specifications and not others, and you may use a combination of these methods. If you do make a statement, whatever you say will be considered and weighed as evidence by me the same as the testimony of other witnesses.

"Do you understand your right to make a statement at this preliminary hearing?"

"I do, Admiral."

"Finally, I remind counsel that they may make objections to the evidence presented here. Note, however, that the rules of evidence applicable to courts-martial are not generally applicable at this proceeding. I will also respond to objections based on relevancy grounds, and I will not admit evidence that is not relevant under Military Rule of Evidence Four-Zero-One. Does either counsel have any questions about this?"

"No, Admiral," Louvois said.

Ezor added, "No, Admiral."

"Very good. Attorney General Louvois, is the government prepared to present evidence?"

"We are, Admiral."

"Proceed."

"Admiral, the government calls to the stand . . . Captain Jean-Luc Picard."

A susurrus of excitement rose and fell among the spectators. Ezor leaned over to Picard and whispered to him, "Decline."

"I'll do no such thing." Picard started to rise.

Ezor pulled him back into his seat. "She's goading you. Don't take the bait."

Admiral Liu's cool manner betrayed a hint of annoyance. "Mister Ezor? Is your client going to testify or not?"

Ezor stood. "Admiral, I request a two-minute recess to confer with my client."

"Make it quick, Counselor."

Picard made no effort to conceal his own irritation as Ezor pulled him into a huddle at their table. "Refusing to testify is the shelter of a guilty man."

"No, Captain, it's the self-sustaining act of a *wise* man."

"Invoking a privilege of silence implies I have something to hide."

"Haven't you been paying attention? That's explicitly *not true* in a court of law. Refusing to be used as a witness against yourself is just good tactics."

"I've done nothing wrong."

"No, you only *think* you haven't. Which means you have the foolish courage of the self-righteous—and in this forum, that can get you life in prison."

"I won't be muted for the sake of convenience."

"Then at least choose to speak on your own terms. Let her make her case without your help. Later on, you can make an unsworn statement, lay out your side of things."

"And excuse myself from questions or cross-examination? How

much weight can my testimony have if I'm not willing to give it under oath?"

"Captain, please think about what you're doing. If you let her swear you in, she can keep you on that stand for as long as she likes. Hours, maybe even *days*. And once you're up there, you can no longer invoke your right against self-incrimination. That's a suicide play."

"I'm not afraid of her."

"You *should* be. The Federation didn't send its AG to prosecute this case just for grins—they're throwing you to the wolves. And it's no mystery why the government sent her. They knew she'd rile you up. This is a trap. Don't fall for it."

Everything that Ezor said made logical sense. But Picard couldn't accept any of it. He stood. "I'm sorry, but a Starfleet officer's first duty is always to the truth."

"This is a court of law, Captain. *Truth* is less important here than you'd like to think."

"Be ready with objections." Picard stepped around his lawyer and headed for the witness box, muttering to himself, "We're going to need them."

Please don't let this be a mistake.

A deep quiet suffused the bridge of the *Enterprise*. The ship lingered in the magnetic pole of a gas giant, operating in low-power stealth mode to avoid registering on other ships' sensors. For the moment it relied instead on passive sensors, including unaided visual monitors, to observe the nearby Talarus Shipyard, a starship-construction facility located in deep space.

Šmrhová wandered from one duty station to the next, sneaking looks past her fellow bridge officers to see if there had been any change, any indication that her prediction of the Nausicaans' next target had proved correct. Each one was as dark as the next, leaving her with a mounting embarrassment that she struggled to hide.

It's so damned hard to stand out on this ship. To make a difference, to get noticed. All my life, people have told me I was born to excel, to do great things. And until I got to the Enterprise, *I believed them. But here,* everybody's *amazing. All of them were born to do big things.*

Here I'm just average. And average doesn't get promoted.

She didn't realize she was pacing next to her command console until she ran into Worf. He looked down at her, his expression as stern as always.

"Lieutenant. You seem . . . anxious."

"Sorry, sir." She turned toward her console, as if miming activity would fool him into thinking she was doing something useful. "It's just hard to sit and wait."

"Yes. It is."

She abandoned her charade, grabbed the sides of her console with both hands, and slumped as if a great weight had landed on her back. "They should have been here by now." Her lament garnered no response from Worf, and that only stoked her insecurity. "I crunched every bit of data we had on the Nausicaans. Patterns to their past attacks, what they stole in previous heists. I even factored in their tendency toward escalation and the proximity of high-value targets within three subsectors of Stonekettle Station, and then I asked myself, 'What would these bandits do with a Husnock cannon and a PMAR?' And the only thing that made sense was that they'd try to steal a half-built warship, use the PMAR to run it, and the cannon to arm it."

Worf turned his head to look at the shipyard on the main viewscreen. "Logical."

For reasons she couldn't explain, she found his lack of criticism damning.

"But now I'm wondering if I read it all wrong. If I missed something. I mean, sure, I had intel. But in the end it was just a hunch. What if I brought us here for nothing?"

That drew a pointed stare from Worf. "*You* did not bring us anywhere. You made a recommendation. I concurred. *I* brought the *Enterprise* here."

She nodded once and hung her head, abashed. "You're right, sir. Sorry. I didn't mean to say that I— I mean, that you—" She found herself unable to finish her thought. Everything she considered saying would only make matters worse.

With a tilt of his head, he indicated she should follow him. He led her to an unoccupied duty station on the port side of the bridge and dropped his voice. "To serve as XO, you must project confidence. Strength. Calm."

"Of course, sir. Any suggestions?"

"Do not wander. Do your job, and trust your peers to do theirs."

"Yes, sir."

"And do not pace." He thought for a moment. "There is an old Klingon saying: When a storm comes, it is better to be a tree than a leaf."

Šmrhová nodded, even though she had no idea what that meant. "I understand."

"Good." He looked around the quiet bridge. "Perhaps we should both take some time off the bridge. Clear our heads."

"Yessir. That sounds—"

An alert shrilled from the security console. Konya silenced it with a tap. "We have a sighting of the Nausicaan bandits." Worf and Šmrhová both hurried to stand on either side of Konya as he assessed the incoming data. "They're attacking a convoy—" His face fell with disappointment as he added, "Two subsectors away."

Worf moved to the command chair and sat down. "Helm, intercept course, maximum warp, engage. Mister Konya, take us to yellow alert."

The overhead lights brightened, and the hum of the engines traveled through the ship like a quickened pulse. A single *whoop* of the ship's alarm signaled the ship's change of alert status, and within moments the bridge was abuzz with activity and expectation.

On the main viewscreen, the Talarus Shipyard slipped out of frame as the *Enterprise* changed its heading, and then the field of stars were pulled into long streaks as the *Sovereign*-class starship accelerated to high warp.

In the middle of it all, Šmrhová stood at her command console and did her best not to let her shipmates see so much as a shred of the angst roiling inside her.

So much for my hunch.

Picard's first few hours in the witness box had been consumed with dull routine. Statements of his name, rank, and service number. Ezor ate up a chunk of time by motioning to have Picard's lengthy record of official commendations, honors, and achievements read into the record—an effort the preliminary hearing officer allowed on the grounds of establishing Picard's credibility as a witness in his own defense. Then Louvois had worked her way through a tedious series of questions, all to establish the timeline of events that had led Picard and the *Enterprise* crew to subdue the military forces and subsequently lead the long-term occupation of the non-aligned world of Tezwa in the Tezel-Oroko system.

He had grown so accustomed to the rhythm of her bland question-and-answer format that he blinked in surprise when she asked without preamble, "Captain, at what point did you initiate or join the criminal conspiracy to oust President Min Zife from his elected office?"

Ezor interjected, "Objection! Prejudicial, and assuming facts not in evidence."

"I disagree," Louvois said. "Clearly there was a discussion of this matter before the actual confrontation with Zife took place, and we know from the deposed statements of other conspirators that Captain Picard was a party to that conversation."

Admiral Liu lowered her chin and cast a skeptical look at Louvois. "Perhaps you could try to rephrase your question, Counselor?"

"Of course, Admiral." Louvois took a second to collect her thoughts, then she faced Picard. "Captain, when, and with whom, did you first discuss the possibility of asking Min Zife to resign his presidency?"

Knowing that the question had been inevitable did not make it any easier for Picard to answer. He thought back to that hushed conference more than seven years earlier, and the vow of silence to which he had agreed. Now that vow would have to yield to the law.

"My first discussion of that possibility was with Ambassador Lagan Serra, the Federation's ambassador to Tezwa, on November the seventh, 2379."

"Was this the same conversation that enlisted the participation of Starfleet admirals William Ross, Tujiro Nakamura, Edward Jellico, Alynna Nechayev, and Owen Paris?"

"No. My conversation with Ambassador Lagan preceded that."

"And is that when your conspiracy against President Zife was hatched?"

Ezor raised his voice. "Objection. It's not for government counsel to determine whether their conversation constituted an act of conspiracy."

"Sustained." To Louvois, Liu added, "Stick to establishing facts, Counselor. Let me draw the conclusions."

"Yes, Admiral." Addressing herself to Picard, Louvois continued. "Captain, to the best of your recollection, what was said during your and Ambassador Lagan's subsequent conference with the aforementioned admirals?"

Ezor said, "Objection. Overly broad. It's not reasonable to expect my client to have memorized a multiparty conversation that occurred more than seven years ago."

"Sustained."

Louvois took the mild rebuke in stride. "I'll try to be more specific. Captain, to the best of your ability to recall, did any of the admirals with whom you and Ambassador Lagan spoke on November seventh, 2379, discuss, either specifically or in general terms, aiding and abetting a slew of now-documented war crimes committed by President Zife and two of his senior advisors, as a means of blackmailing him into surrendering his office? Specifically, did any of the admirals discuss covering up the illegal emplacement of nadion-pulse artillery on Tezwa, as well as the illegal efforts Zife and his advisors made to frame other parties for those actions, in the hope that keeping Zife's crimes a secret would persuade him to resign?"

Once more, Picard felt a pang of guilt at the prospect of smearing the reputations of his fellow officers, particularly his superiors. But he had sworn an oath, and he would not break it.

"Yes, they did."

"And after President Zife resigned his office on November ninth, 2379, were those crimes concealed by means of a joint effort by the admirals who had asked him to step down?"

"They were."

"To the best of your knowledge, were Starfleet resources and personnel used to carry out those obstructions of justice?"

"In some cases, yes, I believe they were."

"Did you ask any members of your crew to suppress information or evidence relating to Zife's war crimes on Tezwa?"

"I was informed by my supervising officer, Admiral Alynna Nechayev, that all matters related to the Tezwa crisis and its precipitating events had been declared top secret, by order of the Chief Admiral of Starfleet. At that time, I had no reason to doubt her order was genuine, and I directed my officers and crew to comply with what I thought to be a lawful command."

"I see." Louvois kept her tone neutral. "Who was the first among your select group to propose that a threat of force be used to persuade President Zife to resign?"

Picard looked at Ezor, but this time his counsel had no grounds on which to object. Casting his mind back to that grim conversation seven years earlier, Picard remembered the chill that had run down his back at the first mention of the use of force.

"It was Admiral William Ross."

"A dead man. How convenient."

"You asked for the truth, Counselor. I gave it to you."

A fraught silence hung between Louvois and Picard. The mute battle of wills was ended as Liu declared, "That's our time for today. This preliminary hearing will continue tomorrow in these chambers at ten hundred hours, Pacific Time. Until then, this hearing is adjourned." She rang the bell on her table once, and then she stood and left the room by the back door.

Louvois turned her back on Picard, gathered her padd from the prosecutor's table, and made a quick exit without a backward glance.

As he stood and stepped out of the witness box, Picard felt drained and shaken. He plodded back to the defense table. Ezor and Crusher bookended him and ushered him out of the courtroom, through the gaggle of civilian news media that packed the corridor outside. Remembering what Ezor had told him, Picard did his best to maintain his air of calm despite the crowd of strange faces shouting rude questions at him. He wanted to rage in response, but he knew that would only make matters worse.

By the time he, Crusher, and Ezor piled inside a private transport pod for the return trip to La Barre, Picard felt exposed. Abused. Violated. All he wanted now was to find someplace far from other people, somewhere dark and quiet, and hide himself away.

But first, he knew, he would have to talk with Ezor.

The defense lawyer sat with his hands folded on his lap, watching clouds rush past outside. It was clear he was trying to give Picard the space he needed to regain his composure.

"Jonathan," Picard said. "How would you assess our first day?"

Ezor sighed. "Like life in the Dark Ages: short and brutal." He leaned forward, rested his arms atop his knees. "This is why I didn't want you on the stand. You barely got a taste of what can happen up there. Once we get to cross-examination, followed by redirect and recross, you'll want to beat yourself unconscious with a copy of the SCMJ."

"I think I'm past that point. By the end, all I wanted was to throttle Phillipa."

"I could tell. And so could the PHO and the spectators. You need to do a better job of hiding that. When you're in that chair, you need to be downright Vulcan. No emotions."

"Easier said than done. But I'll try."

"Good. And another thing: Don't be afraid to ask Louvois to rephrase questions. It's a good way to stall and give yourself time to regroup. And when she speaks, listen carefully. In court you want to answer truthfully but narrowly. Respond to her questions as literally as you can, without expounding or embellishing. Don't volunteer *anything*. Answer only what was *specifically* asked. If you can do that, it might just save your career—and your freedom."

Picard nodded. It rankled him to have to submit to verbal attacks, but he refused to betray his faith in the rule of law. "Thank you."

"Go home and get some rest."

"Because I'm going to need it?"

"Unfortunately, yes. Today was bad. Tomorrow . . . will be worse."

11

The image on the *Enterprise*'s main viewscreen was hashed with static. There was no obvious cause for interference in the signal—the residual radiation left over from the attack on the convoy was fresh, but nothing the ship's sensors were unable to filter out—so Worf concluded that the problem must lie with the transmitters aboard the convoy's lead vessel, the *Palembang,* a large but mostly automated cargo ship out of Coridan.

On-screen, Lieutenant Commander Taurik followed the ship's master, Captain Senalda, a short, sinewy Tiburonian whose finlike ears looked too large for his narrow head. The vid signal was from the tricorder of Senior Chief Petty Officer Betai, a Zakdorn engineer who had accompanied the *Enterprise*'s deputy chief of engineering, along with a team of mechanics, engineers, and medics, to assess the damage and casualties aboard the *Palembang.*

"Main power is out on all decks," Taurik said, talking over his shoulder as he, Senalda, and Betai moved through a dark and narrow corridor. The tall Vulcan ducked a jet of red sparks that leaped from a ragged breach in the bulkhead to his right. *"Multiple ruptures in the EPS conduit system. Plasma fires on all decks below three. The Nausicaans hit this ship hard."*

Šmrhová looked up from her console. "Taurik, do you have any intel on casualties?"

Taurik looked at his own tricorder, which had been set to gather updates from the rest of the away team on the *Palembang.* *"Doctor Harstad reports eleven dead, sixteen wounded. She and Nurse Amavia are assisting the* Palembang*'s surgeon with triage and treatment."*

Worf asked Konya, "Have you completed your analysis?"

Konya glanced up from his work. "Aye, sir. Transmitting my report to you and Lieutenant Šmrhová now." With a tap on his panel, he relayed his findings to the tactical panels beside the command chair and the XO's station. The file arrived with a soft electronic *ping.*

On the main viewscreen, Taurik conferred in private with Captain Senalda, and then he returned to address Worf over the open channel. *"Captain, after conducting a walk-through of the ship, it's my professional opinion that rendering the* Palembang *fit to return to port under its own power will require twenty hours of labor by a team of no fewer than fifteen engineers. Only five of this ship's engineers are currently fit for service, and all but three of the others are dead."*

It was a pessimistic report, but it was also what Worf had expected. "Do they need any parts or equipment?"

"Yes, sir. My team is sending a requisition to Lieutenant Dygan now."

"Very well. Mister Dygan, expedite that request."

"Aye, sir."

"Commander Taurik, delegate the supervision of repairs to the *Palembang* as you see fit, but I want you back on the *Enterprise* as soon as possible."

"Understood, sir. Taurik out." The transmission ceased, and the image on the viewscreen reverted to the battle-scarred hull of the *Palembang,* which was dark, adrift, and leaking plasma.

With a tilt of his head, Worf invited Šmrhová to meet him at the command chair. They huddled over his tactical panel as he opened the report from Konya. Its top-sheet summary surprised him. "Captain Senalda's report says the Nausicaans fired only once."

"That's all they needed." Šmrhová pointed at the technical specs for the freight hauler. "Simple disruptors could've beaten those shields. So why did the Nausicaans use a Husnock cannon that can break a capital starship in half?"

"It might have been a test of the new weapon. But with that kind of power, why hit the convoy at all? Why not a bigger target?"

"I have to admit, that's what I figured for their next move. But since this is where they struck, we need to figure out why."

"Where is the rest of the convoy?"

Šmrhová called up more detailed information about the *Palembang*. "Looks like the lead ship was the only one with a crew. The rest were drones, being pulled along like cars on a train."

"And the Nausicaans decoupled those 'cars' and hijacked them."

Šmrhová paged through the report to the convoy's manifest. "This is weird. I assumed the convoy was hauling fuel, or something else in demand on the black market. But this says they were loaded with heavy construction equipment."

Worf leaned in to study the screen. "What kind?"

"Construction vehicles. Earthmovers, thermoconcrete mixers, variable-g cranes. Industrial replicators. Fusion cores. Deuterium pods."

"What could they build with that?"

"Just about anything, as long as it's on a planet's surface."

"A planet-based structure," Worf said, thinking out loud. "Such as a fortress?"

"Definitely."

"That raises two questions: Why? And where?"

"No idea. But I think we'd better find out—*fast.*"

One of T'Ryssa Chen's favorite perquisites of being an *Enterprise* senior officer was that she was able to commandeer exclusive use of any of the ship's dedicated science labs whenever she had a valid reason to do so. As a junior officer she had often been required to wait hours or even days for the necessary facility to become available. Even then, getting a decent time slot in the lab's schedule often depended on how close a relationship one had with the ship's senior operations or science officers.

I joined Starfleet to practice science, and I ended up learning politics. Go figure.

Today she and science specialist Lieutenant Corinne Clipet had the run of science lab one to pursue a broad-ranging inquiry into the nature, function, capabilities, and vulnerabilities of the Husnock OPC that just hours earlier had disabled the freight-hauler *Palembang*. Clipet had set herself up on one side of a shared long table with multiple overhead holographic displays, and Chen sat across from her, running her own independent tests and analyses.

A look of disappointment crossed Clipet's delicate features. "A shame the freighter's sensors aren't more advanced. I hate to think how much more data we might've recovered if they'd been using the gen-twelve suite instead of an old gen-seven." She shook her head in frustration. "This model doesn't even collect transphasic frequencies, never mind isolate channels for multidimensional transient particles."

"Yeah. It's almost as if no one expects a cargo puller detailed to the core systems to be asked to do cutting-edge research."

Clipet shot a sarcastic smile at Chen before resuming her work. Chen grinned. She understood Clipet's reaction to the limitations of the *Palembang*'s hardware and software, but she couldn't help but tease her colleague for her outsized expectations.

The lab's dedicated computer finished calculating a set of data extrapolated from the *Palembang*'s limited sensor logs, based on filters and algorithms Chen had programmed and applied. She expanded the holographic display with a parting gesture of her hands, to enlarge it for easier review. "Corinne, check this out. It looks like the energy waveform for the OPC retains its relative modulations even as it increases or decreases its output."

"Almost as if its power matrix has a fractal mode of amplification. How odd."

It was hardly a breakthrough, but it captured Chen's imagination. "The Husnock really were fascinating, in a terrifying kind of way. Just think: We were on the verge of first contact with them in '66. If they hadn't been exterminated by the whim of a single Douwd, we might have had a chance to see their culture in person, rather than try to piece it together from artifacts and untranslated databases."

Clipet frowned. "You shouldn't romanticize them just because they're extinct. In case you forgot, the Husnock *did* make first contact in '66—by exterminating every living thing on the surface of Delta Rana IV. Frankly, they don't sound like a species or a culture we'd have wanted as a neighbor."

"We can't really know that, can we? I mean, if we thought that way, we'd never have set up diplomatic relations with the Gorn, or the Sheliak, or the Ferengi."

Looking up from her work, Clipet was visibly irked. "Trys, first contact with the Gorn went sour because we accidentally colonized a planet they considered theirs. Hostilities with the Sheliak occurred because we were slow to realize how literal minded they are, but later we found common ground in the law. And the Ferengi? That's a can of tube grubs I'd rather not open."

"But the Husnock weren't like *any* of them. The Husnock wanted us dead because we *weren't them*. If they'd thought of Delta Rana IV as theirs, why'd they sterilize its surface? If they meant to claim it, why'd they glass it? Trust me, the galaxy is better off without them. I just wish the Douwd had melted down their weapons when he swept them into history's dustbin."

Chen worked quietly for a moment, feeling chastised. "There might have been a *few* who were nice."

"Seriously?"

"We don't know! Species aren't monolithic, Corrine. There are variations. Outliers. Cultural shifts. Yes, the Husnock were a traveling nightmare when they came knocking on our door, but I think it's pretty closed-minded of a Starfleet officer to say that just because an alien culture did something terrible, they were never going to be able to change or grow. I mean, what if humanity had been judged based only on the cruel and stupid things it did before the twenty-second century? It's not like the Vulcans didn't know about humans before first contact. What if they had decided in Earth's twentieth century that the galaxy was better off without humans?"

"For starters, the galaxy would have been spared the Borg."

"Now you're just being difficult." Chen muted a function alert from her console. "There are some interesting energy patterns swirling around inside the OPC. It looks as if it could, in theory, channel nearly any amount of energy into a focused attack without overloading, since it collimates its blast effects in subspace and then manifests them at a distance."

"That would explain why the OPC didn't just vaporize the *Palembang*. But it doesn't tell us why the Nausicaans would have used the OPC for something they could've done without it."

"Like Worf said to Šmrhová, maybe it was a dry run." Chen called up the freighter's log of the attack. "Think about it: The Nausicaans never had a Husnock weapon before today. So instead of risking their necks by using it for the first time in a serious battle, they test it on a soft target. Not just to learn how to use it, but to see what it can do." She halted the playback of the sensor log. "And what a test it was. One shot, at minimum power, crippled a hardened freight hauler."

"Good point." Clipet patched her console into the ship's subspace transceiver. "It makes me curious, though. How does the OPC compare to other Husnock armaments?"

"Are you running a comparison against records in the Starfleet Intelligence database?"

"Yeah. Why?"

The lab went dark, as if someone had sliced its link to the ship's power network and stolen all of its backup batteries. Without

emergency lights or even the faint glow of starlight, Chen couldn't
see so much as her hand in front of her face.

She sighed. "I was afraid that might happen."

Lieutenant Naomi Wildman aimed an accusatory look at her Starfleet Intelligence supervisor, Commander Sam Lavelle. "That was
a tad heavy-handed wasn't it?"

"Don't be so dramatic. It's not like I made you kill someone."

"It's not as if I would, even if you put a phaser to my head."

"Then what're we fighting about?"

Wildman pointed at her console. "You just made me trigger a
hard crash and a full system wipe in a Starfleet vessel's science lab.
Kind of a jerk move, boss."

"We have a chain of command, Wildman. Call me 'sir.'"

"Yes, *sir.*" She gestured at her bank of wraparound monitors,
which filled most of the space in her dark, windowless private office. "I'm just saying, I think *this* was a mistake. Sir."

"I don't recall asking you, Lieutenant."

"Well, *sir,* as an intelligence analyst and operations officer, part
of my job is to anticipate your needs and try to prevent errors before they occur. In fact, I seem to recall that my skill set was why
you talked me into reversing my decision to drop out of Starfleet
Academy."

"A choice I regret more with each passing day."

"Oh, *sir.* You don't mean that."

"Just tell me you understand why I don't want technical data
about the OPC propagating all over subspace."

"It was on a coded Starfleet channel!"

"So what? Are you willing to gamble the safety of the galaxy,
trillions of lives, on the assumption that no one's broken the encryption on that channel? Not the Romulans? Or the Breen? Because it wouldn't be the first time."

"Wow. And I thought blacking out the *Enterprise*'s science lab would be your biggest drama moment of the day. I stand corrected. *Sir.*"

"Are you *trying* to get busted for insubordination?"

"Just offering you a dose of perspective, *sir*. If it gets me a ticket back to civilian life, I can't exactly say I'll be disappointed."

"It'll get you a ticket to the stockade, first."

"Fine. I could use time to catch up on my reading."

"You know you can resign your commission at any time, don't you?"

She spread her arms and looked at her four blank walls. "What? And give up all *this*?"

"Look, we had no choice. We told the *Enterprise* crew to keep their hands off this case."

Wildman shook her head. "That's the part I just don't get. You served on the previous *Enterprise*. You know what kind of officers Picard cultivates: the kind who don't let things like this go. If you'd given me a few minutes, I could've tanked their query and fed them a bunch of nonsense redacted to practically nothing. They wouldn't have liked it, but they might have believed it." She gestured at the blackout protocol on her panel. "But *this*? This'll just piss them off. You served with some of these people. You know them. They're gonna dig and dig until they hit pay dirt. Unless"—she mustered a coy pout—"you want me to run a bit of interference?"

"Absolutely not. Keep the blackout protocol in place."

"For how long?"

"Until I rescind it."

"Must be hard being a hammer."

"What?"

"Because you treat every problem like a nail."

Lavelle buried his face in his hands. Groaned. Massaged his temples. "Before I do something I'll regret, please tell me you know Okona's current location and status."

"Location? A Class-M dirtball known as Faustus Prime. Status? Probably drunk."

"I *always* assume he's drunk. I need to know what he's *doing*."

"Last I heard, following a new lead to our Nausicaan friends."

"Let me guess: in a bar."

"Good guess. You should be a spymaster. *Sir*."

He shook his head. "What did I ever do to deserve being stuck with you and Okona?"

"No idea, sir." She wanted to tell him, but that would've meant confessing she had read his classified Starfleet dossier. Instead, she shrugged and smiled. "I guess you just got lucky."

12

———

True to the implications of its name, Faustus Prime was kind of a hellhole. I'd expected as much before I landed. After leaving the *Tain Hu,* my harshest assumptions had been quickly validated.

Unpaved streets. Skies full of pollution from ore smelters the size of large hills. And a seemingly omnipresent effluvium, a gift from the open sewers that ringed its perimeter in a fetid moat. Those were the highlights of Coker Flats, a mining settlement that had all the charm of a neglected Klingon penal colony. It was the kind of place hope and dreams go to die.

I knew that finding this forsaken excuse for a town would be only the beginning. This planet was the armpit of the sector; the town was the armpit of the planet. Now I'd arrived at the armpit of the town, Ankha's, a seedy watering hole where you could rent a date, hire a gun, or sell your soul, possibly all at the same time. It was the sort of joint that didn't welcome people in uniforms or those who liked to wave badges around. I expected to fit right in.

Two steps inside the door, the heady perfume of narcotic smoke hit me like a velvet slap. I stopped and drank it in. Within a few seconds I was no longer bothered by the over-amped music. I sauntered toward the bar, in no hurry. I caught a few glances in my direction, but for the most part my entrance passed either unnoticed or willfully ignored. Just the way I liked it.

I sized up the room's occupants on my way to the bar. Compared the folks I saw to what I'd already noted in the landing field outside. It was an easy room to read.

More than half the people in the place had sidearms. Low-power stunners, mostly. The kind of weapon civilians can carry without attracting harassment from the law. But a few of the patrons stood out: one had a Klingon disruptor on his hip. He wore it proudly, like a warning or a challenge. The gal trolling the *dom-jot* players for paid dates had a Nalori slimline blaster hidden under her jacket. And one guy at the bar had a compact weapon hidden under his coat, tucked at his waistline in the small of his back. I was pretty sure it was a stolen Starfleet type-1 phaser. Tiny but with enough power to punch a hole in a wall—or disintegrate a person in a flash.

The rest of the room's exigent threats were brawlers rather than shooters. And they had plenty of improvised weapons waiting to happen: *dom-jot* cues, bar stools, empty bottles, cutlery left on tables yet to be cleared, the water-cooled pipes filling the air with a fruit-scented haze that could knock a Denebian slime devil on its ass. It was a target-rich environment.

Matching faces to the ships outside was no great feat, either. There was only one Gorn in the place, and I tied him to his species' trademark junk heap, one of which I'd seen in the landing field. Hotshot *dom-jot* boys? They were slumming it, probably came to Faustus in the tricked-out Tiburonian starjumper. The hired gun at the bar would want to travel incognito. I pegged him as the owner of the dusty TC3 Space Arrow with the cracked tailfin—which, as it happened, was also the ship I considered most likely to be harboring a hidden combat rifle.

I took a seat at the bar. Flagged down the barkeep, a fetching Caitian lass. "Tranya."

She shook her head, ruffling her striped mane. "Sorry, hon. We don't carry it."

"Don't carry it? It's the single most popular alcoholic beverage in the galaxy!"

A shrug of her furry shoulders. "Don't get much call for it around here."

"Okay. What *is* popular hereabouts?"

"Aldebaran whiskey."

"I'd rather drink my own piss."

"If you do, there's a five-credit corkage fee."

"Just pour me a double of the Tsingtao vodka. Neat."

She slapped a grimy shot glass onto the bar. Grabbed the bottle from the shelf behind her, and then she poured. About half of my double ended up on the bar top. The bartender didn't seem to care, and I wasn't in the mood to start a fight, so I let it go. As I watched her work, I got the sense that she wasn't what one would call a "people person." She also didn't seem concerned about whether she was earning tips or goodwill. I got the feeling she was new on the job, and that she likely wouldn't be around much longer.

Which meant she wasn't the one to pump for information.

The bouncer, on the other hand? He was huge for a humanoid. If I'd had to guess, I'd have said he was a Capellan. Well over two meters tall, almost as broad at the shoulder, pale blond hair, a cleft chin that looked as if it had been hewn from a granite block. You'd think a figure that imposing would have kept folks at bay. But this guy had a steady stream of quick visitors. Short whispered conversations. Clandestine passes of currency under his table.

Yeah, this was a person with his finger on the pulse of local events.

I downed the half of my drink that had reached my glass and waved my Federation credit chip to pay for it. After I tucked the chip into my pocket, I grabbed up six strips of gold-pressed latinum. Then I left my rock-hard bar stool and weaved through the crowd to steal my moment alone with the big man. He looked past me, over my head, as I approached.

Without waiting for him to ask, I slipped my fistful of latinum under the table. "I'm looking for some friends of mine, but they aren't here. Maybe you could tell me if I missed them?" It took a moment before he glanced at me. Then he snatched the latinum.

"What do your friends look like?"

"Nausicaans."

The latinum vanished into his pocket. "They were here."

"Any chance you might know where I could find them now?"

"Directions cost extra."

I gathered up more latinum, and then I bent down and pretended to collect it from the floor. I passed it to him without trying to hide it. "I think you dropped this, friend."

He shoved the bribe into his pocket. "Tika Starport. Docking bay ninety-two."

I started to leave, and then I turned back. "Don't tell them I'm coming, okay? I'd like this to be a surprise."

He crossed his arms and put on his *I don't care* face. "Tell who what?"

"Perfect."

The walk across town to the docking bays was long and cold. I usually didn't mind a crisp, bracing cold, but this was a windy, aggressive, stab-you-in-the-face kind of cold. By the time I reached the docking bays—a massive cluster of prefab concrete structures, each shaped like a torus, with a retractable roof over its open center—the fronts of my thighs had gone numb.

The only way into each docking bay from ground level was a three-meter-wide main entrance secured by a single locked set of doors. This tended to cause bottlenecks, and it would never be allowed on a Federation-controlled planet due to fire-safety regulations. I counted myself lucky that the locks on most backwater dirtballs like Faustus Prime were a few decades obsolete. Getting through them usually posed little or no trouble.

I stopped a few dozen meters from docking bay 92 to check it out from a distance. My miniaturized tricorder detected no hidden security systems on the entrance or in the passageway beyond it. I couldn't get a clear reading from the docking area. I tried tweaking my settings. It didn't help. As I'd expected, the Nausicaans' ship was probably jamming sensors.

Despite that interference, my scanner still picked up several

Nausicaan life-forms inside the docking bay facility. I had the right place, at least.

The place looked dark from the outside. It was the middle of the night in Coker Flats. Most working stiffs were already in their bunks for the night. The streets were deserted. As I considered how to go about breaking into the docking bay, it occurred to me that I hadn't seen a single civilian police patrol since I'd arrived. I wondered if this place even had any full-time law enforcement—and, if they did, whether they'd be the kind to kill first and ask questions never.

Worst of all, I didn't like the layout. I had long made a point of not walking into any place that I didn't know how to get out of— and this was a dead end accessed by a long, narrow choke point. Seeding explosives in the passageway would only put me in more danger. And with the Nausicaans' ship jamming sensors, I knew I could forget about using my transporter recall signal to beam out if this went sour. If the docking bay's dome was open, going up to escape might be a viable strategy—assuming I could climb out before they could shut it.

Then I heard Lavelle's voice in my thoughts, goading me: *Or you could just toughen up, go in there, and do your job.* Which is what people say when it's not their ass on the line.

I hugged the walls and stuck to the shadows until I reached the entrance. The lock on the door was a joke. I bypassed it in less than ten seconds, with not an alarm triggered. The doors parted, revealing a long, empty passage leading to the landing area at the heart of the torus. A quick scan with my tricorder didn't reveal much, thanks to the Nausicaans' jammers, but I was able to confirm with a simple acoustic scan that there were no cloaked bodies in the tunnel. It was well and truly empty. For the moment, that would have to be good enough.

I made sure the main doors remained unlocked after they'd closed. If I had to retreat, I wouldn't have time to bypass the locks again.

Halfway down the passage I drew my blaster. Not in reaction to anything in particular. Just because it made me feel better to head into the unknown with a weapon at the ready.

The inner doors to the landing pad were not locked. They slid apart at my approach. I put my back to the wall inside the passageway and searched for any signs of company coming my way. Like the tunnel, the landing pad was deserted and quiet. Massive stained tarpaulins of synthetic fabric were draped over something big and starship-shaped parked in the bay.

I raised an eyebrow at that. *Tarps? What in blazes for?*

I took a fresh look around the bay. Its overhead dome had been closed.

Its perimeter was cluttered with rusted old fuel tanks. Littered among them were some broken cargo containers, an antigrav pallet lifter, and several sloppily gathered coils of cable that hung from hooks bolted into the concrete walls. The poured-concrete floor was scuffed and stained from years of hard use, and long fissures snaked away from its many built-in drains.

A chill breeze snuck in through a large crack in one wall. Fluttered the bottom of a tarp, but didn't lift it high enough for me to see what was underneath.

I imagined Wildman's and Lavelle's voices arguing inside my head, like an angel and a devil vying for control of my actions. On the side of caution, Wildman's voice was telling me, *Get the hell out of there!* And throwing that caution to the wind was Lavelle: *See what's under the tarp, Agonist! That's what we pay you for, isn't it?*

Blaster at the fore, I walked to the mysterious draped hulk. Grabbed the bottom edge of a tarp. And lifted it just far enough to look underneath.

What I found was a lot of empty space, and a welded framework of pipes and beams whose shape formed the rough approximation of a starship. That was when my suspicion became surety—I'd walked into a trap.

As I dropped the tarp, the docking bay's interior landing lights snapped on, so bright as to be painful. I felt their heat, as if I were being slow-cooked. Whoever had control of the lights dimmed them a few seconds later, so that they were merely blinding. Then I heard the doors to the passageway slide open. I turned that way and squinted. Through nearly closed eyes I saw a gang of silhouettes march toward me, with battle rifles raised and aimed in my direction.

The lights faded, and at last I saw what I'd suspected. I was surrounded by Nausicaans. A few of the soldiers stepped forward. Two covered me while one took my weapons and gear.

When they fell back, their leader came forward. "Hear you looking for us." He mocked me with a fang-filled grin. "But we find you."

"That's disappointing. I paid for this tip. Paid well."

"We paid more."

"How very Ferengi of you."

One of the grunts lurched forward with a blade to flense me alive. His leader caught him, threw him backward. "No kill. Orders." To me he added, "Kinogar want you alive."

I grinned with a confidence I absolutely didn't feel. "Lucky me."

13

———•———

"I'm sorry, Commander Worf. I really don't know what to tell you."

Worf glared at the image of the lieutenant from Starfleet Command and wished he could reach through the ready room's holoframe and rip out the man's lungs via the subspace comm channel. "Start with the truth, Mister Spiers."

"That's the issue, sir. The facts of the matter aren't entirely clear."

"They seem quite clear to me. One of my ship's science labs was sabotaged. My tactical and operations officers traced the cause to a signal sent from Starfleet Command to this vessel. I want you to explain why this happened."

"I can't say for certain, sir."

Every word from this *yIntagh*'s mouth made Worf long to cut out the man's tongue. "You could start by acknowledging that it happened."

"Not at this time, sir. We have your report, and we'll look into it. Any report of sabotage is treated as a matter of the utmost importance, and I can assure you that we'll be conducting an inquiry to ascertain what happened. Until that inquiry is completed, however, this incident has to remain classified, and its instigating event designated 'unknown.'"

"So you think it was a coincidence that my ship fell prey to a Starfleet-sponsored cyber-attack at the exact moment my officers tried to analyze the effects of a Husnock weapon?"

Spiers's bureaucratic droning remained unflappable. *"Until now I had no idea what your people were working on, nor had I formed any opinion regarding the timing of the alleged attack. Re-*

gardless, I assure you that your request will be addressed with the utmost priority."

"Meaning what, exactly, Lieutenant?"

"*We should have a preliminary report for your review in four to six weeks.*"

"Weeks?" Worf leaned in, hoping that his simmering rage would overflow the frame of Spiers's holographic display at the other end of the conversation. "I do not have *weeks.*"

"*Sorry, sir. The wheels of justice turn slowly here at headquarters.*"

Worf imagined what Spiers's head would look like if he turned it slowly until its cervical vertebrae shattered and the man's chin faced his shoulder blades.

"Maybe this will help. My acting chief of security identified the signal pulse as having originated from a subspace tower controlled exclusively by Starfleet Intelligence."

"*Interesting. I'll be sure to make a note of that for follow-up, sir.*"

"What will it take to get an admission of responsibility and an apology from Admiral Batanides of Starfleet Intelligence?"

His question left Spiers flummoxed. "*That's not really my department, sir.*"

"Lieutenant. I know *who* sent the pulse. I know *where* it originated. I just want someone at Starfleet Intelligence or Starfleet Command to tell me *why* it happened at all."

Spiers looked tired. "*Sorry, sir. I'm told you don't currently hold a high enough security clearance for that information.*"

"I am the commanding officer of a *Sovereign*-class starship. I am a former Federation ambassador to Qo'noS. I held the diplomatic rank of a vice admiral."

"*You did then. You don't anymore.*" Perhaps sensing that he had set Worf's blood to a high boil, he tried to backtrack. "*I don't set the clearances, sir, but I need to abide by them.*"

Worf was beyond furious, but he knew far too well the intractable nature of Starfleet's command-level administration. Red tape was the bane of every officer's existence, and there was no point taking out his temper on a man who had no choice but to dole out excuses on behalf of the upper brass. He took a breath and forced himself to accept that explanations and apologies were out of reach and would remain so. Instead he focused on what his ship and crew needed in the here and now. "Is there anything you can do to expedite the restoration of our science lab?"

"Possibly. How severe is the damage?"

"The lab's systems were blanked. Their backups in the main computer core were corrupted, as were active copies in the other labs."

"Have you tried downloading clean copies from Starfleet Operations?"

"We have. Someone has throttled our subspace data channel's bandwidth. A download that should take minutes is expected to take more than a day."

Spiers looked truly shocked to hear that. *"Hang on. Let me see what I can find."* He turned away and keyed information into his console. Moments later he turned back. *"I might be able to help. I'm sending you an encrypted data packet on this channel. Use the credentials in that packet to access a priority secure channel to Memory Alpha. That should get your people the clean files they'll need, and in less than five minutes."*

The data packet came through on the comm's subchannel. Worf routed it immediately to Dygan's station on the bridge, and then he said to Spiers, "Thank you, Lieutenant."

"You're welcome, sir. And for what little it's worth, I'm genuinely sorry there isn't more I can do to help you today."

"The help you just provided will make a significant difference."

"Of course, if anyone asks where you got those credentials—"

"I will tell them the truth: that I cannot remember."

"Godspeed, Commander. Starfleet Command out."

Spiers closed the channel. Worf turned off the comm and got up from the ready room's desk. He would have to tell Dygan what the credentials on his panel were for.

And as soon as the science labs were back online, Worf planned to get some answers.

Whether Starfleet Command likes it or not.

It was the long-held and duly informed opinion of Chief Admiral Leonard James Akaar that the people of Earth were overly fond of their cities and not fond enough of their world's wild spaces. Its Chinese deserts, Peruvian mountains, African plains, and Australian outback . . . those were the places that reminded Akaar of his homeworld, Capella IV.

But by necessity he spent the majority of his time on Earth in its urban centers. His role at Starfleet Command kept him in San Francisco most of the year. It was pleasant enough. He preferred its older, more historical quarters over its sleek modern sectors. Downtown was too much duranium and transparent aluminum, too many skyscrapers and glassy-smooth roadways. He loved the rustic qualities of Haight-Ashbury and the long architectural memory of the Castro.

He harbored the same criticisms for most cities on the continent of North America, and for those in Asia. New York, Chicago, Tokyo, Singapore, Kuala Lumpur, Hong Kong . . . aside from a few tiny enclaves of old beauty preserved against the flood tide of modernity, none of those cities held much appeal for him. The only city he truly enjoyed in the Americas was New Orleans, for its cuisine as well as its music. In the cities of Europe, on the other hand—there he felt the weight of history, reveled in the textures of antiquity. His favorite places to visit were mostly in Italy and Greece, and he had developed a grudging fondness for Paris.

Alas, his affinity for the City of Light was tarnished by one inescapable fact: it was the seat of government for the United Federation of Planets. The Palais de la Concorde, which had been built near the Louvre in the early twenty-fourth century, stood over the Place de la Concorde, the largest open square in Paris, where centuries earlier the people of France had executed members of their aristocracy as part of their revolutionary turn toward democracy.

Akaar's official responsibilities brought him to the Palais, on average, a few times each year. He did not dread those visits; he merely disliked them because he found the Palais itself too large and garish. Though the great cylindrical tower of the Palais had been elevated well above ground level to preserve the plaza, obelisk, and fountains beneath it, Akaar felt that it sent the wrong message. Though it contained meeting chambers for the full Federation Council, as well as offices for the cabinet-level officers of the government, and private offices for the Federation president, it looked to him more like an edifice of empire than a house of the people.

None of which was Akaar's problem this evening.

Tonight he had to fight against the cinch of his dress uniform's jacket collar, so that he could navigate the predator-infested waters of a state dinner without suffocating.

The Roth Dining Room, which, along with its support facilities, occupied the entire twelfth floor of the Palais, was packed with dignitaries, all of them in dress uniforms or formal black-tie civilian attire. The tables were decorated with peculiar sculptures of flowers embedded in ice—or was it crystal? Akaar couldn't tell if any of them were melting—and set for what promised to be a long multicourse meal with several types of beverages, each of which would, apparently, need to be served in its own unique form of stemware.

Akaar planned to be gone by then. Years earlier, he had been appalled to learn that being promoted to chief admiral of Starfleet, far from affording him privileges, saddled him with more obligations than he could count. Being paraded about at state dinners like some kind of prized stallion was merely one of them.

Decorum be damned. If not for the hors d'oeuvres, I would not be here at all.

One tactic he had found helpful in minimizing his boredom

and irritation at such affairs was to remain always in motion. It was not easy. Bottlenecks, sudden clusters of people, a shift in the room's general flow of foot traffic—any of these could leave him trapped, surrounded by people who then felt obligated to engage him in small talk. But he did his best to blade through the Gordian knots of mingling dignitaries, raid the trays of passing waitstaff for jumbo shrimp or bacon-wrapped scallops, and then make another lap around the room's edge.

His bid to deplete the Earth's supply of shellfish was proceeding to plan when he dodged to avoid colliding with a fragile-looking young Elaysian woman in a full-body exoskeleton—and found himself facing Ralph Offenhouse, the Federation's secretary of commerce. The human man held a nearly empty flute of sparkling wine. "Admiral! Quite a soiree, don't you think?"

"It seems festive."

"That's right—you're not one for chitchat, are you? Always liked that about you. All business, no bullshit." He tugged at his bow tie. "Who's this party for, anyway? The Petarians?"

"The Pandronians," Akaar corrected. "To celebrate their new treaty of alliance with the Federation."

"Sure, sure. Lovely folks, those Pandronians. Which ones are they again?"

"The ones dressed in all white." He could tell from Offenhouse's confused look that he would need a bit more information. "The ones that can separate into discrete organisms and then reunite. They refer to themselves as 'this one.'"

"Ah, yes. Fascinating. Just amazing." He nudged Akaar. "They've got a crazy amount of dilithium. I mean, you wouldn't believe it. This is gonna be a good get for us."

Abrasive and outspoken, the human man had retained his cabinet office through a change of presidential administrations. First appointed to his post by the late President Nanietta Bacco, he had been retained in that role first by President Pro Tem Ishan Anjar, and then by the current president, Kellessar zh'Tarash.

Akaar had no idea why.

Offenhouse tipped his glass almost vertical and poured its contents down his throat. "You're from Capella IV, right?"

"Yes."

"It also has a metric ass-load of dilithium, right?"

"No, topaline."

"Right, topaline." Offenhouse's posture wavered. Akaar wondered how many drinks the man had consumed. The secretary continued, "What was your life like on Capella IV?"

"I left my world at the age of five. I've never gone back."

"Really? Never? I mean, do you ever just want to roll up with, like, the whole Ninth Fleet and just tell whoever's in charge down there, 'Hey! Guess who! I'm Leonard—'"

"Forgive me, Mister Secretary." He handed Offenhouse his empty hors d'oeuvres plate. "There is someone I need to speak to. Good night." Akaar walked away with no regrets.

I had to hit the eject button on that conversation anyway.

He moved with purpose through a gap in the shifting crowd, toward the Federation's attorney general, who faced him as he finished his approach.

"Admiral Akaar," Phillipa Louvois said with a practiced smile. "To what do I owe the pleasure?"

"Let us not be coy, Madam Attorney General. I need to speak with you about Captain Picard's Article Thirty-Two hearing, and your involvement in it."

She bristled. "A most inappropriate topic of conversation, Admiral."

"When I agreed to refer charges, I was made to understand that it would be treated as a routine inquiry." He moved closer so that he could speak in a more private tone. "Sending the attorney general herself to act as the government's counsel is far from routine."

Though he towered over her, she was not the least bit intimidated. Truly, she had a spine of steel and a gaze to match. "There is *nothing* routine about the crimes of which Captain Picard stands accused. Because of a Starfleet coup, a former Federation president was *murdered*."

"That was the work of Section Thirty-One, not Starfleet."

"I'm beginning to wonder if there's any daylight between the two."

Akaar struggled to keep his demeanor professional and his volume discreet. "There is no basis for that accusation. And no reason to treat Captain Picard like a common criminal. Need I remind you how many times he has personally saved this planet? And the Federation?"

"Is that how you think the law works, Admiral? Rack up enough hero points and one gets to commit high crimes with impunity?"

"Captain Picard is a man of good character. I know it. *You* know it."

"What I *know*, Admiral, is that even good men can do terrible things—*monstrous* things—if they think they're doing so for a good reason. But that doesn't make their actions righteous. Or legal." She handed her empty champagne flute to a passing server. "Just because Captain Picard saved the Earth from the Borg, that doesn't give him the right to force a sitting president from office without due process. Or hand him over to assassins to be killed."

"Are you serious? Is that really what you think Picard has done?"

"*That*, Admiral, is what I intend to find out."

14

I had to give the Nausicaans credit: they really knew how to throw a punch.

They'd strung me up with chains wrapped around my wrists. I was dangling about ten centimeters off the ground, from the framework of pipes they'd rigged up inside docking bay 92. I had started screaming with the first hoist that lifted me off solid ground. The instant full-body stretch made the skin in my armpits feel like it was being ripped apart. The muscles in my chest and back rebelled at being pulled taut and held there, and the pain radiating from my shoulders made me pretty sure they had been yanked out of their sockets.

For good measure, the Nausicaans had tied my ankles together. I guess they didn't like getting kicked in the face any more than anyone else does.

Swinging like a side of meat on a hook, I grinned at the thug in charge. "We should set a safe word before we get started. How 'bout 'garbanzo'?"

He tilted his head like an animal being shown a sleight-of-hand trick. "Huh?"

"Bondage really isn't my bag. Usually I charge double for this kind of action."

He didn't know what I was saying, but he knew he was being mocked. He punched me in the groin, and I nearly threw up on him. Saliva spilled from my mouth as he grabbed my face in one huge hand and made me look him in the eye. "Talk when I ask questions. Understand?"

My voice shrank to a strangled croak. "Garbanzo."

Two more punches in my gut knocked the air out of me.

One of his men punched me in the kidney, hard enough that I felt all my organs shuddering against one another for seconds afterward.

Another four-fanged goon stepped in front of me and landed a right hook to my jaw. It snapped my head hard to the side and launched a spray of blood from my mouth. Dizzy and sick to my stomach, I went limp. Resisting the beating was out of the question. I'd bought the ticket, and now I had to hang on until the ride was over.

Boss thug made his next bruiser stop and wait, and then he grabbed my shoulders to halt my chaotic twisting and swinging. "Who you work for?"

I could barely breathe with my arms distended above me, but I forced out a reply. "Who's hiring?" He landed one-two punches on my ribs, and I heard a few crack. With my next attempt to draw breath, I felt needles of pain in my side.

His hand locked around my throat. "Why you look for us?"

He relaxed his grip enough to let me speak.

"Okay, fine . . . I'm a process server. A Denebian slime devil named Molly hired me 'cause she's suing you for paternity."

The other Nausicaans laughed, but the boss didn't think it was funny—I could tell by the way he picked up a length of pipe and swung it like a golf club against my left foot. If not for my boot, my foot would have broken in three places instead of just one.

He traded the pipe to one of his men for an electrified shock prod. Greenish-white energy crackled on its metallic tip and filled the air with the scent of ozone. Mister Tough Guy waved the prod's business end in front of my face. "Tell who you work for, or this goes up your *dupa*."

I would have asked him to translate *dupa*, but I didn't need to.

"Orion Syndicate," I lied. "Offered to double my fee if I stole back the cargo a bunch of Nausicaans took from them on Kam-hawy Freehold. Said they'd triple it if I killed the morons responsible." The big guy glared at me. "But I told them I don't do that kind of work."

That gave the ugly bastards something to talk about. There was just enough truth salted into the lie to make it palatable. I hoped.

They huddled. Conferred in grunts and snorts that I supposed passed for whispers among their species. As far as I could tell, they seemed to be buying the Orion Syndicate legend.

If I had thought about what that would mean, I'd have come up with a better story.

Moving as a group, they broke from their huddle and returned to surround me.

And then they beat me within an inch of my damned life.

In a matter of seconds I'd lost count of how many punches had landed in my gut, my ribs, my back. Jabs pummeled my face. A bottle cracked and broke against the top of my head. Warm blood ran down my face. I squinted as my blood dripped into my eyes— and that's why I didn't see the fist that flattened my nose and filled my brain with a flash of electric violet.

The smartass in me wanted to mutter *garbanzo* one more time, but my body was done taking directions for a while. I went limp as the blows continued to fall. A few seconds later—or maybe it was a few minutes, I couldn't tell anymore—the Nausicaans stopped hitting me.

One of the grunts complained, "He stop make funny noises."

I'd be lying if I said I'd felt any sympathy for his disappointment.

Eyes closed, I let inertia have my body—but I used every trick I'd ever learned to keep my mind awake inside its bruised and bloodied shell.

The Nausicaans, assuming I was on the other side of consciousness, finally spoke freely, just a few meters away from me. Though I should have expected this, they spoke to each other in their native tongue. Without the aid of the universal translator, I had to rely on my limited and admittedly flawed understanding of Nausico to figure out what they were saying.

It was hard. They spoke quickly, in an obscure dialect I didn't know. But I picked out a few key words and proper names, and as I listened, I pieced together their meaning from context. They were connected to a ship called *Seovong*. They had just hit a convoy. After that the slang became too thick for me to know what they had planned next—but in the flurry of gibberish, I caught one more name that I recognized: Gliza. A shot caller. A heist planner.

I'd never met Gliza. Didn't know if Gliza was a he, a she, an it, or something else entirely, or what species. But I knew the name because Gliza was one of those figures who kept the criminal underworld from devouring itself. A power broker who made the rules—and enforced them. That was the lead that would help me find their boss Kinogar, I was sure of it.

All right. Enough fun. Time to go.

I had hoped to leave the moment the Nausicaans stepped away and gave me a measure of privacy beneath the tarps . . . but then I looked up and remembered that my wrists were still wrapped in chains, and that every part of my body was wailing in agony like the villainous cowards who get put to death at the end of every Klingon opera.

This, I belatedly realized, was going to be a problem.

Admiral Akaar had undone the collar and opened the jacket of his Starfleet dress uniform in the shuttlepod on the ride to his home atop a hill overlooking a lake in Montana. Two steps through his front door he shed the jacket and dropped it on the bench in his mudroom. His residential aide would collect it and the rest of the uniform the following morning to have it cleaned, pressed, and returned to his wardrobe.

His home was quiet, serene. Moving through it he made almost no sound, despite his size. Like many Capellans, he had a natural talent for being light on his feet.

His shoes he doffed in his bedroom. He left them at the foot of his bed to be polished.

In stocking feet he padded through his home's open-concept main floor. Stopped at his replicator nook. It powered up at the sound of his voice. "Mexican hot chocolate, seventy-five degrees Celsius." The beverage and its mug—complete with an oversized handle to fit his large hand—materialized in a swirl of energy. As the last particles faded, Akaar took the mug and carried it to his sofa, one of the few pieces of furniture in the room. He eased himself down into its plush embrace.

Sipping the cocoa, which had a pleasant kick of chili spice, he put up his feet and admired the view of the moonlit lake outside his living room's wall of windows. The beauty of that vista was one of the reasons he had eschewed wall decorations in this room. In his opinion, there was nothing he could display that could compete with the splendor of nature.

The cocoa was soothing in its sweet decadence. All that Akaar wanted to do was wind down and bring his night to a close, but he had too much on his mind to sleep.

"Computer. Open a holovid channel to criminal lawyer Jonathan Ezor."

"Hailing Mister Ezor now," his home's virtual daemon replied in a soothing feminine voice. Soft feedback tones signaled that the transmission was ringing Ezor's comm.

Ezor answered after the third ring. *"Admiral Akaar?"*

"Yes, Mister Ezor. Please forgive the hour. I hope I didn't wake you."

"Not at all, sir." The transmission switched from audio-only to a full holographic image of a visibly groggy Ezor, who blinked the sleep from his eyes. *"What can I do for you?"*

"I was at a state dinner this evening." He sipped his cocoa. "I had a troubling conversation with Attorney General Louvois."

The news honed Ezor's focus. *"Troubling in what respect, sir?"*

"She seems to be sharpening her longest knives for Captain Picard."

Ezor frowned. *"I got much the same impression in court yesterday."*

"I had hoped this hearing would be treated as a polite inquiry, not a witch hunt."

"I'm not sure I would characterize it as a 'witch hunt,' sir. Not yet, at least."

"Perhaps. But it's vitally important that we not let it reach that point." Suddenly aware of a mild chill in the room, Akaar wrapped his hands around his mug to warm them.

The hologram of Ezor rippled as he seemed to wrestle with his conscience. *"Sir, I'm not sure what you're asking me to do here."*

"We're just talking, Mister Ezor. If you're worried that this might be seen as an ex parte communication—"

"I'm not. An Article Thirty-Two hearing isn't a trial. We're free to speak."

"That was my understanding, as well." Akaar set his mug on his coffee table. "Let me ask you this: How do you rate Captain Picard's chances so far?"

"I'd be more optimistic if he had listened to my advice and not testified under oath."

"Yes, that does complicate the picture. But what's done is done. What I want to know is, what can we do now to extricate him from this mess?"

The lawyer shook his head. *"That's hard to say, sir. Now that he's on the stand, my fear is that Louvois will keep him there until she breaks him."*

"Don't let that happen. There is more at stake here than one man. Not only is Picard a celebrity throughout the Federation, after thwarting the Borg Invasion, he's almost become synonymous with Starfleet itself. If Louvois disgraces Picard, the damage will reach much further than the end of his career. It could lead the Council to dismantle the fleet at a time when it's more urgently needed than ever before. We cannot let that happen, Mister Ezor."

"With all respect, Admiral, we might not be able to stop it."

"Not if Louvois keeps us playing defense, that much is certain. You need to throw her off-balance, Mister Ezor. Disrupt her momentum."

His advice only seemed to agitate Ezor. *"I'm trying, sir. But I don't have much to work with. Captain Picard's logs don't cast him in the most sympathetic light, and I can tell that Louvois means to hammer him for placing the most serious blame on the late Admiral Ross."*

"What would give you leverage in court?"

"Seriously? Anything even remotely exculpatory would be a good start. I had every partner, associate, and intern in my office dig through every word of Picard's logs, and all of the depositions that Louvois conducted since the Section Thirty-One story broke. So far we've come up empty. And I'm starting to think that's Thirty-One's delayed-reaction payback."

"How so?"

"The only files to which I lack full access are the records of Thirty-One itself. From what Ozla Graniv made public, they seem like they had an organization-level fetish for documenting absolutely everything about their activities. But every time I've requested access to those files, I'm told they're 'not relevant' to Picard's case, and that I don't have sufficient security clearance to view them, not even redacted versions accessed under supervision."

Akaar folded his hands together as he pondered that. "You think someone is suppressing exculpatory evidence from the captured records of Section Thirty-One."

"I think it's a distinct possibility. I also think the outcome of this case, and the rest of Jean-Luc Picard's life, might be decided, for good or for ill, by what's in those files."

"In other words, if we drag them into the light and their evidence damns Picard instead of exonerating him—"

"Then I'll have single-handedly sunk my own case and done Louvois's job for her."

"A risk I think we need to take, Mister Ezor." Akaar stood. "I'll look into this—discreetly—from my end. Until I find something, please try to keep Captain Picard from self-destructing his own case."

"If only I could, Admiral. If only I could."

15

After more than twenty hours of nonstop work, the reactor control center of Stonekettle Station looked more like a scrapyard than a cutting-edge power-generation facility. Great swaths of its deck plating had been pulled up, and several bulkhead sections had been torn down, all to expose the hardware within. The interface node for the PMAR alone stood untouched in the center of the vast space. It was surrounded by civilians and Starfleet personnel, all of them exhausted and bewildered by the riddle of how to connect the two runabout warp cores intended to save the station and its residents from a fiery death in just a few hours' time.

La Forge leaned against the edge of a companel in front of the PMAR node. He palmed sweat from the back of his neck and found it soaked. As soon as he wiped away one sheen of perspiration, more trickled down from under his close-shorn hair. "We've got to be missing something." He looked around. "Who has the schematics?"

The station's chief engineer, Doctor th'Fehlan, handed La Forge a padd. "Here."

"Thanks." With quick swipes of his fingertips, La Forge paged through the latest updates to the station's PMAR system design. "Did we try patching into the reserve EPS matrix and shunting back to the main grid?"

Elfiki nodded. "We fried half the safeties on the EPS matrix. It's a no-go."

"What about patching the new cores directly to the shield emitters?"

"Won't work," th'Fehlan said. "It's a distributed system, no main emitter. It relies on the station's primary grid to balance the load. We have to patch into the main grid."

Nothing but dead ends. La Forge was losing patience. "How long 'til sunrise?"

"Less than three hours," said one of the civilian engineers.

The pressure drove Elfiki to massage her forehead with her thumbs. "This is crazy. Every system we try to change breaks something else." She shot a perplexed look at th'Fehlan. "Doesn't your station have underground bunkers for an emergency like this?"

"As far as I know, that was never part of the design." The Andorian shook his head in quiet dismay. "In hindsight, a poor decision—one made before my time, I should point out. Most likely it was one of many corners cut in the name of saving time, money, or both."

Her rebuke wasn't done. "Why even *build* a dome on a planet like this? Whoever thought that up had to know they were begging for trouble. So why do it?"

La Forge snorted in grim amusement. "Why does anyone do anything, Dina? Because they can. The dome was this station's way of showing off." Possessed by an idea, he faced th'Fehlan. "Just out of curiosity, does the station have any industrial mining equipment? Anything that could be used to dig an emergency shelter?"

"If we did, we'd have been digging before your ship arrived."

An eye roll from Elfiki. "So much for that."

"Which brings us back to this." La Forge stepped toward the PMAR node, which was shaped like a circular cradle. "A round hole into which we're trying to force two square pegs."

As soon as he'd said it, a new idea lit up his imagination.

"I have an idea." He pointed at a nearby civilian. "Hand me that electrospanner, please." The woman passed the tool to La Forge, who went to work stripping apart the shell of the PMAR's cradle. "Some of these outer pieces are functional with the PMAR, but useless to us. A few are just cosmetic. Either way, we can lose them for now." More pieces of the cradle's casing hit the floor. La

Forge kept going. "The hole might be round, but we don't need the hole."

With a swift kick, he knocked away the last of the node's outer casing, revealing all of the machinery, circuitry, cables, and delicate components inside. "The PMAR fits into this sleeve on top, and that guides its connection points to the main relay contact." Working with almost surgical delicacy, he disassembled the PMAR's sleeve, exposing the power-relay contact. Then he stepped back so everyone could see it, and he raised his voice to address the room.

"Everybody, listen up. We have less than three hours to build a new receiver for this contact point. I'm gonna pull a connection node from the engine of one of our runabouts. I need all of you to design and build an adapter that will let us patch our runabout warp core into the PMAR's main node. It's the only way we can make this work."

Th'Fehlan frowned. "I hate to point this out, Commander, but that would still connect only one of your two warp cores to our main grid. And the math says we'll need at least two if we want to keep the shield up until sundown. So unless you've invented a wireless means of interplexing the output from two cores, we're only halfway out of the frying pan."

La Forge nodded, but his mind was racing. "Yes, that's true. But I'm running the numbers in my head, and if we push the cores into overdrive, we can power the shield over one sector of the station plus its core for just over thirty hours. Which means we'll need to gradually buffer a reserve charge in the station's grid over the first thirty hours, one that'll buy us time to do a hot-swap of the warp cores when the first one starts to burn out."

Mumbles of worry and disbelief rose from the working group, Starfleet and civilians alike. Ensign Ryan Giler was the first one brave enough to voice a protest. "Sirs? I hope I'm not out of line here, but I think pushing a runabout warp core all the way to critical failure sounds like a really bad plan. I mean, one solar flare or plasma ejection, and that core could overload in a hurry. What if it fails before we're ready for the hot-swap?"

Elfiki fixed Giler with a sardonic look. "In that case, Ensign? I hope you're in the mood for one *hell* of a tan."

For the second time in two days, I was running for my life from a gang of Nausicaans.

Running might have been an overstatement. My gait was more of a panicked jog mixed with dazed staggering. Every step sent arcs of pain through my body. My joints protested, my ribs ached, and the bulk of my guts felt like a giant liquefied bruise that I feared I might vomit up at any moment. The pounding in my head was out of synch with my footfalls, which only made it hurt worse. I wanted to lie down and die but I had to keep moving.

I had trouble keeping both eyes open at once. They had swollen in such a way that forcing one open compelled the other to close. I chose not to dwell on it. I'd always thought that depth perception was overrated anyway. Besides, I saw doubles of everything with either eye. If I had been able to open both, I probably would have been seeing quadruple.

Getting free of the docking bay had been both easier and more tedious than I had expected. All I'd had to do was swing back and forth like a gymnast building up to a trick. That accomplished two things: first, it shuffled my bound wrists along the overhead pipe to its nearest fitting, which thanks to shoddy Nausicaan workmanship had been on the verge of sliding free, and second, it had sprained or cramped damned near every muscle from my neck to my toes.

Once the pipe had popped out of joint, my chains slid right off it. Back on solid ground, I freed my feet, and then I found a stray piece of metallic debris with which to pick the lock on the chains about my wrists. Then I hid under a urine-stained tarp next to the docking-bay entrance. When the Nausicaans returned, I skulked out before the inner door closed. By the time they got under their draped pipework and saw that I was gone, I had already made it to the street.

Now all I needed to do was keep them at bay long enough to get clear of their sensor jammer, just like I did on Kamhawy. One or two blocks' head start—I'd thought that would be all I'd need. But half a kilometer from the docking bays, my recall switch was still flashing red. That meant it had no signal from my ship. No signal meant no transporter lock. All I could figure was that the Nausicaans must have turned up the juice on their jammer.

Which left me in a bit of a pickle, as humans would say. Though to be honest, I'd never understood that phrase. Most pickles were quite small, so how could a whole person fit inside one? And why would that be dangerous? I liked the folks from Earth, really, but I found a few of their idioms baffling.

I tried outsmarting the Nausicaans by running away from my ship rather than toward it. There was no reason to show them where my ship was parked, and I figured that the dense woods on the outskirts of Coker Flats would provide me more cover than the town's wide-open streets and dead-end alleyways. But once again the Nausicaans were right on top of me. All I could figure was that they must have had amazing olfactory senses.

Either that or they were able to hear the labored wheezing that had replaced my normally quiet breathing, or the hacking coughs that had me spitting out blood, or the clumsy patter of my running feet snapping through low brush and dry twigs.

Or maybe they were just following my blood trail.

I was bleeding fast. I had no idea how much blood I'd already lost. Or how long I'd be able to keep running before my body would just quit and plant me face-first into the ground.

Disruptor pulses screamed past me, scorched holes into the thickest tree trunks, split the saplings in half and brought them down around me. Collapsing piles of branch and bark and leaf blocked my path and nearly buried me alive.

I dodged left—not on purpose, but because I lost my balance. To my right a flurry of crimson pulses raked the ground, kicking up dust and smoke and filling the air with the smell of burnt peat. Two more shots flew past over my head—again by luck, thanks to a rock I tripped on—and my nose was filled with the acrid stench of my own singed hair.

Flailing and stumbling in the dark, I didn't see the downward slope in front of me until I was tumbling down it, ass over elbows, a runaway slave to gravity. Near the bottom I slammed into a tree and let out a grunt of agony. On all fours I crawled away, hoping to find cover. My hand landed on slick mud and shot out from under me. I plunged headfirst into a cold creek that stank of rust and chemical waste.

I surfaced with a gasp—and heard the soft ping of my recall switch locking in on my ship's signal. I dug it from my pocket and thumbed the trigger.

The dematerialization sequence began immediately. I went limp and sank into the grip of the confinement beam. A vortex of brilliant motes spun around me, and as the forest dissolved, I saw the Nausicaans fire in vain at my dissipating transporter ghost.

The transporter nook of the *Tain Hu* took shape around me.

I solidified on the pad and crumpled into a sitting position. I was sopping wet and in more pain than I could catalog all at once. My body craved painkillers. My brain cried out for oblivion. I figured a bottle of Romulan ale would satisfy both needs.

But first I had to get my ass off of Faustus Prime, and fast.

"Computer," I said, my voice slurred by pain and distorted by split, swollen lips. "Engage autopilot. Initiate launch. Break orbit and get me away from here, warp six."

"Course plotted. Requesting clearance for takeoff. Stand by for launch."

The ship came alive all around me. The engines rumbled awake. Computers purred and chirped. Semi-musical tones wafted down the center passage from the cockpit. It would be just a few moments before I felt the tug of artificial gravity taking over inside the ship, in tandem with the inertial dampers. There was a chance the Nausicaans might chase me, but I didn't think it was likely. If anything, from Faustus Prime they would try to rendezvous with their leader—the one they called Kinogar.

I figured I had at least five hours before *Tain Hu* reached the next inhabited system. If I was lucky, it wouldn't take me more than half an hour to crawl the five meters from the transporter nook to the medical bay.

I pulled myself off the energizer pad, put my hands and knees on the deck, and started my slow scuttle toward relief.

The clock ticked down as the sun came up.

Wright stood in the middle of the operations center, her focus torn between the dwindling countdown and the rising ruby-red glow on the horizon outside the station's dome. Her senior personnel were at their stations, doing all they could to coordinate the final preparations for the coming disaster. And that's what she knew it would be, even under the best of circumstances. What else was she supposed to call losing nearly ninety-five percent of the facility in a single event? Years of labor, the collective effort and dreams of thousands, were all about to vanish.

Nothing can stop that now. The focus now has to be saving lives.

Ops was crowded with night-shift and auxiliary personnel, most of whom had no other place to go now that they had abandoned their quarters in a mad dash for survival. The corners and empty spaces underneath consoles were packed with duffels and luggage—her crew's personal effects, which had been limited to toiletries and two days' changes of clothing.

Thanks to the heaps of baggage, there was little room to move about the operations level. Wright coped by staying inside the semicircle described by Pov's wraparound companels. It also happened to be the best vantage from which to assess the progress of the station's retreat into sector nine as well as the impending deadly daybreak.

"Two minutes to sunup," Pov declared, as if no one else were watching the countdown. He opened a channel to the security office. "Gilmour! Status on the bulkheads."

"Almost sealed," the security chief answered over the comm. *"Locking in now."*

From the engineering station, Denn stared with dread at the crimson glow on the horizon. "Those bulkheads won't mean squat without the energy shield."

Wright glared at the Arkenite. "Thanks for the reminder. I'm sure we'd all forgotten."

Chastised, Denn made himself small behind his bank of companels, but his paranoia had infected Wright. She reached past Pov and opened a channel to reactor control. "Doctor th'Fehlan? What's the status on that warp core? You've got ninety seconds until we burn."

"We can see the clock," the chief engineer snapped. *"Stand by."*

It was all Wright could do not to scream in frustration. *Stand by. As if there's anything else we could do.* She looked toward the coming dawn. She had grown up thinking of sunrise as a metaphor for hope, for rebirth. Now it meant certain death.

"Sixty seconds and counting," Pov declared.

A terrified hush fell over the room. Precious moments melted away . . .

"Warp core patched in," th'Fehlan announced over the comm. *"Raising the shield!"*

Outside the windows of Ops, the familiar golden shimmer of the energy shield rippled into existence. It enveloped the station's cylindrical core first, and then it spread outward, along the sealed inner bulkheads and across the dome overhead, until it surrounded all of sector nine, which Wright had designated as the station's emergency shelter zone. As soon as the shield was fully engaged, the protected portion of the dome darkened to block the blinding radiation from Skarda's red giant.

"Kootis, close the core's blast shields," Wright said. "Keer, engage internal cams. Put it on wall panel two, please."

Heavy shields descended to cover the windows.

"Activating cams," Pov said. "Routing feeds to wall panel two."

The massive full-wall companel switched its content from systems diagnostics to several rows of vid feeds from the station's internal sensors. With each passing second the images grew brighter, as the planet rotated toward the red giant.

Alerts sounded on Denn's panel. He muted them. "Temperatures rising fast in the unshielded sectors. Seventy-five Celsius and climbing."

Pov asked, "How about inside the shield?"

"Also rising, but not as fast. Up two degrees." Denn looked at Wright. "And before you ask—no, we can't increase power to life-support to compensate. Everything we've got is going into the shield. If anything, we might have to reduce life-support before the day's over."

That provoked vulgar grumbles from the assorted personnel in Ops. Wright didn't blame them for being discouraged. She could already feel the air getting warm, and knowing it was only going to get worse ate away at the few crumbs of hope she still clung to.

But hope or no hope, she still had a job to do. "Keer, check in with all levels. Make sure the blast doors are holding. If anything inside the shield starts warming faster than the average, be ready to coordinate evacuations."

"You got it, boss." The Tellarite set to work, turning Wright's order into action.

At five minutes after sunrise, Denn announced, "Surface temp is six hundred degrees and rising. Inside the dome but outside the shield, we're at three hundred and rising."

There was nothing left to do now but watch and pray.

As the minutes passed, the temperatures soared.

At the one-hour mark, the sensors closest to the dome began to fail.

Just shy of two hours after sunrise, the unshielded sections of the dome buckled and collapsed. Half-molten slag rained down on the empty buildings below, crushing some, melting others. Brutal, merciless solar wind from the red giant poured in and bathed the exposed areas of Stonekettle Station. Wright's heart broke as she watched one building after another succumb and implode. Entire regions of the station melted down and sublimated into vapor while she watched in horror—and then the sensors melted down, turning the wall of vid feeds to static, which then switched over to black standby screens blinking the words SIGNAL LOST.

Except for a sliver of humanity huddled under a faltering shimmer of jury-rigged protection, the community for which she had so long worked and sacrificed . . . was gone. Burned away as if it had never been.

She stood behind Pov and sighed. "I guess that's it, then."

"I wish," the Tellarite said. "Now we have to hope that La Forge's warp cores can go the distance—and that he can make the swap at the halfway mark without getting us all killed."

Wright shot a dejected look at the dark companel. "How do you like our chances?"

"I'm not a betting man, Juneau. But if I were . . . this is one wager I wouldn't take."

16

———

Putting myself back together after a first-class ass-kicking was a part of my job I had never been good at, and it only got harder as I got older. For one thing, injuries lately seemed to hurt more than when I was young. And they took longer to heal, even with all the spiffy gadgets that Starfleet Intelligence had loaned to me along with their other upgrades to the *Tain Hu*.

The medbay scanners told me what I already knew: that the Nausicaans had beaten the stuffing out of me. Cracked ribs, other fractures, internal injuries, a concussion—I had come back with enough damage to make three people miserable. When I was young my mom had always said I was an overachiever, but I don't think this was what she'd had in mind.

I had to admire Starfleet's technology. They'd invented some kind of neural damper that could block pain signals from being recognized by the brain. That made it possible to do all kinds of surgical repairs on oneself even while conscious. Ingenious, really. All the same, I still preferred to numb myself with booze. Call me old-fashioned.

I winced at the sting of a hypospray on the back of my neck— the injection of medical nanites to repair my internal injuries without invasive surgery. I was thankful for that, though I'd been put back together at the molecular level so many times that I wondered how many of my organs were still composed of my original cells rather than replicated replacements.

I was also starting to wonder if Starfleet Intelligence would ever consider my debts to them repaid and cut me loose. After all, I wasn't getting any younger, and the universe wasn't getting any kinder. How many more years of this did Lavelle think I had left in me? Or was he just planning to work me until my luck ran out?

A double chirp filtered down from the overhead speaker. My ship's computer had news for me. *"Incoming transmission on the secure quantum channel."*

"Put it through to me down here."

"Channel open."

I took another swig of blue ale. "This is Agonist, go ahead."

"Thadiun? It's Naomi."

"Hey, there. Real names? Is Sam gone for the night?"

"Something like that. How're you doing?"

"The osteofuser's knitting my ribs back together."

"Rough night?"

"I've had worse. I just wish Starfleet made a gizmo that could fix my wounded pride."

"Or reduce the swelling of your ego."

"Says the woman with no bruises and a cushy office job on Earth. Speaking of which, did you run those names I sent in?"

She answered while I worked my way through the rest of my rotgut.

"As a matter of fact, I did. The first one, Seovong, *produced a number of hits, but only one that cross-references with your new Nausicaan friends: it's a ship, probably Kinogar's."*

"Good to know. Any chance we can track it?"

"Working on it. We'll let you know if it comes up on sensors. As for the second name, Gliza—*just a few hits, but only one that matches your description of a shot caller. Details are few, but I've got a ninety-seven percent likelihood that your target is based out of the city of Dulevo on Garada in the Delaroz system."*

It was a decent lead, but I was feeling greedy. "Can you be more specific? Or should I just beam down to Dulevo and go door to door?"

"I'll keep digging. With any luck, I'll have something more solid by the time you reach Garada. Think you'll be sober by then?"

"Not if I can help it."

"Need anything else before I sign off?"

"Tell Sam I want a raise."

"Technically, you're not on the SI payroll."

"I didn't say it had to be a *big* raise."

The computer voice informed me, *"The transmission has been terminated."*

I stretched out on the biobed. "Computer, wake me when we reach Garada. Until then, I want comms and lights *off*." The medbay went mostly dark, and my headache sucked a bit less.

I finished off the ale, and then I looked at my life and my choices.

Apart from the booze, I regretted them all.

The witness stand was no more comfortable for Picard on the second day of his hearing than it had been on the first. Though he did his best to remain calm in the face of Louvois's verbal assault, being able to see her rhetorical traps coming had not made them any easier to evade.

She stood in front of the witness box, ostensibly directing her questions to Picard, though he sensed she was, at least in part, playing to the packed crowd of spectators and media. "Captain, I direct your attention to page twenty-six of the deposition now shown on your padd. In a deposition taken on December the eleventh of last year, Admiral Tujiro Nakamura quoted you as saying to him and the other admirals involved in your subspace conference that you felt President Zife had acted against Starfleet. Did you express such a sentiment at that time?"

"I did."

"Did you also, as Admiral Nakamura testified, say in that same conversation that Zife's actions in connection with the Tezwa crisis and the subsequent cover-up constituted acts of, and I quote, 'depraved indifference tantamount to murder'?"

He wanted to deny it, but when he searched his memory he remembered himself saying those exact words. "Yes, I said that."

"I direct your attention to the top of page twenty-seven of Admiral Nakamura's deposition. He further testified that you discouraged the group from considering impeachment as a remedy to President Zife's alleged offenses. Is that also correct?"

"Because of the potential political and—"

"Yes or no, Captain: Did you discourage your superiors from pursuing a legal remedy to President Zife's alleged offenses, one that was available through the civilian government?"

Boxed in, Picard hoped that Ezor would be able to reframe these points during cross-examination. "Yes."

"Would it be correct to say, Captain, that you set this coup in motion?"

"Objection," Ezor cut in. "Characterizing the event as a 'coup' is prejudicial."

"Sustained," Liu said. To Louvois she added, "Do you wish to rephrase?"

"Yes, Admiral. Captain Picard, you convened the subspace vid conference with Starfleet's senior admirals, did you not?"

"In cooperation with Ambassador Lagan, yes."

"Did you and Ambassador Lagan present the admirals with all of the evidence your officers and crew had obtained concerning the alleged Zife conspiracy on Tezwa?"

"We did." *Where is she going with this?*

Feigning confusion, Louvois asked, "What, precisely, did you think would happen as a consequence of that discussion, Captain?"

Picard took a breath to stall for time. This was the sort of open-ended query that Ezor had warned him about. He volleyed it back to Louvois. "Could you be more specific?"

He caught a tiny flash of anger in her eyes. She knew he was playing games. "Very well. Captain, what action or response did you expect to provoke from the admirals by sharing your findings and suspicions with them?"

There would be no deflecting this query. It would need to be answered with great care and circumspection. Picard put on his most diplomatic air. "It was my hope that my superior officers, being informed of the facts of the president's crimes, and the potentially disastrous consequences of their public revelation at that time, would be able to reason with President Zife, and to persuade him that it would be in the best interest of the Federation and his presidency if he were to resign his office and depart permanently from the political stage."

"That strikes me as an overly optimistic appraisal of the potential fallout, Captain."

Ezor snapped, "Objection: argumentative."

"Sustained. Do you have further questions, Counselor?"

"I do," Louvois said. She collected herself quickly and with ease. "Captain, based on your statements to the admirals and the fact that you dissuaded them from seeking legal remedies through the proper civilian channels, isn't it true that you sought to foment the violent removal of Zife from his elected office?"

"No, I did not."

"But you were aware that conspiring with Admiral William Ross, who had advocated the use of force to oust President Zife, would lead to Zife's assassination."

"I was not. No such proposal was made or even suggested during that conversation."

"But you did understand that if President Zife resisted your superiors' invitation, that the next step in this action was to employ a threat of force to compel his cooperation?"

"I'd hoped it would not come to that. I did not personally advocate such action."

"But neither did you object to the involvement of Section Thirty-One."

"I was unaware of their involvement until the publication of Ozla Graniv's exposé."

Louvois regarded Picard with contempt. "Why don't I believe you, Captain?"

"Objection," Ezor said. "The witness is not obliged to speculate on the government counsel's state of mind or her credulity with regard to his testimony."

"Sustained."

From his privileged vantage in the witness box, Picard saw Louvois clench her hands into fists, a clear betrayal of her mounting frustration.

"Captain, did any member of your crew on the *Enterprise* have any dealings with Section Thirty-One during the Tezwa crisis?"

"Not that I'm aware of."

"Did any of your former *Enterprise* crew, particularly members of your senior staff, have any dealings with Section Thirty-One as a consequence of the Tezwa affair?"

"None that I knew of at the time."

"Not at that time? What about now?"

"No. I have no knowledge of any persons who were current or former members of my crew on the *Enterprise*-D or *Enterprise*-E having any dealings with Section Thirty-One during the Tezwa crisis in 2379."

"Do you deny that your current first officer on the *Enterprise*-E, Commander Worf, had significant interactions with Section Thirty-One director Vasily Zeitsev on Qo'noS, including the commission of numerous illegal acts of espionage against our ally the Klingon Empire, in order to aid your mission to Tezwa?"

"This is the first I've heard of it."

"In light of the role Section Thirty-One played in assuring your mission's success on Tezwa, do you really expect us to believe that you were unaware of their intentions toward President Zife during its aftermath?"

Ezor stood. "Objection! Admiral, the witness has already stated that he had no prior knowledge of this information. Continuing to harp on this point is badgering."

"Sustained. And on that note, I'm declaring a one-hour recess for lunch. Attorney General Louvois, I suggest you be ready to pursue a new line of inquiry when we return."

"Yes, Admiral."

Liu tapped the bell on her desk. "And we're in recess." She stood and left the room, and the crowd in the rear and upper galleries dispersed.

Ezor walked over to the witness box to collect Picard. "Let's get you out of here."

As his lawyer led him past the prosecution's table, Picard noted the pinched expression of rage on Louvois's face. "A capital idea."

Ezor handed Picard off to Crusher at the banister gate. Not wanting to know what Louvois might have on her mind, Picard offered his arm to Crusher. As soon as she took it, he led her out of the hearing room, eager to be anywhere else, even if for just an hour.

Jonathan Ezor pretended to be slow in gathering his effects from the defense table. He wanted to give Captain Picard some much-needed space and privacy with his wife, but even more importantly, he wanted to make sure he positioned himself as a buffer between Picard and Louvois, who seemed to be spoiling for an ex parte conversation.

He reached the exit a few paces behind Picard and a few ahead of Louvois. The attorney general called out, "Counselor? A word with you and your client, please."

Her request was enough to stop Picard and Crusher, who turned back to see what was going on. Ezor motioned for them to keep going. "Head for lift two and get in. I'll meet you on the landing platform." They hesitated, so he added more firmly, "Go."

They resumed walking toward the nearby bank of lifts. Ezor turned back to confront Phillipa Louvois. A tall woman even without the aid of fashion, in heels she was able to look down upon him—an experience he found a little unnerving. She sounded upset. "Mister Ezor. I wanted to speak with Captain Picard."

"I think you'd have to agree it's probably best if you speak with me instead."

"Best? Less problematic, perhaps."

"For the moment let's consider those ideas synonymous." He glanced over his shoulder, confirmed that Picard and Crusher had boarded the lift to the shuttlepod landing pad, and then he turned back toward Louvois. "What's on your mind, Counselor?"

"I think we both know this is a mistake."

"This hearing? I couldn't agree more."

"No, I'm talking about your insistence on prolonging this farce. You can't halt the inevitable, Mister Ezor. At best you can delay it. But sometimes that only makes it worse."

He lifted his chin, refusing to be cowed. "I disagree on all points, Counselor. In my experience, nothing is truly inevitable where the law is concerned. And I believe that an injustice delayed is . . . well, just peachy, actually."

"You don't really think you can win this, do you?"

He met her arrogance with skepticism. "And you do? I've read the same depositions you have. Heard the same testimony, seen the same evidence. I like my client's chances."

"Then you're a fool. After I'm done, he'll be called to face a general court-martial, and from there he's going to a Starfleet stockade for the rest of his life."

"I doubt that. Don't get me wrong, you've done a fine job of spin so far on direct. But I haven't even started my cross, much less my affirmative defense. Once I get going, I plan to bury you and the PHO in mitigating factors, character references, and exculpatory evidence."

"There is no exculpatory evidence."

He shot her a dubious look. "Oh, come on. I know you don't believe that." He dared a half step forward, to intrude upon her personal space. "Why are you pushing this so hard? You have to know that sedition is a major reach. My client didn't act out of malice or self-interest, and he certainly didn't act in the interest of aiding a foreign power."

"Then why did he lead a coup?"

"He did no such thing. His only concerns were for the greater good of the Federation, the preservation of the peace, and the defense of innocent lives. That must count for something."

Louvois smirked. "In a court of law? Not so much."

"Except this isn't a trial court, Phillipa. Admiral Liu expressly said as much."

"The venue doesn't matter. Whether this hearing takes place under Federation civil law or the SCMJ, the law remains clear. And I will see Captain Picard stand trial as a criminal conspirator, an accessory to murder, and a traitor to his oath of service."

"Tall order." A troubling notion occurred to Ezor. "I can't help but notice that Captain Picard was the first of the alleged conspirators you chose to pursue."

"So what?"

"Why isn't your office conducting Article Thirty-Two hearings for the three surviving admirals who were part of that conversation? Why hasn't Ambassador Lagan been made to face a civilian hearing? You deposed all of them, but only Picard gets put in the hot seat."

"Are you building to a point, Mister Ezor?"

The more he thought about it, the angrier he became. "You knew he wouldn't be able to resist testifying under oath. Didn't you?"

Louvois looked pleased with herself. "Let's just say I know Captain Picard quite well."

"This isn't about railroading him. It's a fishing expedition, isn't it?"

She shrugged. "Either-or. If Picard's testimony and evidence sets the stage for the prosecution of three Starfleet flag officers and a career diplomat whose name was recently floated as a possible replacement for the secretary of the exterior, then so be it. But if all I have to show for this at the end is Picard's head on a metaphorical spike, that would be okay, too."

"May I pose a hypothetical scenario?"

"I'm all ears, Mister Ezor."

"What if my client were able to offer testimony and corroborating evidence that would facilitate prosecutions and convictions in those pending cases? Might that be worth an offer of immunity from prosecution?"

"Immunity? That would need to be some truly cosmic testimony, and it would need to be backed up by the most incontrovertible evidence in history. If you want to be realistic, you might want to think about asking for a recommendation of leniency at your client's sentencing."

All this drama in the hope of flipping him, turning him into state's evidence. What a debacle. Ezor plastered a phony smile onto his face. "I'll take it to my client."

"You do that, Counselor. But I'll warn you right now: If I get what I need without your client—all deals are off." She shouldered past Ezor on her way to the lifts, adding as she made her exit, "I'll see to it that Picard *burns*."

Cold breezes tousled Crusher's hair as she walked hand in hand with Picard down the dirt path to the Satterlee Breakwater. Located just a short walk from Starfleet Headquarters in Sausalito, the engineered path helped shield the marina of Horseshoe Bay from the Pacific's tides. The afternoon sun had transformed the waters of the bay and the ocean beyond into shimmering wonders, but Picard felt cut off from their beauty.

He noted the tied-down sailboats in the marina. They had been secured months earlier at the close of sailing season. Part of him felt a tug of sympathy for those old seacraft—they had been left out to face the elements, abandoned to the cruelties of winter.

Some would succumb and be junked come the spring. The fortunate ones would depart these shores once more to test their mettle on the open ocean.

Looming large and bright before Picard and Crusher was the Golden Gate Bridge, its rust-red majesty bending across the bay to San Francisco. The damage done to it during the Dominion War had long since been repaired, and its restoration had been done with such attention to detail that even Picard couldn't tell which parts of the bridge's span were original and which were new.

Crusher gave Picard's hand a gentle squeeze to commandeer his attention. She wore a look of fearful concern. "You're awfully quiet today."

"Can you blame me?" He breathed in the fragrance of the sea, brine and sulfur, and then he frowned. "I'm starting to doubt myself, Beverly."

"About what?"

"About everything." He looked seaward to the horizon, as if the answer to his crisis might suddenly manifest there, fully formed. "This hearing . . . all the memories it's brought back . . . they have me rattled." He stopped, and Crusher halted with him. He turned and cast a melancholy look back at Starfleet Command, and at the Federation banner that waved above it, snapping in the brisk winter air. "What made me think I had the right to act as judge and jury for a sitting president? Was it hubris? Or foolish idealism?"

Crusher clasped his hand in both of hers. "Don't try to shoulder all of the blame for this, Jean-Luc. You didn't act alone, and for good reason."

"I remember. But did that lessen my culpability? Or merely implicate others? I was the one who shared Data's findings with Ambassador Lagan. And when she asked me what I meant to do about Zife's crimes, I was the one who suggested she contact Starfleet Command."

"Which was exactly what you were *supposed* to do."

Doubts and regrets plagued Picard. "Was it? I'm not so certain anymore." He turned away from Starfleet headquarters to regard the city across the water. "Perhaps I should have kept the whole thing a secret. Buried what I knew."

"Could you have lived with that?"

"What would have been the alternative? Go public and risk inciting a conflict with the Klingons when we and they had both barely stanched our wounds from the last war?"

Crusher shook her head. "Who knows? After the Section Thirty-One exposé, the Klingons said they would've accepted the life of Min Zife alone as penance for his crimes and those committed in his name. But I have to wonder: Would the people of the Federation really have accepted their elected leader being handed over to the Klingons for a public execution?"

"I'd seriously doubt it," Picard said.

"I'm inclined to agree." With a grimace of resignation she added, "Still, it would've been a far more reasonable response than a new war."

"True. But what they say *now* that they *would* have done *then*— and what they actually would have done in the heat of the moment— there's no telling what really would've happened."

His wife nodded in agreement. "True. But what matters now is clearing your name."

"I'm not sure we can. Louvois has done a spectacular job of casting me as a villain."

"Maybe, but the hearing's not over yet. She has to rest her case sometime. And when she does, your lawyer is going to turn this around."

Picard had to stifle a cynical laugh. "If only that were true." Noting Crusher's inquisitive look, he continued, "He sent me a message on my padd shortly after we left the building. He thinks that Louvois wants me to volunteer testimony against Admirals Nakamura, Jellico, and Nechayev, as well as against Ambassador Lagan."

"In exchange for what, Jean-Luc? Immunity?"

"Hardly. It seems the best she's willing to float is a recommendation of leniency when it comes time for me to be sentenced, following a general court-martial."

The notion seemed to offend Crusher. "I hope you told her to go to hell."

"She hasn't officially offered me *anything* yet. But I share your sentiment, all the same." He watched the sun sink a few degrees closer to the sea. "It sickens me to think of bearing witness against people who became involved in this debacle only because I *asked* them to."

Crusher reached out and took Picard's hand. "In the end, all you're being asked to do, by her or by your lawyer, is to tell the truth. Which you would have done anyway. You did nothing wrong, so we have nothing to fear."

"True. But as I'm learning the hard way, what seems right in the moment, and what is considered right under the law, aren't always the same thing. *Lawful* and *just* aren't always synonymous. And sometimes . . . truth alone cannot save us."

"Then where does that leave *you*, Jean-Luc? Where does that leave *us*? And René?"

Confronted by the reality that his long-buried role in a crisis with no heroes and no good options had come back to haunt not only him but also his wife and his young son, Picard felt guilt and shame pass through him in sickening waves. "I don't know, Beverly. All I know for certain . . . is that I'm sorry you and René had to see this."

Crusher pulled Picard into an embrace meant to give him comfort, but there was no solace left for him to find. In about an hour he would have to return to his Article 32 hearing, and he feared that nothing he still cared about—his honor, his career, or his family's faith in his integrity—would emerge from that room intact.

Louvois means to ruin me . . . and the truth will not *set me free.*

There were many kinds of invitations that Commander Sam Lavelle enjoyed: dinners with cocktails, birthday celebrations, and promotion parties, to name just a few. Being called to the office of his division's commander, however, was not a summons he ever relished.

He had double-timed his pace from his office through the corridor to the nearest lift, and then out of the lift on level three, all the way to the office suite of Admiral Marta Batanides, the chief of Starfleet Intelligence. At the entrance he waited while the computer subjected him to a biometric scan. After his identity and appointment both were confirmed, the doors opened, and he entered the admiral's waiting room. A Vulcan woman wearing a lieutenant commander's uniform looked up at Lavelle. "The admiral will see you in a moment, sir. Please have a seat."

Great. Because nothing takes the dread out of meeting with your boss like being made to wait without an explanation.

Lavelle did his best to put on a relaxed front. He sat, kept his posture straight, did his best not to fidget. But beneath his uniform he was sweating bullets. The minutes passed slowly, each one more agonizing than the last. He spent them trying to imagine a scenario in which this hasty summons could lead to good news. He failed.

Anxiety had turned his guts to hot mud by the time the Vulcan woman said, "The admiral will see you now, Commander."

He stood and smoothed the front of his uniform tunic. "Thank you." Doing his best impersonation of a dignified officer who wasn't petrified, he walked past the aide, to the office beyond. The door slid open ahead of him. He walked in and put on a polite smile.

"Wipe that smile off your face," Batanides said before Lavelle took his third step inside. "I didn't call you in here for witty banter." She pointed at one of her guest chairs. "Sit."

He sat facing the admiral. The human woman cut an imposing figure, in spite of being in late middle age. She had a lean, athletic physique and chiseled features. Her hair was bright like platinum, her eyes pale blue, and her voice as sharp as a Klingon's war blade. Her attention was on the padd in her hand—and then it was on him.

"Do you know why I called you in here, Lavelle?"

"No, Admiral."

With dramatic flourishes, she flung data from her padd to the large wall-mounted companel behind her desk. One by one, detailed files appeared from left to right: the Husnock OPC. A report about the botched bait and switch against the Orions at Kamhawy Freehold. The theft of the PMAR from Stonekettle Station—and the facility's subsequent meltdown. The long-distance scrambling of the *Enterprise*'s main science lab.

And, last but larger than life, a mug shot of Thadiun Okona.

Batanides skewered Lavelle with a look. "Okona's your asset, yes?"

He nodded. "One of them."

A sweep of the admiral's arm wiped away all of the other data points, and then a single motion replaced them with the *Enterprise*'s report of a Nausicaan attack on a freight convoy, using the OPC. "And *this* is fallout from your bungled op?"

"Well, that's hard to say for certain without knowing all of the variables that—"

"Don't bullshit me, son."

If only I could lie and get away with it.

"Yes, Admiral. The weapon used against the convoy was the one my asset lost on Kamhawy. But the good news is we're pursuing a promising new lead that we—"

"Spare me the holonovel. Just grab a mop and clean it up. On the double."

"Yes, Admiral."

She cleared her companel, picked up her padd, and swiveled her chair away from him, as if he had turned invisible and no longer mattered to her. "Good talk, Commander. Get out."

17

—•—

Morning light spilled across the vineyards of Château Picard like a memory of better days. Picard looked out upon the rows of vines, which were naked of fruit in their off-season. The paths between them were patchworks of mud and puddles; it had rained overnight in the small hours, and though the ground was mostly dried, a sweet scent of petrichor lingered as the sun crested the low hills that sheltered the vineyard's tiny microclimate, its sacred slice of French terroir.

Marie had risen early to prepare breakfast for Picard and Crusher. He had told his sister-in-law that no such effort on her part was expected or needed, that he and Crusher were content to make their own meals and clean up their own messes, but Marie had insisted. "You're guests in my home," she had said, "and I won't hear another word about it."

He and Crusher sat at the kitchen table, both of them dressed in comfortable civilian clothing. In the scant hours that separated his appearances at the Article 32 hearing, Picard had found it necessary to remind himself to take comfort in life's small pleasures. In the soothing flavor and aroma of a perfectly brewed cup of Earl Grey. The decadent sweetness of a raspberry scone, especially one as light and flaky as these that Marie had made from scratch. The restful melodies of birdsong and buzzing insects, a symphony of nature.

The warmth of his wife's hand, tenderly holding his under the table while they each read the morning's news from their own padd.

Crusher and Ezor had suggested to Picard that part of his exhaustion stemmed from his insistence on commuting between two distant time zones on Earth's surface. Early morning in La Barre was still the middle of the night in San Francisco. To a certain degree, they were right. Had he and Crusher chosen to stay in San Francisco—or anywhere along the western coast of North America—he would not have been expected to rise for hours yet. But the truth was that Picard had found it all but impossible to sleep for more than a few hours at a time since he had been ordered back to Earth to face the hearing. In a way, living on La Barre time was simply a convenient disguise for his anxiety-driven insomnia.

Through an open kitchen window he heard approaching footsteps. He looked up, expecting to see one of the vineyard's workers on their way out to tend the vines, or to the racking house to run tests and draw samples on the latest vintage committed to oak barrels. Instead he was surprised to see Jonathan Ezor make his way across the earthen path outside.

Picard got up, and Crusher watched him walk to the back door. By the time he reached it, Ezor had just started to knock. Picard opened the door. "Jonathan!" He stepped sideways to usher the man inside. "Come in."

"Thank you, Captain." Ezor wiped his feet on the mat outside the door, and then he stepped inside the house and pulled off his patchwork tweed flatcap. He smiled at Crusher. "Doctor." To Picard he added, "I was afraid I might wake you, coming so early."

"Not at all. We were just finishing breakfast." He led Ezor toward the kitchen. "Come, please. Have a seat."

Ezor followed him to the table and sat down opposite Picard. As he settled in, Crusher said, "We were expecting you to call around noon. Any chance your visit means good news?"

It was easy for Picard to read the dismay in Ezor's expression. "Unfortunately, no. It seems Louvois and her team are burning the midnight oil. I got a comm from them about thirty minutes ago. She's decided not to offer you any kind of immunity deal."

The news felt like a leaden weight upon Picard's chest. "Did she say why?"

"No. But if I had to guess, I'd say she thinks she has enough evidence to take down Ambassador Lagan and the three admirals without your cooperation. Which means she has no incentive to cut you even a millimeter of slack."

Crusher's mien was sharp, focused. "Has she uncovered new evidence? New witnesses?"

"I don't know." Ezor pulled his padd from his coat pocket and tapped it awake. "She hasn't filed any new exhibits into evidence, or made any new requests for discovery. And for now, your husband remains the only witness scheduled to testify today." He looked baffled. "She might try to spring a surprise at the hearing, but I doubt Admiral Liu would let that fly. She tends to be a stickler for rules of procedure."

Picard sighed. "So much for negotiating a swift end to this charade."

"Don't lose hope." Ezor switched off his padd and set it on the table. "I know it feels like you're being pilloried out there, but she can't go on forever. Once it's our turn, we'll put up our own witnesses and tear down her case piece by piece."

It sounded too optimistic for Picard to believe. "Is that even possible at this point?"

Ezor regained a measure of his confidence. "Trust me, Captain. We don't need to refute every single point the prosecution makes. We just need to give Admiral Liu a good reason to doubt that you acted with a criminal mind. At this point, Louvois's entire case hinges upon the presumption that you wittingly masterminded a political coup followed by an assassination. If we can introduce evidence that proves Section Thirty-One acted without your knowledge, much less your consent or cooperation, her entire premise falls apart."

"That all sounds fine in theory," Crusher said, still skeptical. "But how do you plan on turning that into action that'll make a difference to Admiral Liu?"

Ezor stood, picked up his padd, and smiled. "The practice of law and the practice of magic have one important thing in common: the power of misdirection. And though magicians never reveal their secrets, I don't mind telling you both: I still have a few tricks up my sleeve."

It was Jonathan Ezor's learned experience that, like so many things in life, lawyering was all about timing. Objecting before a witness answered something out-of-bounds. Lulling a hostile witness with a dull cadence of routine questions before sandbagging them with a follow-up that put their backs to a rhetorical wall. And, sometimes most important of all, knowing how and when to mess with the opposing counsel's rhythm.

The hearing had reconvened. Admiral Liu had taken her place at the front of the room, behind her table on the dais. The bailiff had granted everyone permission to sit, and with a ring of the bell, Liu signaled that the Article 32 hearing was officially back in session. Out of the corner of his eye, Ezor saw the shifting of Louvois's feet beneath her table: she pulled them back under her chair and pressed her toes to the floor—something she had done at the start of each previous day in court, before calling Picard to the stand to testify.

Ezor held up his stylus and spoke first. "Admiral? At this time the defense motions to suppress a number of items submitted as evidence by government counsel."

On the edge of his vision he noted Louvois's glare—and then he kept going.

"The defense asks that Captain Picard's logs, from the stardate at which the *Enterprise* was ordered to intervene with military force to prevent a Klingon invasion of Tezwa, through the conclusion of that military operation, be stricken from the record."

Liu cocked an eyebrow. "On what grounds, Counselor?"

"Relevance, Admiral. Upon detailed review, nothing contained in those logs relates in any way to the prosecution's case, nor does it further the government's interest for those logs to be made public."

The admiral looked mildly annoyed. "Anything else?"

"Yes, Admiral. Government counsel entered into evidence several other official logs from that same period of time. None of those recorded by personnel aboard the *Enterprise* have been shown to have any evidentiary relevance. Defense moves that those logs also be stricken."

Louvois's temper flared. "Admiral, what the hell is defense counsel doing?"

Liu held up a hand to ward off Louvois's protest, and then she asked Ezor, "What else?"

"Government counsel has issued a witness subpoena, as yet unfulfilled, seeking to compel the testimony of the android Data Soong. Defense moves that this subpoena be quashed."

That prompted the admiral to lean forward in curiosity. "Pray tell, *why*, Counselor?"

"Because the android Data Soong was not present for the events in question, ma'am."

Liu picked up her padd, tapped it once, and mustered a dubious frown. "According to my records, Mister Ezor, Lieutenant Commander Data served as the acting first officer of the *Enterprise* during its supervision of the occupation of Tezwa."

"That's true, Admiral. But legally, Lieutenant Commander Data is *not* the same person as Data Soong. According to Starfleet personnel records, Lieutenant Commander Data was killed in action aboard the hijacked Romulan warbird *Scimitar*, in the Bassen Rift, on December twelve, 2379. The synthetic entity presently known as Data Soong did not exist until his inception on January sixteen, 2384."

Liu briefly pinched the bridge of her nose. "That's as may be, Counselor. But it's my understanding that the android Data Soong inherited the memories of Lieutenant Commander Data of Starfleet. So while his current form was not present during the events in question, he does possess the memories of his former self's service, yes?"

"Possibly, Admiral. But there's no way we can be certain of that. We must also take into account that the android Data Soong is believed to have inherited the memories of his creator, Doctor Noonian Soong, as well as some of Doctor Soong's personality. If we were to subpoena sensor logs or comm logs from a computer server that had been lost, and then years later restored from a backup onto a new core compromised with unknown contents and software, and had no way to verify the integrity of the original information, would we not move to suppress that source as being inherently unreliable?"

Eyes wide, Louvois almost shouted, "This is absurd! Admiral, the testimony of—"

"I'll take it under advisement," Liu said.

Louvois looked as if someone had just kicked her in the stomach. "Are you serious?"

"Ms. Louvois, I suggest you refresh your understanding of the SCMJ's rules of evidence." Liu turned an apprehensive look at Ezor. "Will that be all, Counselor?"

"Almost, Admiral." He tapped a transmit button on his padd to send his next motion directly to Liu's device. "At this time, the defense moves to demand the immediate recusal of Ms. Louvois as government counsel."

Louvois's expression was half rage, half horror. "On what grounds?"

Liu ignored Louvois's outburst and repeated the query. "On what grounds, Counselor?"

"Admiral, when we swore our oaths two days ago, I was prepared to accept Attorney General Phillipa Louvois's affirmation that she would be able to conduct herself in this forum without prejudice or other disqualification. I granted her this benefit of the doubt in spite of the fact that she previously—and unsuccessfully—prosecuted the defendant in a summary court-martial following the loss of the *U.S.S. Stargazer* in 2355. She subsequently presided over an Article Thirty-Five hearing that challenged the sentience and freedom of Lieutenant Commander Data, at that time an officer under Captain Picard's command aboard the *Enterprise*-D. It is my contention that these previous legal conflicts with Captain Picard—neither of which was concluded in the manner for which she had hoped—left Attorney General Louvois with a lingering resentment of Captain Picard, one that she failed to declare at the start of these proceedings, as required by oath and affirmation."

Liu's patience was expiring. "Why did you not raise this objection *then*, Mister Ezor?"

"As I said, Admiral: I had granted government counsel the benefit of the doubt. I'd hoped she would be able to approach these proceedings in a fair and impartial manner. But after observing the vindictive, openly hostile manner with which she has treated Captain Picard, while dragging out his period of direct examination into what would now be a third full day, I cannot help but harbor grave doubts with regard to her objectivity."

The admiral sighed. "Very well, Counselor. I'll take this and your remaining motions under advisement. Until I'm prepared to render my decisions, this hearing is in recess." She rang the bell on her desk, stood, and left the room while slowly shaking her head.

Ezor did not need to look at Louvois to know that she was livid. He felt her rage boring a hole into his back, like a drill made out of heat and rage.

He leaned down to Picard, who was conferring over the railing with Crusher. "I just bought you a reprieve, Captain. Could be minutes, hours, or a day."

"Thank you, Jonathan." Picard looked at Crusher, then asked Ezor, "What now?"

"Go to the Fairmont, get a suite, order room service, and take a nap." He switched off his padd and blocked Picard's view of Louvois's hateful glare. "You're both gonna need it."

18

Sitting in the command chair of the *Enterprise* made Šmrhová feel like an impostor. It didn't matter to her inner critic that she was the ship's acting first officer, or that she had spent years earning her rank and commendations. All she could think about were the moments when she had failed to live up to her own lofty expectations. When she had come up short of the goals she had set for herself so long ago. All the times she had failed to live up to her potential.

During her days at Starfleet Academy, she had imagined herself becoming a captain by the age of thirty-five. Now her thirty-first birthday was two months behind her, and she had started to wonder if she would ever be promoted beyond the post of security chief. At the same time she dreaded the weight of responsibility that would come with climbing the ranks. She was good at being a tactical officer, arguably an expert in matters of strategy, defense, and criminal investigation. But did any of that really qualify her for command?

I should have pushed to lead more away teams. Spent more time studying diplomacy. Done just about anything to get Captain Picard to notice me.

She tried to shake off her old mantra of self-negation. *Stay focused on the mission. On where you are and what you're doing. Be here. If things aren't happening, make them happen.*

"Mister Dygan. What's the status of the science lab?"

The svelte, charming Cardassian man looked back from ops. "On schedule, Lieutenant. All damaged components have been replaced, and clean uploads of software and firmware are being installed now. The lab is expected to return to service in forty-one minutes, as scheduled."

"Any chance we could shave a few minutes off that time?"

"Not unless you know some way to accelerate the transmission and decryption of coded data packets from Memory Prime. Though if you do, I'm sure Starfleet Operations would be most interested to learn your secret."

She let his sly, winking sarcasm pass unremarked.

That's what I get for trying to pep-talk a Cardassian.

Masking her wounded pride, she swiveled her chair toward the security console. "Mister Konya. Have there been any further reports of burglaries or heists that match the MO of our renegade Nausicaans?"

Konya shook his head. "Not yet, Lieutenant. I'll continue to monitor all channels."

"Very well. Thank you." Šmrhová let the command chair return to its natural, forward-facing position. Staring at the slow streaks of starlight on the viewscreen, she felt trapped.

They're all just humoring me. Worf tells me just to let them work, but then what am I doing? How am I supposed to be in command if all I do is sit and wait? How is that leadership?

A quick double beep from the overhead speaker was followed by Worf's voice. *"Lieutenant Šmrhová, please report to the ready room."*

"Aye, sir." She stood from the center chair. "Konya, you have the conn."

The Betazoid man left the security console and was immediately relieved there by Lieutenant Chen. By the time Šmrhová reached the door to the ready room, Konya had settled into the command chair with a level of grace and calm that filled her with envy.

Šmrhová entered the ready room to find Worf standing with his hands folded behind his back, facing the compartment's sole viewport. Outside, stars streaked past, distorted by the ship's warp field. Šmrhová stood in front of the desk. She heard the door slide shut behind her. Without looking at her, Worf said, "Sit down."

She planted herself into one of the guest chairs. And she waited.

Worf brooded in silence for several seconds. "I do not like being taken for a fool."

Good lord, what have I done now? "Sir?"

He left the viewport and sat down at the desk, his brows knitted in anger. "Starfleet Command will not give me straight answers. They demanded I release Okona, but would not say why. They told me to wipe his arrest from our logs, but won't explain why Starfleet Intelligence sabotaged our science lab. Someone there knows why the Nausicaans attacked that convoy. But they will not talk. *Not enough security clearance*, they tell me."

He rotated his holoframe so that Šmrhová could see it, and then he called up an image of Okona. "But it all comes back to *this* man. Thadiun Okona. I am certain of it."

She nodded. "I agree. But what are we supposed to do? He's off-limits."

Worf eyed the image of Okona as if he were picturing the man's grisly demise. "Is he? If Starfleet Intelligence can break the rules, so can we." He called up a screen of additional intel about Okona. "According to the Federation's sensor network, Okona's ship is on a direct heading for Garada, in the Delaroz system."

"Nothing illegal about that."

Worf shook his head. "Find Okona and you will find a crime. I want him in custody on the *Enterprise,* quietly, and as soon as possible. And this time we hold him until we get the answers we need. Do I make myself clear, Lieutenant?"

"Clear as crystal, sir. Should I delegate this?"

"No. See to it yourself."

"Understood. With your permission, I'd like to put together a small strike team. Civilian clothing, covert ops. Nonstandard small arms, deployed from the runabout *Cumberland.*"

"Approved."

Šmrhová stood to leave, and then she turned back. "Sir? If Mister Okona should ask us why we're arresting him, what should I say?"

Worf mustered a thin, cruel smile. "Tell him . . . I want a word with him."

I stood outside in the rain and wondered what I had done to make the universe hate me.

And by "stood in the rain," know that I wasn't talking about a drizzle or a light spring misting. This was the kind of rain that hits like a million tiny hammers, that scours the rooftops and storefronts and the pavement and strips it all clean—of dirt, rust, and history. It was a deluge to make a man forget his name and wash away his past. If only I'd been so lucky.

I tried to double-check the lead from Wildman, but the downpour made my padd's screen impossible to read. Not that it mattered. I knew I was in the right place. I was just stalling and cursing my dumb luck. There are certain clichés that owe their existence to dismal facts of life. Now, standing in Dulevo's red-light district, I was confronted by one that had dogged me and every other seeker of truth in modern history:

Why does every investigation involve at least one visit to a strip club?

The problem wasn't that I was a prude. Far from it. I was a man of the galaxy, if I'd said so myself. I'd been around, done it all. A bit of flesh on parade, a peek at the sordid side of the skin trade—I'd seen it all before. Male or female, humanoid or xenomorph, it made no difference to me. I'd come to do a job, and the fact that the Nyxos Club featured an all-male review was not going to deter me.

I kept telling myself that until I opened the door and went inside.

It was exactly as advertised. Pulsating music that could stun small insects at a dozen meters, a light show designed to overwhelm optic nerves. Watered-down drinks poured by bartenders with eyes full of suspicion and delivered by servers with phony grins plastered on their faces by desperation or a dose of Moly-Five. And up on the stages, males of various species, not all of them bilateral in their symmetry—or symmetrical at all—swung around metallic poles or gyrated very nearly in time with the music's beat. Taking the edge off it all, a thick haze of narcotic smoke, shredded into layers and illuminated by flashes of neon laser light.

Three steps through the door, I just stopped. Not because I had any objection to the evening's entertainment, but because seeing so many perfect young male bodies in various states of undress only reminded me of my own encroaching decrepitude. Every undulating set of abdominals reminded me of how many kilos I had put on since my own beautiful youth; the flips of perfectly conditioned hair made me reflect upon my thinning mane and receding hairline. I gazed upon perfection as if it were a cruel kind of mirror.

Then I shook my head and took the nearest open seat at the bar.

A humanoid bartender with no discernible neck, just a block of head sprouting from his monstrous torso, wiped something off the countertop in front of me. "Whadda ya have?"

"Three fingers of Argelian scotch, neat."

He planted an almost-clean glass in front of me and half filled it with amber liquor. Then he stepped away, giving me an unparalleled view of an Eskinoid shaking both his upper and lower *flurmen* sacs right in my face. That wasn't the kind of thing one saw every day. At least, not unless one had made some truly horrendous life choices.

Meanwhile, I had to endure a sarcastic wolf whistle from Wildman, thanks to my implanted subaural transceiver. There was a teasing lilt in her voice as it echoed inside my head: *"Oh, damn, Agonist! You always take me to the nicest places."*

I lifted my drink in front of my mouth to make it harder for the people around me to think I was talking to myself at the bar. "Just keep scanning faces and tell me if we get a hit on Gliza."

"Pan around. Give me a good look at the place."

Under my breath, just for her, I said, "Are you even old enough for this kind of smut?"

"I grew up on Voyager, *a ship full of people who thought they'd never see home again. Trust me, I peeked some of the nastiest holodeck sims you could imagine. Nothing shocks me."*

"If you say so." I swept my eyes leftward, so that Wildman, spying on the scene through my ocular implants, could process the vid data through the Starfleet Intelligence database. If any of these scumwads worked for Gliza, we would know it soon enough.

"Wait. Go back a bit. A few degrees right."

I did as she'd asked. "Got something?"

"I'll say. A straight shot at the sweetest booty I've seen in years. Mm-yeah!"

"Would you please focus on work?"

"Spoilsport. Resume panning left, please. Slowly."

I put my head on a slow swivel to the left. I made sure to linger on anyone guarding a doorway or who looked like they might be hiding a weapon. "Anything?"

"The Gormelite by the red door. Face recog pings him as Molikmor, a piece of muscle known to be on Gliza's payroll. Looks like he's your gatekeeper tonight."

"How do I get past the door? Does our furry friend take bribes?"

"Hang on. I'm running a filter on the local comm relays. If I can isolate his device's unique ID, then sort through its history, I might— bingo! Walk up to him and say, 'Don't bite the hand that feeds.' That should get you through the door like a boss."

"You sure about that?"

"Trust me."

"You said that on Beta Lankal, and I had to blow up an opera house."

"Are you still on about that? Quit bitching and get a move on, sport."

I downed the rest of my drink, savored its sweet burn in the back of my throat, and dropped a strip of latinum on the bar to cover it. I made my way through the crowd of hooting aliens to the red door at the back of the club. Even though I had Wildman's assurance that this would work, I couldn't help but tense for a shoot-and-run scenario as I stepped up to the Gormelite—basically, a gigantic apelike thug with flat-black orbs for eyes, slits for nostrils, and a mouth packed with way too many teeth—and smiled.

"Don't bite the hand that feeds," I said.

Sweat soaked the back of my shirt while I waited for fuzz-face's universal translator to parse my greeting. I braced myself for the mother of all punches.

Molikmor opened the door and waved me through.

Grateful to leave behind the roomful of other beings' flopping junk, I strolled through the open doorway with a confidence I hadn't earned, to meet with a known homicidal crime boss who wasn't expecting my visit. I wish I could say this was the moment when I finally realized that my entire life was predicated on bravado and overcompensation, but it wasn't.

Buzzed and feeling smug, I walked right into the trap.

The *Cumberland* banked hard as it cut through the storm front, its nose angled downward on a landing vector. Strapped into the command chair, Šmrhová white-knuckled its armrests. Next to her, the half-human, half-Argelian pilot Lieutenant Parker Kendzior was preternaturally calm as she guided the runabout through slashing curtains of rain and lightning.

A crash of thunder rocked the tiny starship, prompting moans of displeasure from the team in the rear compartment. Šmrhová didn't envy them. They were enduring the same rough ride that she was, but without the benefit of a view or an instrument panel. All they could do as the ship's artificial gravity and inertial dampers cut in and out was close their eyes and try to keep their last meals down.

Anxious to avoid errors of carelessness, Šmrhová checked the command panel again. The runabout's sensor-jamming systems still appeared to be functioning correctly. Given the remote location of Garada, and its relative lack of industrialization, its space-traffic control system was antiquated, as was its sensor network. On the other hand, knowing the unsavory types that spies were likely to encounter in a place like this, Šmrhová had come prepared to thwart the paranoid precautions of black marketers and smugglers, who tended to be fairly tech savvy.

Forks of lightning bent past the rain-slicked cockpit window. The storm was proving to be downright biblical, even as they neared the surface.

Šmrhová squinted into the maelstrom. "How long to the LZ?"

Kendzior adjusted her instruments. "Ten seconds." She engaged the antigravs and cut the heavy thrusters with a single pass of her hand across the overhead controls, and the ship lurched to an abrupt halt in midair. "Taking her down."

Šmrhová reached up and activated the ship's internal comm to help the team in the rear compartment hear her over the storm. "Strike team on the ready line, ten seconds."

The *Cumberland* floated downward, steady despite being buffeted by wind and rain. Šmrhová freed herself from her seat's flight harness and headed aft. She reached the rear compartment to find her civilian-garbed team ready to go.

Nearest to the door was her point man, Lieutenant Robert Mars. He was short for a human man, but what he lacked in height he made up for with bravery, cunning, and sharpshooting skills.

Behind him were the strike team's other three grunts: Ensign Lila Sharp, a fresh-faced young blonde straight out of Starfleet Academy and looking to add a combat mission to her file; Chief Petty Officer Granok Bolin, a hardheaded, take-no-crap Bajoran woman who was two years shy of her Starfleet pension; and Petty Officer Third Class Szegurra, a male Saurian who loved to tell anyone who would listen about his hundred-year plan for his Starfleet career.

At the back of the ready line were Ensign Nathan Kurtz, their squirrelly but technically gifted combat engineer, and Lieutenant

Zseiszaz, a Kaferian who had recently been promoted after completing his training as a combat-qualified field paramedic.

The ship's hull resounded with the steady patter of torrential rain. Šmrhová inspected her line of troops with approving nods. "Looking good, people." She patted Granok's shoulder, then hooked her thumb at Sharp. "Keep an eye on this one. Teach her everything you know." To Sharp she added, "Don't let me catch you doing anything she teaches you." She moved on, smiled at Szegurra. "Sounds like your kind of weather out there." He shrugged.

The ship landed with a gentle bump, and then the hum of the engines and the antigravs went quiet. The lights inside the runabout shifted to a dim red.

As Kendzior arrived from the cockpit, Šmrhová addressed the group. "Listen up. Kendzior, Zseiszaz, you're both staying here. Zsei, you guard the ship and keep sensor locks on all of us in case we need emergency beam-out. Parker, you'll be using the sensors to guide us to our pal Thadiun Okona. But if something goes wrong, if you come under attack, lift off and get the hell out of here. We need to protect the ship even above op-sec, clear?"

"Perfectly."

She gave the pilot a thumbs-up, and then she faced the strike team. "We can't be seen using Starfleet equipment down here. Everybody check on your subaural transceiver."

One by one, they made a fast equipment check of their comms, which were implanted into their jaws just below their ears, and their weapons, which were Andorian military-grade phaser pistols and stun-level photon grenades. The only one of the group carrying serious ordnance was Kurtz, the engineer. Šmrhová hoped that his skills wouldn't be necessary.

Because if they are, this op's gonna get a lot more press than Worf wants.

She looked at Kendzior. "What's our bearing?"

"Exit through the aft hatch, then straight on for a hundred

meters until you hit the edge of town. I'll give you turn-by-turn once you get oriented."

"Sounds like a plan. Let's go."

Šmrhová hit the button to open the aft hatch.

As the rear bulkhead descended to serve as a ramp, wind and rain gusted into the runabout. Outside, the night was black and cold. Lightning flashed, revealing the barren sprawl of mud that lay between the team and the faint orange glow of the ramshackle city of Dulevo.

Šmrhová led the way down the ramp and through the mud.

Freezing rain pelted her face, each drop stinging worse than the last. Mud squelched under her boots, and she was grateful when the howling wind drowned out the cadence of deep slop disturbed by marching feet.

She imagined a scenario in which she might need to shoot Okona. And she smiled.

Under her poncho, her hand tightened on the grip of her weapon.

This sonofabitch better be worth the trouble.

"C'mon, Gliza. This could be a win for both of us. All I need is a lead, and I'm ready to pay a small fortune for it." I put on my most charming smile and hoped Gliza's species wasn't one that would read it as an act of aggression.

The massive, toad-like shot caller floated in her pool of steaming brine, surrounded by a trio of skinny vermicular creatures that took turns dunking their top halves into the bathwater, filling their throats, and then regurgitating it down Gliza's back. Apparently, she considered that service a value-add. Don't get me wrong; I'd always made a point of not being judgmental, but this hit my squick factor, and not just because of the room's dense odors of musk and sulfur.

Gliza tilted her huge dome of a head backward. Her gullet

yawned open, and some clown decked out in turmeric-yellow robes leaned down to fill it with creamy sludge from a massive pitcher. From a distance its contents smelled like a mix of seafood and compost.

After gulping down her mouthful of garbage chowder, Gliza cleaned her broad chin with a lick of a tongue as wide as my torso. "Why should I make enemies for you?"

"Enemies? Who said that? If you know the name Thadiun Okona—"

"I don't." She punctuated her denial with a malodorous belch that blew back my hair.

"Fair enough. But if you did, you'd know that I am the very model of discretion."

"So am I. Which is why I won't help you."

One of her mitt-like extremities twitched, cueing her guards to move in.

The first to grab my arm had a head like a knuckle with eyes. I shook him off and risked stepping closer to Gliza's frothy pool of alien bacteria. "Don't be hasty, Gliza. If a small fortune won't win your help, what about a large one? I represent some well-capitalized power players. They'd reward you well for a lead to the Nausicaans who pulled the Kamhawy job."

"Nausicaans are crazy. And vengeful."

"So are the people they stole from." I deepened my voice, hoping that it would register as menacing. "If my patrons can't get satisfaction from the Nausicaans, they'll take it from anyone who protects them."

Gliza raised both her flippers, halting the worm-dudes' spit takes. Even her bruisers backed off half a step. I had her attention.

"This was no simple heist, Gliza. The Nausicaans took something powerful. Something *dangerous*. And right now every major power in the galaxy is hunting them for it. Trust me when I say that's not a cross fire you want any part of. So help me keep it far from your doorstep: tell me where to find Kinogar and his ragtag army."

The Sheliak bathhouse went quiet. I heard the low thrumming of the liquid jets inside Gliza's tub, and the chaotic percussion of raindrops on the roof and the window behind her.

The lids of her bulbous eyes drooped half-shut. "I'm not sure I believe you."

Wildman's voice cooed in my ear, *"Keep her talking. I'm cracking that portable comm on the back table. Gimme a minute to break its firewall and analyze its contents."*

I spread my hands, purely for the sake of theatrics. "Then permit me to make my case." I began to pace. "A few weeks ago, on the edge of Breen space, I recovered a rare and valuable cargo." I gave her my most winsome grin. "At great personal risk and expense, I might add. Then, with my customary discretion, I set up a meeting with one of my longtime clients." Playing to the room, I shrugged. "Who am I kidding? You knew all about my meeting with the Orion Syndicate. Because somebody talked. Told you I was bringing in a motherlode. But they didn't tell you what it was, did they? Because they didn't know. But that didn't matter. You saw an easy mark. So you sent the Nausicaans—am I right? You subcontracted to them, didn't you?"

Gliza laughed. It sounded like someone choking a manatee, or a whale fighting to vomit. "What if we did?"

"If you did, you messed with the wrong people."

"We do not fear the Orions."

"I wasn't talking about them."

"Not afraid of you, either."

I waved away her words. "What? Of course not! No, no. I'm not a fighter, dear Gliza. I'm a deal maker. A middleman. But I also represent persons of a most terrible nature—the kind who wouldn't think twice about killing us all, and vaporizing this town, just to make a point."

"Almost through the firewall, Agonist. You're doing great."

I felt the transponder warming beneath my skin. Until that moment, I hadn't even thought to ask Wildman whether it was safe for her to route a two-way subspace signal through this tiny circuit in my jaw, using the quantum comm on the *Tain Hu* as a hub and booster.

Gliza shifted in her steamy pool of milky broth, as if she were taking the silent measure of her gang of Knuckle-heads. Then her disturbingly large eyes settled once more upon me. "All a shot caller has is their reputation. Without it, I might as well be dead. So if your dangerous friends want to come here looking for trouble, I, for one—"

Deep buzzing alarms drowned out everything else. Harsh white lights set near the ceiling pulsed in quick flashes. Gliza's Knuckle-heads sprang into action, checking handheld devices. One hurried to a companel on the wall near the door and checked its readout. "Intruders!"

Gliza stood from her bath, exposing her bloated, foam-shrouded form. "Who?"

"Mixed species," said Knuckle One. "Humans. Bajoran. Saurian. Federation-made military-grade small arms."

Gliza understood at once. "So either Starfleet or Federation Security. Kindosic! Fast-wipe my computer!"

I cursed under my breath and reached into my pocket, in search of my transporter recall trigger. Then one of the Knuckle-heads clocked me across the back of my skull with something heavy and rock hard—probably his fist. I face-planted on the floor.

Wildman's voice sounded oddly far away. *"Agonist? Are you okay? Where—"*

I heard glass break. Shards scattered across the tiled floor, splashed into the dirty water. Then a blinding flash of light and an earsplitting bang that felt like an ax cleaving my skull—

Time became fluid, light turned to shadow.

Then I blinked, and the room was filled with smoke. People were shooting. Phaser pulses shrieked past above me. I winced as I saw a stray shot lance through the comm unit at the back of the room. It exploded into sparks and shrapnel as Wildman complained inside my head, *"Damn it! I lost the signal! And I was almost in!"*

One by one the Knuckle-heads were mowed down. Last to fall was Gliza. It took three phaser beams to knock her back on her massive hindquarters, into her soon-to-be-tepid bath.

When the shooting stopped, a team advanced through the shifting veils of steam and smoke, weapons held level and ready. None of them were familiar faces until I saw the one in charge. Šmrhová holstered her weapon, reached down, and lifted me by my jacket collar.

"Thadiun Okona. You're coming with me."

"You could've just asked me to dinner. No need for all *this*."

She waved over a couple of her people. A Saurian and a Bajoran woman grabbed me, one by each arm, and dragged me to the center of the room. Šmrhová gave orders on the move. "*Cumberland*, we have the package. Prepare for dust-off."

Dazed and aching, I looked up at the no-nonsense brunette. "Lieutenant?"

"Save it, Okona. We found your ship in orbit. We'll tow it back to the *Enterprise*."

"Thanks. But that's not my question."

She fixed me with a look that could kill. "What is?"

I smiled. "Did you get the flowers I sent?"

She rolled her eyes and sighed as the runabout's transporter beam took hold.

The strike team and Okona materialized inside the *Cumberland*'s aft compartment, and Šmrhová couldn't wait to get off Garada and on her way back to the *Enterprise*. She caught the pilot's eye. "Kendzior, get us out of here." Then she looked back at her strike team and their prisoner. "Mars, Bolin, secure Mister Okona. Zseiszaz, scan him for implants, hidden devices, ingested tech, anything he might use trying to escape custody."

Okona took the abuse in stride. He put up no resistance as Mars and Bolin secured his hands with magnetic manacles and strapped him into a flight seat.

As soon as he was locked down, Zseiszaz started scanning him with a medical tricorder. The Kaferian's small mandibles—which had evolved for extracting juice and pulp from fruit—twitched slowly, betraying his concern. He leaned closer to Okona. "My scans show you have suffered numerous serious injuries in the last twenty-four hours. Not all of them are fully repaired. Do you require medical assistance?"

"Now that you mention it, a gin and tonic with lime would be great. But I think I'm gonna need a straw. Or an intravenous line."

Šmrhová waved off her medic. "He's fine. Did your scan find anything?"

"A subspace transceiver implanted in his jaw, and optical transceiver lenses on his eyes. Both are Starfleet-issue, so I deactivated them."

"Good work. Go strap in for lift-off."

Zseiszaz returned to his flight seat on the starboard side of the compartment. As Šmrhová checked to ensure that Okona's bonds were secure, he said, "I guess I'm not getting that drink."

"You're lucky you're not getting your ass kicked."

"Weren't you listening? That happened already. A few times, actually. Unlike some folks who spend their lives on cushy state-of-the-art starships, I have to *work* for a living."

She glared at the rumpled, tousled rogue. "Don't you know when to shut up?"

"Don't you know when to stand down? You and your shipmates were ordered by Starfleet Command to stay the hell out of my way. What part of that wasn't clear?"

Šmrhová leaned down to invade his personal space. "If *your* people had stayed out of *our* way, we'd have been happy to let you do what you do. But somebody at Starfleet Intelligence—and I'd be willing to bet you'd know who—remotely sabotaged our main science lab and our main computer. Since no one'll tell us who did it, or help us fix it, my commanding officer has decided he'd like another word with you."

The runabout's engines came to life with a deep rumbling purr. There was a moment of awkwardness as the ship engaged its anti-grav thrusters, but then the inertial dampers and the artificial gravity kicked in, and conditions inside the ship stabilized.

Seething with quiet rage, Okona shook his head. "Worf. I should've known." He glared at Šmrhová. "Do you idiots have any idea what you've done? The lead you just wasted? The intel that SI just lost because of you?"

"Enlighten me, hotshot."

"I shed a few pints of blood to get that lead to Gliza. And if you hadn't barged in with weapons blazing, my Ree-Oh—"

"Your what?"

"Remote intelligence officer," he said, enunciating each word to stress how angry he was. Hearing it explained, Šmrhová realized he had been pronouncing the acronym RIO. "She was cracking the security on Gliza's comm unit through my transceiver. Another few seconds, and we'd have been in. Could've accessed every message she'd sent or received since she got that unit." A sour smirk. "But then one of your sharpshooters blew it up."

"You were surrounded by armed criminals. We thought you were in trouble."

"I'm *always* in trouble! Trouble's the water I swim in! It's the air I breathe!"

Kendzior announced from the overhead, *"We've cleared atmo. Putting a tractor beam on Okona's ship now."*

"Acknowledged," Šmrhová said. "As soon as it's in tow, set course for the *Enterprise*, warp seven, and engage."

"Copy that." The overhead channel switched off with a low *click*.

Okona wore a smile of subdued fury. "Good work. Now you're kidnappers *and* hijackers! This mission's a real twofer, guys. I'd ap-plaud, but—" He raised his manacled hands. "Instead I'll just salute you: hip, hip, hooray for Starfleet—the galaxy's greatest *blunt instrument!*"

Šmrhová grabbed Okona by his jacket's collar. "Keep running your mouth, Okona, and I'll shut it with a blunt instrument I like to call *my boot.*"

His expression mirrored hers, but only for a moment. Then all his anger vanished, and he laughed. "Damn, you're *gorgeous* when you're angry!"

She let go of his collar and stalked off to the runabout's cockpit.

Don't kill him, she advised herself. *Not here. . . . Too many witnesses.*

19

The crowd settled into expectant silence as Admiral Liu took her place at the front of the room.

At the opposing counsels' tables, tensions were equally high. Louvois and her associate from the Starfleet JAG were all but champing at the bit, eager to get on with their agenda for the day. Meanwhile, though there were only a few minutes left in the court's regular schedule, Ezor and Picard would have been happy to see the proceedings pushed to the next day.

Admiral Liu seemed committed to not letting that happen.

She rang the bell on her desk. "This hearing is now in session." She lifted her padd and considered its contents. "After careful deliberation of the arguments presented earlier, I have chosen to deny defense counsel's motion demanding the recusal of government counsel on the grounds of prejudice. Though many of defense counsel's points were well taken, in the end I found their cumulative value to be less than convincing, especially in light of what it would mean for these proceedings. It should also be noted that, in keeping with a long history of precedents, the correct time for this objection to have been raised would have been at the start of this hearing. Though I likely would have rejected it then, as well.

"With regard to the defense's motion requesting the exclusion of logs recorded by Captain Picard, and others recorded by various members of his crew and members of Starfleet's admiralty, that pertain to the invasion and occupation of Tezwa: that motion is denied. It is my opinion that those logs might contain information that would provide essential context for other evidence that might be deemed essential to a proper understanding of this case.

"Finally, with regard to defense counsel's motion that the android known as Data Soong be removed from the government's list of witnesses, that motion is granted.

"Upon consideration of the legal arguments presented, it is the opinion of this officer that the android Data Soong is legally a distinct individual from the android who was last known as Lieutenant Commander Data of Starfleet. As such, Data Soong cannot be compelled to fulfill any legal obligations or be made to assume any debts for which Lieutenant Commander Data might have been liable at the time of his death in 2379.

"With those decisions recorded, I note that we still have about ten minutes left on our schedule today. Attorney General Louvois, do you wish to make use of that time?"

"I do, Admiral."

"Proceed."

"If it please the court, at this time the government wishes to continue with its direct examination of Captain Picard."

Picard stood, walked to the witness box, and sat down. As he settled, Admiral Liu said, "Captain, be aware that you are still under oath."

"I understand, Admiral."

Louvois got up and moved to stand beside the witness box. "Admiral, at this time I would like to enter into evidence Government Exhibit Seventeen, a deposition of Admiral Tujiro Nakamura, in which he discusses the aftermath of the Starfleet coup against President Zife."

"Objection." Ezor waited for the admiral's attention before he continued. "Once more, the government's use of the term 'coup' is prejudicial and assumes legal conclusions not in evidence. Second, I've reviewed the transcript of Government Exhibit Seventeen and move that it be excluded on the basis that it has no relevance."

Liu looked intrigued. "Why isn't it relevant?"

"Because Captain Picard was not a participant in the conversations detailed in that deposition, none of the details of those conversations shed any light on what my client did or did not know before, during, or after the alleged events concerning the resignation of President Zife, and unless he hears the details of those depositions now, my client has no idea what they contain. They are, therefore, irrelevant to the question of whether he acted with *mens rea*."

Louvois was in a combative mood. "Admiral, the deliberations that took place between the admirals who were briefed by Captain Picard are the direct result of his involvement, his instigation of events, and his introduction of evidence of Zife's crimes into this conspiracy."

"Be that as it may, Admiral," Ezor countered, "when these subsequent conversations transpired, Captain Picard was *literally* hundreds of light-years away. If we're to judge whether he acted in good faith, we must consider his role only in the conversation to which he was party. Anything after that is beyond the scope of his knowledge, control, or legal culpability."

Animated with rage, Louvois gestured dramatically. "That's absurd! That's like saying he suggested his accomplices should burn a building, told them how to do it, provided the fuel, lit the match, and walked away—but then claiming he played *no role* in the arson!"

Ezor waggled a finger in denial. "That's not a fair comparison, Admiral. Captain Picard never directly advocated any specific course of action or any desired outcome, beyond the idea that President Zife should resign his office out of respect for the law and the good of the Federation. That's not even remotely equivalent to calling for armed action, and it absolutely is not the same as advocating for violence or murder."

Almost shouting, Louvois shot back, "He set the whole damned conspiracy in motion!"

"No," Ezor said, refusing to yield one centimeter of rhetorical ground. "Based on not only Captain Picard's own testimony, but the respective depositions of Ambassador Lagan and the flag officers who are known to have taken part in the conversation, Captain Picard's role in this debacle was quite limited. He shared with his superiors evidence of crimes committed by and in the name of Zife and his administration—evidence legally acquired and reported by officers and other personnel under his command. He recommended corrective action be taken, but he never specified what form that correction should take.

"Captain Picard did *exactly* what he was supposed to do. He was *obligated* by his oath of service and by Starfleet regulations not to suppress evidence of criminal wrongdoing, but to elevate it for review via the proper chain of command, to let his superiors dictate the official response, and to abide by their lawful decisions, to the degree that he was aware of them. Under the circumstances, Admiral, his actions were not only lawful, but imperatively so."

Liu cocked an eyebrow. "Counselor, that sounded suspiciously like an invocation of 'He was just following orders.' For all our sakes, I hope you don't plan to invoke *that* defense."

"No, Admiral."

Weary from just a few minutes of debate, Liu shook her head. "I think we've heard enough for today. Madam Attorney General, please be prepared to move on to a new line of questioning tomorrow morning. Mister Ezor, consider the grounds of your defense very carefully. Until tomorrow at ten hundred, this hearing is adjourned."

She rang the bell, got up, and made a fast retreat from the courtroom.

Louvois threw her padd into her briefcase and left with equal haste.

Ezor stood and noted Picard's and Crusher's frowns of displeasure.

"That could've gone better," Crusher said.

"It could've gone *worse*." Ezor put away his padd. As Picard and Crusher followed him out he added, "If I were you right now, I'd consider every day not spent behind bars as a gift."

It felt strange to Šmrhová to walk the corridors of the *Enterprise* while out of uniform. She and Lieutenant Mars had escorted Okona off the *Cumberland* shortly after landing, and now they were following the shortest route to the ship's brig. The prisoner was taller than either she or Mars, but he seemed relaxed, even genial, as they marched him toward captivity.

The overhead lights flickered erratically, sometimes ahead of them, sometimes behind. Šmrhová did her best to ignore it, but Mars and other *Enterprise* personnel they passed in the corridor seemed distracted by it. As the trio passed a companel, it fritzed for a moment before resetting to its default configuration.

Okona noted the malfunctions with curiosity. "What's with the lights?"

Šmrhová tightened her grip on his biceps. "Shut up."

"They weren't doing that when I left."

She quickened her pace and sharpened her tone. "I said: Shut. Up."

The lanky rogue chuckled. "It's funny. Right now you're telling me to shut up, but once you lock me up, you'll start shouting at me to talk. I wish you'd make up your mind."

"You really love the sound of your own voice, don't you?"

"As compared to what? A Klingon opera? Sure. But I'd rather listen to waves crashing on a beach, or wind whispering through trees, or the crackle of a campfire under—"

"Please stop talking."

He frowned and kept pace with her and Mars. His silence lasted all of about ten seconds, which Šmrhová figured was probably a record-best for Okona. "You realize we're wasting valuable time, right? I mean, c'mon. We're on the same side. We're tracking the same enemy. We ought to be working together, not getting in each other's way."

"You think we're getting in *your* way? Tell that to Worf. He'll *love* that."

"Why do you find it so hard to believe we're both working for the greater good?"

Šmrhová resisted the urge to reach for her phaser. "Because I've read your file, Okona. I don't buy you as a 'noble servant of a higher calling.' I've seen your kind before."

"What am I, then? In your expert opinion."

"You're a wild card. A random variable with a prejudice for chaotic outcomes." She yanked him to a halt in front of the door to the brig. "It's my job to protect my crew, my ship, and the Federation from your brand of havoc." With her free hand she pressed the door signal. Half a second later, she heard its magnetic bolts retract. The door glided open, and she and Mars ushered Okona inside.

Just beyond the door was a guard's station, a single seat surrounded by a C-shaped bank of screens and bio-monitors, a virtual panopticon for all of the cells in this brig block. The security officer on duty was Lieutenant Barsk glov Shon, one of the largest and most thickly muscled Tellarites that Šmrhová had ever met. He looked up and wrinkled his snout at Okona. "Where'd you get this one? The sewer?"

Šmrhová smiled. "Sewer's too good for him. What's open, Shon?"

He invited her past him with a broad wave. "Take your pick."

"Thanks." She and Mars nudged Okona into motion. They led him down the left passageway, and then shoved him into the first open cell. As soon as Okona stumbled past its threshold, Mars activated the cell's force field. It snapped on with a loud buzz, and for a moment it flashed into sight—an artifact of airborne dust particles ionizing as they became trapped in the field. Then the golden veil disappeared, leaving only the brightly lit emitter band around the cell's entrance—and its buzzing—to serve as warnings of its presence.

Okona walked right up to the invisible barrier and stopped just shy of getting himself a nasty shock on the tip of his nose. "You think you know me, but you don't."

"Is that a fact?"

"It is. To tell the truth—"

"As if you ever could."

"—I'm of the opinion that you've completely misjudged me. You look at me and see a lawless ruffian, a ne'er-do-well, a lovable scoundrel—"

"I never called you lovable. Or a scoundrel."

"Because you don't know me. So let's rectify that. I'll answer any questions you or your captain might have, if you'll agree to ask them over a candlelit dinner. We can dine here in my cell if that would make you more comfortable."

"It would make me retch."

"I promise, I clean up well. And I happen to know a few of the better 'secret recipe files' programmed into your ship's replicator database. We could start off with some bacon-wrapped, Manchego-filled roasted dates, paired with—"

"You don't get it, do you?" She folded her arms and regarded him with contempt. "I don't find your flirtations funny or cute, Okona. I find them disrespectful. When you speak to me this way, you demean me as both a Starfleet officer and as a sentient being."

He looked profoundly hurt. "I apologize, Lieutenant. That wasn't my intention. I—"

"Stop. This is what I hate about you: You don't *listen* to other people. All you do is wait for your turn to speak. You're so busy being witty and slick that you fail to see the people around you as beings worthy of dignity. You treat everyone you meet like a commodity to be won or an obstacle to be overcome. You're a joke, Okona. And not a funny one."

She reached over the cell's master control panel, accessed the replicator control, and conjured up a bowl of basic humanoid nutritional solution: a bowl of bland, grain-based gruel.

Okona took the bowl from the replicator. Lifted a spoonful of its contents to his nose and gave it a whiff. Disappointed, he carried it to his rack and sat down.

Šmrhová shut down the replicator and closed its panel. "And just in case anything else you think is funny or clever starts coming out of your mouth—the toilet's behind that panel over there. Bon appetit, Romeo."

The situation was far from ideal. Throughout the ship, overhead lights and bulkhead companels stuttered on and off, seemingly at random, and three consecutive diagnostic sweeps had failed to identify the cause of the problem. Under normal circumstances, that would have been reason to convene the talents of the *Enterprise*'s chief engineer, senior science officer, and top specialists. Unfortunately, they were all currently attached to La Forge's away mission to save Stonekettle Station. That meant that Lieutenant Commander Taurik, in his role as acting chief engineer, had to make do with the personnel who were still on the ship.

Taurik stood hunched over the central hub in main engineering, flanked by a dozen of his colleagues. Unlike most of the men, Taurik had a build that was slender and wiry, but he was tall and his voice was deep, both of which he had found helpful in asserting himself in command situations. "We must isolate these errors," he told his team. "Right now they are inconvenient. If they start to affect mission-critical systems, they will become a threat to the ship's survival."

Lieutenant Taro Trinell, a twenty-something Bajoran woman who was a newer member of the engineering department, spoke up in frustration. "How do we isolate something whose cause we can't identify? Do we take the EPS grid offline? Purge the main computer?"

Ensign Nathan Kurtz, who was still out of uniform following his return minutes earlier from a covert-ops away mission, highlighted a sequence of command lines on one of the status monitors. "Have we considered the possibility that the error is in the firmware drivers? I'm seeing a lot of strange code cycling through that system."

"I'm already working on that," interjected enlisted engineer Maureen Granados. She swept a tangle of her brown hair out of her eyes in between keying commands into a companel. "I plugged in a code patch, but something fragged it the second it hit the server."

Taro looked hopeful. "That suggests the problem is in the drivers. But then why didn't the diagnostics catch that?"

"If they, too, are corrupted," Taurik realized aloud, "their results would all be suspect."

"Damn." Petty Officer Egerton looked queasy. "That would *not* be good, bruh."

Around the crisis team, computer displays began to distort, flicker, and stutter to black. Taurik noted the mounting errors with the requisite degree of concern. "It would appear the problem is intensifying. Does anyone have a suggestion for slowing its rate of spread?"

Ensign Oliver Trimble, who had come down from the sciences division to lend a hand, was keying commands into a computer interface. "I'm trying to raise firewalls between all of our systems. It'll slow down coordinated crisis responses, but it should keep tainted systems from infecting others—assuming that's been the problem."

Taro shouldered her way past her peers to stand next to Taurik. "Sir, did these errors propagate outward from science lab one?"

"Possibly. But we restored the lab's software and firmware with clean downloads from Memory Prime. Those systems should be clean now."

"Yes, they might be. But if the original problem spread from the lab before we purged the code and downloaded clean copies . . . ?"

Once she said it, Taurik knew that, in all likelihood, that was what had happened.

"We have a serious problem." His imagination conjured a worst-case scenario. Then another. And then he realized there were so many ways for this inconvenience to become a catastrophe that he was unable to easily count them all. "Mister Trimble, prioritize isolation of the antimatter-containment system, followed by the intermix controls and the inertial dampers. After that, secure life-support, and then focus on—"

Main engineering went dark. The thrumming pulse of the ship's main warp reactor halted, as did the low but steady white noise of the ventilation system. In the blackness a few computer screens hiccuped with flashes of code or a glimpse of the standard interface. Then the battery-powered emergency lights kicked on, filling the cavernous space with dull orange light from the deck, painting everyone's faces with peculiar, sinister shadows.

"That's not good," Taro said.

From overhead came the double chirp of the comm, followed by Worf's near bellow: *"Bridge to engineering! Report!"*

All that Taurik could do was stick to the facts. "Bridge, this is Lieutenant Commander Taurik. We appear to have suffered a cascade system malfunction."

"As have we. The bridge is offline."

With a gesture, Taurik dispatched Taro and Egerton. "Understood, Captain. I am sending up a pair of engineers to assist you with repairs."

"How long to restore main power?"

"Unknown, sir. We are still evaluating the scope of the—"

"I want it restored immediately."

"Understood, Captain."

"But first I want a damage report. What caused this?"

All eyes in main engineering were upon Taurik. As a Vulcan, he rarely had reason to feel emotions such as anxiety or self-consciousness, but this moment tested his hard-learned stoicism. "Our current working hypothesis is that the virtual attack which disabled science lab one was able to spread to other departments and systems before we had a chance to purge the corrupted software. Because part of the corruption occurred in our main computer core, this malware could, in theory, have infected every system on the *Enterprise.*"

Worf sounded aghast. *"Every system?"* Then he growled in frustration.

The next voice on the comm was Lieutenant Dygan's. *"Engineering, this is ops. If we assume a worst-case scenario, with total contamination of the main computer, what protocols do we have in place for restoring the core before critical failures ensue?"*

"Because the memory banks are isolated from the rest of the computer, we would need to restore only the operational segments of the core. But to do that would require a manual shutdown of the core, followed by a hard purge back to default settings, and then a—" He stopped himself. "Suffice it to say that this would be a task better performed in spacedock."

"Noted," Dygan said. *"So, just to recap: You don't know how to fix this?"*

"Not as such, no."

Taurik's acute ears heard Worf grumbling over the comm, *"I suspect the spy in our brig knows someone who does. Number One, get me that name."* Then Worf raised his voice for the comm: *"Mister Taurik, we may soon have help for you. Until then . . . try to keep us all from being ejected into space. Bridge out."*

20

Alpha shift was winding down on the *Starship Titan,* which was cruising at low warp through the UFP's core systems. The ship had left Earth a couple of days earlier and was still breaking in new personnel and new technology during a shakedown cruise, but already Admiral William Riker had begun to feel as if he could breathe easier and sleep more soundly now that he was once more in his element: interstellar space, bound for exploration and adventure.

It had felt good to see the crew again, after so many weeks apart. The ship felt new and slightly unfamiliar after a thorough refitting in spacedock, to repair the brutal damage it had suffered while fighting to prevent the proliferation of Husnock military ordnance in local space. But the crew, who made the *Titan* the place that Riker, Troi, and their daughter Tasha called home, all had come back. Even, to Riker's mild surprise, Doctor Ra-Havreii, who had found it necessary to seek psychiatric counseling during the ship's refit. The chief engineer—who also had been the *Titan*'s lead designer—had returned to duty quieter, calmer, and more introspective than Riker had ever seen him. In a way, Riker realized, Ra-Havreii was a changed man.

Here's hoping that change proves to be for the better.

Riker was looking over his calendar, to see what Troi had planned for him and their daughter that evening. For once the schedule was blissfully free of commitments. Tonight he could revel in the simple joy of sharing dinner with his family, and then helping Deanna read a bedtime story to Tasha. The notion made him smile. *I really can't imagine a better life than this.*

The urgent beeping of an encrypted comm signal from Starfleet

Command wiped the smile from Riker's face. *Only one person could bypass the bridge to hail me directly . . .*

He opened the subspace channel. His holoscreen blinked on to show him a close-up of the well-lined visage of Admiral Akaar. *"Will. I hope I'm not disturbing you."*

"Not at all, sir. How can I be of service?"

"This conversation is sensitive in nature. Are you alone?"

"I am. Please speak freely, sir."

The white-haired admiral looked troubled. *"I need a favor, Will."* He collected himself, reclaimed his air of pride. *"I need access to L'Haan, the former Section Thirty-One director."*

Riker searched his memory. "I read that she'd been arrested."

"She was, on foreign soil, by Starfleet Intelligence. They brought her back to Federation space, but then they put her in some kind of black-site prison." He looked annoyed. *"Its location was classified by presidential order, so only people with operational necessity know where it is."*

"Let me guess: The president decided you didn't need to know?"

"Correct. And that's only the start of my troubles." He sighed. *"Not only can I not visit L'Haan, SI won't let her be subpoenaed as a witness. They won't even let her record testimony for use in court. They've got her locked down tighter than antimatter."*

Riker processed that. "All right. But can't you talk to the president? I hear she likes you."

"Not this much. You need to understand—this business with Section Thirty-One has people scared. Careers are being ended. People at all levels of society are going to prison. The last thing the president wants is to get caught up in yet another scandal peripheral to all of this. And I can't do that to her, Will. She's a good leader. That's rare, in my experience. I won't see her tarnished by what I need to do."

"I understand that. But what can I possibly do to help?"

"A few weeks ago, you told me that you and Captain Vale had recorded a conversation that might prove rather damning to Admiral Batanides."

"Yes, we did." At once Riker's thoughts were cast back to the end of the Husnock-suppression mission. Captain Christine Vale's first officer, Commander Dalit Sarai, had confided to him and Vale that she had been being extorted by Admiral Batanides to act as a spy against them, to serve some personal suspicion or political grudge harbored by Batanides. They had not yet settled upon a course of action to address this grave breach of protocol and regulations, but now it seemed that Admiral Akaar meant to force Riker's hand.

"Forgive me, Will. I know that's a drastic card to play, and one that we can't take back once we put it on the table. But I don't have any other leverage I can use against Batanides, and Captain Picard's career and freedom are both on the line. So it's now or never."

All doubt and hesitation left Riker's mind. Knowing that this favor was being asked for the sake of Jean-Luc Picard was all he'd needed to know.

"Say no more, sir. I have Commander Sarai's deposition recorded and ready to go, along with corroborating recordings she made of her check-ins with Admiral Batanides during her period of extortion. I'll encrypt them and send them via secure subspace channel right away."

Akaar bowed his head by the smallest degree, a gesture of humility and gratitude. *"Thank you, Will. Here's hoping it's enough to persuade Batanides to do the right thing."*

"Agreed. But, sir? If you could also see your way clear to helping free Commander Sarai from the admiral's control—"

"Consider it done." For the first time since Riker had known him, Akaar smiled. *"It's the least I can do for someone who helps me save a friend."*

21

———

"I need more cable," Taurik said, his tone level but his voice loud to convey urgency. "Another thirty meters, and five more splitters."

He, his engineering team, and every spare set of hands they had been able to draft into service were busy running kilometers of hard-line comm cables up from the main subspace antenna in the forward dish assembly, out of open hatchways, down corridors, through hastily cut openings in bulkheads, and up through the *Enterprise*'s superstructure—a part of the ship usually visited only by automated repair drones—up to the main hangar on deck five.

Lieutenant Commander Linn Payne, Taurik's gamma-shift counterpart as deputy chief engineer, arrived with a massive coil of comm line on her shoulder. "This ought to do it. Can I help you splice it in?"

"Please," Taurik said, and together they made quick work of the task, fusing the new length of cable to the end of the previous one in a matter of seconds.

Someone up in the hangar tugged on the main line. A man's voice echoed down through the empty pockets in the starship's spaceframe, "We need more slack up here!"

"It's coming!" Payne shouted back, a hoarse edge in her voice. "Keep your pants on!"

Taurik raised an eyebrow to telegraph his perplexity. "Why would Lieutenant Cole have removed his trousers in the middle of a critical op?"

Payne winked at Taurik. "I just have that effect on men."

He wasn't sure whether he should take her at her word or if she was, as she so often liked to say, just messing with his head. *Probably safest to assume it is the latter.*

They threaded the new cable extension into the gap, taking turns at making sure the coil on the deck between them didn't kink or snag as it unspooled.

Roughly half of the new coil had been pushed to the hangar bay when Lieutenant Taro came running up to Payne and Taurik. "The main computer's starting to glitch."

Still working with his hands to supply slack cable, Taurik shot a castigating look at Taro. "Could you be more specific, Lieutenant?"

"It's glitching really bad. All over the place. And nothing's working right."

Payne regarded the young Bajoran woman with a disappointed frown. "Nothing like a laser-sharp summary to point the way to a solution."

Taurik was running too short of time to waste any of it on rebukes. "Shut down the main computer. Take the engineering backup core offline and send it a flash-reset pulse. If it glitches, even for a moment, shut it down."

"Aye, sir." Taro took off like a shot, no doubt because she knew she needed to relay all of Taurik's orders in person, since the intraship comms were no longer reliable.

The uptake of slack on the comm line ceased. Payne shouted up through the gap, "Got what you need up there?"

"Aye, sir," came the reply. "We're good."

"Hang on, we're patching into the main antenna line now." Payne nodded at Taurik to indicate that she was ready for the next step. With her help, he fused the line that had been run up from the main array with the end of the one they had just supplied to the team up in the aft quarter of the ship's saucer section. A few final checks confirmed that all of the links were secure and functional. Taurik placed the loose cable flush against the bottom of the bulkhead.

"That should hold," he said to Payne. "Let's go check the work in the hangar."

On any other day they would have boarded a turbolift and been on deck five in a matter of seconds. Today would not be so easy. Taurik and Payne walked to the nearest service junction. Like most on the ship, it appeared to be a dead end. But if one opened the hatches in the deck and the overhead, it led to insulated ladderways between decks. Whenever it became unsafe to use the turbolifts, emergency movements through the ship could be accomplished this way.

Payne reached the ladderway first. Taurik, being a few centimeters taller than her, thought he might need to give her a boost to reach the lower rungs and start her climb. To his mild surprise, she made the vertical leap with ease, grabbed a couple of rungs, and pulled herself up into the ladderway. Being confronted by the unexpected jogged Taurik's memory.

I should have realized—she grew up on Alpha Centauri B-IV. Her muscles developed in a stronger gravity well than Earth's. She likely has the same physical strength as a Vulcan.

He sprang upward, grabbed a couple of rungs, and climbed up the ladderway behind her.

Minutes later the vertical ladderway gave way to a steep but traversable stairway that hugged the dorsal section of the ship's hull. Taurik and Payne quickened their pace here, and at the top of the cramped accessway they reached an open hatch. They stepped through it and out onto the main hangar deck of the *Enterprise.*

Located one deck below the shuttlebay, the hangar was a cavernous space. It occupied most of the aft half of the saucer section on decks five, six, and seven. Here the ship stored its vast array of small spacecraft and support vessels—everything from runabouts and shuttles to crewed work pods and automated repair drones. In addition, there were terrestrial vehicles stored here, aquatic and submersible craft, as well as spare parts, fuel pods, and repair bays.

Most of the time, the majority of small starships and shuttlecraft were tucked away, stacked in elevator grids until they were ordered to deploy. Today, nearly every ship that had a subspace comm had been hauled out to any open space on the hangar deck. An army of mechanics and engineers moved between the small ships, frantically working to patch in hard lines for the purpose of interplexing all of their subspace transceivers, in the hope of being able to generate a strong-enough signal to drive the *Enterprise*'s main antenna—and transmit an SOS before it was too late for help to make a difference.

Supervising the work on this deck was Master Chief Petty Officer Temkin. The lean, bearded noncommissioned officer had trained as an engineer and was the *Enterprise*'s hangar deck supervisor. Taurik had also heard that Temkin was one of the ship's craftiest card players, but he had never had the opportunity to learn the truth of that claim for himself.

"Let's go!" Temkin barked at his gang of enlisted mechanics. "Get those cables patched in! The line to the main array is hot, so get a move on!" He noted Taurik and Payne's approach, and he walked toward them. "Sirs, we're almost set. Just a few more seconds."

"Good work, Master Chief," Taurik said.

"Thank you, sir."

Temkin met them and shook their hands. When they stepped past a nearby shuttle that had obstructed their view of the deeper quarters of the hangar, Taurik noted the presence of a non-Starfleet vessel. He pointed at it. "Is that—?"

"The *Tain Hu*," Temkin said. "Impounded and therefore fair game."

"In that case," Taurik said, "I stand corrected: *Outstanding* work, Master Chief."

"Glad you like it, sir." One of the hangar crew jogged into Temkin's field of view and gave him a thumbs-up signal. Temkin looked at Payne and Taurik. "Good to go."

Payne nodded. "Fire it up, Master Chief." As Temkin left to

activate the jury-rigged replacement for a comm system, Payne added to Taurik, "Just pray we don't have a burnout."

Three steps more and she would have been out the door. Had she left her station three seconds earlier, she would have been on her way home to an empty apartment, a replicated meal, and a few hours of "cozy" mysteries on holovid. But the secure comm line on her desk buzzed as her office door slid open, and Lieutenant Naomi Wildman was torn between her quiet night at home and being drawn back into the seemingly endless morass of duty.

She looked back, frozen with indecision. The line buzzed again. *I could just go home. No one would know.*

A third buzz. Whoever was reaching out to her wasn't giving up easily.

Wildman went back to her desk. *I'm going to regret this, I can tell already.*

A glance at the metadata for the incoming signal indicated that it was being transmitted from the *Starship Enterprise*, an automatic red flag. No member of that ship's complement should have known how to patch a secure signal directly to her action station inside Starfleet Intelligence. The established protocol for situations such as this was to block the incoming signal and report the attempted contact to her spymaster without delay. She was about to do precisely that when she noticed the status tag embedded with the other metadata:

DISTRESS SIGNAL—PRIORITY ONE

Her conscience nagged at her. *How desperate would they need to be to reach out to me? And what if this is actually from Okona? What if he's in real trouble this time?*

She opened the channel with a tap on her console's glassy black surface. "This is Expositor. Go ahead."

A strangely familiar male voice replied, *"Is this Naomi Wildman?"*

Paralyzed at the mention of her name on the secure channel, Wildman had no idea how to answer. To identify herself positively would be a breach of operational security, or "op-sec," as Commander Lavelle liked to say. But the fact that her caller was even asking the question suggested to her that op-sec had already been compromised, and that the only way she could find out how, why, and by whom would be to keep this conversation going.

"This is Naomi Wildman. To whom am I speaking?"

"I am Lieutenant Commander Taurik, the deputy chief engineer of the Starship Enterprise. *My twin brother, Commander Vorik, served as an engineer on the* Starship Voyager, *on which you were born."*

Talk about a blast from the past. "Yes, I remember Vorik well."

"In that case, I hope your associations with him were of a positive nature, because I and the Enterprise *are in need of your assistance."*

What was she supposed to say? She followed her first impulse, which was to tell Taurik the truth. "I'm sorry, Commander, but according to regs, I shouldn't even be talking to you. I should have blocked your signal the moment I saw that it came from your ship."

"That is what Agent Okona told us you would say. He recommended that we tell you that your 'spike' has 'metastasized.' I can only presume he is alluding to the sabotage you wrought on our science lab having spread to every critical system on the ship. We—" He was interrupted by a loud bang, followed by crackling sounds and pained shouts in the background. *"My apologies. Another EPS conduit overloaded. We estimate loss of antimatter containment within the hour, at which point we will have no choice but to abandon ship."*

Sounds of chaos echoed beneath Taurik's voice, painting an auditory picture that filled Wildman with guilt and shame. *Am I really going to hide behind regulations tomorrow when Admiral Batanides asks why my "targeted" software spike destroyed a major ship of the line?*

"All right, Commander. I might be able to help you. First things first: Do you have enough bandwidth on this channel for a data subcarrier?"

"Affirmative, though it will push our capacity to its maximum."

"Set up the subcarrier for me on port one-eleven." She set down her satchel and dropped back into her work chair. Its armrests adjusted to support her elbows, and it floated as if weightless, supported by its main gimbal, drifting left or right along her U-shaped bank of consoles in response to the slightest shifts in her weight or eye line. Her hands flitted across the black interfaces, summoning information and executable applications like a virtual army rising to her command. "Before I work my magic, I need you to promise your crew will stop researching Husnock weapons. That's a verboten subject, right up there with the you-know-what molecule."

"Understood," Taurik said. *"If you have a remedy at hand, please proceed."*

She keyed in the last few command strings. "Stand by, *Enterprise*. I'll need to take remote control of your main computer. Don't interfere with that, or this won't work."

"I am signaling all personnel to stand down from computer ops."

"Okay, here we go. I'm pushing a patch now. Once it integrates into your main computer's OS, it should start correcting all the other system errors, in order of mission criticality." She tracked the upload's progress. "Forty percent . . . forty-five . . ."

It took effort for Wildman not to complain about the sluggishness of the channel. She had become accustomed to using the quantum comm that linked SI to the *Tain Hu*. Not only was it more secure, it was orders of magnitude faster. *If there had been no other way to get this patch into the* Enterprise's *systems, I might have had a justifiable reason for exposing the existence of quantum comms to the* Enterprise *crew. But if helping them is a breach of op-sec, exposing our most top-secret comms tech would probably be grounds for a charge of treason.*

"Seventy-five percent, *Enterprise*. Eighty and counting."

"Just in case we lose contact after the upload is finished," Taurik said, *"my commanding officer wants me to thank you on our behalf."*

"Thank me by not including any mention of my help in your

logs. But, seriously . . . it was my pleasure, Taurik. After all, we're on the same side, right?"

"So I am told, Lieutenant. For the moment, however, I am reserving judgment."

"Fair enough." She checked her console. "Ninety-five percent . . . and complete. The patch is in place. Your main computer should stabilize within thirty seconds, key systems should come back within five minutes, full system restoration within an hour."

"We appreciate your help, Lieutenant."

"You're welcome. Good luck, and pretty please: lose my number and never call again."

The overhead lights stuttered back to life on the bridge of the *Enterprise*, and within a few seconds it was clear that they would be staying on, at least for the time being. Worf noted the susurrus of mumbled thanks and other sounds of gratitude that attended the return of steady illumination and functional companels, though he personally refrained from adding to it.

From the command chair he took the measure of operations on the bridge. At ops, Dygan dispelled the hash of static from the main viewscreen with a few commands keyed into his panel. Lieutenant Joanna Faur ran through a standard preflight check of the ship's flight controls. Konya was at the security chief's post, monitoring signal traffic while conducting tests of the ship's defensive systems. Engineers Taro and Egerton, their on-site repairs completed, closed up a bulkhead panel near the portside aft turbolift. Lieutenants Šmrhová and Chen, meanwhile, conferred at the master systems display along the bridge's aft bulkhead.

Everything appeared to be running smoothly. But Worf wanted confirmation.

"Number One. Damage reports."

Šmrhová gave a few parting instructions to Chen, and then she moved forward to stand beside the command chair. "As promised, sir, the main computer is back online. All traces of the corruption have been purged. Critical systems restored in engineering and tactical. Our only remaining glitches are in secondary systems, but those are resolving quickly. No injuries or permanent damage reported. Ship and crew should be ready for action in forty-five minutes."

"Good. Have we learned anything else of value from our prisoner?"

"We have. Chen and I downloaded his sensor logs, and we just compared them to new information from the FRO. Long story short, we know where the Nausicaan bandits are."

That news intensified Worf's focus. "Where?"

"They're on the surface of Nausicaa, sir."

"Nausicaa? But the Borg laid that world waste."

"I know." She rolled her eyes in mild disbelief. "Honestly, it's the last place I would've thought to look for them, but there they are."

"Is the stolen cargo also there?"

"Yes, sir. Chen spotted it in long-range scans, and I just confirmed it. Looks like they've put together a sizable encampment."

"To what end?"

Šmrhová beckoned Chen. The half-Vulcan contact specialist hurried to her side. "Chen, tell the captain what you told me."

Chen faced Worf. "My review of the cargo drones' manifests, combined with those from previous heists by the Nausicaans, suggests they're setting up a terraforming operation."

"Terraforming?" That didn't sound like any Nausicaans Worf had ever known.

"It all fits," Chen said. "Industrial replicators. Construction-grade fabricators. Fusion reactors. Deuterium pods. Earthmovers and tons of other construction hardware, along with raw materials. They've been gathering equipment and supplies for this for years."

Worf pondered these new details. "Then why steal the Husnock weapon?"

Šmrhová shrugged. "Insurance? Maybe he didn't want to commit to a long-term operation until he was sure he could defend it."

"Perhaps." He asked Chen, "Is their terraforming project viable?"

She and Šmrhová traded grim looks, and then Chen said, "Probably not. Even if they ramped up their ops by seven percent year after year—which would be almost impossible—it would still take them nearly three centuries to render the surface of Nausicaa even remotely habitable. But the odds are they won't live that long. Our most optimistic models suggest they'll be dead of starvation or radiation poisoning within a few years, a decade at most."

That sounded needlessly grim to Worf. "The Borg leveled Risa and Deneva. Both are scheduled for recolonization in less than twenty years. Why is Nausicaa different?"

"Because," Chen said, "Nausicaa was still using dirty fission reactors for power in some of its less developed regions, and it also had several munitions factories and depots on its surface. It didn't just get wiped clean by the Borg—it got poisoned by its own tech."

Worf remembered every day of the Borg Invasion with terrible clarity. He tried to imagine it from the perspective of the Nausicaan people. He wondered if any of them had realized in their last moments how much of their terrible fate they had brought upon themselves. Then he thought of the Klingon Empire's best-known self-inflicted cataclysm, the destruction of Qo'noS's moon, Praxis—a disaster that once had threatened to extinguish all life on the Klingon homeworld.

My people were lucky enough to be offered a way to recover from that calamity. A chance to change their direction, their culture. But what hope did the Nausicaans have?

Lieutenant Konya stepped into view on the other side of Worf's command chair. "Sir?"

"Speak freely."

"As tragic as the Nausicaans' situation might be, it doesn't give them license to commit armed robbery, or to hijack starships, or to engage in acts of terrorism. And even if their plan to rebuild Nau-sicaa were viable—which it isn't—that still wouldn't justify letting them keep stolen equipment, especially when that tech is urgently needed elsewhere. I'm not saying we shouldn't feel sympathy for the Nausicaans' situation, but we can't let their crimes go unpunished."

Just to test the man's conviction, Worf asked him, "What if we did?"

The question surprised Konya, but he answered quickly. "If they dig in on the surface, they'll be stuck. As long as they have the Husnock weapon, they'll have to be denied access to space travel. Their planet—if not the entire star system—would have to be interdicted if not bombarded. They'd be cut off from trade, interstellar comms, and any form of diplomacy. Which would mean no new shipments of water, food, fuel, or medical supplies. My best guess? Even with replicators and fusion pods, they'd all be dead inside five years."

"At which point," Chen interjected, "we'd be free to reclaim the stolen technology."

"Real compassionate," Šmrhová chided her. "And also irrelevant, because the folks at Stonekettle Station can't wait five years to get their PMAR back."

The three officers all looked at Worf, awaiting his final word on the subject.

He scowled. "The Nausicaans' plight is tragic, but Stonekettle needs that power core. Number One: as soon as the ship is ready, take us to Nausicaa—maximum warp."

22

Dim and sweltering. Those two words kept running through La Forge's mind. With the shield up but most other systems inside Stonekettle Station offline to conserve power, reactor control was a shadowy hothouse. Now and again a palm beacon would snap on somewhere nearby, abruptly flooding a small area with harsh bluish light. Then it would switch off again, usually within a few seconds. Everyone understood that when the palm beacons and other small tools ran out of energy, there would be no recharging them.

The same rules applied to the *Enterprise* team's tricorders. It took effort for La Forge to resist the temptation to check trivial details constantly. At one point he had caught himself switching on his tricorder three times in less than two minutes—first to check the time, again to confirm the current temperature inside reactor control, and then to review the status of the runabout warp core presently feeding into the station's power grid at the PMAR node. All in spite of the fact that he had set automated alerts to notify him of the start of each new hour, warn him if the ambient temperature in his vicinity exceeded forty degrees Celsius, and trigger a full-team alert if any part of the warp core malfunctioned beyond safe operating parameters.

La Forge, Elfiki, and the other personnel laboring on this level had long since shed their uniform jackets and now were down to sweat-soaked undershirts. Because of the heat and humidity that choked the station's lowest levels, even light work could wear someone out in just a few minutes. Consequently, La Forge had ordered everyone to rest and hydrate whenever possible between tasks. He had no intention of succumbing to heat stroke, and he didn't want any of his people to risk that, either.

Someone sat down on top of the EPS conduit housing. When he heard the person's sigh of exhaustion, he recognized it as Elfiki's. "Dina. Holding up okay?"

"I'm fine. But this weight-loss spa sucks."

"Look on the bright side—"

"If you say, 'At least it's a dry heat,' I'll push you through the force field and surrender myself for court-martial. They'd never convict me."

"I was going to say, 'Where else can you get a free sixty-hour pore cleanse?'"

"Sure you were."

He was about to defend his honor when something close by made a loud metallic shriek, followed by a leaden *thunk*. A moment later, the most serious of the preset alerts on La Forge's tricorder shrilled in the dark. He raised the scanning device and checked its readout. "Not good."

Elfiki reacted to his dread with her own. "What just happened?"

"The warp core's intermix regulator is failing. I'd say we've got about five minutes before it breaks down completely."

Other personnel gathered around La Forge and Elfiki, most of them just dark shapes among the shadows. From the group he heard the voice of the station's chief engineer, Doctor th'Fehlan. "Did you say we're losing the intermix regulator?"

"Yeah. I have a workaround, but it'll make a new problem."

"Let's fix the problem in front of us," th'Fehlan said, "and we can deal with the next one when this one's finished."

"All right. Here's the quick fix: we'll need to power up our second runabout core, patch its control system into the first core's main bus, and then slave the first core to the second core's controls. If we do this right, we can run core one's regulator with core two's controls."

Fear tinged Elfiki's skeptical reaction. "What's the catch?"

Doctor th'Fehlan answered, clearly having deduced the problem before Elfiki. "Once we slave core two's controls to core one's hardware, it will complicate our switchover to core two when core one's portable fuel reserve is depleted."

"Exactly," La Forge said. "Now, instead of a simple hot-swap that we could do in three minutes, we'll need to disconnect the cores from each other before we can remove core one from the PMAR node. Then we'll need to reset core two's controls to their defaults before we can install it in core one's place." He cast a worried look at th'Fehlan. "Can your station's emergency capacitors store eight minutes of charge for the shield before we make the swap?"

"I'm still not sure they can hold three."

"All right. I guess we'll burn that bridge when we come to it."

Confused, th'Fehlan asked, "Don't you mean 'cross that bridge'?"

"That was just Starfleet engineering gallows humor," Elfiki explained. "Ignore it."

"I see." The Andorian engineer checked his chrono. "Commander La Forge? We now have four minutes to slave core one to core two. Perhaps we should get started?"

"Agreed." La Forge raised his voice, since he had no idea where his own personnel were in the crowd around him, Elfiki, and th'Fehlan. "Holt! Jeffords! Get core two and bring it to the PMAR node. Giler, bring me the optronic patch kit. Elfiki, call up the wiring schematic for the *Danube*-class warp core and meet me at the node."

La Forge turned and used his shoulder to blade through the wall of bodies blocking his path to the PMAR node. He reached the first core at the same time as Elfiki. They both kneeled in front of the failing device. He opened its main access panel as she summoned its schematics on the screen of her tricorder.

She leaned over and whispered to him. "Geordi?"

He whispered back. "Yeah?"

"Do we have any chance in hell of slaving this thing to core two before it shuts down?"

"I guess we're about to find out."

"And what happens when we need to make the swap?"

For reasons La Forge couldn't fully explain, he no longer felt afraid. He felt motivated to save the lives around him, but he had no fear of losing his own. The only response he could give Elfiki was a confident smile. "Ask me again in ten hours."

It had been a long morning. Picard had stepped into the witness box shortly after eleven hundred hours, and Louvois had gone to work grilling him to account for nearly every word he had recorded in his personal logs since the beginning of January 2379. It hadn't mattered that none of his entries had pertained to the matter of Min Zife's removal from office; all of Ezor's attempts to object to Louvois's line of inquiry had been overruled.

I once lived an entire life in twenty minutes because of an alien probe's neural link, and even that felt more focused and concise than this.

At last she circled back around to something that felt marginally relevant. "Captain Picard, when you and Ambassador Lagan reached out to five senior members of Starfleet's admiralty, were you aware that Admiral Ross was an established asset of Section Thirty-One?"

"I was not."

"Do you recall when you first met Elias Vaughn of Starfleet?"

He had to think on that. "I believe it was in May of 2343."

"Did the two of you discuss his investigation of Section Thirty-One at that time?"

"No, we did not." Picard saw Louvois thinking out her next question, so he took advantage of the brief pause to take a sip of water from the glass that had been provided for him.

"Did you and Elias Vaughn ever talk about Section Thirty-One?"

"Not that I recall."

"What was the first time you became aware of the existence of Section Thirty-One?"

"March of 2373." He was ready to spill out a whole narrative, but he remembered Ezor's advice: *Answer all questions as narrowly as possible. Volunteer nothing.*

Louvois paced slowly in front of him, and then she stopped. "Captain, please describe the circumstances that led to your knowledge of the organization."

He cleared his throat. "The *Enterprise* was ordered to Chiaros IV, to find the *U.S.S. Slayton*, a Starfleet vessel that had gone missing in action. At first we believed the *Slayton* had been destroyed by an unknown spatial anomaly. We later determined that the anomaly was a creation of Romulan technology, and that renegade Romulan forces had destroyed the *Slayton*. The *Enterprise* was ordered to complete the *Slayton*'s mission, which was to persuade the Chiarosians to ally themselves with the Federation rather than with the Romulan Star Empire.

"Vice Admiral Marta Batanides joined the mission aboard the *Enterprise* because one of the officers believed lost aboard the *Slayton* was our mutual friend and Starfleet Academy classmate Commander Cortin Zweller. During the course of our mission, we discovered that Commander Zweller was still alive, and that he had betrayed the crew of the *Slayton* to the Romulans. His motivation for doing so was that he had been acting in the service of Section Thirty-One, with orders to persuade the Chiarosians to join the Romulan Star Empire. In return for doing so, he was to be rewarded with a list of deep-cover Tal Shiar operatives active inside Federation space."

Louvois faced Picard. "Did you take Commander Zweller into custody?"

"We did."

"Then why is there no record of his court-martial?"

"Because he was released and his crimes were expunged, on the orders of Admiral Connaught Rossa. Who, I believe, was also recently arrested."

"She was. Captain, did you have any subsequent encounters with Section Thirty-One?"

"Yes, though I was unaware of it at the time."

"Please elaborate."

"In 2375, the crew of the *Enterprise* investigated a report of irregular behavior by our former shipmate Lieutenant Commander Data, who had been assigned to a cultural-research team on the planet Ba'ku, inside the Briar Patch nebula. We soon learned that Admiral Matthew Dougherty was coordinating an off-the-books operation to illegally displace the Ba'ku from their homeworld, whose metaphasic rings were found to have regenerative effects upon a range of humanoid species. Though Admiral Dougherty insisted we were in violation of our orders, we later discovered that *he* was the one operating without legal authority. It was only in recent weeks, after the publication of Ozla Graniv's exposé, that I learned Admiral Dougherty was, in fact, then acting as an agent of Section Thirty-One."

"Interesting. Would it be fair to say, then, Captain, that you've had more experience with Section Thirty-One than most other Starfleet officers have had?"

"Not necessarily. More than some; less than others."

"Were you ever approached by Section Thirty-One for recruitment?"

"I was not."

"Odd, then, that you conspired with them during the Tezwa crisis."

He replied with more vigor than he intended: "I did no such thing!"

"Are you sure? We have records recovered from Section Thirty-One's own files that show one of its senior directors, Vasily Zeitsev, conspired on Qo'noS with Federation Ambassador Worf, Son of Mogh, House of Martok, to steal Klingon Imperial Fleet command codes, which were then relayed to the *Enterprise*, and used by your crew to halt an impending Klingon bombardment and surface occupation of Tezwa. Do you deny this?"

"I had no knowledge of the codes' provenance, or of the means by which they were acquired."

"So is it your contention, then, that Ambassador Worf—who now serves as your first officer aboard the *Enterprise*—conspired independently with Section Thirty-One?"

Ezor called out, "Objection! Counsel is asking the witness to speculate on events to which he did not bear witness."

Admiral Liu looked almost relieved to say, "Sustained."

Louvois remained calm. "I'll rephrase, Admiral. Captain Picard, given how readily and how profoundly you and your crew benefited from the intervention of Section Thirty-One, would it not be reasonable to assume you would be willing to accept their participation in your subsequent conspiracy to illegally remove a sitting president?"

"It would not."

"Really? It seems well within the bounds of your moral compass."

"Objection," Ezor cut in. "Captain Picard is one of Starfleet's most decorated officers and a man of good character. Counsel's estimation of his moral compass is groundless."

Before Liu could rule, Louvois jumped on Ezor's words: "I'd like to address that, if I may, Admiral. Since defense counsel saw fit to introduce the question of Captain Picard's record and, presumably, his character as matters worthy of review, I'd like to take a moment to do so."

Wary but curious, Liu said, "Proceed."

Louvois walked to her table and picked up her padd. "Forgive me for resorting to notes, but I don't want to miss anything." She returned to face Picard. "Please answer the following questions with either 'yes' or 'no,' Captain. Was the *Starship Stargazer* lost in action under your command in 2355?"

"Yes."

"Did you, in 2366, wittingly violate the Prime Directive on planet Mintaka III?"

"Yes."

"Did you, in 2367, allow Romulan spy Subcommander Selok to escape from the *Enterprise* and return to Romulan space?"

"Yes."

"Did you, in 2368, defy a direct order from Starfleet Command to use the liberated Borg drone known as 'Hugh' to deploy an attack that might have destroyed the Borg Collective, thereby sparing dozens of worlds and the lives of more than sixty billion people thirteen years later?"

"Yes."

"Was the *Starship Enterprise*-D lost in action under your command in 2371?"

"Yes."

"In 2375, when you thought that Admiral Dougherty was acting with proper legal authority, did you lead your officers and crew in a mutiny against him?"

"Yes."

"And were you temporarily relieved of your command in 2378 for the negligent destruction of an allied starship in Ontallian space?"

"Yes."

Louvois pivoted toward Ezor, looking quite self-satisfied. "It would seem, Counselor, that you and I define 'good character' quite differently."

Admiral Liu backed her chair away from her table. "I think we've heard enough for now. I'm declaring a recess for lunch. We'll reconvene here at fourteen hundred." She rang the brass bell on her desktop, bringing the hearing to a temporary halt.

Picard stood and tried to keep his chin up as he left the witness box. *Saved by the bell.*

Louvois, her associate counsel, and the spectators filed out of the room. When everyone else had gone, only Ezor, Crusher, and Picard remained.

Ezor wore a look of remorse. "Captain, I am so sorry. She goaded me, and I opened the door. I honestly don't know what the hell I was thinking."

Picard rested a reassuring hand on his lawyer's shoulder. "I won't let you blame yourself for this, Jonathan. Look at me." He waited until Ezor met his gaze. "These are *my* sins, Counselor, and mine alone. I need to *own* them. And one way or another, before this is over, that is *precisely* what I am going to do."

23

—•—

Warp-distorted starlight filled the main viewscreen of the *Enterprise*—and then, as the droning of the engines diminished and faded, the streaks shrank to points, signaling the ship's return to impulse-level velocities. Worf noted the change from the command chair. "Helm, report."

Lieutenant Faur replied, "We've reached the edge of the Nausicaa system, sir. Holding position just outside the bandits' maximum sensor range, as ordered."

"Well done. Tactical, visual scan, full magnification."

Konya entered the commands on his panel. "Aye, sir."

The stars on the main viewscreen were replaced by an image of the northern hemisphere of Nausicaa. Worf had visited the planet only once, decades earlier, as a freshly minted Starfleet officer. He recalled having been impressed by the planet's lush rainforests, dark blue seas, and thick cloud cover. Now he stood from his chair, horrified by what was left of Nausicaa.

Its sheltering clouds had become a smothering blackness. Where rich jungles once had sprawled, there now stretched trackless wastes of black, brown, and gray. He tried to see where the land ended and the seas began, but either the two had bled into one, or else the planet's hydrosphere had been cooked off. The Borg's sterilizing inferno had reduced Nausicaa to a scorched orb, like a face burned down to the bone.

Staring at the charred remains of a murdered world filled Worf with anger and awoke a sick sensation in his gut. It overwhelmed him with memories he had long hoped to forget—worlds he had watched burn in the wake of the Borg Invasion: Ramatis III,

Acamar, Barolia, Korvat, Deneva. He had borne witness to the slaughter of billions.

Thinking back, he recalled having seen Nausicaa listed among the worlds that had been wiped out by the Borg Invasion fleet on February 9, 2381. At the time it had just been one among dozens of worlds. Only now, seeing it with his own eyes, did its tragedy become tangible to him.

He looked aft, toward the science station. "Lieutenant Chen. What vessels defended Nausicaa during the Borg attack?"

Chen called up a file on her console. She read it quickly, then looked back at Worf, her face ashen. "None, sir. Nausicaa had no fleet of its own, just orbital defenses."

"Did it send out a distress signal?"

She checked the report. "Several, starting about six hours before the Borg arrived."

"What allied vessels responded?"

There was shame in her expression. "None, sir."

Worf looked back at the desecrated world on the viewscreen and tried to imagine what a nightmare its surface must have been in the hours and days following the Borg's bombardment. "What vessels provided aid *after* the attack?"

This time Chen couldn't even look at him as she replied, "None, sir. We're the first Federation vessel to visit Nausicaa since it was destroyed."

Once she'd said it, Worf noted that none of his bridge officers wanted to look one another in the eye. Like him, they all felt suddenly burdened with shame at learning of their society's collective neglect and denial of an entire world's destruction, and the near-total extermination of a sentient species. Forced to confront the truth, Worf regarded the ruination of Nausicaa with a changed perspective. He imagined being a Nausicaan survivor, returning home to find his world blasted into radioactive ash, and knowing that not only was it done by a foe that had come in response to provocation by the Federation, but that the Federation never saw fit to send a single morsel of food, a drop of water, or so much as a word of contrition for the calamity it brought down upon its closest galactic neighbors.

We ignored their cries for help. Left them defenseless before the Borg. And then, as we rebuilt our worlds, we turned our backs on this one. As if its death means nothing.

In his heart, as both a Klingon warrior and a Starfleet officer, Worf felt ashamed.

We are supposed to be better than this. . . . We need to be.

Šmrhová quietly interrupted his remorseful introspection. "Sir?"

"Number One?"

"We have coordinates for the Nausicaans' camp. How do you wish to proceed?"

Worf put aside his feelings of guilt and sympathy and focused his mind upon the mission. "We have two objectives. First, recover the PMAR. Second, recover the Husnock weapon."

"You sure you want them in that order, sir?"

"I am. We need the PMAR to save what is left of Stonekettle Station."

"Understood. Can I make a suggestion?" Worf nodded, so Šmrhová continued. "If we're keeping the strike team small, we might not have the strength to haul the weapon out. Considering the current condition of Nausicaa's surface, I'd like permission to destroy the OPC on-site with a timed demolition, as a backup plan if recovery proves impossible."

"Permission granted."

"And what about the hijacked convoy drones? Do we care about those?"

"Try to reach their helm controls. Set them for remote piloting. If we can get them into orbit, we can tow them out of the system."

"Sounds like a plan. One last thing. The Nausicaans: Avoid? Arrest?"

"Avoid if possible. Use force in self-defense only."

"So, no arrests, then."

"It is not worth the risk." He sensed Šmrhová tensing to argue with him, so he cut her off. "These are not small-time thieves. These are trained mercenaries. Do not underestimate them."

His advice seemed only to steel Šmrhová's resolve. "Trust me, sir—we won't."

The surface of Nausicaa was dark and wasted, an endless scar of burnt rock. Šmrhová and her strike team plodded across it, traversing kilometers of ground blanketed ankle deep in black ash. Clouds of coal-colored dust drifted over the landscape, obscuring the horizon and blotting out the midday sun. There were no shadows on the surface, just a bleak, impenetrable gloom.

She checked her helmet's holographic display. Her strike team had marched just over eight kilometers since leaving the runabout *Cumberland,* which had approached the planet on a stealth vector to avoid being picked up by the Nausicaans' sensors. A glance over her shoulder confirmed all of her people were still with her. She was on point. Behind her were the five best-trained and most combat-experienced members of the *Enterprise*'s security division.

Directly behind her were Santiago, a Cuban woman with a neurotic tendency toward perfectionism, and Peralta, the group's top shot and ranking smartass. Trailing them were Boyle, a nebbishy type who was great at cooking up explosives, and Diaz, a taciturn woman who had lost her home and her entire extended family when the Borg destroyed Deneva. Bringing up the rear was Szegurra, her Saurian go-to guy for high-risk missions. Just as she had done on Garada, Šmrhová had left medic Zseiszaz and pilot Kendzior to guard the runabout.

Each strike-team member's name was projected above them in Šmrhová's HUD, enabling her to confirm that everyone was present and in position.

Her helmet's HUD responded to her eye-blink command and opened a secure channel to the other five members of her unit.

"Look sharp, folks. The Nausicaan camp should be just over this next rise. Fan out as we approach the edge. Szegurra, hang back a few meters, just in case."

She left the channel open as she checked the settings on her phaser rifle. Its power cell was fully charged, and the weapon was set for short, pulsed bursts at maximum stun.

I hope that's strong enough to put down a Nausicaan in battle gear.

Climbing the gradual incline to the ridge, she heard her breathing loud and close inside her helmet. It was a testament to Starfleet engineering that their faceplates had been designed not to fog up, and the rest of their tactical environment suits provided thermal regulation as well as limited protection against beam attacks, puncture weapons, and a variety of projectiles. Their suits' closed life-support systems were the only reason she and her team were able to function in the toxic soup that now constituted Nausicaa's atmosphere.

Šmrhová was the first to the ridge line. She dropped to her hands and knees before getting close enough to be spotted from below, and she crawled the last few meters to the edge. Within moments, Santiago and Peralta had flanked her, and a few seconds after that, Boyle and Diaz took up position on the outer ends of the line. As instructed, Szegurra kneeled a few meters behind them, to keep watch on the path they had taken and to scout the area for new threats.

Looking down into the crater, Šmrhová adjusted her faceplate's holographic filters to compensate for the dust and smoke that choked the air. Her helmet's built-in computer assembled a new composite image from infrared, ultraviolet, and sonic data. Starships ranging from small scrub fighters to midsized corsairs bristling with armaments came into view.

"Looks like a bigger party than we expected."

"This is definitely not gonna be a cakewalk," Santiago said over the comm.

"I count about a dozen ships down there. What about you, Peralta?"

The sharpshooter studied the mini-armada. *"Fourteen, I think. The good news? Only one is big enough to be any trouble to the* Enterprise, *and six others are the stolen cargo drones. The bad news? The Nausicaans separated the drones and spread them all over the place, so we can't reprogram them as a group—we'd have to do 'em all one by one."*

"Diaz, how many Nausicaans are down there?"

"Checking." Diaz pulled up her tricorder and ran a fast scan. *"Radiation's fouling the scan, so I can't give you an exact number. But based on total biomass and heat signatures, I'd say there has to be at least a few hundred down there out in the open, and maybe as many as another five hundred inside the parked ships."* She turned off the tricorder and put it away. *"Bottom line? It's safe to say we're outnumbered."*

"That's okay," Šmrhová said. "We didn't come down here for a firefight anyway."

"Speak for yourself," Peralta said. *"I think we can take these guys."*

"Put a sock in it, Peralta. Boyle, do you have a lock on the PMAR?"

Boyle tweaked the settings on his own tricorder. *"I think so. Looks like it's inside the big ship, the* Seovong. *Deep in the engineering section."*

"Great. The lead ship, parked smack in the middle of the cluster, surrounded by a thousand Nausicaans. What about the Husnock weapon? Any sign of that?"

"Hell, yeah. Can't miss it. It's on the same ship, up in the main magazine with the rest of the ordnance." He lowered his tricorder. *"Could be worse, I guess. At least both our major targets are on the same ship. Our only problem now is how to get in."*

As usual, Santiago was the first to offer an idea. *"What about a distraction? Maybe we could set off a few charges around the rim of the crater. Trigger a landslide?"*

"That would just put them on a defensive footing," Šmrhová said. "We need to get inside their command ship without being seen. Through the gaps under its landing gear, maybe."

"So something to obscure their sight lines," Diaz said. *"Blow up something that makes a lot of smoke, and use it to cover a run for the ship."*

"Problem is," Peralta said, *"the Nausicaans are wearing gear like ours. Which means if our HUDs can see heat signatures, so can theirs. And the last time I checked, we're all a bit short to pass for Nausicaans. Even their kids are taller than most of us."*

"Man," Boyle said, *"I wish we had some of those Breen battlesuits. You know, the ones with the chameleon circuits they invented based on the Jem'Hadar's natural cloaking ability?"*

Diaz nodded. *"Yeah, those would be pretty sweet right about now."*

Šmrhová was losing patience with the banter. "Does anyone have an idea that makes use of the equipment we actually have with us? Szegurra, what about you? You've been awfully—"

She looked back to see Szegurra facedown in the dust.

Behind him stood a trio of Nausicaans aiming heavy disruptor rifles at the strike team. They wore body armor and full-head helmets. Flurries of ash fell from their limbs, blown free by the ceaseless poison wind. To either side of them, four more Nausicaans rose silently from beneath their world's blanket of desolation, like corpses climbing out of their graves.

The one in the center of their group pointed at the strike team. His guttural voice was amplified and distorted by his helmet's external speaker. *"Weapons. Ground."*

"Guys, do as he says." Šmrhová tossed away her phaser rifle.

Her team obeyed, discarding their weapons into the dust beside hers.

The Nausicaan squad leader appeared to relay orders to his men, most likely on their own private comm channel. One of his men picked up Szegurra and draped the unconscious Saurian across his massive shoulders. Another gathered up the strike team's weapons. Then the leader pointed toward the crater and ordered Šmrhová and her team, *"Walk."*

Walking with the Nausicaans at her back, Šmrhová changed

her comm settings with a blink via her HUD. "Kendzior, do you copy?"

"Copy, team leader. Go ahead."

"You win the bet: Plan A is one-hundred percent FUBAR."

"So, time for Plan B?"

"Affirmative. And Parker? Be quick. I'm pretty sure these guys are gonna shoot us in about five minutes."

I see them coming and I laugh. "Look at the prisoners!" I point at the captured Starfleeters, and my people laugh with me. "Came to conquer, got captured!"

They plod like scolded younglings, their heads down. My people hurl garbage and rocks, pelt them like banished heretics. The Starfleeters take their punishment in silence. Weaklings. Not a word of protest, not one threat of revenge.

By the time they stand before me, they are spattered with refuse. I look them over, try to guess which one is in charge. To me they all look small and pitiful. I give one of them a shove, and he takes it. "These are Starfleet's best? Cowards and women?"

My people guffaw. This is the laugh we've needed. Too much hard work these days. It's good to laugh, remember why we struggle. Kradech lines up the prisoners in a single rank. I walk past, review them. They fill me with the urge to spit, but I am wearing a full helmet, and I'm not some *kooluk* who would foul his own nest.

I stop at the middle of the line. "Who leader?"

The woman-child in front of me looks me in the eye. Her voice sounds thin and flat filtered through her helmet's speaker. *"I am."*

She is silly and delicate. Like a toy lost on a battlefield. But I look deeper. Something in her eyes. She is not afraid. Tiny thing has *guramba*. I like that.

I turn up my helmet's speaker. I want my men to hear what I tell woman-child and her friends. "Know my name, Starfleet?"

"Should I care?"

"I am Kinogar. And you are first Starfleet on Nausicaa since this world *died.*" I continue while circling her and her band of fools. "First to come since Borg murdered our people. Does Starfleet send you to help? No. They send you to steal. To kill." Angry jeers wash over us; my people bellow wordless hate at the Starfleeters. "You not on mercy mission. Just thugs like us. Only thing that make you different? You belong to a bigger gang. Call yourselves Starfleet, or Federation. But you no different. Take what you want. Forget who you hurt."

"That's not true," the woman-child argues. *"We—"*

"Left my family to die! Turned your back while the Borg burned my mates! My younglings! My *world*!" The crowd shouts for the Starfleeters' blood. I yearn to give it to them, and to drink my fill, too. "My people call for help. *No one comes.* Borg bathe us in fire. *No one comes.* Make promises. Say you fix broken worlds. Fix Risa. Fix Deneva. Fix Vulcan. But Nausicaa? . . . *No one comes.*"

I see the shame on the Starfleeters' faces. They know I am right. It is not enough. Don't want their pity. Too late for their help. All I want now is justice.

Woman-child musters her steel. *"That doesn't give you the right to kill and plunder."*

"Have *every* right. I walk in a desert. Find water. But Starfleet says *I can't drink.* Water not mine to take. But who is dying? Me? Or Starfleet? We take what we *need.*"

She wants to argue. I see it on her face. So much *guramba* in this one.

Then everything explodes. Plumes of fire erupt from nothing on either side of us. A shock wave hits us all like a charging *bünca*, plows us flat into the dust and ash. I lift my head from the grime, but it sticks to my helmet's faceplate. I wipe it away—just in time for another explosion's blast wave to throw me backward into the air. I smash against something hard and feel the air knocked out of my lungs. It doesn't matter that I know what's happening, that I know it will pass in a moment—I can't breathe, and I panic. Fear clouds my mind, and I flail like a madman, all while I gulp and struggle to draw breath, suffocating like a landed fish.

I slam my fist into my abdomen to force my chest to inflate.

Air floods in, relief follows. I gasp, and then I suck in a greedy mouthful.

Then I get my bearings. My people scatter, run in all directions, harried by fire from above. I look for the source—and then I see the Starfleet runabout, but only for a moment. It streaks past in a high-speed strafing run, hectors my people with phaser blasts, pummels our defenseless ships with its microtorpedoes. I count six ships on fire. A dozen people wounded.

And in the middle of it all, the only people not running? The Starfleeters.

They lie on the ground, huddled like cowards.

I set my helmet's comm to an open channel. "All ships! Shields up! Fire on the Starfleet runabout!" Then I draw my *klika,* its gleaming blade as long as my forearm, and stalk toward the Starfleeters. If they won't run, I will butcher them where they lie.

My parked fleet starts to shoot back at its buzzing pest. One shot hammers its shields, but the tiny craft keeps going. The ground beneath my feet trembles as my fleet's engines come alive. Within moments, our ships will be aloft, and then this shrill nuisance will be silenced.

I am just paces from the prone Starfleeters. Idiots, burying their heads in the sand like *maalats.* I will not regret taking their lives. I charge and raise my blade—

Shimmering golden specks envelop the Starfleeters, and too late I hear the song of their transporter beam through the chords of the wind. Still, I try to take the leader's head—but my blade passes through her as though she had never been there, as if her body had departed this world and left only a brief and fading echo of her *tegol.*

The wind stirs the dust around my feet, but the Starfleeters are gone.

I march toward the *Seovong* and pledge a solemn vow.

I will make the Federation pay for what it did to my world.

I will make all of them pay.

Šmrhová strained against the fading transporter beam, even though she knew she would be trapped on the energizer pad until the annular confinement beam released her. A moment later, fully materialized inside the aft compartment of the *Cumberland*, she shouldered past the rest of her strike team and scrambled forward to the cockpit.

To her relief, Kendzior was still circling above the parked fleet of Nausicaan vessels in the crater, rather than having broken for orbit as soon as the team had been beamed aboard. "Kendzior, can you get a transporter lock on the PMAR inside their lead ship?"

"With their shields up? Not a chance."

"So I guess the Husnock weapon's off the table?"

Her question was answered by a disruptor barrage from one of the ships beneath them. The salvo slammed into the *Cumberland*'s shields, which began to lose integrity.

"One more hit like that and we're toast," Kendzior said.

"All right, get us outta here. Head for orbit, full thrusters."

"Copy that."

Disappointed and feeling more than a bit humbled, Šmrhová settled into the command chair and opened a comm channel. "*Cumberland* to *Enterprise*, do you copy?"

Konya replied. "*This is* Enterprise. *Go ahead,* Cumberland.*"

"*Enterprise,* the strike op is a fumble. We are in retreat, and the Nausicaans are in pursuit, with both mission objectives still on board their lead vessel. Prep the main shuttlebay for an emergency landing, we might be coming in hot. And get ready to greet our new friends. They'll be the ones right behind us, beating our ass with disruptors."

I stride onto the command deck of the *Seovong*, eager to join the hunt. I can tell there are missing faces, but I don't have time now to count casualties. Not with the scent of prey so fresh and so near. "Close all hatches! Thrusters full! Capture the runabout!"

Haylak works the conn, spurs our ship upward into the chase. "Lifting off," he reports. "Ten seconds to orbit. Charging impulse drive, priming warp coils."

Taking my place in the center of the action, I hunger for information. "Tactical! Report!"

Grendig has the weapons console. I had expected Zenber to be there, but now I see he's absent. Grendig will have to do. He is slow to answer. "Sensors locked onto the runabout. It's running away at full impulse."

"Weapons hot. As soon as we close to targeting distance, lock and fire at will."

The young hothead nods but says nothing, too focused on trying to make sense of a console he hasn't worked before. I let it slide. I don't care about his words, as long as I'm pleased by his actions. I take my place in the command chair.

On the viewscreen, the dark veil of mourning that surrounds Nausicaa parts to reveal the endless black of space. Within moments the stars appear, cold and distant. Just like the Federation and its neighbors, the cosmos gave Nausicaa no warning of its fate, and it has shed no tears for its dead. The indifference of the void is a lesson to us all: No one cares for Nausicaans but Nausicaans. No one else hears our cries. No one else will help us. We are alone.

But today I will make the Federation share a small taste of our pain.

"Helm, plot the runabout's course. Where is it going?"

"Edge of the system," Haylak says. "The outer gas giants."

I check my command panel. "Yes. That makes sense. A run-about would not come this far alone. It must have a support ship close by. Tactical! Find it."

The impulse engines kick up to full power as we break free of the atmosphere. I revel in the shudders of the deck plates beneath my boots, the resonant vibrations humming in the ship's space-frame. Around me, my people confer in the hushed tones of hunters. We are close and we know it. We all want to taste fresh blood.

Kradech leans in next to Grendig. Checks the data on his console. And then my second-in-command walks to my side. He keeps his voice down. "We found the parent ship."

"And?"

"It's the *Enterprise.*"

There is worry in his voice. I should smack him down for showing weakness on my command deck. For daring to doubt me to my face. But I need him. Our kind are too few now. We cannot afford to waste anyone, not when our flame is so close to being snuffed. Instead, I clap my gloved hand on Kradech's shoulder. "Well done, my brother."

"Kinogar?"

"Tactical, lock scanners on the *Enterprise.* Put it on-screen. Full magnification." I wait until Grendig executes my command. "This is the ship that brought us the scourge of the Borg. I can think of no better symbol for the Federation's blame. No better target for our revenge. Helm, set intercept course for the *Enterprise.*"

Drogeer, my ice-blooded comrade, sidles over to me, his voice a whisper. "Are you sure that's wise, Kinogar? The *Enterprise* is a formidable target."

"Which is why its destruction will put the galaxy on notice."

I use my command chair's control panel to open a channel to the engineering deck. "Majaf, this is Kinogar. Answer."

"*This is Majaf.*"

"Did you link the station's power device to the Husnock weapon, as I ordered?"

"I did. But I've not had a chance to test it."

"There is no time. We need it to bring the selfish to justice. Will it work?"

"Fire it and we'll find out."

"So be it." I close the channel.

Justice or infamy. Which one I receive is up to chance now. Whether my name will be sung upon the Four Winds, or my *tegol* delivered to them, all will know soon enough.

Until then, I stand tall—and count the seconds until I face the *Enterprise*.

24

———

"*Cumberland*'s coming in hot," Konya reported, as if Worf were unable to see the runabout on the bridge's main viewscreen, racing toward the *Enterprise* with a Nausicaan frigate, the *Seovong*, in close pursuit, hammering the tiny ship's aft shields with disruptor blasts.

"Helm, move to intercept," Worf said. "Prepare to cut off the Nausicaans' pursuit."

"Aye, sir." Lieutenant Joanna Faur increased the *Enterprise*'s speed and adjusted its course to put it into a head-on confrontation with the Nausicaan vessel.

Worf watched, hopeful that the *Enterprise*'s arrival would deter the Nausicaans' pursuit.

Even they would not be so foolish as to force this confrontation.

His expectations were quickly confounded. Something was wrong.

He swiveled his chair toward Konya. "Tactical. Report."

"The *Seovong* is increasing speed." Konya reacted to new sensor readings. "And she's shifting her targeting sensors—off the runabout, and onto *us.*"

Worf stood and stared at the pirate vessel on the viewscreen. *They are moving into an attack posture. Has its commander gone mad?* "Ops, stand by for emergency recovery of the runabout. Tactical, target the *Seovong*, all weapons. Shields to ready standby."

"Shields precharged, weapons locked," Konya said. "Sir, is it safe to target the *Seovong* with the Husnock weapon and the PMAR both still on board?"

It was a valid concern, one that Worf had already planned to address with his next order. "Make our first volley phasers only. A warning shot across their bow."

"Aye, sir."

This does not feel right. Worf had seen enough David-versus-Goliath scenarios to know that ships that seemed tactically inferior rarely challenged more powerful ships unless they were prepared to back up their bravado with action. *This could be a bluff. But with the weapon they've stolen, I cannot take that chance.*

The runabout passed out of frame on the viewscreen. Through the hull Worf heard the resonance of the *Enterprise*'s tractor beams towing the small craft into the shuttlebay. Dygan looked back from the ops console. "The runabout's aboard, sir."

It was time for Worf to finish this. "Shields up!"

"Raising shields," Konya confirmed. "Ready to fire on your mark."

"Open hailing frequencies," Worf said. He doubted that diplomacy would be of any use with hardened criminals such as these, but Starfleet's rules of engagement were clear. He had to give the Nausicaans every chance to stand down before he resorted to violence.

Konya looked up from his console. "Channel open."

"Attention, Nausicaan vessel *Seovong*. This is the Federation *Starship Enterprise*. Adjust your course to avoid collision with this vessel, and terminate your weapons lock immediately. If you fail to comply, you *will* be fired upon."

The main viewscreen was filled with an image from the command deck of the *Seovong*—the fierce, black-eyed visage of its commander. *"Not scared of you, Starfleet. I am Kinogar! And you will pay. For Nausicaa. For my people. For your cowardice."* Kinogar looked at someone off-screen, made a slashing motion with his hand. The transmission ended, and the image on the screen reverted to that of the *Seovong* closing in on the *Enterprise*.

Konya looked up in alarm. "They just charged their weapons grid to full power."

"Fire the warning shot, Mister Konya."

The deputy security chief tapped his console once—and on the viewscreen, brilliant beams of orange phaser energy slashed through the void, narrowly grazing the forward shields of the *Seovong*, which lit up with sparks and feedback, revealing its oblate capsular form around the Nausicaan ship. Then the salvo ended— and the *Seovong* pressed on, full speed ahead.

From the sciences console, Chen noted with alarm, "Looks like they want a fight."

"Enough," Worf said. "Target their—"

"They're firing!" Konya cut in. "It's the Husnock—!"

The main viewscreen went white, and the *Enterprise* pitched into a violent roll.

The engines whined, and the spaceframe groaned in protest. Worf clung to the command chair's armrests. Chen and several junior officers at the auxiliary stations tumbled like dice across the bridge, while the viewscreen showed nothing but blurred streaks twisting and pinwheeling like mad. A secondary blast rocked the ship and flickered the overhead lights.

It was as if the ship had slammed into an immovable object. Everything went dark for a split second, and then sparks rained from breaches in the overhead, baptizing the bridge crew with white-hot motes. Plasma fires erupted inside bulkheads, and three of the auxiliary consoles on the starboard side spat out static and machine-language gibberish before going black.

The strained sound of the engines fell away.

Silence descended upon the bridge. Which in Worf's experience was the last thing a commander wanted in the middle of a combat situation. "Damage report!"

"Bridge consoles not responding," Dygan said, slapping the side of his panel.

Worf was out of his chair and heading aft. "Chen! Show me the master systems display!"

"Offline, sir." She tapped her combadge. "Bridge to Taurik, please respond."

Taurik's voice issued from her combadge, rather than from the overhead speakers. *"This is Taurik. Go ahead."* Chen nodded at Worf, handing off the conversation to him.

"Mister Taurik, damage report."

"Main power is down, engines are offline. Fighting fires on multiple decks."

"Do we still have life-support?"

"Barely. Navigation, shields, and tactical systems are all down. We appear to be adrift in a chaotic tumble. And overloads in the secondary grid are preventing the launch of lifeboats."

Worf imagined Kinogar on the command deck of the *Seovong*, lining up his killing shot at that very moment. "Mister Taurik, I need either weapons, shields, or navigation, *right now.* Any one of them will do."

"I regret that none of them are available."

"Understood. Bridge out." Worf walked away from Chen. Returned to the command chair. Sat down. The other bridge officers looked at him, waiting on his next order. He refused to surrender, or to give in to despair. If they were about to die, so be it. They still had jobs to do.

"Ops, coordinate damage-control and firefighting teams. Lieutenant Chen, prioritize repairs with engineering. Helm, use manual thrusters to halt our spin. Tactical, stand by to fire the log buoy with a ten-hour delay on its beacon. Then get me casualty reports from medical."

His officers went to work, all of them focused and professional.

All that Worf could do was sit in the command chair and wonder:

Why doesn't Kinogar fire the killing shot? What is he waiting for?

I can't see. My ears are ringing. When I try to move, my limbs won't obey. The air is thick with the smell of charred wiring, burnt flesh, scorched hair. Something has gone wrong, but I can't remember what it was. Pain hammers inside my skull with a steady beat.

Fire kisses my face. Hot needles of pain pierce my cheeks, sting my forehead. I blink by reflex, and my sight returns, at least a bit. Layers of gray smoke linger above me, floating blankets in the air. They tatter, twist, and break apart as my men move through them.

I struggle to focus: Garbled voices on the comms. Distorted shapes on the viewscreen.

Strong hands seize the breastplate of my environment suit. Kradech and the physician, Doctor Veekhour, pull me up to a sitting pose and prop me against the side of the command chair. Veekhour cracks open a small ampoule and holds it under my nostrils.

A blast of chlorine odor hits my sinuses and I jolt back to full awareness, swat the ampoule away. "What happened?"

"Overload." Kradech nods toward the tactical console. "The PMAR killed our grid when we fired the Husnock weapon."

"How much damage?"

My trusted second makes a sideways chopping motion with his hand. "Total. All guns fried. Tactical systems dead. Shields gone. Need new ones. No fixes."

I can't believe it's this bad. "No shields?"

"Emitters overloaded. Main coils melted. No spares."

It's worse than I'd feared. I'd expected some feedback, a few burnouts. Nothing like this. I put out my arms. "Help me up."

Kradech and Veekhour pull me to my feet. I assess the state of the command deck.

Most of my people are still up and working. A few need help. No one looks dead.

Major systems are offline. The tactical console is dark. Life-support is on backup. Ship-to-ship comms are down. A tang in the air tells me plasma fires were burning here until a few minutes ago, but my crew has put them out.

If only the main viewscreen showed me more than wavy lines.

"*Enterprise*? Status?"

"Major damage." Kradech hands me a small data tablet. It has a link to our sensors. He continues his rundown as I look over the hard numbers. "Shields down. Engines offline. Main power down. No comms. No weapons."

I point at the tablet's screen. "They are correcting their roll. Restoring control."

"Not without main power. *Enterprise* is an open target."

"So are we." I point at the crippled tactical station. "No disruptors. No torpedo launchers. No shields. Can't fire the Husnock weapon. Can't ram them without killing ourselves."

Kradech taps the tablet's screen with fierce urgency. "We *board* them!"

His *guramba* attracts Grendig the hotspur: "Yes! Board the Starfleeters!"

Their excitement riles up the others. My men stomp on the deck and chant for blood.

I use both hands, slam their heads together. That silences the war chants.

"Fools! They have eight hundred people on that ship! We have a hundred. Need half to run the ship. Send fifty to fight eight hundred?" I look around the command deck. "Need a real plan. How long to fix the ship? Can we fire before they do?"

One of my fighters steps forward to stand before me. It's Drogeer, the *venolar*. If anyone can give me sound advice while my temper boils, it will be the snowblood.

"We can navigate. They cannot. We should make best use of that advantage."

I look him in the eye. "Tell me more."

"We are missing vital supplies. Medicine. Fuel. Spare parts. Raw materials. Things we need to make repairs, heal our wounded, and expand our project on Nausicaa."

"Continue."

"If we want these things, we must either take them, or give the enemy reason to hand them over. To do that, we must take something they consider valuable, and hold it hostage."

"We have only one fighting ship," I protest. "A hundred men at most. What could we capture that the enemy would pay to ransom?"

Drogeer grins, his fangs wide. "They told us the answer. Tracked us all the way to Nausicaa to steal it back. The PMAR plus the Husnock weapon. Merge them in a matrix that can handle the load, and you will have a weapon that can reach between the stars."

Now I understand. A target weak enough for us to dominate. Small enough for us to control. The perfect place to ground our attack and take our revenge. "Yes," I say. "That's good. We take it. Then we get everything our people need."

Kradech seems less excited by this notion than I am. "Bad idea. 'Never fight from a fixed position. Always stay mobile.' *You* taught us that. Get trapped in one place and we die."

My gorge rises. I hate having my own words thrown back at me. "Situations change. So must our attack." I raise my voice to address all of my people and put down this insubordination. "The enemy lives in fixed positions. We will take one—and with it, hold them *all* hostage."

Still not satisfied, Kradech puts himself in front of me. "And if we get trapped?"

"Get our people what they need. Then we go down fighting."

I shove him out of my way. I'm done negotiating. My mind is set.

"Forget the *Enterprise*. Helm, plot a course back to Skarda. Maximum warp. Commit."

There are no protests as our ship maneuvers away from the crippled Starfleet vessel. No one rises to challenge me as I take my place in the command chair. We have much to do, and very little time left. I cannot brook any more of these uprisings. It's time for me to make a change I should have made long ago.

"Kradech, go below. Take command of Rifle Company One." I

look for and find the snowblood. "Drogeer. You are now second-in-command. Take your place here." I point to my right, the place of honored counsel beside my chair. "We go now to secure a future for our people. May the Four Winds grant us victory—or take our *tegoli* and praise our sacrifice."

In typical Starfleet fashion, no one bothered to tell me what was going on when the *Enterprise* started taking fire and getting its ass kicked. Granted, the latter portion of that complaint was speculation, but when all the lights went out after what felt like a planet-sized mule kicking the ship dead center in its saucer, it wasn't that hard to figure out what had happened.

I had just settled in. Over the years I'd learned not to mind incarceration. I'd come to think of it as a chance to get some sleep and catch up on my reading. In a way, being stuffed into a cell was like a free vacation, and on a scale from Risan *jamaharon* resort to Gorn gladiator pen, time in a Starfleet brig was one of the better options. They tended to be fairly conscientious about providing up-to-date reading material, a decent selection of music, and a clean head. I've long said that their bedding left much to be desired, but you can't have everything.

The shaking and rumbling had stopped by the time Šmrhová barged into the brig. She looked worse for wear, to be honest. Her environmental suit—one of those sleek black Starfleet tactical models, not the baggy civilian kind—was caked in dust and muck. She had shed her helmet someplace else, and her dark hair was a tousled mess. She stormed past the brig sentry and parked herself, seething like a wounded *targ*, in front of my cell. It was one of the few moments I had ever been glad to be stuck behind an impenetrable force field—and then I remembered she could turn it off whenever she wanted.

The overhead lights weltered, throwing evil shadows across her elegant features. She glared at me like I had murdered her parents and sold her new puppy into Tholian slavery. "Did you know? Tell me, you piece of crap! Did you *know*?"

I was keen to play her game, but I needed more information first. "Know what?"

"Don't be cute. Did you know the Husnock weapon could do this to the *Enterprise*?"

I shrugged. "I thought it would cut you in half. I'd say you got off easy."

She growled like a wild animal and paced in front of my cage. "We just got this ship working again, and the Nausicaans crippled us in one shot. If you knew what that thing could do, why the hell didn't you warn us?"

What did she expect me to say? "No one asked me."

She slammed her forearm against the force field, which flashed, buzzed, and spat sparks. If not for the insulation in her tactical suit, she would almost certainly have shocked herself unconscious. Still pacing, she looked feral. I wanted to feel thankful that she didn't appear to be armed, but I could tell that wouldn't matter if she dropped the force field.

Even so, I remained a glutton for punishment. "You never answered my question."

She halted and stared daggers into me. "What question?"

"Did you get my flowers?"

Her features contorted, as if all of her emotions were warring for face time and no clear winner was able to emerge. Then she shook her head and let anger win the day. "Are you kidding me? That's what's on your mind? You narcissistic *twit*. You egomaniacal *moron*." She punched the force field again, hard enough to make me step back. "If we end up having to abandon ship, I promise you, no one is *ever* going to find your body."

She turned and stalked off toward the brig's main door.

I called after her. "I can help."

She stopped. Her expression was skeptical. "Help with what?"

"This mess with the Nausicaans." I don't know what came over me. A feeling of pity? A sense of duty? An attack of chivalry? An urge born of desperation? But I spilled the answers to questions she hadn't even asked. "If you go to my ship, log into the main computer with the password 'Shambalala dash alpha dash nine seven five.' Look for a file directory named 'Bonfire.' It has all the specs on the Husnock OPC."

She looked annoyed. "What good is that gonna do us now?"

"It won't fix the damage done. But it will tell you how to configure your EPS grid so that a shot from that thing won't knock it out again. It might not seem like much now, but it could be enough to keep your shields up next time."

"That's great. Let's just hope there *is* a next time."

On that cheerful note, Šmrhová turned away and left me to stew in my regrets.

To tell the truth, I didn't really blame her. And I took her words to heart: I hoped there would be a next time. Because that was probably the only way I'd ever get another shot at recovering the OPC—and keeping my ass out of a Starfleet Intelligence black site for the rest of my natural life.

25

———•———

The sky above La Barre was clear, and the stars were bright. A gentle breeze whispered through the rows of vines. Dinner was long done, the kitchen cleaned and readied for the next morning. It was oddly warm for a winter night, almost ten degrees Celsius. Clad in a fall jacket and a knitted scarf, Picard stood on the porch and resisted the inclination to worry about his legal jeopardy. Instead, he focused on the pleasant surprise that was the 2383 vintage of Château Picard.

It had been over six years since he had last sampled his family's label. That time he had opened a bottle of the 2372 and found it disappointing. He hadn't held that against Marie; the '72 had been her first vintage as the winemaker, the year after Robert and René had died. He had been surprised to hear that she had even tried to continue the label without interruption. No one would have blamed her if she had simply sold the vineyard's grapes to other winemakers for a few years—or perhaps even sold the winery outright. After all, she was a Picard by marriage rather than by birth. But she had insisted on preserving the family legacy.

I underestimated how much it meant to her. And how much it still means to me.

Sip by sip he savored his pour of the '83. It renewed his faith—in Marie, in his family name, in his brother's memory, in the beauty of wine. From the moment he had filled his glass he had known this would be the wine he recalled from his youth. Deep crimson in color, it had a bouquet that promised delicate smokiness, dark fruit, and spice. Though it was translucent, it had the lush mouthfeel of a more opaque varietal, and its flavors were sophisticated and well-balanced. Hints of blackberry and cassis, complex earthy undertones, and elegant tannins all had been married to perfection by Marie's two-step maturation process in new French oak casks.

Technically, Château Picard was now a Jura wine by region, but climatic shifts in the aftermath of World War III had changed the characteristics of many growing regions. Before the war, Château Picard had been housed in Saint-Estèphe, much farther west. In pursuit of an elusive and favorable microclimate, Picard's ancestors had moved the vineyard here in the mid-twenty-first century. The relocation had proved so successful that it had earned La Barre its own coveted AOC—*appellation d'origine contrôllée*—designating it as a unique wine-growing area.

The only change in the formulation of Château Picard subsequent to the move to La Barre had been to adjust its blend of grapes, reducing its portion of Cabernet Sauvignon from eighty-five percent to eighty percent, and allocating that five percent to Trousseau, a local grape with a sour-cherry flavor but superb tannins. Cabernet gave the wine its body, and Merlot provided smoothness and acidity, but the Trousseau imbued Château Picard with complexity and a backbone. Those tannins were what gave it decades of longevity in the bottle.

He treated himself to a long draught from his glass.

This is one of the finest vintages our label has ever produced. Simply marvelous.

His hope of finishing the glass in peace was spoiled by the crunch of approaching footsteps on the gravel path that ringed the house. He no longer had to wonder who it was that would come calling, unannounced, at such an hour. Steeling his nerve for bad news, he turned to face Ezor as he stepped out of the shadows into the porch's light and climbed the steps.

"Jonathan. Can I pour you a glass of the '83? It's quite sublime."

"I couldn't. Not when I come bearing bad news."

"Does this case produce any other kind?"

Ezor gestured toward a pair of nearby chairs. "Can we sit?"

Picard took one chair and motioned for Ezor to take the other. "What's happened?"

"My mistake today, opening the door for Louvois to trot out a parade of your professional missteps—it did a lot of damage. More than I'd realized."

"We knew that. And even if you hadn't said it, I saw Admiral Liu's reaction."

"So did I. And I'm pretty sure she called the break when she did out of pity. Which is not a good sign for how she'll decide your case." He reached inside his coat and pulled out his padd. "Louvois saw it, too. Which probably explains her latest offer." He offered the padd to Picard.

Picard demurred. "Just read it to me, please."

He put away the padd. His countenance was that of a beaten man. "She says that if you'll change your plea to guilty on the lesser charges, she'll drop the sedition charge."

"Only that charge? What about the murder-related charges?"

"No, those stay."

"Did she dangle a carrot of leniency at the end of her stick?"

"She offered to recommend that you not be sentenced to more than twenty years in a Federation penal colony." Puzzled, he crinkled his brow. "You're not actually considering this?"

Picard shook his head. "Of course not. I just want to gauge Phillipa's state of mind based on how much she's prepared to give up in order to secure a conviction."

Ezor nodded. "All right. You know her better than I do. What's your take?"

A deep sigh left Picard feeling empty. "She feels confident. If she were worried, she would have offered to drop the murder-related charges. But her willingness to let go of the sedition charge tells me she was never serious about that count. I suspect she hoped she could use it to apply pressure and break us on some other front."

"Makes sense." Ezor stood to leave. "Do you want me to make a counteroffer? Try to negotiate a more favorable plea?"

"Absolutely not." Picard's resolve was firm. "Phillipa tries to make my surrender sound fair, even merciful. As if she were extending me a personal courtesy by mere dint of its offer. But it's just gamesmanship. It wouldn't matter to me if she recommended my sentence be reduced to ten years, five months, or even one day. She's asking me to kill my own reputation. To destroy my career and all for which it's stood. She wants me to willingly visit disgrace upon the name of Picard." A righteous anger bloomed inside him. "If that's my fate, let *her* be the one to inflict it. I refuse to do it *for* her."

As he approached the door of Admiral Batanides's office, Admiral Akaar paused to gather his courage. This was going to be a gamble, and he knew it. A confrontation such as this could backfire with potentially disastrous consequences, but with so much at stake, he had to try. He wouldn't be able to live with himself if he ignored any chance to serve the truth and save a good man like Jean-Luc Picard.

His hand paused in front of the visitor signal beside Batanides's office door. He knew that she was in—her aide had told him so just a few minutes earlier.

If I'm wrong about this . . . if I've been misinformed . . . this could end my career.

He pressed the visitor call button and waited.

Batanides's voice issued from the speaker beside her door: *"Come."* The lock on the door released with a soft *click* inside the bulkhead, and then the door slid open with a silken whisper.

Akaar stepped inside Batanides's sanctum. It was sparse in its furnishings. Shades of gray defined the room—a fitting motif for the director of Starfleet Intelligence, Akaar mused. Batanides was seated at her desk, reviewing information on her holoscreen. The jacket of her duty uniform was open at the top, a not uncommon look for flag officers at the end of a long day. She looked up as Akaar crossed the room and planted himself in front of her desk.

Her steel-gray hair was pulled back tight against her head into a neat and simple ponytail, which only served to accentuate her angular features and pale blue eyes. "Sir! I wasn't expecting you." She started to get up.

"As you were. I'm hoping this visit will be brief."

Batanides settled back into her chair and switched off her holoscreen. "If I may ask, sir, what brings you down here?"

"I hope you'll forgive me if I skip the usual pleasantries, Marta. I need something that is yours to provide, and I need it quickly, without SI's trademark red tape and runaround."

His frankness, rather than allaying Batanides's suspicions, heightened them. She sat up a bit straighter, and her body language became stiff and defensive. "I suppose that will depend upon what it is you've come for, sir."

"Put simply, I need to arrange immediate access to a Section Thirty-One prisoner whom you placed in an SI black-site prison. The Vulcan woman known as L'Haan."

The SI director reclined her chair a few degrees while eyeing Akaar. "Why her?"

"I believe she can lead us to evidence related to the current inquiry into the resignation of President Min Zife, and his subsequent fate."

Batanides narrowed her stare. "You mean the Starfleet coup that led to his assassination."

"I haven't come to debate terms or argue semantics, Marta. I have reason to believe that L'Haan can give us information that might serve to exonerate Captain Picard, and if so, I need that information uncovered as soon as possible."

His plea garnered no sympathy from Batanides. She folded her hands atop her lap. "I wasn't aware we were invested in salvaging the careers of traitors."

"I was led to believe you considered Jean-Luc Picard a friend."

"I used to. Back when I thought I knew who he was. Now I'm not so sure."

This is just as I had feared. I wish she hadn't forced me to do this.
"I know what you did, Marta."

Her expression turned aggressive, and she leaned forward as if to meet his accusation head-on. "To what, exactly, do you refer, Admiral?"

"I know you were the one who leaked multiple classified internal files to Attorney General Louvois. You provided her with access to Captain Picard's sealed personal logs, in violation of the SCMJ. I know you did the same for the personal logs of Admirals Nakamura, Nechayev, Jellico, Ross, and even the late Owen Paris."

"The Federation had a right to know what they thought of their crimes."

"Maybe. Maybe not. But you had no right to release those logs without my consent. Which you neither sought nor received."

"If you're that upset, bring me up on charges. See if they stick."

"If I bring you up on charges, I won't limit it to the unauthorized release of personal logs. I'll make sure that I also charge you with the blackmail and extortion of Commander Dalit Sarai, and with running an unauthorized surveillance against a Starfleet flag officer, Admiral William T. Riker, and a Starfleet starship commander, Captain Christine Vale. Would you like to review the recorded evidence of your crimes? Or peruse the official sealed complaint filed with my office by Admiral Riker, Captain Vale, and Commander Sarai?"

Batanides's posture relaxed, but her expression was one of seething contempt. "So. Commander Sarai sold me out, did she?"

"And then some." He leaned on her desk. "Tell me where L'Haan is. *Right now.*"

"We're keeping her close. She's in our black site at Wolf 359."

"Send me the coordinates and any codes required for private access to the prisoner. Admiral Riker will be there within three hours."

She picked up a padd and tapped in a few commands. "Done. Anything else?"

"Yes. First, cease and desist all unauthorized contact related to official Starfleet inquiries and courts-martial. If this ever happens again, I'll see that you spend the rest of your life in one of your own black sites. Second, you are to immediately terminate all surveillance of Admiral Riker, Captain Vale, Commander Sarai, and the crew and operations of the *Starship Titan* and its exploratory group. Whatever you thought you were accomplishing with that op, you failed. And now it's over. Do I make myself absolutely clear, Admiral Batanides?"

"Perfectly, sir."

"Good." Akaar turned and walked out of Batanides's office, not daring to look back.

Someday she'll make me pay for this. I'll just have to hope that L'Haan actually knows something that can help Captain Picard—and that Riker can persuade her to share it.

It had come as a mild surprise to William Riker when he was ordered by Admiral Akaar to have Captain Vale bring the *Starship Titan* to the Wolf 359 system. So far as Riker knew, there had never been much of anything there—nothing except the haunting memory of nearly eleven thousand Starfleet personnel slain or assimilated and thirty-nine vessels destroyed by the Borg.

Then had come an encrypted message from Admiral Akaar, one marked for Riker's eyes only. Once decoded, its first portion had provided him with a set of instructions for how to solo-pilot a small shuttlecraft into the system's asteroid field and navigate to an unmarked and officially unknown Starfleet Intelligence black site. Its second portion provided access codes that had earned him admittance to the site, which was concealed inside a hollowed-out asteroid, and then granted him permission to meet alone with former Section 31 director L'Haan.

Armed guards escorted him from his shuttle in the landing bay, through angular corridors that were as immaculate as they were cold. Windowless portals marked only with numerals lined the long walk from the landing bay to an interview room that had been set aside for Riker's impromptu meeting. No signage indicated what one might find behind any of those doors. They might have been storage lockers, guard barracks, or just an endless array of cells. There was no way of knowing—and that, Riker realized with a chill, was the point.

No one except a handful of people inside Starfleet Intelligence knows how many people are held here, or in any of the other black sites. This isn't just imprisonment. To be sent here is to be disappeared. Erased. Forgotten.

The guards ushered Riker inside the interview room. It was just a few meters square, gray and featureless. A solid wall of transparent aluminum divided the room across its center. Set into the ceiling on either side of the wall were transceivers that Riker presumed were directly linked. There was no furniture on either side of the barrier, but on the other side Riker saw another door.

It slid open. A second pair of guards escorted a middle-aged Vulcan woman into the other side of the interview room. She was tall with long legs, a slender swimmer's physique, and a coppery complexion. Her eyes were dark beneath brows like the slopes of distant mountains, and her jet-black hair was styled in a Cleopatra cut, complete with dramatic bangs that covered her forehead. She was dressed in a plain gray jumpsuit that bore no markings other than a prisoner number above her left breast. Her wrists were bound in front of her with magnetic manacles.

The guards who had led her in retreated through the door on their side, which closed.

One of the guards who had brought Riker to the meeting eyed L'Haan with suspicion. "Be careful, Admiral. We're flooding this room with signals similar to Tholian thoughtwaves, to prevent the Vulcan woman from using her telepathic abilities on you from a distance, but do not touch the barrier. We think her touch-telepathy skills are degraded, but we can't guarantee your safety if you touch the barrier."

"Understood. Thank you."

The guard left the room, and the door slid shut behind him.

From the other side of the wall, L'Haan's glare cut like a knife into Riker's soul. "What do you want?"

"My name is—"

"I know who you are. What do you *want*?"

"I want you to help me find and access information in the Section Thirty-One archives that could help clear Captain Picard of criminal culpability in the murder of President Zife."

He noted the slightest lift of her left eyebrow. "Why should I help you?"

"What do you want?"

"Nothing I can ever have." She cast a desperate look around their drab, featureless space. "*This* is what now constitutes intellectual stimulation in my life."

"There must be something you want that I could help you acquire."

"Since the only thing I want is to escape this rock, I would disagree. So I ask you again: What possible reason could I have for helping you? Or Picard?"

She was, unfortunately, correct. Riker considered what little he knew of Section 31. What it had done. Why its agents had done what they did.

He decided to play a hunch. "All I can do is appeal to your sense of duty as an agent and director of Section Thirty-One."

Her eyebrow lifted a tiny bit higher this time. "Explain."

"You and your fellow agents had one mission: to defend the Federation from those who would see it harmed or destroyed, and to serve that mission at any cost, no matter what it took. Even to the point of removing a criminal president whose continued tenure threatened the Federation's future safety."

"Your time is almost up, Admiral. Get to the point."

"There's nothing more that Federation law can do to you. But even from this forsaken place, you can still carry out your mission—by defending the Federation from the self-harm it would do by destroying a good man like Captain Picard."

"Why should I care what happens to him?"

"I'd submit that you already do, and you did, even six years ago. There was a reason you insulated him from the truth. A reason you made sure he was kept at a distance, with his hands clean. You weren't afraid he'd stop you. You knew no one could at that point. No, I think you protected Captain Picard because you knew the Federation would *need* him. I would argue that it still does. And you know that, L'Haan. Which is how I know you're going to tell me how to find proof of his innocence in the Section Thirty-One archives."

The Vulcan woman eyed him, her countenance a mystery.

"Are you a gambling man, Admiral?"

Unable to help himself, he flashed a wide grin. "I've been known to play a little poker."

She lifted her eyebrow in a high and dramatic arch. "It shows."

The deadly sunlight faded beyond Skarda's still-scorched horizon. Once more facing the cold emptiness of space, the knot of humanity jammed inside the last surviving sliver of Stonekettle Station breathed a collective sigh of relief as the energy shield was deactivated.

Sweltering heat still reigned in reactor control, but La Forge and Doctor th'Fehlan had already set to work on a remedy. "Opening external vents," th'Fehlan said.

La Forge flipped toggles on the life-support console. "Engaging primary heat exchangers." He pressed the start switch and hoped the system was still working. To his relief, the great fans and compressor engines rattled and whirred to life. The first gusts from the ventilator system were hot like a turbojet's exhaust, but within ten seconds the air cooled.

A few meters away, Elfiki sat on the floor, her back to a console.

Her eyes fluttered at the return of cool, filtered air. She muttered through chapped lips, "Are we really not dead?"

"Not yet," La Forge said. "C'mon. Get up. We've got a lot to do."

"Later. First, I need a gallon of iced tea. Then, a two-day nap."

He considered chiding her for setting a bad example for the junior officers, but he was interrupted by engineer Ryan Giler. "Sir? Should we dial back the second warp core?"

"Yes, we should. Do me a favor and take care of it, will you?"

"You sure you want me to, sir? After I nearly blew us all up swapping it in?"

La Forge gave Giler a reassuring pat on the back. "Forget that, Ryan. Could've happened to any of us. Besides, this is just throttling its output. No need to identify wires this time."

"Aye, sir. I'm on it." Giler trudged away to the warp core.

Doctor th'Fehlan had taken up his post in front of the station's enormous master systems display. Because most of the station had been lost to the red giant, the entirety of the wall-sized monitor was filled with a detailed representation of the surviving one-sixteenth of the station, as well as the facility's cylindrical central core. La Forge joined th'Fehlan and a few of the station's civilian engineers in front of the massive schematic. "How'd we do, Doctor?"

"About as expected." The Andorian engineer pointed out flashing red areas in the diagram. "Hiccups in the shield left us with damage in a few spots. I'd like to send out survey teams to inspect the station's footprint and core as soon as they cool to a safe temperature."

"Makes sense." La Forge opened an internal channel. "Reactor control to Ops. How are you folks doing up there?"

"Better now that the air's back on," Juneau Wright replied. *"How soon can you guys give us power for repairs?"*

"We nearly fried our borrowed core," th'Fehlan said. "It needs time to cool down." He checked his numbers. "We can give you fifty percent now. Seventy-five in about an hour."

"Okay, solid. That works. Also, Commander La Forge? We want to

send an updated distress signal, but our subspace transmitter's dam-
aged. I think part of it might have melted. Can we borrow a few of
your people to go out and have a look at it?"

"Absolutely. Any updates on the possibility of an evacuation?"

"Not yet. Last we heard, Starfleet's still trying to round up ships
with enough combined free space to take us all aboard. They keep tell-
ing us to be patient, but I—"

A crash like thunder shook the station. Alarms wailed. People
scrambled to duty stations.

Looks of dread passed among the team in reactor control. For a
moment even La Forge feared the worst. Did the heat compromise
something structural? Did an outer bulkhead fail?

He made sure the channel to Ops was still open. "Ops! What's
going on?"

"Perimeter breach," replied Pov, the Tellarite second-in-command.
"Somebody just shot their way into one of the docking bays."

That seemed to shock th'Fehlan. "Shot their way *in*? Who'd
want to be in here?"

"Hang on, we're still trying to bring the security network back on-
line. The vid feeds are all a little slow right— Wait! We've got an image.
Breach is in docking bay fifty-one. And our uninvited guests are—"
After a long pause, Pov added in a flat tone, *"I don't believe it."*

La Forge had no time for this sort of drama. "Ops! Talk to
us! What's going on? Who breached the station? Where are they
going?"

"Nausicaans," Pov said, sounding stunned. *"Pretty sure it's the*
same ones as before. And this time they came in a bigger ship, and
there's a whole lot more of them."

Even th'Fehlan was becoming impatient for actionable intel.
"How many?"

"Almost a hundred. All of them with rifles, sidearms, tactical muni-
tions. Not sure what these guys want, but it looks like they came ready
to make a stand."

La Forge shook his head at the mad improbability of it all. *Why would they come back? What the hell is going on?* He walked over to Elfiki, who was awake now, and helped her up. "Dina, we've got trouble."

"I heard. What's our play?"

"Zone defense. Keep the Nausicaans out of reactor control, and away from any system that would let them hold the station's people hostage. Take our people back to the runabouts, open the small-arms lockers, and give everybody a weapon."

Doctor th'Fehlan interrupted, "Commander? Should we put the shield back up?"

"We can't. The core would burn out within minutes, and then we'd have no power at all. Besides, why raise the shields once the bad guys are already inside?" He feared th'Fehlan might try to answer that rhetorical question, so he added, "Tell Ops to send a new mayday. We don't just need rides anymore. We need re-inforcements."

26

More than once Worf had heard people refer to "flying a ship apart," but this was the first moment he had ever feared he might do so for real. Barely operational after the restoration of its major systems hours earlier, the *Enterprise* shuddered, groaned, and creaked like an old house being buffeted by a windstorm. Primary and secondary consoles had stuttered momentarily at random a number of times, and the ship's lights seemed to become less reliable the nearer it came to catching up with the Nausicaan bandits at Skarda.

The *Enterprise* had received Stonekettle Station's new distress signal less than an hour earlier, and Worf was keenly aware that each passing minute served only to benefit the Nausicaans. The ruthless brigands were no doubt entrenching themselves, fortifying their position, and preparing to pillage the facility down to empty floors and bare walls.

If I believed the ship could handle it, I would go to maximum warp. But even warp seven is threatening to overload main engineering. I cannot risk pushing us any further.

Though he had counseled Šmrhová not to haunt her subordinates' workstations, this time he had sent her around with specific orders to demand constant updates on damage reports and repair estimates. She had just finished another circuit of the bridge duty stations and returned to her place at Worf's right hand. They leaned toward each other and kept their voices down.

"I wish I had good news, sir. Most of our major systems are still offline." She checked the padd in her hand. "Transporters, targeting sensors, phaser collimating arrays, and torpedo launchers are at the top of the repair list, but right now they're all down."

"How long until we can increase speed?"

"Taurik is twisting himself in knots keeping us at warp seven. And he's making that work only because we're traveling in a mostly straight line. If we try to make any maneuvers at high warp, we'll end up as a light-year-long smear of wreckage."

It wasn't the update Worf had hoped for, but he accepted it and moved on to the next matter. "When we reach Stonekettle Station, we will need a plan for containing and neutralizing the Nausicaan intruders." He cast a critical look at Šmrhová. "Do you have an attack plan?"

"I'm going to lead one of four strike teams. We can't trust the transporters right now, so we'll take runabouts to the station and deploy from there. The station's last message says they're leaving their shields down so we can send people in."

"Are you sure another confrontation is wise?"

Šmrhová looked offended by the question. "I don't see that we have much choice, sir."

"I ask because last time, you and your team were captured. By these same Nausicaans. Another hostage situation, inside the station, would be . . . unfortunate."

"Yes, sir. I'm aware of that." Hints of her mounting anger slipped out as she continued. "But with all respect, the Nausicaans had sensor-blocked sentries hidden under the sand down on Nausicaa. I doubt they'll find that kind of cover inside the station's engineering levels."

As much as Worf admired Šmrhová's fighting spirit, he had to consider a larger picture than one tactical engagement. One that would call upon the skills he had acquired not just as a Starfleet officer, but also those he had learned as the Federation ambassador to Qo'noS many years earlier. "Brief me on your plan's details before you deploy. But do not engage the Nausicaans unless I order it. I must try to resolve this matter through diplomacy."

"Ah, yes. The mandatory negotiation with an implacable foe, as required by Starfleet regulations." There was a winsome gleam in her eye. "You envy me right now, don't you?"

"More than somewhat." He steeled himself. "Prep your strike force. Be ready to launch on my command."

"Aye, sir." She moved aft, toward the turbolifts, and was about to leave when a signal chirped on the security console. Its sound halted Šmrhová in midstep.

Konya muted the alert and then he reviewed its contents. "Captain? We're being hailed on a priority channel by Starfleet Intelligence."

"Classification level?"

"General comms. Should I put it through?"

"On-screen." Worf stood, so as to present a more imposing visage to whoever was hailing him from the shadowy environs of Starfleet Intelligence.

The image of Admiral Batanides appeared on the main viewscreen. *"Commander Worf. I've been made to understand your ship is en route to Stonekettle Station."*

"Correct, Admiral. We are the closest Starfleet vessel."

"And are you once more in pursuit of the Nausicaan bandits who absconded with a Husnock Omega-particle cannon?"

"We are. Our ETA is sixteen minutes."

"Will you be sending armed personnel to contain the incursion?"

"That is the plan."

"Release Agent Okona from your brig at once, Captain."

Knowing it would always be easier to obtain forgiveness than permission, Worf played dumb. "I do not understand. We have not seen Mister Okona since—"

"Since you arrested him on Garada? Please don't try to bluff me, Commander. I know you sent a team there, and that they abducted Agent Okona. Now I want him back."

Worf raised his chin, a display of pride. "It is good to *want* things, Admiral."

"*Commander, this is not a game, nor is it a debate, or a negotiation. This is an order: Release Agent Thadiun Okona from your ship's brig at once. Return to him all of his possessions, as well as unmonitored access to his ship. Furthermore, include him in whatever operation you plan to conduct inside Stonekettle Station. I want him on the ground with your people when they recover the Husnock weapon. Is that clear, Commander?*"

"Yes, Admiral."

"*Good. Obey my orders at once. Batanides out.*" She terminated the transmission, and the bridge's main screen reverted to an image of stars elongated and curved by the warping and compression of space-time.

Being strong-armed made Worf's blood course hot in his veins. It left his face feeling flush and his ears burning, and when he curled his fist he imagined it closing around Batanides's throat. He looked at Šmrhová and did his best to maintain his mask of aloof control.

"Release Okona and take him with you to the station—but do *not* trust him."

"Haven't so far. Won't start now." She bounded up the bridge's tiers to the aft turbolifts, where she paused and looked back at Worf. "Sir, I don't recall the admiral saying we weren't allowed to *shoot* Okona, do you?"

"Dismissed, Lieutenant." Worf watched Šmrhová step inside a turbolift car, and then he raised his voice to add, "The rest of you? Forget what you just heard. That is an *order.*"

As much as she expected it to gall her to have to let Okona out of his cell, Šmrhová had always enjoyed the moment of releasing someone from the brig. Even more than the act of shoving them in and raising the force field, being able to play the part of the liberator made her feel powerful, benevolent, and merciful all at once. Such moments comported with her image of herself as a woman in control, an officer to be respected, a force with which to be reckoned.

Most of all, I want to hear that smug jerk say "thank you" just once.

She stepped through the main door of the brig, full of anticipation for moments she expected to savor for the next few days at the very least—only to see that Okona was already out of his cell, had recovered his personal possessions from the brig's central storage lockup, and was putting his sidearm back into its holster as she arrived. He greeted her with a broad, white grin. "Hey, you! Good to see you again—looking forward to working with you!"

Her temper broke free, like a rush of champagne launching a cork. "Brig officer! Front and center! Now!"

Clumsy scrambling sounds behind the brig officer's panopticon were followed by running footsteps. Moments later, a flustered and frightened young female ensign snapped to attention in front of Šmrhová. "Ensign O'Meara, reporting as ordered, sir!"

Šmrhová pointed at Okona. "O'Meara! Who gave the order to release this man?"

The young purple-haired woman stared in terror at Okona. "I don't know, sir."

"Are you telling me you didn't see him walk out of his cell, stroll over to the lockup, remove his personal effects, and then stand here dressing himself? You're surrounded by state-of-the-art sensors and vid screens! How did you not see this?"

All the woman could do was shrug and look petrified.

"Return to your post!" As she watched O'Meara hurry away, Šmrhová added under her breath, "For whatever good it'll do." Then she turned toward Okona. "You sonofabitch. How did you get out of that cell?"

"A good magician never reveals his secrets. Now, I understand we have work to do?"

"Follow me." She led him out of the brig, and then down the corridor. "I'm supposed to take you back to your ship and let you grab whatever gear you think you'll need."

He beamed. "Splendid! I'm glad someone's finally thinking straight around here."

"Thank Admiral Batanides. She's the one who shoved this down our gullets."

They stepped into a turbolift. The ride up to the hangar was brief and, to Šmrhová's relief, quiet. When they stepped out into the hangar, and they caught sight of Okona's ship, his gums started flapping again. "So what's the op? I'll need intel to shape my load-out."

Struck favorably by his no-nonsense attitude, Šmrhová handed him her padd so he could follow along while she briefed him. "Stonekettle Station. Core section, lower levels. Nausicaan intruders. Their objective: unknown. Our mission: contain, then capture or neutralize."

"Do we know how many troops they have?"

"Around a hundred, give or take. Various small arms, limited antipersonnel ordnance."

Okona nodded, paged through the info on the padd. "Any hostages?"

"Unknown. Station security was trying to clear sections ahead of the Nausicaans, but space is tight. No telling if things went wrong."

"*Always* assume they've gone wrong. You'll rarely be disappointed." He handed back the padd. "Infil is by runabout? Why not beam in?"

"Transporters are still blitzed thanks to the OPC."

They reached the ramp to his ship. He paused and raised a hand, blocking Šmrhová's path. "Stay here."

"The hell I will."

For a second he looked as if he might argue with her, but then he shrugged. "You're right. Starfleet's obsession with security clearances is a waste of time. C'mon aboard."

He led her inside the starhopper. Its interior was even less impressive than its beaten, cosmically weathered exterior—until he walked into his sleep nook and said in a loud, clear voice, "I reserve the quiet defense." At once the bulkheads retracted, his bunk folded away upon itself, and the lighting from the overhead panel changed to a bright frost blue, casting an unearthly glow on the broad assortment of sleek, terrifying-looking weapons that now surrounded them on three sides. Beam weapons, gauss rifles, and monofilament blades of various sizes and styles were displayed beside miniaturized pieces of equipment whose functions Šmrhová couldn't even begin to guess. It was an armory unlike any she had ever seen.

Okona chose a long hunting knife with a monofilament edge, inside a specially designed sheath, and attached it to the left side of his belt, under his coat. Then he traded his cheap Nalori blaster for a chunkier-looking pistol, which he affixed to his belt over his right hip. He grabbed a fragile-looking, finger-sized capsule filled with clear liquid, tucked it inside a metallic canister, pushed a lid onto the end of the canister, and then he put that inside his coat pocket.

He pressed his left index finger to his left temple while looking at the overhead. Then he turned away from the armory and said with precise enunciation, "Love and life are deep."

In just a handful of seconds, the room reverted to its previous state, and all trace of the high-tech weapons was gone. He faced Šmrhová. "All right, let's roll."

He led her out of the ship, and then he gestured for her to take the lead. "Ladies first."

She walked him out of the hangar, toward a turbolift. They stepped into a lift car and rode up to the shuttlebay. He shot her a look: "Runabouts have transporters, don't they?"

"Short range. For emergencies only. Why?"

"You should amend your strike plan. Once the runabouts land, you can use their transporters to deploy your teams quickly throughout the station. Might make it easier to surround Kinogar and his men without them getting the drop on your people in transit."

"I'll consider that. Just make sure you don't get in our way down there."

Exiting the lift, they walked together toward a row of parked runabouts. Okona struck a suddenly militant tone. "Let's get something straight, Lieutenant. I'm not part of your chain of command. I don't answer to you. I have my own mission, set by Starfleet Intelligence."

"That's true. Which is why there are now two security officers behind you." It took effort for Šmrhová not to grin as Okona realized that Peralta and Diaz were both at his back with phasers drawn. "Diaz, take his weapons. He's got a blade on the left, a blaster on the right, some kind of surprise in his right coat pocket." She waited until Okona was disarmed, and then she waved him toward the open hatchway of the runabout *Cumberland*.

"Climb aboard, and do us both a favor, Okona: don't do anything stupid."

He walked up the runabout's short ramp. "Define *stupid*."

"Don't risk your life. Don't endanger ours. Don't put the safety of the station or its personnel at risk, and don't get in our way. Think you can handle that?"

Okona flashed his trademark smirk. "You're a real lights-on kind of gal, aren't you?"

"Addendum," Šmrhová said. "For you? *Speaking* counts as doing something stupid."

27

It was a credit to Starfleet's Special Operators' training that more than twenty of its commandos were able to march single file down multiple flights of a narrow switchback emergency staircase deep inside Stonekettle Station's core hub without making a sound.

The commandos moved quickly in the dark, their rifles held close to their chests, muzzles angled downward and away from their feet. Each of them practiced what was known as "good trigger discipline"—their index fingers remained outside the trigger guard, flat against the rifle's body, to reduce the risk of accidental discharges and casualties. There was little risk of the commandos hitting one another, thanks to the "identify friend or foe"—IFF—circuits in both their weapons and their armored battlesuits, whose ablative plates could stop most stun-level blasts and reduce many lethal energy bursts to survivable wounds.

At the head of the line was Šmrhová, who relied on her helmet's holographic HUD to pierce the perfect darkness beneath her and render the stairwell in crisp detail, complete with its best approximation of the location's true colors. At her back was Okona, who had proved to be less of a liability than she had expected. Like the Spec-Ops commandos, he moved without a sound and seemed able to orient himself in the darkness despite not having been provided with a battlesuit. A few steps behind Okona were Peralta, Santiago, Diaz, and Boyle. The rest of the *Enterprise*'s Spec-Ops detachment snaked up the staircase behind them.

"Hold up," Okona said as Šmrhová reached the door for sublevel 42. "This is it."

She stopped next to the door. "Peralta, you're up. Diaz, move up, cover my six."

Diaz and Peralta stepped past Okona, who moved aside to let them pass. Peralta kneeled in front of the locked door, which led to the maintenance passages beneath the station's reactor control area, and started working on bypassing its lock. Diaz continued past him and Šmrhová, and she took up a covering position on the next flight of stairs below them, watching for any sign of attack from the station's bottom-most levels.

Peralta beat the door's lock in a matter of seconds, without a sound or an alarm. It slid open ahead of him, and he pressed a button on its control panel to hold it open. Then he made a swift and soundless scan of the area ahead with his suit's built-in tricorder-like sensors. His voice was low but clear over the team's shared comm channel. *"Clear."*

Šmrhová stole a look around the corner, down a long, empty passage of steel-grate floors, exposed pipes, and dangling cables. "Peralta: Any sign of the Nausicaans?"

"Not on this level." He pointed at the environment. *"But there's plenty in here to scramble the sensors. We might not read 'em until we run into 'em."*

From higher up the stairs, Okona asked in a stage whisper, "Can I help?"

Šmrhová glared up at him. "What?"

He looked put-upon. "My RIO has a lock on the Husnock weapon. Looks like the Nausicaans brought it with them."

That was the worst news Šmrhová had heard since they'd landed. "Why'd they do that?"

"No idea. But I can tell you that it's on the main reactor control level, range sixty-one point nine meters, bearing three-eight mark eight-seven."

Šmrhová still wasn't sure she could trust Okona, but she programmed those details as a target marker into her HUD's targeting system. "All right, everybody listen up. We're splitting into four teams of six and spreading out on this sublevel." She sent the weapon's position out on the data subchannel. "Squad leaders, program these coordinates for the Husnock weapon. The moment anyone has a confirmation on that reading, let me know." She backed away from the door and moved down a few stairs to stand beside Diaz. "Squad One, regroup on me. We'll guard the low road. Squads Two, Three, and Four, advance into the maintenance sublevel."

Overlapping responses of *"Copy that"* filled the comm channel.

The commandos moved with speed and quiet precision into the sublevel. Each team remembered its zone-clearance orders from Šmrhová's briefing topside, and there were no questions as each team deployed and took its own route into the industrial labyrinth beneath the station. A few moments after Squad Four was inside, a voice crackled over the comm.

"Strike Team Leader, this is Squad Two Actual. Confirming your coordinates for the Husnock weapon. Our range is nineteen point six meters. Over."

Before she could reply, another message cut through the static: *"Strike Team Actual, Squad Three Actual. Confirming target position. Range, seventeen point four meters. Over."*

"Well done, squad leaders. Secure the sublevel and converge on the target."

"Copy that," the squad leaders replied in quick succession.

Šmrhová turned to share the good news. "Nice work, Okona. We got a lead on—" She let her praise trail off as she discovered that he wasn't behind her. "Okona?" She made a fast head count. Her four handpicked commandos were all with her, but she found no sign of Okona.

He never passed me and Diaz, so he can't be beneath us.

She used her HUD to sweep the staircase above her with a scan for life signs. Okona, bereft of the protection offered by a battle-suit, should have shown up easily. But her HUD indicated that no life-forms had been detected.

Is it possible he slipped past us?

"Squad leaders, this is Strike Team Actual. Is Agent Okona with any of your units?"

One by one, her three team leaders replied with variations on the word *Negative*.

"All personnel, this is Strike Team Actual. If any of you have seen Okona in the last ninety seconds, sound off now. That's an order."

There was no reply to her demand except silence.

"Diaz, tell me you still have Okona's weapons."

"*Of course,*" she said, reaching toward her belt. "*They're right—*" Her hand landed on empty spaces. "*I mean, they should be right, um . . .*"

"Never mind." *This is the last thing I need.* She checked her suit's sensor log to determine when Okona vanished. *If that twit gets away, Worf will kill me himself.*

And I'll deserve it.

I didn't blame Šmrhová for taking my weapons. I hoped she didn't blame me for stealing them back. Lifting my gear from Diaz's utility belt had been easy. Not letting Peralta see me do it had been the tricky part.

Getting out of their clutches had been a simple matter of leveraged confusion. When Šmrhová started sending her people through the door, I kept politely stepping aside, around, and behind each of the advancing commandos. By the time Squad Four was on its way inside, I had retreated four flights upstairs without Šmrhová or her team any the wiser.

And that's where I went to work.

Moving quickly and with light footfalls, I crossed sublevel 38 with my experimental smart phaser set on heavy stun. A tap on my subaural transceiver produced a soft tone that only I could hear—a confirmation that even though the *Tain Hu* was still inside the

Enterprise's hangar, I had a clear signal to its quantum comm, and with it, an active link to Starfleet Intelligence.

"Expositor, this is Agonist. Do you copy?"

Wildman replied immediately. *"Right here, Agonist. You okay?"*

"I've been better." I checked the holographic tracking data provided by my retinal implant. It gave me wireframe schematics of the station around me, direction and range data to the Husnock weapon, and all the intel that it could siphon from the station's information network. "Can you tap the station's main computer? Get me more info?"

"I've got my hands full blocking your signal from the Starfleet commandos' battlesuits. By the way, that trick'll be blown the moment one of them shuts off their suit and restarts it."

"Then we've got no worries. You know these Starfleet types. They'd rather build a whole new suit from scratch than just restart one they already have."

"Do you have the route I sent?"

I updated my holographic overlays with a blink. A path through the station's maze of engineering spaces was delineated with bright red lines. "Got it. On the move."

My pistol led the way.

At the next corner I paused long enough to gather my nerve. Then I sprang around the turn, straight into a surprised guard from the station's security detail. I smacked him in the face with my pistol. That put him on his knees, burbling like a Pakled. Another swat across the back of his melon laid him out on the floor. I stepped over and around him.

"Expositor, can you get me any readings on the Nausicaans? I've got to be close."

"You are, but they're jamming sensors. No transport locks, no comms down there. You're lucky we're on a quantum frequency, or else you'd be flying blind right now."

"I'll count my blessings later. What's waiting for me in there?"

"Turn left and find out."

I took the left turn, down a short passage that ended at a window into a yawning space. As I neared the end of the path I crouched. The last couple of meters I waddled and then I crawled to the half wall. Then I lifted my head and looked over the waist-height partition, into the atrium-like compartment on the other side.

Clusters of engineers—some civilian, others Starfleet—were up against walls or pressed into shallow nooks, all held there at gunpoint by Nausicaans with disruptor rifles. I made a fast head count. There had to be over three dozen Nausicaans, and probably just as many hostages. This was going to be a bloodbath, I could feel it.

In the center of the room was a strange, cylindrical device plugged into a stripped-down node in the deck. I got the feeling that its inner workings weren't meant to be so exposed.

I whispered to my ever-watchful handler, "Expositor? You seeing this?"

"Copy that, Agonist. We've got a good look. Analyzing now."

"Well, analyze faster. Because I get the feeling this is about to go south."

"We're working as fast as we can," Wildman said, obviously annoyed at me.

Then I heard Lavelle's voice on the quantum comm. *"Agonist, are you in position to eliminate the Husnock weapon? Or neutralize the Nausicaan assets?"*

"Are you kidding me? I'm outnumbered forty to one here. Even with the fanciest phaser pistol ever made, I'm not starting a firefight with those odds."

Down below, one of the Nausicaans was arguing with La Forge, the Starfleet engineer in charge here. I tensed, fearing that I was about to see La Forge's head torn off and used for sport, but whatever he said to his Nausicaan captor, it made the ugly brute step away to think for a bit.

Wildman snapped me back into the moment. *"Agonist? Still there?"*

"Still here. Talk to me. Fast."

"We're digging through the station's schematics, and we've got an idea."

"Lay it on me."

"If you can get to sublevel forty-one," she said, *"you could access the main power buffer beneath the PMAR assembly. It's the machine beneath that cylinder right below you."*

"I see it. So I hack into that. Then what?"

"Then you sabotage the capacitor and trigger a major feedback pulse."

At that point, I was pretty sure that either Wildman or Lavelle was messing with me. I stole another look down at the core. "You guys do see the Husnock weapon tied into the station's primary power grid, right?"

Lavelle sounded surprised. *"See it? We're counting on it."*

"Want to run that by me *again*, Suzerain?"

Lavelle sighed. *"Look. We crunched the numbers. Ran a million sims. There's no way you can take out all those Nausicaans and reach the PMAR or the weapon alive."*

"What're you saying?"

"We need you to get to that power buffer and blow the station."

"You're serious?"

"It's the only way to be sure," Lavelle said.

A sick churn of acid in my gut nearly doubled me over. I wanted to retch at the very idea of slaughtering so many people in cold blood. "No. There's gotta be another way."

"We need you to do this. There's no time to argue."

It took every bit of restraint I had not to shout. "Dammit, *no*. There are sixty thousand people on this station! If I make that core go maximum flash, they all die. And if this stunt sets off the Husnock weapon, we might destroy the *Enterprise*, too."

"Trust us, Agonist," Lavelle said, *"that would be the least of our problems. If the Nausicaans fire that weapon using the PMAR's power*

and the station's array to focus it, they'll unleash a subspace pulse that'll shatter a planet. And right now, they're aiming at Earth."

Worf found it hard to believe that the scorched sliver of a dome, the huddle of structures beneath it, and the core tower to which the dome was connected were all that remained of Stonekettle Station. Where the rest of the facility had stood, there was now an uneven footprint of molten shapes, many of them married by the intense heat of the planet's star.

If not for La Forge and his team, there would be nothing left standing at all.

It had been several minutes since Worf had last seen a malfunction in the bridge's consoles. He hoped that everything would remain stable long enough to finish this operation without further complications.

Konya reacted to an update on the security console. "Sir? The Nausicaan vessel *Seovong* has been captured without fatalities."

"Good. Any prisoners?"

"Forty-one. Being held on-site until the crisis is over."

"Civilian casualties?"

"A few injuries during the shield failure, but nothing combat related. At least, not yet."

"Keep it that way." Worf stood from the command chair, impatient. He missed the scents of sweat and smoke, the adrenaline rush of charging into danger, the euphoria of victory.

Once, I would have been the one in the line of fire. Now I stand and wait.

Another signal broke through the ambient sounds of the bridge. Dygan muted the alert and looked back at Worf. "Sir, we're being hailed from the surface. It's the Nausicaan leader, Kinogar. He wants to speak with 'the one in charge.'"

"On-screen," Worf said.

The Nausicaan's face filled the viewscreen, rendering enormous his four-fanged double mandible. Even through the universal translator, his voice was loud and guttural. *"I am Kinogar, leader. Give your name, Klingon."*

Worf suspected Kinogar might react better to his Klingon identity. "I am Worf, son of Mogh, House of Martok, commander of the *Starship Enterprise*. State your demands."

"My raiders seize reactor core. Link mini core to Husnock weapon. Patch it into station's subspace transceiver." Kinogar reached off-screen and pulled La Forge into the frame at his side. *"Tell him what that means."*

"It means he can supercharge that weapon to a hundred times its normal output and fire a blast through subspace that can crack a planet in half."

Lieutenant Chen drifted forward, horrified. "Would that work?"

La Forge grimaced. *"Oh, yeah. Count on it."*

Kinogar pushed La Forge back out of view. *"One word and I break Earth. Break Vulcan. Break any world I say. Your ship locks weapons? Worlds die."*

All that Worf wanted in that moment was to sink a blade into Kinogar, but this was not a moment for the easily provoked. He took care to strip the aggression from his voice. "I hear your threats. I believe your words. Tell me your demands."

Chen sounded shocked. "Sir? We don't negotiate with—"

One glare from Worf ended Chen's protest.

He faced the viewscreen and waited for Kinogar's response. The most helpful thing Worf could do at that moment was keep Kinogar talking, to buy time for Šmrhová and her strike team to find some means of neutralizing Kinogar's offensive options.

Another Nausicaan handed Kinogar a padd, at which he glanced repeatedly while he spoke. *"On behalf of all surviving Nausicaans, I demand Federation apologize. Admit it caused the great Borg Invasion. Admit that Nausicaa died because of Starfleet arrogance."*

Worf nodded once. "Continue."

"Survivors of Nausicaa demand reparations. Compensation for all we lost."

Curious to hear this demand reduced to a number, Worf asked, "In what amount?"

"Ninety-eight trillion, four hundred sixty-one billion bars of gold-pressed latinum."

Worf signaled Konya with a subtle gesture to mute the channel. "Mister Konya? How much latinum has ever been refined and pressed in all of known space?"

A shrug. "Nowhere near ninety-eight trillion bars, I can tell you that."

He motioned for Konya to reopen the channel. He told Kinogar, "Continue."

"Nausicaa demands Federation install terraforming technology. A hundred atmosphere reactors. A thousand water-cleaning plants. Radiation scrubbers. Wildlife regeneration."

From the helm, Faur muttered to Dygan, "It'd be cheaper to set off a Genesis device."

"Federation drop all criminal charges against me, my people. Guarantee immunity for all actions we took to save Nausicaa."

Konya was incredulous. "Is he for real? What's next? Rig a beauty pageant for him?"

"And we keep PMAR," Kinogar added, *"plus Husnock gun. Need them to keep Nausicaa safe. No invaders. No reprisals. Or we break worlds."*

Worf understood his officers' reactions. Kinogar's demands were outlandish.

I suspect they mean for this ultimatum to justify a deadly end they think is inevitable.

He limited his reaction to another single nod. "I will relay your demands to the Federation government. Stand by to receive our counteroffer. *Enterprise* out."

Dygan closed the channel, and the main viewscreen reverted to the image of Stonekettle Station's heat-blasted remains and its lone slice of survivors, like a compass with its needle forever pointing due north. Worf stepped forward to stand behind the Cardassian officer's shoulder. "Mister Dygan, please send a transcript of Kinogar's demands to Starfleet Command, the Federation Council, and the Federation's secretary of the exterior."

"Aye, sir." Dygan prepped the message with his trademark speed and precision. "Sent."

As Worf walked back to the command chair, he was intercepted by Chen. "Sir? Why even relay his demands?"

"If he monitors comms, he will know if we contact Earth. If we do not, he will know we are lying. That could provoke him into using the Husnock weapon. We cannot take that chance."

"But why send his actual demands to the secretary of the exterior?"

"Because he and his people deserve to be heard."

Chen's face scrunched with frustration and confusion. "But— he's *insane*."

"No . . . he is desperate." Worf sighed. "There is a difference."

28

—•—

"Into the Jefferies tube," Wildman prompted me via my implanted quantum comm transceiver.

The crawlspace was narrow, nowhere near the generous width of a Starfleet-standard maintenance passage, and it was filled with components that were insulated poorly or not at all. Sparks leaped from cross-wired junction boxes, and dancing forks of electricity that looked like spiders made of lightning crept along the sides of the tube.

"Expositor, please tell me there's another way in."

"Sure. Want to fight a few dozen Starfleet commandos and a few dozen Nausicaans? 'Cause if you can do all that before *the Nausicaans blow the Earth to smithereens—"*

"I'm proceeding into the Jefferies tube."

Glowing motes of hot plasma set my hair to smoldering as I shimmied on my belly through the crawlspace. As I neared the arachnid-like clusters of lightning, the hairs on my forearms stood to attention—and then forks of white energy struck me in rapid succession, like serpents with fangs of flame. I swallowed my curses and kept going, pulling myself with my bare palms and pushing with my booted feet.

I came to a four-way junction. Surrounding it was a larger box-like space. I crawled inside it and reveled in the chance to draw a full breath. "Expositor? Which way now?"

"Down."

I was pretty sure I must have heard her wrong. "Repeat your last, Expositor?"

"Your next direction is down. Enter code four-tango-six-one-red on the octagonal keypad next to the hatch by your feet."

"Copy that. Entering the code now." As I typed the last command, a panel I had mistaken for a solid plate retracted to reveal a dark, vertical shaft less than a meter wide—and then a gust of dry, hot air hit me in the face. My eyes watered, and I winced as I turned away in search of cooler air to breathe.

Wildman's voice echoed inside my head. *"Agonist? Is the hatchway open?"*

"Affirmative. But there's no ladder. No rungs, no handholds, nothing."

This time, my complaint was answered by Lavelle. *"Put your palms flat against one side, your boot soles flat against the opposite side. Use outward pressure to control your descent."*

"Easy for you to say. Your palms aren't sweating a liter per minute."

I sat down with my legs over the edge, into the drop. Then I wiped my hands dry on my shirt, lowered myself into the shaft, braced my feet against the far side, and pushed my hands against the other side behind me. Tucked in a semi-fetal position, I tried to shimmy downward.

I slid nearly four meters before I halted myself, my hands and boot soles squeaking loudly against the smooth metal. Motionless in the middle of the shaft, I waited—mostly to see if anyone had heard me through a bulkhead and decided to shoot me full of holes.

No one perforated me with disruptor blasts or phaser beams, so I kept going.

I stood as I reached the bottom, and I relaxed—but I still couldn't draw a decent breath, since I was being roasted slowly in the galaxy's worst convection oven.

"Expositor, I'm at bottom. What's next?"

"Cut through the bottom panel. You should drop into the maintenance bay directly beneath the PMAR's chassis."

"What if someone's in there? Won't they see me cutting through?"

"Don't sweat it. All our taps on station security show that compart-ment's clear."

I drew my sidearm and set it to simulate a high-power, narrow-beam plasma torch. *"Don't sweat it?* Is that what you said? You trying to be funny?"

"Why should you get to make all the jokes?"

"Because I'm the one out here risking my ass."

I set my feet against opposite sides of the shaft, and then I cut open a square in the panel beneath me—one just large enough for me to fit through, but leaving a narrow lip to stand on. I once cut through a panel like this by slicing a circle around my feet, and found out the hard way that there was a twenty-meter drop beneath me. I wasn't making that mistake again.

The fresh-cut panel fell three meters before it landed with a dull *thunk* on a bare floor. I crouched, braced my hands on the broad lip inside the shaft, and lowered myself into the octagonal com-partment below.

As promised, it was empty of personnel. It had two doors on opposite sides. The floor was bare, but the walls were packed with the kind of tech one normally found in the power plants of major cities or Federation spacedocks. The ceiling, likewise, was lined with bundles of high-capacity solid cable, super-dense capacitors, power transformers, and loads of other gear that I couldn't begin to identify. All of it was aglow with an eerie green radiance, and just being inside that sealed room made me feel like weird cosmic energies were coursing through me—and not in a good "awak-ening secret powers" way, but in a bad "I have a new incurable mutation" way.

But at least the air was cool enough to breathe without caramel-izing my lung tissue.

"All right, Expositor, I'm in. What's next?"

"Find the toggle for the main capacitor and flip it to its open *position."*

I turned in circles, overwhelmed by symbols—and tried not to think about the fact that I was about to blast myself, hundreds of Starfleet personnel, and thousands of civilians into vapor. Then I saw the main capacitor. I walked over to it. Put my hand on it. And I froze.

"Suzerain? Do we really need to do this?"

Lavelle was pissed. *"Do you want to wait for the Nausicaans to blow a planet in half and kill billions, and then ask me that again? Or should we fix this mess before it goes any further?"*

"Have the Nausicaans made any demands?"

"Of course they have. But they're all insane. *These aren't the kind of thugs you can reason with, Agonist. This is the kind of threat you neutralize. With prejudice."*

"Maybe we can make this a time-delay kind of thing. Give them a countdown. A chance to evacuate the station—"

"Or a chance to fire the weapon? No, thanks, Agonist. Last I heard, they have it aimed at Earth. And guess what? Expositor and I are on Earth. Along with twelve billion other people." Lavelle took a breath to calm himself. *"Listen, I get what you're saying. This is hard, and I'm sorry. But it needs to be done. This is the mission. To work, it needs to be a surprise—and it has to be preemptive, or else billions of innocent people die. I know that's cold, but that's the way it is. Sometimes our job comes down to a numbers game. Now, can you do this or not?"*

I felt sick to my stomach. Ending my life didn't trouble me. There were plenty of times I'd thought about doing it, just for my own peace of mind. But taking so many other souls with me, some of them allies . . . the guilt was too much. So many possibilities snuffed out, so many stories robbed of their endings, all because of me. But then I forced myself to see things from Lavelle's side. Entire worlds in the Nausicaans' cross hairs. Tens of billions of lives at stake. How much worse would I feel if I let them die because I was too paralyzed by my conscience to act when I had the chance? Either way, innocents would perish. It was all a matter of degree.

I put my hands on the capacitor toggle and closed my eyes. Tears rolled down my face. "May the Great Bird forgive me."

I tensed to pull down—

—and then powerful hands tore mine from the toggle.

A boot kicked me behind my knee, and I fell on my face.

Someone pressed a weapon's muzzle to the nape of my neck.

Out of the corner of my eye I saw a Vulcan man kneeling on my back, trapping me on the floor—and beside him was Lieutenant Šmrhová, with her phaser rifle at my head.

"Okona," she said, "you're under arrest."

I sobbed with relief into my sleeve. "Thank the Great Bird."

"Hail him," Worf said from the command chair.

The bridge crew of the *Enterprise* tended their stations and stole looks in Worf's direction, all of them clearly wondering what he was doing. They all knew there had been no response yet from the Federation government or Starfleet Command. So why would he want to talk with the Nausicaans' lead rabble-rouser?

Worf folded his hands in his lap. *Why, indeed.*

It took a moment before Konya looked up from the tactical console. "I have him, sir."

"On-screen."

Once more the main viewscreen was filled by an imposing close-up of Kinogar. Behind his voice was the steady grumbling of his cohort. *"Starfleet! Will your council give us our due?"*

"They have yet to respond."

Overcome with rage, Kinogar shouted, launching flecks of spittle from his fangs. *"Then why hail me? You need proof our weapon works?"*

"We do not. But I *do* wish to speak with you."

Now the Nausicaan squinted at Worf, as if confused. *"Done talking."*

"But I am still listening. And I think you have more to say."

Kinogar waved off the very notion. *"What good are words now?"*

"That depends on the words." He took a moment to think. "Before either of us does something we cannot undo, tell me this:

What did you want to achieve when you started this? What did you hope to accomplish?"

His question angered Kinogar. *"Stalling! Told you our demands!"*

"I did not ask for your demands. I ask for the truth. What is your true goal?"

Kinogar's bafflement was followed by surprise, and then by poignant understanding. Now when he spoke, he no longer shouted. *"Wanted justice. For my people. Wanted . . . hope."*

Worf stood, and then he nodded slowly. "I understand. Some of my people do not. In your words, tell my people why you blame the Federation."

All of Kinogar's fellow Nausicaans fell silent.

Kinogar drew a breath, and then he stood tall, his chin raised with pride. *"Nausicaa was a free world. Provided for itself."* He looked back at his bedraggled comrades. *"Then Starfleet made enemies of the Borg. Provoked them. Brought the great invasion."*

Behind Kinogar, some of his people nodded in affirmation. Others bowed their heads in sorrow. He acknowledged them, and then he continued. *"When Borg came to Nausicaa, no one helped us. No Starfleet. No Klingons. No one. Left us all to die.*

"But some of us lived. Came back to a home laid waste. Found our people murdered. Our skies on fire, our seas turned to poison." Words caught in Kinogar's throat, stuck on barbs of long-swallowed rage, and a bitter fury blazed in his eyes. *"Waited for help that never came. Asked for help and were ignored. Watched your worlds rebuild. Saw your people heal. But no one came to save us. My family? My people? My world? Federation forgot about us."*

Worf stood in front of the forward duty stations and looked back at his bridge officers. On every face he saw the dawning of understanding, coupled with the burden of guilt and shame.

Just as I felt. As we all should feel.

He faced Kinogar. "Your anger has merit, Kinogar. What you say is true, and it is long past time that my people were made to hear it."

"And what if they do?"

"I do not know. But as one warrior to another, I will not make promises that I know cannot be kept. Your mission to restore Nausicaa . . . will not succeed. The damage is too great, and the resources to fix it do not exist. I am sorry, but your planet is lost."

The news landed on Kinogar like a crushing blow. He dropped out of frame for a moment, and when the vid sensor found him again, he was sitting on the floor in the reactor control room, surrounded by his shattered friends and kinsmen. *"If all is lost—"*

"Not all," Worf cut in. "If you would put your trust in me, I give you my word I will do all I can to offer you and your people a path to a better future."

Kinogar seemed to be considering Worf's offer—and then he sprang to his feet, freshly infuriated. *"A trick! Trying to lower our defenses! We put down weapons, then you strike!"*

"No. I have ordered our people to fall back. There will be no ambush, Kinogar."

The Nausicaan reached toward the firing control for the Husnock weapon, which Konya had warned was locked onto Earth. One shot, and billions of lives would be snuffed out within seconds, victims of an attack fired through subspace, originating here but manifesting almost instantaneously above Earth. Kinogar's hand hovered above the trigger pad.

"Want what we came for! Reparations! Apologies! Our home restored! No more lies!"

"I have not lied to you, Kinogar. Nausicaa *cannot* be saved. Your people *can.*"

Kinogar's hand trembled above the firing controls. *"Why would you help us?"*

"Because I am not just a Starfleet officer. I am also a Klingon warrior, and a member of the House of Martok. The Federation's neglect of your people *dishonors* our government, and all those who serve it. To regain our honor, I *must* see this injustice corrected." Seeing the glimmer of possibility in Kinogar's expression, Worf added, "Before you act—will you let me try?"

The Nausicaan leader searched the faces of his own people, but in the end he found himself just as alone in the moment of decision as Worf.

"After all I have said, all I have done, it is hard for me to . . . compromise." Slowly, he pulled his hand away from the firing controls. *"But as one warrior to another—I am listening."*

29

———

As the spectators in the courtroom settled, Picard wished that he could quiet the nervous tides of acid sloshing in his stomach, or quell the sick pangs of anxiety snaking through his guts. He couldn't remember the last time he'd had to wear his dress uniform this many days in a row. Worst of all, he couldn't stop imagining what trail of past indignities Louvois intended to drag him down today. The notion of stepping once more into the witness box filled him with dread.

At the front of the room, Admiral Liu took her place and rang the ceremonial bell. "Attention, this hearing is now in session." She picked up her padd. Squinted at it. Set it down. "Madam Attorney General, I have what appears to be a message from you, received in the small hours of this morning, Pacific Time. Is this communiqué authentic?"

"It is, Admiral." Louvois turned a quick look at Picard, and then she continued to Liu, "At this time, the government counsel rests its case."

Picard masked his profound sense of relief. He closed his eyes and slowed his deep intake of breath, and then even more slowly let it out through his nose, shedding days of pent-up stress.

Liu looked at Ezor. "Is the defense prepared to present its case?"

"We are, Admiral."

"Please begin, Mister Ezor."

"Thank you, Admiral." He picked up his padd. "At this time, the defense would like to submit a newly acquired piece of evidence, a recording that—"

"Objection," Louvois cut in. "We've been given no notice of new evidence."

"As I said," Ezor continued, "we obtained this only last night. Notice was filed with government counsel through proper channels this morning"—he shot a cold smile at Louvois—"but perhaps it hasn't been processed yet."

"Regardless," Louvois continued, "we've had no opportunity to vet this evidence or verify its provenance."

Ezor remained insistent. "Government counsel will have ample opportunity to review this evidence and vet its source. However, Admiral, once you hear it, I believe you'll agree that its exculpatory value far outweighs the inconvenience it presents to government counsel."

Liu put her index finger to her lips while she considered their arguments. "Madam Attorney General, you will be afforded an opportunity to have experts review, and if necessary rebut, the evidence to be presented, but for now I'm going to let the defense proceed. Overruled."

Ezor nodded at Liu. "Thank you, Admiral." He picked up his padd and keyed in a few commands. Picard watched the lawyer work and wondered what was going on.

I wasn't informed of any new evidence. What is he playing at?

The lights in the courtroom dimmed, and an overhead holoprojector activated with a barely audible hum. Ezor gestured toward a blank pillar of blue holographic light in the middle of the room, between Liu's dais and the two tables for the opposing counsels.

"Admiral, what I'm about to present is a holovid recording from the archives of Section Thirty-One. It is one of many thousands of such recordings made by the organization's agents and directors. This one was produced by Section Thirty-One director L'Haan of Vulcan. It documents a conversation that took place on November sixteenth, 2379, between herself and Admiral William Ross, who at that time was still an active senior flag officer of Starfleet, and by his own confession, a co-conspirator with Section Thirty-One."

Ezor tapped his padd, and soft alert tones chimed on Liu's and

Louvois's devices. "I have just submitted to you and to government counsel a letter from Starfleet Intelligence that verifies the authenticity of this recording, as well as documenting its provenance and chain of custody while in their possession. Admiral, with your permission, I'd like to play the recording now."

"Proceed."

With a single tap on his padd, Ezor played the holovid. Ghostly figures appeared inside the blue light, which widened into a broad cone. On one side was the image of Admiral Ross. A broad-shouldered and burly man, he somehow looked small and cowed by L'Haan. Though she was slender of build, she was tall for a Vulcan woman, and her presence was intimidating.

Their recorded voices echoed inside the courtroom.

"It all seems to have gone according to plan," Ross said.

L'Haan wore a dubious frown. *"It was sloppy. And done in haste."*

"At least Zife is gone—along with his accomplices."

The Vulcan woman paced and looked away, as if staring out of a window. *"Control is concerned about Picard and Lagan. They know too much."*

Ross tensed. *"They know nothing."*

"Picard led the investigation. Lagan led the coup. Do either of them know that we killed Zife and his lackeys?"

The admiral shook his head. *"I told them nothing but what they wanted to hear. They think Zife and his men are heading off to comfy retirements in exile."*

"Are you sure? We can't have luminaries like Picard or Lagan asking questions."

"I give you my word: Neither of them knows anything."

"See that it stays that way."

The recording ended there. Both figures faded away, and then the room's lights came up.

From his seat, Picard saw that Louvois looked utterly shocked. Her mouth hung slightly agape, and her eyes seemed frozen open. When Picard glanced at Admiral Liu, he found her wearing the same stunned expression. Then he realized he must look exactly the same.

The only person in the room looking confident was Ezor.

"As you saw and heard, Admiral, two of the chief players in the conspiracy confirmed that not only did Captain Picard have no prior knowledge of their intent to kill President Zife, they made it an imperative to conceal such knowledge from him after the fact. Furthermore, L'Haan herself states that it was Lagan—meaning Ambassador Lagan Serra—who 'led the coup.' Not Captain Picard."

His declaration was met by gobsmacked silence.

Liu recovered a small measure of her composure and made a note on her padd. "The recording is accepted as Defense Exhibit Twenty-Nine."

"Thank you, Admiral. Now, with your permission, I'd like to call my first witness."

On the outside, Jonathan Ezor projected pure confidence, but everything beneath his façade was pure terror—because even as he called the name of his first and only witness, he had no idea whether she would actually appear when the doors opened.

Everyone turned toward the room's main entrance, curious to see whether Ezor was serious or just pulling some kind of outlandish stunt. Gasps and murmurs spread like a virus as the witness entered the room, and then a terrified silence settled over one and all.

Flanked by armed guards and restrained with magnetic manacles, L'Haan of Vulcan strode down the center aisle, through the gallery gate, and into the witness box. Her every movement and glance conveyed menace and danger, in spite of her bonds.

Liu's bailiff approached L'Haan. "Please raise your right hand."

L'Haan glanced at her manacles, and then she fixed the bailiff with a cold stare.

The bailiff continued, "Do you swear by the Precepts of Logic to offer truthful testimony, forgoing obfuscation, omission, or fabrication?"

"I do," L'Haan said.

The bailiff stepped away, and Ezor approached the witness box. "L'Haan. A few moments ago, I played for this court a recording from the Section Thirty-One archives, of a conversation that transpired on November sixteenth, 2379, between yourself and Admiral William Ross. Are you familiar with the recording in question?"

"I am."

"Is it an accurate document of that conversation, as you remember it?"

"It is."

Ezor took a breath and steadied his voice. "Please tell us what you, personally, and, to the best of your knowledge, Section Thirty-One, generally, knew about President Zife's crimes and cover-ups on the planet Tezwa in 2379."

He expected Louvois to object, but when he looked toward her table, she still appeared to be overwhelmed. He turned back toward L'Haan as she answered his question.

"In 2374, Federation president Min Zife, his senior political advisor Koll Azernal of Zakdorn, and his secretary of military intelligence, Nelino Quafina, believed that the Federation was losing its war against the Dominion. They created a fallback strategy by arming the planet Tezwa—a neutral world on the Federation's border of the Klingon Empire—with six surface-based nadion-pulse cannons.

"Technically, arming Tezwa was a violation of the Khitomer Accords, but because the Klingon Empire had severed its alliance with the Federation while secretly under Dominion influence, Zife and others in the Federation government felt the accords no longer applied.

"The following year, when the Klingons restored their alliance with the Federation, the accords once again became legally binding. The Tezwa fallback plan was eventually forgotten—as were the nadion-pulse cannons.

"In 2379, a dictator named Kinchawn seized power on Tezwa. He antagonized the Klingons by attacking their border colonies. The Klingons sent an attack force to retaliate. Kinchawn destroyed it in orbit of Tezwa, using the nadion-pulse cannons.

"At that time, President Zife, Koll Azernal, and Nelino Quafina initiated their attempted cover-up of their role in the arming of Tezwa and the slaughter of six thousand Klingon warriors. They started by sending the crew of the *Starship Enterprise* alone into combat to destroy the cannons, in order to prevent them from being analyzed by others. In other words, they illegally ordered Starfleet personnel to destroy incriminating evidence.

"Second, President Zife issued a direct order for Captain Picard to 'conquer' Tezwa and therefore make it into a Federation possession, as a means of forestalling a full Klingon invasion. This conquest of a foreign world, despite its previous act of aggression against an ally, constituted an act of war on the part of the Federation—a decision that requires a formal act of the Federation Council in order to be legal. President Zife ordered an illegal war of aggression.

"Once Starfleet personnel were in place on Tezwa and controlled the shipping lanes in all sectors surrounding it, Zife's advisor Azernal continued to orchestrate the removal and destruction of evidence, while Secretary Quafina met with and engaged the services of members of the Orion Syndicate, as part of a plot to frame the Tholian Assembly for arming Tezwa. In this manner, Zife and his accomplices sought to obstruct justice.

"As a direct consequence of these many crimes, more than a million Tezwan civilians, six thousand Klingon military personnel, and four thousand Starfleet personnel were killed. Because their deaths can be linked directly to felony-level offenses, Zife and his accomplices were legally culpable for more than a million counts of felony murder. And by engaging in a conspiracy against the United Federation of Planets, they also were guilty of sedition."

Ezor waited until he was sure L'Haan was finished, and then he proceeded to his next question. "To the best of your knowledge, what role did Captain Picard play in this crisis?"

"At first, he and his crew were unwitting tools of Zife's scheme. Later, as his officers began to uncover evidence of criminal conspiracies, Captain Picard authorized his people to pursue their investigations. When they connected patterns of behavior, data from sensor logs, and physical evidence into a cohesive case against Zife and his conspirators, Captain Picard presented their findings to the ranking member of the Federation civilian government on Tezwa, Ambassador Lagan Serra, and sought her counsel. Based on Section Thirty-One's surveillance of Lagan's office and residence, I know that Ambassador Lagan asked Captain Picard to join her in bringing the matter to the attention of his superiors at Starfleet Command, so that he could verify his investigative findings to the admiralty."

"Did Section Thirty-One record the conference discussion involving Ambassador Lagan, Captain Picard, and Admirals Ross, Nakamura, Nechayev, Jellico, and Paris?"

"No. They took sufficient precautions that we were unable to intercept or record it without being detected. I did, however, eavesdrop personally on the conversation, by hiding myself near Ambassador Lagan's office."

"How well do you recall the details of that conversation?"

"I recall it perfectly."

"How did Captain Picard approach that discussion?"

L'Haan considered the question. "He was circumspect, especially at the start. He let Ambassador Lagan set the agenda, and restricted his role to providing evidence at her behest."

"Did Captain Picard, at any time, advocate for any specific response to Zife's crimes?"

"Not as such. He made clear that he, personally, felt that Zife was no longer fit to hold elected office. And that he felt his superiors should not let Zife's crimes go unpunished."

"Did Captain Picard recommend any specific form of punishment?"

"No."

"When the admirals elected to confront Zife directly, how did Captain Picard react?"

"He voiced strong objections," L'Haan said. "He questioned their motives. Forced them to curtail their more extreme inclinations. But even after they mitigated their response, he made it clear that he found their decision . . . less than noble. He called it 'one of the darkest days in the history of the Federation.'" She aimed a chilling look directly at Picard. "Had they not ordered him to secrecy, I suspect he might have turned them all in long ago."

"Objection," Louvois said. "Supposition."

Liu nodded. "Sustained."

Ezor let the verbal stumble pass. "In the recording of your conversation with Admiral Ross, his statements implied that he alone of all the participants in this confrontation was aware that Section Thirty-One intended to assassinate Zife and his advisors. Was that in fact the case?"

"It was, yes."

"And Captain Picard had no knowledge of this, either before or after the fact?"

"No, he did not. He was not present when we took custody of President Zife."

Ezor faced Liu. "No more questions at this time, Admiral."

He returned to his chair at the defense table, while Louvois stood and walked over to the witness box to confront L'Haan.

"Regarding the group conversation you say you monitored: Was it or was it not convened specifically to plot the violent removal of President Zife from his legally elected office?"

"It was not."

"Was the use of violence discussed?"

"Only in the sense that none of those involved wanted it to come to that."

"But none of them were opposed to it, were they?"

"Several were. Including Admiral Jellico, Captain Picard, and Admiral Paris."

"But they came around in the end, didn't they?"

"I cannot speak as to what each party in the discussion thought. I know that Captain Picard did not express support for the use of force."

"But he was the one who set the conspiracy in motion, wasn't he?"

"No. As I said previously, the decision to consult the admiralty was made by Ambassador Lagan. Captain Picard participated in the conversation at her request, to present evidence."

"Are you saying that Captain Picard played no active role in the meeting's outcome?"

"I can tell you only what I heard. He presented evidence to his superior officers. When asked, he expressed his opinion regarding Zife's fitness for office. And when the admirals seemed to set themselves on a legally precarious course, he voiced concern and urged caution."

"Did Captain Picard make any actionable recommendations or decisions?"

"No. Every decision concerning a specific response was offered or approved by one of the flag officers involved in the conversation."

"But by the end of the discussion, was Captain Picard aware that his superior officers intended to remove President Zife by force?"

"Objection," Ezor said. "The witness cannot testify as to what my client was *aware of*."

"Sustained."

"I'll rephrase," Louvois said. "By the end of the discussion, had Captain Picard heard the admirals make statements that might be construed by a reasonable person to mean that they intended to force President Zife from office?"

"It is possible Captain Picard might have inferred that from Admiral Ross's insistence that bluffing would not be an option if they intended to persuade Zife to resign."

Louvois seemed very pleased with that answer. "If so, wouldn't Captain Picard have had an obligation to warn President Zife about his impending meeting with a group of senior military personnel who intended him harm?"

"He was under orders to treat the matter as classified, and to defer to their judgment."

"But if their intention was sedition, a criminal act, then ordering Captain Picard to ignore it would be an inherently illegal order under the SCMJ, and therefore invalid."

"Objection," Ezor said, standing this time. "It would not have been immediately apparent to Captain Picard at that time whether that order was illegal and therefore invalid. If, as he has testified, he believed in good faith that his superiors were going to make a lawful effort to address the crimes of their commander-in-chief, for the good of the Federation, then he would have had no reason to suspect that any sort of criminal action on their part was imminent. Ergo, in the absence of evidence to the contrary, he would have to have considered their order to be both legal and valid."

"Sustained."

Ezor sat down and tried not to look smug when he noticed Louvois was fuming.

She geared up for one more verbal sally at L'Haan.

"If, as the defense claims, Captain Picard believed his superiors were acting in good faith, how do you explain the fact that all five admirals violated their own chain of command by confronting President Zife directly, rather than escalating the matter to their own civilian superior, the secretary of defense?"

"Objection," Ezor said, back on his feet. "Captain Picard had no idea with whom his superiors intended to confer, nor was he present at the meeting in the Palais de la Concorde, as he already stated during government counsel's direct examination. Further-

more, this hearing is intended to examine the actions and statements of Captain Picard, not those of his superiors."

"Sustained."

Louvois shook her head in disgust. "Nothing further," she
grumbled on the way back to her table, trailed every step of the
way by a figurative black cloud of contempt.

"The witness can step down," Liu said.

Picard was still reeling from the rapidity of L'Haan's cross-
examination when Admiral Liu asked, "Mister Ezor, do you have
any other witnesses or exhibits to present?"

"No, Admiral. The defense rests."

Alarmed, Picard grasped Ezor's coat sleeve. Under his breath he
said, "Are you sure?"

Ezor gestured for Picard to remain calm. "It's okay. Trust me."

On the dais, Liu reviewed the information on her padd. "Are
both counsels ready to move to closing statements? Madam Attorney General?"

"Ready, Admiral."

"Mister Ezor?"

"Ready, Admiral."

"All right, then. Madam Attorney General, the floor is yours."

Louvois stood, took a deep breath, and stepped out from behind
her table. "Admiral, the facts of this case are very clear. Regardless
of what motivated Captain Picard's actions, he was a key player in a
sequence of events that led to a military conspiracy to forcibly end
the presidency of Min Zife, the lawfully elected head of the Federation civilian government. Captain Picard presented evidence of
Zife's crimes to his superiors, and voiced clearly his opinion that
President Zife was no longer fit to hold that office—a statement
confirmed by Captain Picard himself.

"He was no mere spectator. No accidental bystander. He was
an active participant in the discussion that set the conspiracy into

motion. It's not reasonable to think that he could have heard the discourse of his superiors and not realized what they were going to do. Which means that he either gave their coup his tacit approval, or else he willfully turned a blind eye to the ouster and murder of a sitting Federation president.

"But even if we accept that he was unaware of the admirals' intentions toward President Zife, even if he never suspected for a moment that they meant to have him killed, he was and remains an accessory before the fact to their conspiracy to commit murder and sedition. And because that murder, to which Captain Picard is inextricably connected, was carried out by Section Thirty-One, a non-state terror group engaged in acts of espionage against the United Federation of Planets, Captain Picard made himself their agent, by presenting to his superiors evidence that Section Thirty-One had carefully arranged for him to find, so that he could trigger the sequence of events that would culminate in their endgame: the illegal removal and subsequent assassination of President Min Zife, and his succession by Nanietta Bacco, who, as it happens, abetted their cover-up more than a year later."

Louvois finished her closing argument while staring directly at Picard. "Captain Picard is an asset of a hostile intelligence agency, a witting accomplice to sedition, and an unapologetic accessory to felony murder. He does not deserve to wear that uniform, nor to breathe air as a free man. And when you review the preponderance of evidence before you, Admiral, I think you will agree that there is more than sufficient cause for Captain Picard to face a general court-martial." She nodded at Liu. "Thank you, Admiral."

As the attorney general returned to her table, Liu nodded at Ezor. "Mister Ezor?"

He stood and smoothed the front of his suit jacket. "Thank you, Admiral." He collected his thoughts as he stepped out from behind his table and took a few steps toward the dais.

"It has been the contention of the government's counsel that Captain Picard took part in an illegal exercise of force against a sitting Federation president. Yet, by the government's own admission, Captain Picard was not present when that crime occurred.

"The government would have us believe that Captain Picard is culpable for the actions of his superiors with regard to the resignation of President Min Zife, merely because those actions occurred subsequent to a conversation in which he presented them with evidence of serious crimes committed by the president, and during which he expressed his personal opinion that President Zife was no longer fit for office.

"From a legal standpoint, Admiral, this argument is invalid.

"First and foremost, in the SCMJ it is black-letter law that no active member of Starfleet can be held legally accountable for the actions of their superiors. This is a fundamental precept of military hierarchy. An officer is always held accountable for the actions of those personnel under their command, but the reverse is never true.

"Evidence presented by both this defense and by government counsel indicated that Captain Picard's role in the conference of the five admirals was limited to the presentation of evidence collected by his officers and crew during the course of their legally required investigation, and to the expression of a single statement of personal opinion. Under the terms of the SCMJ, Captain Picard is accountable only for his own actions up to that moment. He bears no legal responsibility for any action taken by his superiors from that moment forward.

"If one were to argue differently, that Captain Picard was responsible for events that transpired after his involvement was concluded, then we would, by logical inference, have to indict every one of the officers and enlisted personnel who participated in the investigation on Tezwa. After all, did not their actions contribute to the tide of events that led to the admirals' coup? If so, why are they not also charged? If not, then why accuse Captain Picard?

"Concerning the government's assertion that Captain Picard should be considered an asset of the now defunct entity formerly known as Section Thirty-One, we saw and heard evidence, corroborated by a former Section Thirty-One director, that the organization took steps to ensure that Captain Picard was *not* involved, specifically because it feared his attention. That alone should be sufficient to dismiss the charge of espionage.

"As to the government's proposition that Captain Picard should have handled the entire affair in a different manner, in some fashion that they imagine might have been more legally palatable, I would argue that, under the circumstances extant at that time, Captain Picard had *no choice* but to proceed *exactly* as he did.

"Once Captain Picard was made aware of the evidence amassed by his officers indicating the commission of serious felonies and abrogation of a treaty by President Zife, Koll Azernal, and Nelino Quafina, he was *required* by Starfleet regulations to report those crimes. Under the terms of the SCMJ, he had the option of submitting his report directly to his superiors without civilian involvement, or to file his evidence with the ranking member of the civilian government to which he had the most immediate access—in this case, Ambassador Lagan Serra, the Federation's ranking diplomatic official on Tezwa.

"That is exactly what Captain Picard did, in full compliance with regulations.

"He could not, as one might suppose, have taken his evidence to the civilian media. To do so would have been a clear violation of the SCMJ, and it would have meant arrogating unto himself the right to decide Federation media policy, foreign policy, and criminal-justice policy.

"He could not have skipped over Ambassador Lagan and the admirals to address his concerns directly with the Federation Council. To do so would have been insubordinate, and once again a violation of the SCMJ. And because Captain Picard could not have been certain whether other members of the civilian government were involved in Zife's crimes, he would have been unwise to expose them without knowing in whom he should confide.

"By the same logic, he could not have taken his concerns directly to President Zife. Not only would that have been insubordinate, it would have afforded Zife and his conspirators an opportunity to cover up their crimes even more effectively than they did.

"No, Captain Picard had only one path forward after he learned of Zife's crimes. And he followed those protocols to the letter.

"Many pundits commenting on this and related cases have expressed dismay over the admirals' decision to confront Zife in secret. That criticism has merit. Perhaps the five admirals *should* have escalated their concerns to Starfleet's chief admiral, and then let him take the matter to the secretary of defense, for consideration by the cabinet, and then to the Council, for private deliberation by the Security Committee. But those errors in judgment were not made by Captain Picard. They were made by his *superiors*—and he cannot be held accountable for that."

Ezor shifted his pose so that Liu could see his face as well as Captain Picard's. "In the final equation, Admiral, not a single argument, and not a single exhibit presented as evidence in this case, proves any wrongdoing by Captain Picard. None of his actions *before* the conference with the five admirals violated the SCMJ, and none of his actions or statements *during* that meeting violated the SCMJ. Lastly, and most importantly, under the terms of the SCMJ, he bears no legal responsibility for the actions of his superior officers subsequent to that conference.

"In short, Admiral, it is the contention of this defense that the government has failed to present sufficient evidence, testimony, or legal precedent to support *any* of the charges filed against Captain Picard—and on those grounds, the defense asks for your formal recommendation that this case be dismissed. Thank you."

30

———

The only thing rougher than the scarred face pictured inside the ready room's holographic frame was its deep, rasping voice. *"Worf, you can't be serious."*

"I assure you, Chancellor—I am." Most people, even Federation starship captains, would feel at least a bit intimidated while conversing with Chancellor Martok, the leader of the Klingon High Council, one of the most powerful persons in local space. But to Worf, Martok was his kinsman, his brother-in-arms, the patron who had adopted Worf into his House. The two of them had stood together in good times and bad. They were bonded by blood and trust.

On the other end of the subspace comm channel, Martok looked doubtful. *"It's not as if the Empire has a shortage of* novpu' *or* jeghpu'wI'. *How does this benefit me, Worf?"*

"In many ways."

Martok scowled so hard his eye patch shifted. *"Name some."*

"Labor. For centuries, the Klingon Empire planted its flag on every Class-M rock it found, whether it had the troops to hold it or not."

"What should we have done, Worf? Let the Federation have them? Or the Romulans?"

"That is *not* my point."

"Then get to whatever is."

"The Empire has conquered more worlds than it can defend, or exploit. Many of them—in fact, more of them than the High Council wants to admit—are filled with hostile fauna and toxic flora. And some have climates that even our kind cannot abide."

"So what?"

"They go unexploited. Lie undeveloped for centuries. But still they need to be defended against foreign colonization. That costs the Empire time and wealth. But if even *one* of these worlds gave up its riches, the benefits to the Empire would be significant."

"Tell me you're not suggesting—"

"The Empire needs subjects willing to *tame* those worlds. People who can survive on the most extreme planets in the galaxy. Who can thrive in the worst possible environments."

"And you think this gang of yIntaghpu' *fits the bill?"*

"They are more than a gang. More than two hundred thousand Nausicaans scattered across local space survived the loss of their planet. Kinogar can turn them into an *army*. One that wants nothing more than a new world to conquer and call home."

Martok rested his chin on his fist, clearly considering the idea. *"I'm not sure I like the idea of that many Nausicaans squatting in Klingon space. I know the High Council won't."*

"They will not be squatters. They are prepared to work, and to make reasonable tributes to the Empire. All they ask in return is the right to self-rule." Worf saw that Martok was struggling to accept the idea. "The Empire will gain a new source of raw materials, one for which it will spend *nothing*—not blood, treasure, sweat, or time. How is that not a victory?"

The chancellor shook his head. *"Our people have never been keen on immigrants. Or, worse, refugees. It reeks of charity. Of weakness."*

"If anyone is engaging in charity, I am."

A suspicious glare. *"What makes you say that?"*

"I am offering the Empire a massive alien workforce—and I ask nothing in return."

That seemed to amuse Martok. *"Maybe you should."*

"No. Because that is my gift to you, as the leader of my sworn House."

"Some gift. This will have me fighting with the High Council for weeks to come."

"Not when they realize the leverage it gives you." He waited for Martok to cue him to continue with a skeptically lifted eyebrow. "Frame the Empire's grant of asylum for the Nausicaans as a political favor to the Federation. I will do the same. This will put the Federation Council in your debt—and strengthen your position against challengers inside the High Council."

Martok chortled, and nodded in satisfaction. *"Once a diplomat, always a diplomat, eh?"*

Worf accepted the praise with humility. "It was you who taught me that any leader can make war—only a *great* one can make peace."

"You would make us slaves of the Klingons?" Kinogar's rage and disgust were palpable, even filtered through the universal translator and a subspace comm channel to the main viewscreen on the bridge of the *Enterprise.* *"You take us for fools?"*

The band of Nausicaans behind Kinogar howled with indignation. The translation circuits tried to keep up with them, but all Worf could pick out were intermittent vulgarities and a few epithets that he presumed were meant as slurs against his parentage. Meanwhile, the bridge crew of the *Enterprise* remained quiet and mindful of their posts, though he felt the pressure of their attention as if it were a thousand-kilogram weight upon his back.

"Kinogar," Worf said, adding bass to his voice. "Listen to me." He waited until he restored eye contact with the Nausicaan commander. "You would not be slaves. Your world would not be run or occupied by Klingons."

Kinogar spat at the vid sensor—which, Worf realized, from the Nausicaan's perspective must have felt like spitting in Worf's face. *"So you say. My people know how Klingons treat outsiders. Novpu' they call them. No rights. No freedom. Not for us!"*

"This would be different," Worf said. "If you colonize Kremlat, the chancellor will recognize your independence. You would not be a client state, a subjugated world, or a conquered people. You would be imperial subjects, protected under imperial law."

Kinogar sneered. *"If we pay ransom!"*

More hoots of derision from his cohort.

"No," Worf said. "In return for a yearly tribute. A fraction of what you produce, what you mine, what you harvest—would be given to the Empire. In return, the Empire would defend your world from invasion, but would otherwise leave you in peace."

"Prisoners! Sweating to serve a warden!"

"You would be free men. Free to come and go. If you tire of having a world to call your own, you can go back to being nomads. Pirates. Scavengers. Bottom-feeders." He stepped toward the screen. "Or you can build a new world. A new civilization. Remake your culture in the image of your best selves. All free of supervision."

The jeers from Kinogar's troops became a steady grumbling. A few of them muttered complaints to Kinogar, who nodded, as if they weren't telling him anything he hadn't already considered. He returned to his conversation with Worf. *"My people not want to live in exile."*

"To be *exiled* is to be cast out of one's home," Worf said. "We offer you a *new* home."

"Maybe you abandon us on dead ball of mud. How do we know?"

"Look up Kremlat on your ship's database." Worf nodded at Konya, who transmitted a file to Kinogar on the comm's data sub-channel.

T'Ryssa Chen stepped forward—without permission—to join the conversation. "Or read the imperial planetary survey. They say the same thing. A Class-M planet. Gravity within ninety-seven percent of Nausicaa normal. Clean, breathable air. Plenty of potable fresh water. A wide range of climates and ecosystems. And more deadly plants and animals than you can shake a stick at. You guys'll *love* it down there."

The Nausicaans were still reviewing the raw data about the planet as Worf added, "Kremlat is rich in rare mineral elements, including dilithium. And while Lieutenant Chen was correct to note that most plant and animal species you will encounter will be hostile, it should also be noted that Nausicaans are one of the few humanoid species that can safely consume a majority of the species found on Kremlat."

Kinogar squinted at Worf, telegraphing his distrust. *"But some are poison?"*

"We will give you a list," Worf said. "This is not a trick, or a test. We will help your people travel to Kremlat, and we will aid your colonization." He smiled. "It is a world waiting to be tamed, Kinogar—if your people have the *guramba*."

The Nausicaan leader and his men recoiled at hearing their sacred word spoken by an outsider, and then they fell into hushed arguments with one another. Their tone sounded as if it was infused with hope and excitement, but Worf found it difficult to read Nausicaans' emotions.

When Kinogar faced him once more, however, it was easy for Worf to read the emptiness in the Nausicaan's eyes, and to hear the sorrow in his voice. *"Your offer . . . is generous. But no new world can replace what we lost. Not just land, but history. Our myths. Art. Architecture. Our music and poems, our great epic tales, books of wisdom. All that made us more than nomads. All that made us truly Nausicaan."*

"I understand. That is why we prepared *this*." Worf threw a meaningful glance at Chen, who transmitted to Kinogar a small sample of what they had assembled for this negotiation.

"Though your species has never cooperated with our efforts to study your history or culture," Chen said, "the Federation knows a lot about Nausicaa and its people." She nodded at Worf, confirming that the sample package had been sent.

"Much of what you and your fellow survivors thought had been lost forever," Worf said, "was preserved by the Federation, kept safe in our official archives."

Kinogar opened the sample file. His mandible went slack as he perused its contents. Within moments his men crowded in around him, all of them desperate to see artifacts of their shared past restored to life in their leader's hands. Foreign names tripped from their tongues as they marveled over a table of contents.

"If you surrender and turn over the Husnock weapon without further violence," Worf said, "I am authorized by the Federation Council to grant you all amnesty, and to provide you with portable data cores containing every bit of information the Federation has about your history and culture. With that, and a promise of safe conduct to Kremlat, you will be able to rally the galaxy's surviving Nausicaans to help you build a new world. A new home. A future."

Anguish and doubt twisted Kinogar's features. *"How do I know we can trust you?"*

"Because I give you my *word*. I, Worf, son of Mogh, pledge to you that all of this is true, and that the terms I have promised you and your people *will* be honored. This I swear, on my honor as a Starfleet officer, as a Klingon warrior, and as a *kinsman* of the Klingon high chancellor, Martok, son of Urthog."

A silence freighted with hope and fear stretched out over the comm.

Then Kinogar turned and barked a curt command at his men. One of them flipped a switch—and shut off the Husnock weapon. The other Nausicaans holstered or slung their weapons. Kinogar exhaled, and then he faced Worf once more.

"Worf . . . we accept your terms. We surrender."

Fifteen hours after Kinogar's surrender, Šmrhová still found it hard to believe that the crisis had been resolved without another shot fired in anger, or that Worf had somehow persuaded the Klingons, notorious xenophobes that they were, to grant the Nausicaan survivors amnesty and independent control of one of their uninhabited colony worlds.

I guess he learned a few things while he was an ambassador.

She had missed most of his negotiations with Kinogar, since she had been planetside with the strike team, lying in wait for the order to take down the Nausicaans, sacrifice the station, or both. But after she had returned to the *Enterprise* and taken some time to clean herself up, she had accessed the bridge's comm logs. And she had marveled at how calm, patient, and empathetic Worf had been while offering terms to the Nausicaans.

He had the directness of a Klingon, the rationality of a Vulcan, and the compassion of a Betazoid. Now I see what it takes to impress Captain Picard: something I'll never be.

She stood at his side, savoring her last hours as his first officer. Soon, Commander La Forge would return from Stonekettle Station with his emergency team, and he would resume his role as Worf's second-in-command, once more relegating Šmrhová to the security console.

On the main viewscreen, ships of various designs and registries jockeyed for position in orbit on the night side of Skarda. Many of the vessels had come to assist in an evacuation of the station, but now that the PMAR had been returned, the danger to the facility had passed. Its energy shield was back to full power, as was what still remained of the research outpost.

From the command chair, Worf asked the station's leader, Juneau Wright, "Are you sure there is no other help we can provide before we depart?"

On the main viewscreen, Wright shook her head. *"No, we're good. Don't get me wrong, there's lots to do down here. Rebuilding most of the station, for starters. But this time we're going to do what we should've done the first time: build underground."*

Dygan looked up from the ops console. "Forgive me, but may I ask why you originally built above ground in such a dangerous environment?"

Wright smiled. *"What can I tell you? We got cocky. Won't happen again."*

Her colleague Pov stepped into view, and he pulled La Forge along with him. *"We're just glad your engineer La Forge was here to pull our fat outta the fire. If not for him, we'd all be dead."*

Trying to escape the Tellarite's embrace, La Forge grimaced. *"All part of the service."*

"At any rate," Wright said, *"thank you,* Enterprise. *From now on, we'll keep a lower profile—and save our showing off for when it really counts."*

"Smart," Worf said. "Mister La Forge, we need you back aboard as soon as possible."

Still struggling to free himself, La Forge croaked out, *"On my way, Captain."*

Worf smirked at his friend's predicament. *"Enterprise* out." He swiveled his chair toward Šmrhová. "Has the Husnock weapon been secured?"

"Aye, sir. I locked it down myself." Knowing its eventual destination sickened her. "Do we really have to turn it over to *him* when we reach Earth?"

"Yes. It was a direct order from Admiral Batanides."

"But there's got to be *someone* at Starfleet Intelligence better qualified? More trustworthy? Less obnoxious? Of all the people in the galaxy—"

"I agree. But when we reach Earth, we need to turn over the Husnock weapon"—disgust passed over Worf's features—"to Agent Thadiun Okona."

Šmrhová shook her head. "It's just not fair."

"Life is not fair, Lieutenant. Get used to it."

A comm signal beeped on Konya's console. "Sir? Incoming hail from Kinogar."

"On-screen."

The image of Skarda and its orbiting fleet was replaced by the face of Kinogar, who sat proudly in his ship's command chair, in a pose that echoed Worf's. *"Captain Worf. We are now to go. But we scan Kremlat. It is rich. Unspoiled. Kept your promise. My people"*—

he looked around his command deck at his crew—*"will never forget your name."*

"See that they never forget *yours*. *You* are the one who leads them to freedom. To hope."

It was hard for Šmrhová to tell, but she thought she saw behind Kinogar's fearsome double mandible . . . the ghost of a smile. Then he uttered words that she had never thought she would hear any Nausicaan say to anyone, much less to a Starfleet officer:

"Thank you, Captain."

The Nausicaans closed the comm channel, and the main viewscreen reverted to an image of the ship activity in orbit above Skarda. The *Seovong* broke from the traffic pattern, followed by a string of smaller Nausicaan ships. They assumed a loose formation behind a Klingon battle cruiser, the *I.K.S. Navong*, which had come to escort the Nausicaan refugee fleet to its new home inside the Klingon Empire.

Šmrhová stole a look at Worf—and caught the same glimmer of a smile on his usually stern countenance. "Everything all right, sir?"

"This was a good day."

Thinking she was being set up for a Klingon proverb, she replied, "A good day to what?"

Worf's smile widened. "Just . . . a good day."

31

Admiral Liu's deliberation period after the closing arguments was shorter than Picard had expected. He had thought she might take a few days to weigh all the evidence and testimony before rendering a decision. Instead, Ezor had contacted him late that evening to say that they and opposing counsel had been directed to appear the next morning.

The mood in the courtroom was solemn. No one seemed to know what to make of such a swift decision—not even Ezor, who had been able to say only that "this is either very good news, or very bad news." Picard shifted uncomfortably in his Starfleet dress uniform for what he hoped would be the last time for the foreseeable future, but not the last time in his life.

He had just taken his seat beside Ezor, with Crusher directly behind him in the front row of spectators' seats on the other side of the room's divider, when Liu appeared through the door behind and to the left of the dais. Everyone stood until she settled into her chair at the desk, and then the participants and the crowd took their seats.

Liu rang the bell on the table three times, then silenced it with a touch of one fingertip. She wore a grave expression as she folded her hands atop the table and took a breath.

"Before I render my recommendation," Liu said, "I want to state for the record that this was a complex matter to evaluate. Not just because of its legal elements, but because of its moral and ethical implications, and the fact that it will almost certainly serve to set a legal precedent.

"Serious charges have been brought against Captain Jean-Luc

Picard. But in considering the merit of those charges, it was necessary to weigh those leveled in kind against the late President Min Zife, Koll Azernal, and Nelino Quafina. There has been so much conspiracy, wrongdoing, and obfuscation brought to light by these proceedings that it seems few individual acts can be examined in isolation, which makes an overall moral accounting of this fiasco all but impossible. I know that will disappoint some people, but in the end, it is irrelevant.

"From a legal standpoint, the purpose of this preliminary hearing was to examine the evidence and testimony currently available, to see whether it was directly relevant to the charges made against the accused, and to assess whether the provenance and content of that evidence was sufficiently compelling and credible as to warrant a court-martial of Captain Picard.

"It is also my duty as the preliminary hearing officer in this matter to recommend the course of action that I believe to be in best accordance with the laws of the Starfleet Code of Military Justice, and which I think will best serve the interests of justice, Starfleet, and the people and government of the United Federation of Planets.

"In spite of the passion with which Attorney General Louvois argued her case against Captain Picard, she failed to present what I consider to be credible evidence of wrongdoing. The only witness testimony she was able to offer were statements by flag officers currently indicted for their respective roles in the alleged conspiracy. Not only did I find them to be less than fully credible witnesses, nothing in their depositions directly implicates Captain Picard in their crimes. Consequently, I find no evidentiary support for the charge of conspiracy.

"The only recorded evidence introduced came from the defense, and its content was, inarguably, exculpatory. That, combined with the sworn testimony of the witness L'Haan, is sufficient for me to conclude that there is no support for the charge of espionage.

"As for the charge of accessory to murder, the letter of the law would have required that Captain Picard be involved in a prior criminal activity which contributed directly to the homicide. As no such predicate offense is alleged or demonstrated, and because ample exculpatory evidence and testimony has been offered to show that Captain Picard had no knowledge or role in any of the events that transpired after his conference discussion with Admirals Ross, Nechayev, Jellico, Paris, and Nakamura, I find no basis to support this charge.

"That brings us to the final charge, of sedition. This is not an easy question to answer. The very notion of a secret conference of high-ranking military officers, convened to discuss the premature and possibly illegal removal of a sitting president from elected office, troubles me. It would be helpful if we had a transcript of that meeting, but we do not. In its absence, we are forced to piece together its contents from the depositions of some of its known participants.

"In the end, I had to base my conclusions as much upon what was said as what was *not* said. So far as we know, no one present— not Captain Picard, Ambassador Lagan, or any of the flag officers— specifically proposed the use of *violent* force to persuade Zife to resign. No one suggested the implementation of martial law; in fact, such a course of action was actively refused. And while Attorney General Louvois made a point of stressing Captain Picard's expressed opinion that he considered President Zife 'unfit' to continue as president, that opinion alone does not constitute sedition, not even when spoken by a Starfleet officer.

"Nothing concerning Captain Picard's conduct during that conference rises to the level of sedition. As for the government counsel's argument that Captain Picard should be held liable for the actions of the admirals subsequent to that conference, I must concur with Mister Ezor's argument that the SCMJ specifically insulates Starfleet personnel of all ranks and rates from being held accountable for the actions of their superiors.

"Consequently, I find no legal support for the charge of sedition."

Murmurs filled the room, and Picard let go of a deep, tense

breath. Ezor gave him a gentle back-pat of reassurance, and Crusher leaned forward to rest a hand on Picard's shoulder.

At the head of the room, Liu frowned, and then she continued.

"Though I will not be recommending any further court-martial proceedings against Captain Picard, I cannot in good conscience let him walk out of this room without facing some manner of censure, some measure of consequence. Though his specific actions might not have risen to the level of court-martial offenses, I cannot ignore the fact that he played a role, no matter how well intentioned, in the covert termination of Min Zife's presidency and his life.

"Having conferred with Starfleet Chief Admiral Leonard James Akaar, Secretary of Defense Selora Quintor, and the members of the Federation Security Council, I have been authorized to render the following recommendation, which the aforementioned parties have agreed unanimously to enforce: although Captain Jean-Luc Picard will be permitted to continue to serve in Starfleet as an active officer of the line, he will be formally reprimanded for his role in covering up the criminal wrongdoings of President Min Zife and his administration, and he will be consequently and *permanently* barred from holding flag rank in Starfleet.

"With that, we come to the end of these proceedings. I thank all of the parties involved for their professionalism and their candor, and our spectators for their restraint and discretion. This matter is now concluded. These proceedings . . . are closed."

32

—•—

Picard left the courtroom in a daze. After all of the anticipation, all of the anxiety, the outright dread, it felt surreal to know that it was behind him. He had been cleared of the charges against him but reprimanded for others the government hadn't deigned to bring. It felt less like an exoneration and more like a reprieve. A second chance.

He followed Ezor and Crusher through the corridor, past the crowd of civilians asking for his autograph or a photo at his side, into a turbolift that carried them up and away from the tumult of the media and the insatiable appetites of the public. Crusher peppered Ezor with questions about whether Starfleet could or would appeal the recommendation, and whether the civilian legal system might insist on taking its own turn against Picard. Though he was only half listening, Picard caught enough of their conversation to know he had little reason to be concerned going forward. The SCMJ offered the same guarantees against double jeopardy as were found in civilian law, and because Starfleet and the Federation Council had already endorsed the current recommendation, it was unlikely they would pursue the matter further.

Outside the turbolift, sunlight gleamed off the tops of San Francisco's towers, and a tattered blanket of fog stretched across the bay and wrapped around the Golden Gate Bridge. Dizzying streaks of automated aircar traffic blurred past in a number of directions.

As it would have, no matter the decision. Whatever my fate, life would go on.

It seemed a bleak notion, and yet within it Picard found a spark of hope.

The pod halted, and its doors parted. Picard followed Crusher and Ezor out, down a corridor, and through another set of doors onto a landing pad. Wind tousled Crusher's hair.

Parked on the landing pad was Crusher and Picard's transport pod. Standing between them and it was Phillipa Louvois. Her gray hair, gathered in a fashionable 'do, seemed impervious to the wind, though her clothes fluttered madly with each gust.

Ezor strode ahead of Picard and Crusher to intercept Louvois, who kept her attention on Picard. "Madam Attorney General? What are you doing here?"

"Forgive the intrusion," Louvois said. "I know the case is over, but I was hoping Captain Picard and I might speak privately for a moment before he departs."

Crusher glared at Louvois, while Ezor turned a plaintive look at Picard, who nodded his assent. Then he touched Crusher's arm, diverting her attention to him. "I'll just be a moment."

"All right," Crusher said, though her demeanor suggested otherwise.

When she stepped away, Ezor leaned in. "Are you sure, Captain?"

"It'll be fine, Jonathan. Please, wait for me in the pod."

"Okay, then." Ezor caught Crusher's eye and gestured for her to follow him to the automated transport. The two of them continued past Louvois, who remained focused on Picard.

As soon as Crusher and Ezor were out of earshot, Picard broke the fraught silence between himself and Louvois. "What do you need, Phillipa?"

A cynical shake of her head. "For something to make sense? For the law to matter again, to someone? Anyone? I don't know." She looked eastward, into the morning sun. There was anger in her voice. And disappointment. "I really expected to see you leave here in custody."

"I know." He sensed her hostility, which continued unabated even though the hearing was over. "During my court-martial after the loss of the *Stargazer,* I never felt as if you were acting out of personal animus. But that's not been the case here, has it?"

She was unrepentant. "No. It hasn't."

"Why? What's changed?"

"*You* have. Covering up war crimes? Helping to unseat a president? The Jean-Luc Picard I knew would *never* have let himself get caught up in a fiasco like this."

"The man you once knew never had to choose between preserving his moral purity and sparing the quadrant from a war that would have wasted billions of lives for *nothing.*"

Louvois looked away in disgust. "The old 'I did it to keep the peace' excuse. How many atrocities have been swept under *that* rug, Jean-Luc?"

"It was not an *excuse.* I was there, at Tezwa. I saw the destruction. The slaughter. The burning of the Klingon fleet. I heard both sides rattle their sabers for war. We were at a flash point, Phillipa. One spark away from a war that might have consumed us all."

She studied him with a critical gaze. "So you say. And I have to admit, even now, after all of this, part of me still wants to *believe* you, Jean-Luc. Part of me still wants to believe in the best part of you." She winced, as if in pain. "But then I hear those recordings, and I read those depositions, and I imagine the president who led us through the Dominion War being ushered into some dark, empty room, and being shot in the back of the head, executed in cold blood. And all I want is for everyone who played a part in that bloody deed to pay for it in hard time."

A strong slash of wind partly undid her hairdo and set a few long strands of her gray hair whipping about like mad snakes. She swatted them away from her face and held them at bay. "I need you to know that I can accept that I lost this case for any of a hundred reasons, but I will *never* think that I was wrong to pursue it. Evidence and regulations be damned—you knew there was something wrong about what you'd done. If there hadn't been, you wouldn't have been so careful never to speak of it in your logs."

"Perhaps I simply had nothing to say."

"You? The great orator? The acclaimed diplomat? Nothing to say? Don't make me laugh. I had you talking about this for over three days, and I feel as if we barely scratched the surface of what you really know about what happened."

Even without the specter of legal peril to constrain his response, Picard chose to err on the side of discretion. "I suppose we'll never know." He tried to sidestep around her.

She darted left to block his path. "I'm really trying to believe that everything you and your lawyer said in there was true. The truth is, in my heart, I want you to be *innocent.*"

He frowned. "None of us is *innocent,* Phillipa. Not anymore."

"I know. Which is why I'll always have my doubts. About this case. And about you."

"So will I." Picard stepped around her; this time she let him go. "*Au revoir,* Phillipa."

He walked to the transport pod.

All that Jean-Luc Picard wanted now . . . was to go home.

33

After his prolonged and grotesquely uncomfortable mission to Stonekettle Station, Geordi La Forge felt like his old self again. He had snagged two good nights' sleep in a row, back in his own quarters on the *Enterprise*. This morning he had risen early and mustered the willpower to go to the ship's gymnasium. He'd worked up a healthful sweat with a half-hour callisthenic workout followed by fifteen minutes of hitting the heavy bag, before returning to his quarters for a quick sonic shower and a light breakfast of steel-cut oatmeal with fresh strawberries and a cup of black coffee.

Now he was on the move, padd in hand, tracking his progress against the ship's chronometer. He had a few stops to make before proceeding to main engineering to start his shift. The *Enterprise* had arrived in orbit of Earth less than an hour earlier, both to pick up Captain Picard and to coordinate the return of the Husnock OPC to Starfleet Intelligence.

Ten minutes ahead of schedule, he noted as he passed a companel on deck six. *I am a machine this morning!*

The first task on his pre-shift agenda was to round up Agent Thadiun Okona and escort him down to cargo bay one. La Forge's orders were to reunite Okona with the Husnock weapon, permit him to inspect the device, and then secure his signature confirming the transfer of custody before Okona was permitted to load the crated weapon onto his own vessel, the *Tain Hu.* It was easy for La Forge to understand why Worf was so eager to be rid of both Okona and the weapon: both had been nothing but trouble to the *Enterprise,* and Captain Picard would be most displeased to find either one still on board when he returned.

Dotting the i*'s and crossing the* t*'s—that's what I do. I get things done.*

He made a right turn down a transverse passage that led to deck six's guest quarters.

As he passed another bulkhead companel, he noticed the appearance of a flashing message addressed to him. He was receiving a personal comm from someone on Earth, and the ship's computer had tracked his location and routed the call to him here. He stopped and tapped OPEN CHANNEL on the interface projected onto the glassy black panel.

A flat vid image of Doctor Leah Brahms appeared in a small inset on the companel. She beamed at the sight of La Forge. *"Geordi! Good morning! I hope it wasn't too early to call."*

He couldn't help but mirror her wide smile. "Leah! Not at all. What's going on?"

"Fun coincidence! I'm on Earth for business, and I heard the Enterprise *will be in orbit for a day or so. Any chance you and Tamala want to meet me in Berlin for dinner?"*

Her invitation caught him off guard. "Um, maybe." He was going to make an excuse to delay committing to plans, but then he remembered that truthfulness and openness were the cornerstones of the open relationships that he shared with both Doctor Brahms and Doctor Tamala Harstad. "I just wonder, would it feel awkward? All three of us out together socially?"

"No reason it has to. I'm not trying to get in the middle of anything you two have going on, I'd just like to see you. So tell you what: Talk with Tamala. If she's up for it, great—ping me back, and we'll make solid plans. If she isn't, we'll catch up another time. Sound good?"

"Sounds great, Leah. I'll be in touch as soon as I talk to her."

"Perfect. Talk to you then! Ciao.*"*

"Ciao!" Brahms closed the channel at her end, and the companel reverted to its standard "ship's business" configuration. La Forge had to shake his head, amused by the ways his life had changed for the better as he had grown older and more comfortable in his own skin.

The nervous kid who could never get a date suddenly has to juggle two relationships at once. Who'd have ever seen that *coming?*

He checked the chrono and resumed walking. *Still eight minutes ahead. I'm killing it!*

A few junior officers turned curious looks his way as he passed by whistling "Frère Jacques" for no reason other than it made him happy.

He counted down the numbers next to the doors until he arrived at the one assigned to Thadiun Okona. He reached toward the door signal, and then he hesitated.

I am a bit early. Maybe I should wait out here. Let him finish getting ready. La Forge looked around. Watched a pair of noncoms stroll past. Felt self-conscious. *This is ridiculous. I'm the acting XO. If I want to roust Okona a few minutes early, that's my prerogative.*

He reached toward the door signal.

Before he touched it, the door to Okona's quarters slid open.

A lithe, dark-haired woman in civilian clothes darted out of the doorway when it was barely half-open, and she slammed straight into La Forge. He recovered from the surprise of the collision and looked down—into the mortified eyes of Lieutenant Aneta Šmrhová.

She pushed her tousled hair from her face and glared up at him. "Not *one word*, La Forge. I *mean* it." She didn't wait for him to reply. She shoved past him and vanished down the corridor in the fastest "walk of shame" that he had ever seen.

La Forge was still reining in his smile as Okona stepped out of his quarters, fully dressed, bag packed, hair impeccably combed, and in every way as fresh as the proverbial daisy. He grinned at La Forge. "You're early! I *love* that." He stepped around La Forge and headed for the nearest turbolift. "Let's seize the day, Commander!"

Amused, La Forge fell in behind him. "Looks to me like you already did."

34

———

"The good news," Commander Sam Lavelle said, "was that the situation was contained before it became necessary to resort to extreme measures, and Agent Okona recovered the Husnock Omega-particle cannon without further violence or loss of life."

Sweat rolled down his back beneath his tunic and uniform jacket, impelled by the raw, incandescent contempt of Admiral Batanides. The director of Starfleet Intelligence sat behind her desk and regarded Lavelle, her lone visitor on this brisk winter morning, as if he had just farted.

"Commander Lavelle, when you look at me, what do you see?"

Her question perplexed him—not its literal meaning, but its subtext. She was setting him up to be rhetorically emasculated. Hoping to delay the inevitable, he played dumb. "Admiral?"

"Do you see a person of deficient mental faculties? Or perhaps some overinflated rube from a backwater planet who wouldn't know her ass from a phaser coupling?"

"Absolutely not, Admiral."

"Then why are you peddling me this load of bullshit? Do you think I didn't read anyone else's after-action reports before asking for yours? I know full well that it was the *Enterprise* crew that resolved the hostage crisis at Stonekettle Station, not your asset Okona. And the only reason that mess ended without massive loss of life is because they arrested Okona just as he was about to blow the whole thing to kingdom come."

Batanides got up and turned her back on Lavelle to gaze out of her office's window. "I also know that it was Commander Worf who negotiated the safe return of the Husnock OPC—a weapon that your man lost, and which the Nausicaans used to steal Stonekettle's portable reactor, resulting in major collateral damage to that outpost." She turned and fixed Lavelle with an icy stare that felt as if it were skewering his heart. "Did I miss anything, Commander?"

"No, Admiral."

"Is there anything you wish to add at this time? Anything that might possibly cast you, your asset, or his RIO in an even marginally more flattering light?"

Lavelle searched his memory, desperate for any kind of decisive victory on which to hang his proverbial hat, but he came up with nothing. He averted his eyes from Batanides's withering glare. "No, Admiral."

"Then I think you'll understand why you don't get a cookie and a pat on the head for walking into my office and crowing 'mission accomplished' after riding herd on one of the longest strings of screw-ups and own-goals I've ever seen. Do you get me, Commander?"

"I do, Admiral."

"Good." She sat, smoothed the front of her uniform, and then added, "Get out."

Lavelle turned about-face and marched out the door.

He had never before been so grateful just to walk out of a room alive.

"Oh, come on," I said, trailing Lieutenant Naomi Wildman through the sterile gray corridors of Starfleet Intelligence. "An introduction, that's all I'm asking for." I gave her my most imploring wide-eyed look and hoped to melt her human-Ktarian heart.

All I got for my trouble was a side-of-her-eye glare of reproof. "Not happening."

"But I thought you said you and Seven were like family."

"We are. Which is a big part of why I said *no*." She gave me a funny look as we turned the corner toward her office. "Besides, you're not her type. And she's seeing someone."

I played the *I'm-so-offended* card. "Why do you assume my attentions are amorous?"

"Because I know you."

"Maybe I'm just starstruck. Maybe I just want to ask her about her experiences with the Borg, and the Caeliar, and the Children of the Storm, and—" Wildman shut me down with a weary eye roll and a matching frown. "And you're not buying a word of this, are you?"

"Like I said: I know you."

"Have it your way." I reached into my coat pocket and pulled out my padd. "Back to work, then. I've got a good lead on the Dashkari Barons. Word has it they're putting together a major push into the black market on Kavaria." I handed the padd to Wildman as the door to her office opened ahead of us. "All I'd need is a few thousand bars of gold-pressed latinum to buy my way in, and then something sweet to use as bait, and I—"

"Bait for what?" interrupted Commander Sam Lavelle, who was inside Wildman's office, leaning against her wraparound bank of consoles and workstations.

I opened my arms and my smile wide. "Sam!"

He put out a hand to halt my step forward. "Hug me and I'll shoot you. Bait for what?"

Wildman stole my thunder. "Okona thinks he can take a bite out of the Dashkari Barons if we help him worm his way into the Kavarian black market."

Lavelle pressed his forehead above the bridge of his nose and shut his eyes tight. "No, no, *no.* Please tell me you're kidding."

I took my padd from Wildman and offered it to Lavelle. "Look at this intel, Sam! My sources on Dreon intercepted three minutes of SIGINT. The Barons are looking to push the Orion Syndicate out and move their people in. If we time this right, the Barons will do our jobs against the Orions, and then we can cut the Barons off at the knees before they settle in."

"And if you get it wrong, like usual, you'll install the Barons as the new overlords of interstellar crime in the Alpha Quadrant."

"Like usual?" Typical Lavelle—he always saw the risks, never the rewards. "I've been busting my ass in the field for twenty years, Sam. Don't let this latest *targ*-hump fool you. My win-lose ratio isn't just better than most, it's downright phenomenal, and you *know* that."

Lavelle crossed his arms and sighed. "Fine, I'll play along. You want to infiltrate the Kavarian black market to take down the Dashkari Barons. And all you need is three thousand—"

"*Five* thousand."

"—five thousand bars of gold-pressed latinum and a fresh legend?"

I nodded. "Yup. Plus the bait, like I said."

His air of suspicion returned. "And what kind of bait were you thinking of, exactly?"

"The Barons want to carve off a piece of the Ferengi arms market. So if we dangle the Husnock OPC in front of them—"

"No, goddammit, no."

"But it's the perfect—"

Lavelle waved his hands like a crazy person. "Have you lost your mind?"

"I'm not saying we go in fast and loose, like we did with the Orions. I totally understand that we'll need tighter op-sec, and better control over the meet site. But if we—"

"Do you really expect me to trust you back in the field with the same doomsday weapon you lost the last time? After all the mayhem that caused?"

I shrugged. "It really wasn't my fault, Sam."

Wildman tilted her head. "It was kind of a freak accident."

"Unbelievable." Lavelle headed for the door, stopped, and then wheeled back on us, his temper in full flare. "You two are the biggest problem children in all of SI! And somehow I got saddled with both of you at the same time! How am I supposed to do my job with you two throwing spanners in the works every time I turn my back? Him bedding everything remotely feminine that crosses his path, you melting down the *Enterprise*'s computers! The two of you together are a traveling disaster. The best thing you did on this last op was *fail to finish it.* And ten minutes ago I got my ass chewed off and served back to me as pâté by Admiral Batanides, all because SI's greenest RIO and its most chaotic field agent bungled what should've been a dead-simple sting. Now, with our careers and your freedom on the line, you want to do it *again?*"

I projected confidence as I said, "This time it'll be different!"

"*How* will it?"

"I don't know, it's a mystery. But this time it'll work!"

Lavelle's body slumped with fatigue. He turned and walked out the door, muttering under his breath, "Angels and ministers of grace, defend us . . ."

The door slid shut, leaving me and Wildman alone once more.

"That could've gone better," she said, dispirited.

"What do you mean? He's praying for us." I smiled. "He's starting to like me, I can tell."

35

Farewells were never easy, especially when so much needed to be left unsaid. Picard had tried to make his departure from the family vineyard with a minimum of drama, but Marie had made it difficult. There had been tears in her eyes as she'd said good-bye to young René, and Picard had been able to tell that it was because Marie saw some echo of her late son in her nephew's face.

By contrast, Jonathan Ezor had bid Picard and Crusher farewell a few nights before, after dropping them off at La Barre and before continuing on to his own home. The only message he had sent since then had been the bill for his legal services, which Picard had promptly paid.

The flight up from La Barre to the *Enterprise* had been bittersweet. As much as Picard tried to conceal the sentimental side of his nature, he always felt a pang of sweet sorrow when he watched the horizon curve and the blue scatter of the sky fade to reveal the black curtain of space. The majesty of it, and the old melancholy that came from leaving home, continued to resonate in his soul, decades after his first exodus from this world.

But no sight was so beautiful or so welcome as that of the *Enterprise* in orbit, surrounded by repair crews putting finishing touches on the vessel in preparation for its return to deep space. Had he not been informed that his transport pod was on a strict schedule, he might have asked its pilot to indulge him with a few circles around his beloved starship.

Perhaps another time.

The transport pod touched down in the *Enterprise*'s main shuttlebay. It was promptly attended by flight-deck mechanics and personnel from the ship's services division. Picard and Crusher disembarked to find yeomen arranging the transfer of their luggage to their quarters.

As their bags departed on an antigrav, Picard saw La Forge approaching him and Crusher with his familiar broad smile. "Captain! Good to have you back, sir."

"It's a pleasure to *be* back, Geordi."

La Forge leaned in to give Crusher a quick hug. "Welcome home, Doctor."

"Thank you, Geordi." She turned back, helped young René out of the transport, and then said to Picard, "I'll drop him off at the nursery on my way to sickbay."

"Splendid. I'll see you both at dinner."

"You'd better." Crusher gave Picard a quick, chaste kiss.

He squatted down and gave his son a hug. "Be good, René. I'll see you tonight."

René smiled. "Okay. Love you, Papa." He squirmed in a bid for freedom, and Picard let him go. Crusher took the boy's hand and led him away as Picard stood and watched with pride.

La Forge waited until Picard turned to him and said, "Lead on, Mister La Forge."

"Yessir." He led Picard toward a nearby turbolift. "We took a bit of a beating over the last few days, but all repairs are finished, and the ship is ready for service."

"Very good. Any casualties?"

"Some injuries, no fatalities. All personnel are aboard and accounted for."

Picard nodded. "Well done."

They reached the open turbolift and stepped inside. "Bridge," La Forge said. The doors closed and the car filled with a low hum as magnetic coils propelled it upward and away.

They stood silently inside the turbolift. Picard shot a curious look at La Forge, and wondered whether he would take the opportunity to crow about his own recent exploits. When no boasts seemed forthcoming, Picard gave his friend a gentle prompt. "I was told you went above and beyond the call of duty at Stonekettle Station."

As usual, La Forge deflected praise. "I wouldn't go that far, sir. I did my job, that's all."

"Don't be so modest, Geordi. I've read Worf's report. You saved more than sixty thousand lives, as well as preserving decades of advanced research. Lieutenant Elfiki described you as 'cool and confident during extreme circumstances,' and one of your engineers, an Ensign Giler, described your leadership as 'inspiring.'"

The commendations seemed to make La Forge uncomfortable. "I did what I had to do."

"As did Commander Worf." When that comment turned La Forge's head, Picard added, "He's recommended you for the Christopher Pike Medal of Valor. And I've approved his recommendation. I expect Starfleet Command will agree."

The news left La Forge momentarily dumbstruck. He seemed surprised, then abashed, and at last he smiled and nodded once. "Thank you, Captain."

The turbolift car slowed, and the doors opened onto the bridge.

Picard stepped out and let the ambient sounds of the *Enterprise*'s bridge wash over him. Feedback sounds from the consoles, oscillating tones from the sensors, the subaural vibrations in the deck, resonating with the output of the ship's fusion-based impulse reactors. The low chatter of voices over comms, and the hushed conversations of officers conferring at their stations.

Worf noted Picard and La Forge's arrival. He stood from the command chair, faced them, and stood at ease. "Welcome back, Captain."

"Thank you, Number One."

As Picard walked over to greet Worf, La Forge headed for the aft duty stations to speak with Lieutenant Elfiki at the master systems display.

Worf, as usual, cut to business. "We have clearance to depart, sir."

Picard rested his hands on the back of the command chair. "In good time." He lowered his voice to speak confidentially with his XO. "I'm most impressed with your handling of the Nausicaan crisis, Number One. Your solution was in line with the finest traditions of Starfleet."

"Thank you, sir."

"And I'm not the only one who noticed. At this rate, it won't be long before I lose you."

Confusion knitted Worf's thick brows. "Sir?"

"Admiral Akaar put your name on the short list for promotion to captain. I suspect that within a year or so, you'll have your own command." He gave Worf's shoulder a paternal clasp. "And it's about time."

"I . . . do not know what to say."

"No need to say anything, Number One. Though if I were you, I'd start thinking about who you might want to request for your first officer."

A peculiar half smile tugged at Worf's mouth.

"Please tell me you don't plan on poaching Commander La Forge."

Worf shot a quick but decisive glance toward the security console—and Lieutenant Aneta Šmrhová. "I have someone else in mind, sir."

Picard smiled in approval. "A splendid choice, Number One."

He stepped around the command chair, and then he settled into it. He had forgotten how comfortable it was. Relaxing his forearms on the armrests, he straightened his back and lifted his chin. "Everyone?" His bridge officers ceased their conversations and activities, and faced him. "I just want you all to know how glad I am to be here with all of you. No captain could ask for a better crew, or a finer vessel on which to serve. Now . . . stations."

Everyone around Picard snapped into action. Worf took his place beside the command chair, hands still folded behind his back. "Heading, Captain?"

"Second star to the right, and as far from politics as we can get—warp six."

Worf delegated the order to the helm officer with a single nod.

Picard raised his right hand. "Let's go see what's out there." He dropped his arm and pointed forward—toward the stars and the future. "Engage."

The stars on the viewscreen stretched and curved as the *Enterprise* went to warp speed.

Picard tugged the front of his uniform tunic smooth and cracked a wan smile.

It's good to be home.

EPILOGUE
February 2389

———

It has been two years since we came to this mad, wild world. Two years since the last sons and daughters of Nausicaa claimed Kremlat as their own. Since we were reborn.

I stand atop this world's highest plateau, surrounded by mighty peaks of bare granite. Below me sprawls a valley, once a jungle, now the site of Hayao—our first city in this new paradise. Above me stretches an endless sky, wider and a deeper shade of blue than any I have ever dreamed. Mist shrouds the horizon, a veil yet to be lifted.

My old friend Kradech approaches, the ceremonial spade in his hand. Behind him a crowd watches and waits. Kradech draws near and bows his head. "Receive me, Wind-Father."

I take him by his shoulders. "Kradech! My *brother*. To you I am Kinogar. *Always*."

He hands me the digging tool. I take it with reverence.

A breeze wafts over us. Kradech breathes it in, and so do I. He looks to me, his eyes full of hope. "You were right. This is it. I feel it, Wind-Father."

"Yes." I close my eyes and feel the sun's warmth upon my face, even in the alpine cold. "I knew it from the first day I set foot here. This would be the place."

The wind howls. Inspired by its cry, my people start to sing. Deep throaty hums give way to bright, soaring notes, all in harmony. My *tegol* soars with a joy that not long ago I had feared would never return. In the song of the air and the music of my people, I hear our faith in truth renewed. Our faith in promises made and kept. Our debt to sacred words of honor.

I lift my voice and sing to the Four Winds. They live again—in us, in this place. They have found us here, far across the stars, beneath a new sun—and claimed us as their own.

Around us yawns a world of danger—and opportunity. It is all that we were promised and more. And thanks to Worf, son of Mogh, kinsman of Chancellor Martok the Great, our history survives. Our poetry, our art, our music. So much more than I had ever dared to hope—all of it preserved in the archives of the Federation, and given back to us in the name of contrition.

Deep inside I still howl for the mates and younglings I lost on Nausicaa. But I see now I cannot honor them with acts of destruction. To honor them, I must go on. I must ensure that our people live, and remember their heritage. Yawa and Baru, my loves . . . Iraji and Teko, my little fighters . . . the Four Winds will sing your names forever. Because we will not let them forget.

I turn and face the gathered believers. They all wait for me, their Wind-Father.

Closest to me are those who bled with me during the dark years: Drogeer, the snowblood; Grendig, the hotspur; Kradech, the loyal; and Miruni, my new mate, with our newborn, Pindar.

The spade is light in my hands. The ground hard beneath my feet.

I step into the center of the ring of the faithful. Press the spade's point against the cold earth. Set my foot on top of the spade's square back edge. With my weight added to my strength, I force it to break the soil and sink deep. I lift the blade full of dry dirt and rocks—

My people cheer in exultation.

We have, at last, broken ground on a new Temple of the Four Winds.

This is our threshold moment. No longer will we call this world a colony.

This is our new beginning. A chance to rebuild our civilization, and ourselves.

We are home.

ACKNOWLEDGMENTS

First and always, I thank my wife, Kara, for her patience and encouragement. I literally could not do what I do without her constant love and support.

It's important to me to acknowledge the inspiration I found in the work of author Seth Dickinson, whose novel *The Monster Baru Cormorant* includes chapters written in different verb tenses and first-person perspectives. I found this literary technique irresistible, so I used it for scenes written from the points of view of Thadiun Okona (first-person, past tense, because he lives his life as if he were narrating his heroic tale for posterity) and Kinogar (first-person, present tense, because he lives his life in the moment, having been violently separated from his past and led to believe that he has no future). Consequently, several names in this manuscript (Yawa, Baru, Tain Hu, and others) are homages to the work of Seth Dickinson. I encourage you to seek out, purchase, and read his work. You won't regret it.

Propriety demands that I offer a nod of thanks to U.S. Navy veteran and political essayist extraordinaire Jim Wright, who publishes his musings on the state of the world and the American republic in particular on his blog, Stonekettle Station. It was with his kind permission that I named the research facility in this story after his blog, and its commander in honor of him.

I'd be remiss if I didn't thank my editors Margaret Clark and

Edward Schlesinger for their patience. They know why. All you need to know is that they are awesome and I'm lucky to work with them.

Behind the scenes, I owe a great debt to *Star Trek* novels copy editor Scott Pearson for his unstinting encouragement and his keen eye for details both mundane and *Star Trek*–specific, and to my fellow word-monkey Dayton Ward, who nobly handled the first two rounds of Section 31 mop-up in Aisle Picard, in his novels *Hearts and Minds* and *Available Light*. Thanks, *hermanos*.

And lastly, I thank you, dear readers, for making this journey with us. *Qapla'!*

ABOUT THE AUTHOR

David Mack keeps on going,
Guess he'll never know why.
Trek's been good to him so far . . .

Learn more on his official website:
davidmack.pro
Or follow him on Twitter:
@DavidAlanMack